SONG
OF THE
SPIRIT

JOHN JOHNSON

Paperback ISBN 978-1-960007-78-0
eBook ISBN 978-1-960007-79-7

Published by
Orison Publishers, Inc.
PO Box 188
Grantham, PA 17027
www.OrisonPublishers.com
Publish your book now, marsha@orisonpublishers.com

Printed in the United States of America

Other books by John Johnson
The Byzantine Chronicles series
The Blade – ISBN 978-1945169-29-8
The Brothers of the Blade – ISBN 978-1945169-40-3
Sons of Light – ISBN 978-1945169-45-8
The World Chronicles series
In the Shadow of Babylon – ISBN 978-1-945169-55-7
Babylon Revealed – ISBN 978-1-945169-72-4
Christ's Reign and the Last Harvest – ISBN 978-1-960007-12-4
The Silver Cord – ISBN 978-1-945169-87-8

Dedicated to Angie and Christy,

my daughters, who will be with me in eternity.

Angie's computer skills kept this project moving on to completion.

Angie's stories of the oldsters she has met in her health-care field,

and Christie's stories of the youngsters with mental and social barriers

in her field of work have kept within my consciousness

the beauty of frailty and the honor in perseverance.

Then I saw a new heaven and a new earth, for the first heaven and the first earth had passed away, and there was no longer any sea. I saw the Holy City, the New Jerusalem, coming down out of heaven from God, prepared as a bride beautifully dressed for her husband. And I heard a loud voice from the throne saying, "Now the dwelling of God is with men, and he will live with them. They will be his people, and God himself will be with them and be their God. He will wipe every tear from their eyes. There will be no more death or mourning or crying or pain, for the old order of things has passed away."

(Revelation 21: 1–4)

Then the angel showed me the river of the water of life, as clear as crystal, flowing from the throne of God and of the Lamb down the middle of the great street of the city. On each side of the river stood the tree of life, bearing twelve crops of fruit, yielding its fruit every month. And the leaves of the tree are for the healing of the nations. No longer will there be any curse. The throne of God and of the Lamb will be in the city, and his servants will serve him. They will see his face, and his name will be on their foreheads. There will be no more night. They will not need the light of a lamp or the light of the sun, for the Lord God will give them light. And they will reign for ever and ever.

(Revelation 22: 1–5)

PREFACE

The written word of God, holy, infallible, begins with creation history and ends in the prophecy of the book of Revelation, the last written words, insights into the future. What then, chosen of mankind? What will be your destiny? Do we dare think beyond the New Jerusalem and the River of Life? The answer is Yes! I am certain God delights in our dreaming; here, visions are birthed. He smiles upon us as our unknowing minds work to foresee His goodness. As a father, I delighted in telling bedtime stories to my young daughters. How could I involve them in a quest—satisfy their need for justice and fairness and help them learn to conquer every problem and need, growing spiritually in confidence and love? The written word ends, waiting fulfillment, even as a new world—Heaven—awaits us. Explore a vision of the new world waiting. *Let us sing to the Lord a new song. Sing His praise from the end of the earth!* (Isaiah 42:10)

This is the first work, of a planned trilogy, set within the exploration of God's created work-Space. This trilogy has its foundation constructed on the World Chronicles trilogy of: The Shadow of Babylon, Babylon Revealed, Christ's Reign and the Last Harvest. In fact Song of the Spirit was to be the fourth book of The World Chronicles. It deserves companions. The story has not ended and we have yet to know ourselves, or the goodness of our God.

If you dare to pursue this story, you will grow in knowledge and freedom, and you will delight in your salvation and the gift of eternal life.

CHAPTER 1

John and Diana lounged on a large, flat rock in the Susquehanna River. The summer day pressed warmth into their bodies, and the scents of flowering aquatic weeds, island trees and plants carried the sweetest memories of previous times on the river. John lay on the edge of the six-foot high rock and watched the fish below through the transparent water; it seemed the fish moved through air. Most did not move at all, save for their gills, as they formed a line behind a log obstruction of length that fed an area of quiet, protected water into the current. All smallmouth bass, John noted. Diana lay on her back with a soft, thick towel between her and the rock. The sun felt so good. In New Jerusalem, just finished a hundred years ago, the constant light came from the radiance of God's presence—no night, no shadow-covered days. She laughed almost imperceptibly in delight, remembering their visit to the fifteen-hundred–mile by fifteen-hundred–mile Holy City, and the River of Life that flowed within the city limits. John sensed her thoughts and spoke. "Yes, we need to go back. That riverbed was fantastic—every stone a gem of sparkling color."

She answered, "And the water so buoyant no one could sink. And drink where you pleased—such purity." She turned onto her side to face her partner and ran her hand down the side of John's torso. "It is so good to have you with me." John had returned days ago from the Chesapeake Bay project, where the waters of the Susquehanna had been dammed before entering the Atlantic Ocean basin. The Chesapeake Bay had been renewed by the clean waters. The Atlantic waters had been diverted into subterranean channels that scoured and filtered out the pollutants naturally, even as Earth's people employed their ingenuity by adding natural chemicals, electrical therapies, and filters to the process. All the rivers upon the earth, when emptying into the oceans, had met the same fate, as had all ocean waters.

The oceans and seas had died during the Tribulation from environmental catastrophe, human pollution, and atomic weapons, and they had been only partially restored during the Millennium. With the end of seismic activity, Earth's core had been calmed, and full cleansing could occur. Some of the cleansed waters were being redirected to lakes upon the desalinized bedrock of oceans and seas. Some waters were being stored in underground reservoirs. The remaining waters, slowly pulsed through subterranean passages. Sufficient waters were left on Earth's surface to be reabsorbed into the air and fall as rain on the newly planted vegetation of the ocean beds. No deserts caused by insufficient rainfall existed on Earth.

Diana's remembrance of his recent work trip brought up thoughts he had yet to share. He reached out and held her hand as he spoke. "While studying the ocean bed, my group came upon a group of tourists. Ten people, all passengers of the same ship that had sunk in that area in the seventeen hundreds. They had found the wooden bones of the ship, and some had souvenirs—an ink well, a plate, a piece of the ship, a teakettle. They had been immigrants from England, who had briefly stayed in Maine and were relocating to North Carolina, when the storm stopped their earthly lives. Such joyous people, and after all these years, their native eighteenth-century English accents were still present, although just faint whispers of what they had been."

Diana joined her thoughts to his. "Years in Paradise, the Millennium, and five hundred years after; how stubborn are those things we learn in childhood. Is it legal to take souvenirs?" She answered her own question. "It must be, or they would not have taken them—there are no more foolish laws, and there are no more lawbreakers. That weakness just doesn't reside in the human heart in Heaven."

John added to her thoughts. "The maritime salvage laws reflect the sensitivity of the resurrected people and allow, at the least, one souvenir apiece, if the object is not a rare item of historical significance. And addressing your first statement, there are deep ramifications to that thought on the human memory and speech." He would save exploring her words on that subject for another time. He continued, "Five hundred years since the Millennium's end and the brief final conflict."

Diana spoke. "The last five hundred years passed so quickly—don't you agree?—with the oceans project, the core-cooling project, the positioning and integrating of New Jerusalem to the existing landscape...."

John interjected, "Everyone engaged in those tasks."

Diana addressed John's "everyone"—friends and family—and said, "Tim, Mat, Emily, Dan, Tom Sr., and Tom Jr. employed with strip-mining the ocean beds and the retrieval of rare earths and the exploration of Spanish galleons and hundreds of other ships from times past."

John added, "Nuclear bombs, radioactive power-plant waste, tons of barrels of toxic waste, salt deserts. Robbie, Jack, and Sammy were involved in that before moving into ocean-bed–soil revitalization."

"By the way," Diana asked, "what does revitalization involve?"

John answered, "Lots of machinery contouring rough ground for fields, prairies, plains; removing stones and boulders. Creating watercourses, retention ponds. Then the seeding and cutting machines, tilling the new-grown greenness back into the soil, three crops a year—it's like stirring a soup. Adding nutrients, minerals, microscopic organisms, earthworms, and more. Forests are planted on the rocky ground, grasses on the farmable land. We could feed a thousand worlds if we planted food crops."

John's wrist phone buzzed. He glanced at the screen, spoke to Diana. "Andy says the corn is roasted to perfection, and the buffalo burgers were just placed on the grill."

"Let's go." Diana seemed to bounce to her feet. The sweet corn, hand-picked that morning, had been roasting, husks on, in a long trench covered in wet burlap and soil—her favorite corn-preparation technique. Buffalo, her favorite meat. Animal and fish were still favored by the eternal inhabitants; the creatures were raised lean and eaten in moderation. John and Diana had decided long ago on one poultry, two fish, and one red-meat meal per week.

"Transporting?" queried John as he raised his body effortlessly to his feet.

"We have time to wade to shore and walk," said Diana. "Besides, it will help my appetite, and I love to walk in these new shoes." She looked down at her feet, pointed her toes, then turned her feet side to side, admiring her new purchase.

John laughed in happiness at her little-girl delight and understood her satisfaction and comfort—his shoes were of the same make. The process was so simple: cover the bare foot in a light, sticky, protective gel; press on heel pads, a sole, and necessary supports to the foot; choose areas for ventilation by placing venting upon the gel. Choose your material for the shoe from granulated deerskin or leather, buffalo skin, plastics, or cloth; dip the feet into the vat, pull them out, and when the cure is right, blow air between skin and the shell. Zippers are added at the initial stage, or a slit, at the end of the process, for tying or Velcro. All this, the invention of a man and his son and daughter, in a backyard garage.

He took her by the hand, brought her body into his; they kissed. He jumped into the water and felt her splash beside him without asking for or requiring a steadying arm.

***

Andy, the first inhabitant of this shore, watched John and Diana, walk up the gradual, man-made incline cut into the naturally steep riverbank. He had created the incline, raked away the small stones and flood debris yearly after the spring rises, and kept the soil on the upper slope mowed. His neighbors and dearest friends moved like athletes, evidenced by the swing of their arms, the tightness and spring in their steps. John had been in the military as a young recruit prior to the Tribulation and had fought in the European conflict. He and his newfound European friend, Diana, had played a key role in exposing the Satanic church within the supposedly Christian World Church. John had been responsible for the Johnsons knowing Christ.

Tim Johnson, neighbor, friend, and John's older brother by ten years, had heard the gospel message from John, and through seven years of the Tribulation, he and his wife, Mary, and kids, Mat and Katie, came to know the Lord. Hope, their second daughter, was born in the Millennium. Mat and Katie and their former spouses, Barb and Paul, now lived in the small community by the river. Hope and former spouse, William, had moved to California. Pete Johnson, the great-grandson of Mat, and Pete's wife, Grace, lived up river a ways on the same shore (east). Andy knew he was incredibly blessed that John and Diana lived near him, on their mountaintop perch, where the buzzards and hawks circled. Andy's river home was surrounded by homes of Johnsons, and he cherished them all. Andy thanked God for the beautiful day, a warmth that loosened muscles and seemed to bathe bones and ligaments in wellness. All the trees were puffy with growth, the greenness like a blanket on the far island and forested shorelines. God was so good. Still good. Continuously good. Forever good. The Holy Spirit within Andy bubbled within his spirit and joined together in delightful happiness so good that his throat gave rise to a chuckling thankfulness.

Andy, an American Indian of the Susquehannock tribe, was thankful, too, that his family of wife, Leaf, and sons, Tuck and Robin (born disabled and now healed), all lived within their ancestral lands. Leaf was busy uncovering the corn, the heat and some smoke making her dodge and duck. Tuck and Robin were present with their partners; they both had found female friends with American Indian blood. Charlotte, a Delaware, was Tuck's close friend; and Deborah, of Cherokee lineage, clung to Robin. Both were good girls esteemed by Andy and Leaf. What else would they be but good girls? Full of the Spirit of God. Filled with the wisdom and knowledge of the Spirit. Seeing life through the eyes of their Redeemer. How a piece of the mind still lingered in the past, when good and evil contended. They were helping Leaf. Tuck and Robin tended the coals where the meat would be cooked. Tuck still held his water-conservation job on the river, but in his spare time, he had developed a mussel farm along with his sturgeon caviar and eel-harvesting enterprises. Robin had remained in banking but in his spare time found enjoyment in working with his brother on the river.

Although men and women were not creating children, as humankind were "like angels in Heaven" where marriage was concerned, they liked being with their opposites for companionship, and decidedly they enjoyed the sexual differences in appearance, voice, movement, behavior, and thought processes. In truth, women had kept the maternal outlook and men, a paternal mind-set. In the eternal world, no one was wondering what a man was or what a woman was. God defined them. Some men were more emotional than others, some women more stoic than other women. Some women wished to build offices and habitations, and some men wished to build relationships. Men showed deep concern for others, a willingness to engage in emotional support as well as a practical guiding knowledge, as did women. All rested in their creator God for His definition of man and woman and how it defined individuals, and all knew they were true to Him in their lives; He was pleased with them all. No untoward desire ever furrowed a brow or caused worried reflection or dread. Sexual identity was not strained by the absence of intercourse. Nothing needed to be proven; Satan was powerless, squirming in eternal fire; the once-accusing flesh was dead, and therefore, the world knew no lies, no deceit. Hearts were pure, living through and by the Holy Spirit, and therefore justified.

Andy had studied John and Diana's arrival, their physical movement, their bond, the keenness in their eyes, with a purpose in his mind. He had received a formal text, on phone and computer, from New Jerusalem. He had been summoned. No department had been given; the man who summoned him was listed in the directory of officials and department heads as a member of Christ's advisory board. The letterhead had carried the seal of the Trinity and therefore was authentic. The text had mentioned exploration; the letter had hinted of a need for a certain type of experience and personality. Andy was certain that space exploration was imminent. Nothing left to do on Earth. New Jerusalem was seated upon the earth; the River of Life was flowing. Earth's core was stabilized, the magma cooled; the oceans' waters were being cleansed and the oceans' beds, reconstituted. It seemed evident—vast acreage had been created for agricultural output, perhaps to feed beings on other earths, or to establish food caches for space travelers. Perhaps immigrants would come and inhabit the former ocean beds.

Humankind needed a vision—needed work, needed discovery and challenge, purpose. To think an omniscient God who created man in His image would be content to have His children lounging on clouds, singing to harp music to glorify Him was nonsensical. Humankind had the genetic code, the mind, the spiritual code of Abba. Dad was an explorer, a creator, a God who shared the glory of His creation. The old heavenly star scape destroyed in the Tribulation had been replaced by new heavens. Angels, with human help, had mined a distant planet for the gems used for the base of the New Jerusalem wall. Exploratory probes had revealed no form of higher animal life.

Perhaps Andy was letting his imagination go too far, but he thought of his close friends and those on the periphery. Who would make a good explorer? He remembered vividly, in Paradise, reading the journals of Lewis and Clark, when they first appeared in 1815, and how they had selected the men for their exploration of the American frontier. Andy's newly acquired reading skills had opened a new world to him and occupied his mind as he waited for his return to Earth. His readings in Paradise had been extensive, with accounts of discovery of greatest interest. Who would be a good explorer for the world of space? Machine operators and machine creators with biology and earth-sciences backgrounds. Observers who were inventive, collegial, steady, determined, focused on mission. What if humanlike life was discovered? Then people with linguistics skills and minds of understanding, who were nonjudgmental, to a point, would be needed. Were there little Satans, demons, demonic influences left in God's heavens? Was Satan, now burning in Hell with his followers, the only being of his kind? He had been a fallen angel. Were there others who had winged their way to the farthest recesses of the galaxies to hide? Was Jesus the savior of the world only? Or of the Milky Way? Or of the universe? Was Jesus the savior of humankind only or of all cognizant life-forms?

Of this Andy was certain: there was only one God, Yahweh. He had created all that was or ever would be. His goodness and righteousness had been revealed. Who would dare contest Him? Jesus was God, was of His substance, His genetics; why would Christ's salvation not cover all that had been made in the image of God? If this were the case, life-forms with cognizance would bow to the Creator—unless there was a liar of power and persuasion still roaming the galaxies. But even these life-forms may have social bonds that created a false world and fleshly desires rooted in selfishness that needed to be conquered with Christ's power.

John and Diana sat on the double-seated Adirondack chair that faced Andy's seat at an angle, so that all parties could view the river and each other. Andy turned, and Tuck, with plates for all, handed him one. Leaf came behind with a high-sided pan holding at least a dozen ears of corn and with containers of softened butter and salt- and pepper-shakers attached to the sides.

"Thank you from us both," said Diana, taking ears from Leaf. "That's a nifty corn carrier with accessories."

"The shepherd Abraham's second son, Bobby, a coppersmith, is selling those and other clever items," Leaf said happily.

"Bobby? Why isn't he called Isaac?" asked John, alluding to the order of the biblical Abraham's sons: Isaac was the second of Abraham's eight sons, the only son of Sara. Ishmael, the first son, was born of Hagar.

"Isaac is a carpenter," said Leaf, straight-faced, and then she broke into a grin. "Our local Abraham had a dear friend named Robert, so one male child didn't get a biblical name. He has thirteen children. Unfortunately, not all are with us." Leaf deposited the bulky pan on the picnic table behind the individual chairs and sat down, taking two ears for her plate.

"Where are all the Johnsons?" asked Andy. Leaf had been responsible for rounding up participants, as for the past two weeks Andy had been absorbed in his final review of his manuscript, a local study of the last conflict on Earth, "The Return of Satan's Rule to Central Pennsylvania."

John answered. "Tim is still involved in the ocean-bed renewal project somewhere near the tip of the Delmarva Peninsula. Mary decided to visit Hope and that side of the family. Katie and Paul are in California also, at a warehouse for items recovered from shipwrecks. It seems that sheet music bound for California during the gold rush of 1848 was preserved, as well as sheet music created during the 1896 Alaskan gold rush. Mat and Barb and their extended families are visiting New Jerusalem, and Gramps and GG Jeremiah joined them. I think Pete and Grace are at home upriver."

"Here they come now." Andy nodded his head upriver as two kayaks came at blazing speed—competition. Pete's demeanor was one of determined concentration. Grace, trailing by only inches, began to laugh at her Pete's need for victory, even though he had started far behind her. Andy, amused by the drama, laughed.

Diana spoke. "Dan and Emily are in Washington, DC, attending some celebration at Mount Vernon. Something to do with the Potomac. I wish those two weren't so adventuresome; I miss them." Dan was the brother of Barb, who had become a Johnson by marriage, and Diana had come to enjoy her company, and Emily's, too, through the Johnson family. Who could not like orphaned Emily, urbane and down home in the same breath, grafted into the Johnson family during the Tribulation?

"Washington. Now, there was a man who could pick a river site for a homestead," said Andy. "Since the resurrection, George Washington has lived in a modern home, of small size, below the historic home. I met him recently; told him how I had seen him through the trees at Braddock's defeat in 1755. I wasn't participating in the combat; I was just in the area and decided to observe. I patched up a few men but never thought to look them up. Are they living in Hell now or alive with us? Washington was a fearless man—the bullets were thick around his mounted form. We really had a good talk, and he was genuinely interested in my life. He plans to visit. By the way, he was in command of the DC area during Satan's return."

John spoke. "I always wanted to meet him. Remember to inform me when he visits. Did you ever notice that the early presidents are here with us now, but most of the later ones had no clue? On another subject, where are Tom Sr. and Jr.?" John spoke of the Burnells, the only family in the immediate area with African ancestry.

"Both in China. Senior and Tish are visiting Sammy and Robby, who moved out there. Jack's here in the homestead house," answered Andy, his mind turning to Tom Burnell and his extended family. Tom Sr. owned the home and land to the south of Andy's holdings and was a good neighbor, trusted friend, and a very Christian man. His former wife, Tish, was a delight, and hospitality was her forte. Andy had gotten to know Tom's family during the Millennium. Tom Jr. had grown up here by the river and spent most of his time in the family garage, inventing, and keeping the homestead garden producing. At the age of fifteen, he had gone with Carl and Ling, both friends to all, to China, where they launched a business that was now a multibillion-dollar industry. Incredibly smart kid and a lover of the Lord. Three of Tom Jr.'s great-grandsons—Jack, Robbie, and Sammy—had fought on these very grounds at Satan's last hurrah. Jack had decided to stay by the river, after the fighting.

"There's Jack," Diana said, pointing, "coming across the lawn with someone."

From her seat at the picnic table, Leaf said, "That's Stacie, his friend. You'll like her."

"Hallelujah," said John, who had spent many moments in prayer, asking for a friend for his friend Jack. He rose and waved Jack into the gathering.

CHAPTER 2

Andy, John, and Diana stood in line at the boarding gate to the Atlantic Wind River Transportation System, destination: New Jerusalem. John and Diana's first and only visit had been a hundred years ago, before the wind river system had been constructed. Andy had never been to New Jerusalem and had never experienced the wind river system, even at a local level. Leaf had decided to remain at home, due to commitments at church and with family. To Leaf, traveling seemed more like work than pleasure, even in this perfect world. The travelers would be in Jerusalem in nine hours. The portal was located at Harrisburg International, no reservations needed, and only a few minutes of wait time. You could travel with strangers or choose to fly alone.

For people in a hurry, stratospheric flights on modern jets cut the time in half but cost five times as much, and travelers observed less of the earth because of the increase in air particulates at higher flying elevations. These three travelers wished to see the changes on the earth: the dry ocean beds; the pinnacles, canyons of mountain ranges and ridges; the mid-Atlantic ridge, the valley chasm where the magma once flowed, as tectonic plates grated, spread, clashed, subsided. The travelers wished to see newly formed lakes, reforested land, prairies, plains, and the wildlife introduced; the remnant-heritage seas where sea animals were allowed to live, and citizens could experience the ocean floor's history; the salt and rare-earth deserts; the now dormant volcanoes and dinosaur graveyards.

John and Diana had decided just yesterday to accompany Andy to his interview with a high-ranking official in government. Since their last visit, they had always wanted to return, especially to the designated "Old City," locked in time—the city Jesus knew at his human birth. The restoration had only been completed a few years ago. Recreating historic sites had reached new levels of authenticity, as some of those who had lived in those times still lived. Like witnesses at a crime scene (many had witnessed Christ's arrest, interrogations, torture, and death) the former inhabitants had all seen something different and had had difficulty agreeing on anything. With the help of the disciples and Christ, a consensus had been reached with stunning clarity.

Diana grabbed John by the two sides of his open jacket and tugged hard till he bent his head toward her. He had been looking upward at the loading area—it was just like entering a ski lift or a roller-coaster car. "This is so exciting!" Her voice held her delight. "Remember the night the gem stones came down for the foundations of our Holy City? I look forward to seeing them up close."

"Yes, that was spectacular—the sparkling stones bathed in the light of God's presence. Our night turning to day before slipping behind Earth's curvature. Then, the constant glow on the eastern horizon. Wonder what that glow appears like from space," John mused, awe in his voice.

"A city on a hill and now a city on a planet—a light to the universe," Andy said. "The home of God—Earth."

"The shining of the foundation stones as they sparkled in the light…" Diana's mind could not let go of the image. She strode behind the passengers ahead of her as her eyes searched hungrily. She heard Andy yell, "Three!" to someone above their place in line. Just as the group before them disappeared into the boarding building, they saw an unsubstantial vehicle of the wind river, much less bulky than a car of the road, slow down. The passengers ahead of them were now seated in their vehicle, which then shot outward, upward, and was scooped away by the invisible current of air.

Diana, John, and Andy entered the building. The man in charge was courteous and took delight in knowing their destination; he wished them a good visit. He checked their seat belts, stepped away. A brief pause before they were pushed back in their seats by a force launching them forward. Then, the sensation of the swoop of air lifting them into the pull of the unseen wind river. Diana laughed spontaneously, and John grunted without thought. Even Andy was smiling wildly as they were gone from the city in an instant; traveling in complete quiet and seeming stillness as Pennsylvania passed them in the opposite direction.

They could smell New Jersey's forests of pines before they crossed the Delaware River. They could not remember seeing Philadelphia. Diana recalled reading that the city had begun a tree-planting initiative soon after the Satan followers left for their confrontation with God in Jerusalem.

Five-hundred-year-old trees could hide a city. They saw the scar on the northern horizon where old New York City had once stood and the spires of tall, new sky grabbers, where the new city was slowly reforming. The city had been hit hard by the Tribulation earthquake, and again, after a thousand years of peace, by the Satan-worshippers' rebellion. The wind river, which had risen to five thousand feet, descended three thousand feet.

They saw the sands of beaches that now knew no ocean tides or the sounds of surf. A lake of shallow waters had been created, and it spread beyond sight. They saw the new lands of the continental shelf—rectangular fields of seedlings, forests, grasslands, where immense herds of wild horses, cattle, buffalo roamed. Suddenly the continental shelf stopped, dropped thousands of feet to sparse green grasses. Within minutes, the mid-Atlantic ridges and pinnacles appeared, looking like the ribs of Earth. Stark blacks and grays of varying shades and hues were the palette. The air-dropped seeds of human intervention had found no ready place to grow, yet they *did* grow in crevices, ravines. The stench of sulfur deposits and rotting carcasses seemed imbued into the rock. Seabirds—gulls, terns—had created vast nesting areas. Avian populations had flown from their continental feeding spaces and found sufficient materials to make nests and produce offspring on the barrens of ocean mountains. Foxes and coyotes had traveled long distances across the desert ocean beds in search of the feeding place of eggs and newborns. At seemingly random intervals, the travelers saw shipwrecks in various states of dilapidation or restoration.

The traveler's sight searched every crevice, valley, cave opening, plain, horizon; all three wished to experience to the fullest this new world. Surprised by the quickness of time, they stared at the great gap looming at Gibraltar. They dropped into the channel, flying barely a hundred feet from the bedrock. Vast avian nesting colonies inhabited the crevices in the walls. Upon other rock-ledged areas, goats and sheep dotted the expansive cliff faces. They saw the apes of Gibraltar above them, and learned through their phones, dialed to the travel app, that the apes were classified as monkeys. The monkeys, spellbound it seemed, with mouths open, watched the tiny vehicle pass, as if the humans were on animal-entertainment TV.

The Mediterranean Sea was unique for the number of freshwater and saltwater lakes being created. Active paleontological and archeological sites, as well as completed sites with museums, grounds, caretakers and staff, were numerous. Treasures from the past attracted tourists: entire herds of dinosaur skeletons reassembled; unearthed ancient cities rebuilt; treasures of every type, from gems to coprolites; all protected by roofed buildings. The intact or nearly intact shipwrecks spanned the ages: caravels, Viking longboats, paddle-wheelers, steel fighting ships, submarines, Byzantine triremes—one with an intact flamethrower. Weapons and accoutrements of Romans, Carthaginians, Ottomans, Barbary pirates, Crusaders; warships with oars, sails, and engines; plank hulls and steel.

Before them, the massive western wall of New Jerusalem, sitting on its gemmed foundation, rose out of the old seabed. From the sparkling gemstone walls of jasper, it was 750 miles to the New Jerusalem city center. "All this is new to us, Andy!" said John, who wanted Andy to know that they were experiencing this city with as much wonder and naivete as he. They had not left the bed of the drained Mediterranean and could see no end to the fifteen-hundred–mile wall, nor the corners, where the walls both north and south ran east for fifteen-hundred miles. John knew from his readings that the ancient cities of Constantinople, Turkey, to the north and Alexandria, Egypt, to the south were included within the walls. The ancient rivers to the east, the Euphrates and Tigris, ran within the city limits, as well as the Jordan River. The water bodies—Black Sea, Caspian, Mediterranean, Red Sea, Persian Gulf—had been drained, save for areas within New Jerusalem. These lakes had world-heritage status. The propulsion of their small wind-river craft became actively computerized and dropped them out of the wind river, onto a debarking platform before a large gate in the wall. John's last aerial thought was upon the vast, open areas of farmland and forest within the walls—room for future growth of the city. The gate was the middle gate of three gates, equally distanced, penetrating the western wall.

***

The travelers' first and greatest impression was the light within and above the city. Did the light emanate upward from the walls, as if the earth steamed with light and warmth? This light projected up but did not cross over the wall; it seemed to go upward forever. Clouds passed through the city but cast no shadows. They had read that when the rain came, there was no lightning, no thunder. Did the light come from the heavens like the sun had once done—and still did on the entirety of Earth, save for the square of fifteen-hundred by fifteen-hundred miles?

They could see the difference in the light as they stood in the light of Earth's sun and looked at the Holy Light that shone within the city. The Holy Light shone from the opened pearly gates, shimmering gates, sometimes seen with tones of gray, purple, or indigo. As soon as you thought you saw these variations of shading in the white pearliness, the shadings were gone. The mass of travelers on the portico before the open gates moved toward the gates. Light was coming out of the gates. Why did the light not go over the walls of the city? The light coming out of the gate was clearer, warmer than the light coming down from the sun. God's light felt good on the skin; this heavenly light soothed muscle, ligament, bone to the point that people sighed in peace. John and his fellow travelers seemed to bubble with joy and thankfulness. What little anxiety people had—for arriving on time, or not getting lost, or just being in a strange or new place, with perhaps strange customs—dissolved, evaporated.

They stood before the high walls of the city, and the foundation stones underneath the open gate directly before them sparkled; twelve layers of gems of the most delightful colors, jasper, sapphire, chalcedony, emerald, sardonyx, carnelian, chrysolite, beryl, topaz, chrysoprase, jacinth, amethyst. Orange-brown, deep blue, dark-green or gray, light-blue–green, dense white, orange-apricot, white-yellow, light-gray, translucent blue, blue-green, black, orange, purple. Some layered in strata by color, some translucent, some solid, all presented in harmony of texture, design, color.

Beyond the gate they could see a street of gold, transparent as glass. Staring at the gate, they realized that twelve angels were staring back—ten feet tall, with blocklike builds and human musculature, in white robe-like tunics with armor plates sewn within. Their waists were girded with armored belts, and their thighs and calves showed the outline of the same embedded armor as the tunic. Around each waist, a short sword and a long, thin dagger hung; both within scabbards. Whether these were blades or light beams, John could not ascertain. The angels' bearing and their standing, helmeted forms were alike, and military was their movement, when they did move. These were warrior, soldier angels who had fought and prevailed in a civil war against the fallen angels—the angels of Satan. The Pennsylvania travelers knew these angels before them had known combat and desperate times. Their movements carried a gravitas, and the short, bellowed commands that echoed against the stones resonated with all they had seen and experienced of life and victory. No rank, no medals, no unit patches. Humility would allow no medals, no rank, and their unit was one: Jehovah's warriors.

John thought the guard of angels had a reason for its place against the wall. He thought God's light, which bathed them outside the confines of the walls, was a purposeful act. Searching the wall, he became cognizant of two lists carved in the stone: the names of the twelve tribes of Israel and of the twelve disciples (Matthias replacing Judas). The angels were guarding a gate but also a history; they seemed to be protecting the twelves tribes of Israel and the twelve disciples and all the citizens of the new Earth. When the travelers came close to the gate, the angels cried out in deep voices, "Praise to our eternal God!" The sound of their voices was like thunder, and it reverberated from the walls. From the travelers' mouths came the words, "Praise to our Creator, who has given us the freedom to seek Him and worship Him!"

The gathered crowd of pilgrims all felt the electricity of pulsing emotion coursing through their own hearts, minds, souls. The crowd of strangers all carried the same phrase, imparted to their souls by the God who loved them: "Praise to our God, who called to us through the din of Satan's lies." The pilgrims reached out to each other, wrapped arms around each other, grabbed shoulders, necks, came close to steady themselves emotionally. The inseparable, deep voices of the angels declared, "We rest in His eternal love." Just as a silence settled upon the wall, the angels spoke again. "We act in His eternal vigilance."

The unseen Spirit of Holiness within the words struck the huddled pilgrims before the city of God. Something deep and elemental had been dislodged from their souls as their individual hardships and anguish melded with the goodness of their God. They had believed, had trusted, had staked their lives upon His holy words. He had come through; they had come through; they had fought the good fight, sometimes with weapons of war, sometimes with fists, a stone, a butcher knife, a hammer, an axe; sometimes with just gritty resolve to obey only His ways, to forsake the pleasures of the world, deny themselves and carry their cross, return good for evil, and patiently endure. Emotions entered the voices of the redeemed; power came from a deep source into their voices. They called out to the angels and to Him, "Praises to our God! Lover of our souls! Praise to His eternal world!"

The people of God chorused with, felt the song of the Spirit coursing through their nerves, veins, bones. They walked invincibly, with heightened praise; forgiveness and justification and sanctification raised them to accept the gifts of God, and so they knew the ecstasy of promises fulfilled and never ending. People jumped, they bowed, their arms went into the air with fists, with outstretched fingers, with supplication. They cheered and offered their praises till exhaustion stayed their desire. They fell to their knees and wet the stones with their tears of thankfulness. They knew the walls and gates of New Jerusalem would never be needed, for their great God had conquered all their enemies for all eternity. The great fortress walls were a symbol of the security and peace that covered the people within.

In due time, when they had recovered emotionally, they entered the city through the gates of pearly whiteness onto the streets of translucent gold. Palm fronds were given to them, and they cried out, they sang, "Hosannah! Hosannah in the highest!" God was around them, in the air they breathed, within them—in their very souls, within the streets and buildings, the trees.

All of creation shouted the presence of the Holy God. Their desire, their energy had no end. They danced in holiness.

Their eyes widened in wonder and their praises, renewed by the beauty of the city, gushed from their mouths. A river ran beside the main avenue; beautiful fruiting trees and fruiting berry thickets and bushes had been planted. It seemed every fruit tree and berry bush known to the people of Earth was producing. The scent in the air seemed edible, and all breathed deeply as the scent permeated their clothing. As they regained their equilibrium, their bodies slowly entered a normalcy and an expectation. Uniformed people—city workers, grounds-maintenance crews were gathering up the fruits and berries. Refreshing stations were scattered about, and here the fresh fruits and berries were placed into receptacles. A low hum said the fruit was being pulped, the spigots were labeled, "Push," and a cup dispenser invited participation. They drank; the workers were smiling; people passing by—tourists and travelers—wore the same expression on their faces as Andy, John, and Diana wore. The juice dispensers were pointed at, and inviting arm gestures were directed at passers-by.

John spoke to his group as he pointed to the river. "That must be the River of Life."

Andy answered, "A channel. The river divides up at the western wall, all along its length, then travels underground back to the Old Jerusalem, to re-emerge wide and powerful in appearance but with a gentle current and a depth of only inches till it gradually rises to four feet."

"You've been reading up on New Jerusalem." John laughed in appreciation for Andy's thoroughness.

"Of course. What does a tourist do?" said Andy, laughing.

"We sat in that part of the river you described, as awed tourists, on our first visit. Can I assume these are the trees of life?" asked Diana.

Andy spoke. "No, the tree of life—there is only one—is near where the river begins. It bears one fruit, harvested monthly. It appears as two trees, one on each side of the river, but it is one tree. Somewhere unseen is a common root."

A maintenance man pushing a wheelbarrow came by, stooped down, then went to his knees to work on a brick walkway coursing down to the river park. John approached him and said, "Good man, do you have a moment?"

"Certainly." He was a heavily muscled man, straining his uniform's seams. He was deeply tanned. His black hair had a natural waviness. He pointed to his name tag and said, "Paternus is how it is pronounced. How may I assist you?"

"I am John. We are pilgrims from the United States. Does this road lead directly to the old city?"

"Yes, assuredly. You will see a sign soon." Paternus spoke with such a deliberate, natural calm that his placid expression asked and wished for a conversation from the guests.

"Is there a taxi service or bus line?" asked Diana. "It's been almost a hundred years since we were last here. So many changes. At that time, we flew directly to Old Jerusalem; we weren't stopped at the western wall."

"At the sign ahead, you will see the mileage to the old city. The highway will have lanes; the farthest to the right is the express lane. An hour will have you in the old city. The two other lanes to the left will take double and quadruple the time, respectively. Local commuters normally use these. All lanes offer seated cars, but in the express lane, you can opt to stand."

"Thank you," said Diana.

John asked, "Are you a native of Jerusalem?"

"No, born in Italy but spent my time in present-day Turkey, when it was part of the Byzantine Kingdom, around the year of our Lord 800. These government-employment positions in New Jerusalem are of limited duration, so that everyone who wishes can work here, fulfill their gratitude, absorb the culture of the Old Testament, see the historic sites—so many uncovered since the people of those times have returned, including our Lord. There is no guessing where Jesus walked, taught, performed miracles. Or where Elijah and Elisha awed the people, or where the ark sat. On the other side, there's no guessing how many 'venerated relics' are frauds."

"All, I imagine," said Andy.

Paternus laughed. "Yes, all. And all of Christendom could have received the presence of the living God whenever they liked—if knowledge of the Holy Spirit had been preached over the magic of relics." Paternus saw his two coworkers and lifelong friends approaching. He said, "My friends, my battle companions, my brothers through Christ, approach. Woden, the tall one, named for a Germanic god; and Seth, Woden's half-brother. They fought beside me, and they brought me to Christ back in our day, and I am eternally grateful." The two men went each to a side and grasped Paternus's shoulders. "He was worth saving," said Seth.

"Agreed," said Woden, as Paternus's eyes became misty.

John began to shake the hands of the soldiers from antiquity. Diana followed John's lead, and Andy completed the ritual. Andy spoke, "You lived roughly eight hundred years before I was born. What were your weapons?" Andy had sensed, by Paternus's calm, that he had been an old soldier. Only seeing and conquering all the terrors of death and life gave such deliberation to one's every moment. Woden, the tall one with wide shoulders, heard the question and answered, "The sword, the battle hammer or mace, the shield, the bow." The short one, Seth, with thick shoulders and chest, added, "Bloody hell were battles, yet our Lord saw us through."

Andy's voice rose with the remembrance of fear conquered and resonated with the power of his lungs. "Yes, our Lord, our Savior God was everything and is now all. You are country people close to the land, like me, I sense, and the horse and the donkey were our only machines. You must come and visit us, sit at my home by our river bank. We would like to know more. All three of you. Let me give you my information." Andy knew the three had lived simple but rough lives, much like he had. The Spirit was telling the travelers to hold onto these men, and this was done willingly, as a natural bond had formed simply by shared values, experiences, demeanor, mannerisms, and the presence of the Holy Ghost sharing His heartfelt love for God's warriors.

Paternus produced a phone from a back pocket. Andy pressed his right thumb onto the screen. Handed the phone back. Paternus did the same to Andy's offered phone. Andy said, "Come this summer. It is summer now. We have plenty of room. Bring friends, if you like, your partners—they would enjoy the company of my partner and her friends. We will be three days, at the most, in New Jerusalem, and then we will be back home, ready to receive you at any time."

Paternus and his friends were smiling broadly. All had talked of traveling, and the United States had been one destination discussed at length. Meetings and friendships in this age were easy. The Spirit of God had given all an ease, an understanding of others, an appreciation for the life walks of others. All were bound to Christ, and Christ had bound them all to the Spirit. The three travelers shook the rough hands of Paternus and his friends, exchanging smiles, and delighted at the warmth of their newfound friends. They marveled at their ease and the depth of unspoken understanding. They departed slowly, facing east, toward Old Jerusalem, hands raised in good-byes.

***

John enjoyed the view of the broad, stone piazza, the radiance of God pouring down from a cloudless sky. He enjoyed remembering the past. He and Diana had sat on or near this very location fifteen hundred years ago, on the seventy-fifth day of the Millennium. They had gathered with the Johnson family, and here he and brother, Tim, had met Christ Jesus in the flesh. They had not known Andy at that time, and Andy was not with them now—he had gone to his meeting in the governmental area of New Jerusalem. John spoke. "Seems odd that fifteen hundred years later, we are still alive and even healthier than at that time."

Diana joined his reverie. "How filled with beauty those years have been, the mountains, the river, our mountaintop home, and the riverbank homes of cherished family and friends. I never thought, as a sinner in my body of death, that God's creation, His life, could so enrapture me."

He added, "And the wonderful people we have the honor of living with, interacting with."

She added to his thought, "And the work He has us do—the knowledge He gives—and it will never end."

"So back to the present," he said. "Any thoughts?" He laughed at his abruptness—Diana had mentioned this tendency before.

She smiled, knowing why he laughed, and said, "Most have been spoken, but I like the old Jerusalem much more this time—with the removal of all the churches and pavilions that had been built over historic sites for preservation. Even though those newer structures, themselves, were built so long ago and have histories, it was a good idea to move them away from the sites. Posterity wants realism—to see the city as Jesus and the citizens of that time saw it."

"Jesus walked his entire life over again with the disciples," John said, "before the restoration project began, pointing out the mistakes and forgotten incidents and interactions."

Diana continued her appraisal. "I also like how the modern suburbs have kept the same ancient style of architecture, building materials, and even the narrow road design in residential areas. All the parks, water fountains, swimming pools, trees, flower beds, and flowering bushes are a welcome addition. The quaint trolleys on only the main thoroughfares do not detract."

John added, "The thoroughfares were zoned 'modern,' and that modernity does add convenience without marring the old."

John slowly reached over and grabbed her wrist, felt her heartbeat, and said, "To me, the oddest—maybe that's too strong a word—the most *innovative* but perhaps troubling idea is the mentioning by name of the evil forces in the drama, the names of the centurions who crucified Christ and the histories of their crimes before their deaths. Same with the priests who condemned Jesus to crucifixion and the people who voted for Barabbas, rather than Jesus, to be released."

"Well, we're told of the good people, too—the man, Simon of Cyrene, who carried the cross for Jesus, the thief on the cross who went with Jesus to Paradise, the lives of all the disciples and their accomplishments after the crucifixion," Diana said. "It's balanced."

"Too much detail about the evil lives of the damned. I don't really want to remember evil." Maybe it is me, but it just seems out of place. I just want to hear continual victory stories."

"It appears God wants you to remember the bad," she said. "We need to understand the barbarity of the times. Sin was an infection of the human spirit, the mind; and it produced utter folly and stupidity. All of us were just decaying flesh, stinking up life. That needs to be remembered. Jesus approved all descriptive markers at the sites. Talk to Tom Sr. and see if he has changed his mind about remembering the bad in life."

"Good point. It is the bad that delineates the good. Tom Sr. is resolute on that fact. For now, let's order a meal—lunch. Eat. Explore the afternoon away or simply sit and watch the people and their lives go by. If Andy isn't back by the time we're done, we'll go to his place of meetings and then have supper," John said.

"That's the plan," answered Diana.

CHAPTER 3

Andy sat with his group of one hundred on the tiered seats of the lecture room. The televised live presentation, the first offering, had covered the reason for space exploration—because space existed. God had made its vastness for no other reason than creation had been a work of pleasure that He had desired would never end. He loved to create. He loved to surprise and astonish humankind. He had made man and woman to be masters of His universe—all of it. It was for mankind to explore and make of it what He willed. He would not tell mankind what they would find. Although Christ, as God, knew every intimate detail of the creation, Christ, the man, purposely was limited in the knowledge He could reveal.

Jesus's great commission, stated in Matthew 28:18–19, gave a hint, a clue. "All authority has been given to me in heaven and on earth. Go therefore and make disciples of all nations, baptizing them in the name of the Father and the Son and the Holy Spirit." Some wondered why Heaven had been included with Earth when His intent had been to talk of making disciples. Jesus's only comment had been, "I said what I said."

The second presentation reviewed what was now known about space. Rudimentary explorations, some with the help of angels, had already occurred. The mining and quarrying of the "gem planet" for New Jerusalem's foundation and wall had been accomplished with angelic help. "Paradise" and "Hades," once thought to be ethereal holding areas for souls, had been found, with angelic guidance, to be actual planets. A space port and colony had been developed on Paradise, since a holding place was no longer needed for the "saved." Hades had become Hell and could only be viewed at a distance. Since the beginning, only angels had jurisdictional control.

Outside the locally known reaches of space, many unmanned probes and a few manned flights had been launched.

The greatest news to come from these probes was an interstellar map that showed what were termed "space highways." Whether these were truly routes created by other inhabitants of the universe or simply naturally made paths from myriad gravitational pulls and pushes and corresponding collections of planet dust and sands, atoms, isotopes, nuclides, and space gasses was impossible to tell. They appeared, through various lenses and data, more like veins and arteries or root systems scattered across the heavens. Probes seemed to indicate the viability of sending manned flights along these paths. Many of the paths had "velocities" or "currents," either a dominant push or a pull, depending on competing gravitational fields. The "pushes" were difficult to define or even speculate upon, but they did exist. What early mariner knew what the wind consisted of that filled the sails and carried his ship to distant lands?

The audience, now that the second presentation was finished, had been prompted to take a break. People began to talk among themselves, stand, stretch. They knew that in total, three thousand people had collected in lecture halls around Old Jerusalem, had seen the same presentations, and would now be addressed by their own in-room lecturer. That lecturer would be followed by an adviser, who would describe the various new positions being created in space exploration. This goal would be facilitated by a comprehensive set of tests to assess leadership skills, personality, world view, professional skills, opinions, and actual likes and dislikes within various contexts. Next, audience members would meet with a panel that was monitoring and measuring the stress levels caused by the day's activities. Finally, each candidate would go home and wait for a response.

Andy had not been, by nature, a gregarious man, but he had taught himself to be so when defending his young sons against the hatred of the world. He had realized that brute force was not enough. Persuasion could work if he knew the minds of his people. The greatest tool was simply to think of the needs of the people around him and assist them. As he had worth to others as a warrior and a sharing, prolific hunter, they respected his children. Now, in Christ, he enjoyed conversing with people. He looked to his left; a young, dark-haired woman with a kind sparkle in her eyes held the arm of the man next to her, her former husband, he believed. They had stood, and he in turn, stood, hoping to meet them. Something of Native American blood was within the couple. Andy partially faced them, as the aisle was narrow, and squeezed her arm in kindness, even as her friend turned and offered his hand. Andy spoke as he grabbed the hand. "I'm Andy, from Pennsylvania."

The man smiled cordially. "I am Enrique, and this is my friend, Ava, once my wife. Both of us from the country of Mexico."

Andy asked, "And when was your time on Earth?"

Ava answered, "We both lived through the Tribulation as teenagers."

Andy spoke, "I'm much before your time, a Native American, born in 1680. Lived till the year of our Lord 1765. Eastern United States—basically, Pennsylvania."

Ava smiled. "Penn's woods."

Andy's face lit up in surprise; he hadn't heard that phrase recently. He was about to engage in small talk with the couple when the lights flicked, and the speaker took his place behind the lectern. "Back to work," said Andy. Ava and Enrique smiled in empathy as they sat. Andy checked his watch and hoped the afternoon would go quickly. He wished to learn more of the couple.

Ava caught the eye of Enrique. She leaned into his neck, her lips hidden, and whispered, "All seem to know our secret." Enrique waited till Andy's head turned as he scanned the auditorium, then, covering his mouth with his hand, he whispered back. "It's you—paranoia."

***

The last interview of the day was done. Andy shook the hands of the panel of men and women. All had brought different perspectives and different interviewing techniques—from brusque, driven inquiries, seemingly intolerant of mental slowness; to kind, gentle, open-ended questioning, where thought exploration was welcomed. Andy knew they were all speaking the language of love, and they truly cared about the people before them; but they cared more for the people or the cognizant life-forms whose lives—and deaths—might be in the hands of whomever was chosen. The candidates had to fit the tasks. A "can-do, all-things-possible" spirit was essential, for assuredly the task might not fit the person, and negative results would flow if grit and daring was not present in abundance. Andy glanced at his watch; the old planetary sun outside of New Jerusalem had already set over their part of the world, but God's light had not varied in brightness or warmth. Regretfully, he had no time to explore Enrique and Ava's lives—they hadn't anticipated professors going over their allotted time limits, and they said they were late for a scheduled appointment. There was something about those two, he thought. Then the thought was gone.

He could easily eat his evening meal now, and enjoy a diversionary tourist moment, such as a special restaurant. His body had the capability of continuing at any level of thought and action for days—this was common to all the resurrected. He thanked God for his resurrection body—it had performed magnificently in the warfare of Satan's final rebellion. The past victories gave confidence for the future. He entered the hallway, and there were John and Diana, watching him with mirthful eyes, feeding from his glance of delight at their presence, which he had not fully expected. He thought it likely that they had eaten without him, were visiting sites, and expected a call from him.

John approached, skirting the people exiting, who were making decisions as to their next destination and how to get there. "We scouted restaurants on the way here. Diana has them listed." John changed his tone and asked, "Was it about space exploration?"

Andy answered quickly. "Yes."

Diana's eyes widened in surprise. "The nearest is a Middle Eastern-themed eatery," she said. "A quarter mile further is an American restaurant, not of fast foods but of dinners—mashed potatoes, meat loaf and gravy, or turkey-and-gravy type fare. Apple pie for dessert."

Before she could finish, a voice bellowed from down the hall. "John! My Pennsylvania river friend!" A dark-bearded man waved his hand as he strode purposefully to the gathered friends.

"My Lord!" John uttered in surprise, even as he attempted to suppress his emotion and volume. Christ took him by the hand and shook heartedly. Internally, John heard, "Everyone knows me. No need to suppress your voice." Jesus then audibly spoke. "Diana and Andy, we've never formally met. I last saw John by the river before Satan's final rebellion. He was with his disciples, Jack, Robert, and Samuel."

John laughed softly. "I hardly warrant the title *teacher*."

Jesus smiled broadly. "I'm Christ—I can't be wrong. But you are a good man, and I know you were a good teacher, for your students belong to me now."

John thought back to that time, and that very day exploded into a thousand scents, scenes, and the very emotional soul quality of the internal mind at that time. The river-mud smell, the blossoming weed flowers, the nearby pines, the scent and sound of the broad waters passing by. The woodsmoke of Jesus's fire, the smell of roasting fish freshly caught—smallmouth bass. John spoke quietly. "Your presence made the difference. Your gift of your partner, the Holy Spirit, made the difference."

"We wouldn't have come, save for your prayers and the prayers of your little community. Andy and Diana, certainly included." Jesus's thick, muscular hand grabbed John's shoulder and squeezed. "Come, all of you, eat with me. I would like that. Let's go to that American restaurant that serves apple pie and mashed potatoes." Jesus turned to two trailing men, aides, and addressed them. "You may come along and eat with us at the American restaurant, or you may go home. Simply keep phones handy, if the latter."

The aides smiled happily. They already had possible evening scenarios in their imaginations. "To home. We are your children, but our children, even as adults, await us," said one aide.

The second aide said, "Thank you, good boss."

Jesus, smiling, answered. "The thanks are all mine. Another solid day of work. To your families," he ordered softly.

Jesus looked at his friends. "Now only my angels surround me, and they take up no space.

***

They entered the restaurant—the fuselage of an antiquated transoceanic jetliner. The hostess with long, black hair and dark eyes could not stop her work demeanor from turning to a wide-eyed joy. She called the proprietor, behind the counter—her father—who came instantly, his face lit with joy at the Lord's presence. He hugged the Lord, and talk ensued in Hebrew. The party was shown a quiet booth at the back of the fuselage.

"Everything is good here," said Jesus. "The proprietor, Lev, started as a short-order cook in Madison, Wisconsin, while attending college, back in the nineteen seventies. He is an American, who once served in the Israeli defense force and retired after running a successful eatery for forty years. After the resurrection, he took over this restaurant to keep busy and maintain a hand on the pulse of his city." Jesus studied the faces of his three friends as their histories raced through his mind. They were good people; all his people were. Their goodness had salved his wounded body and mind from that day he had suffered beyond suffering and his soul had writhed in agony. He was glad that he had not listened to his desire to escape, if possible, the pain. Only his agony and death could have freed the lives of these captives born into Satan's kingdom.

Orders were taken, and food came quickly. The talk could not compete with the food, and silence came; as forks, spoons, knives busily clinked.

Jesus went back in time, saw Andy crying his heart out on an empty rock in the middle of the Susquehanna River so none of his tribesmen could see his weakness, hear his anguish. How he had cried for his little boys. How he would have given his own life to make them whole. John—teenaged John— so alone in a heartless world that his soul had become desolate before the Spirit had made a home within and guided him into life everlasting. He had given that new life willingly in service to his Lord, foregoing the dream of a companion/wife, children. Diana, with the same loneliness and desolation as John, conned by an evil church into a career of degradation. She, with the hope of a new life with promises of fulfillment, left the world behind to follow John, and so she found and followed her Lord and suffered. His death had made the difference in their lives. They were worth every second of his agony. He would do it again, without doubt, if asked. Abba loved his children, and the Son, one Spirit with the Father, was no different.

Jesus noticed a crowd was gathering in the space before their table. The crowd had purposely waited, thankfully, till they had eaten. What else would His people do? They were mannered, thoughtful people. The people of the diner knew who He was, what He had done for them. They were whole in mind and body, had peace with the past, and anticipated the future with a happy yearning. And the future was forever. They had stories like Andy, John, and Diana. They had all given up something precious—their lives, hopes, dreams—to follow something they felt but could not absolutely prove: that God loved them and that He was worthy of love in return. What a thin, tenuous reality, more a dream, more a fleeting scent on the wind. They had seen the kingdom of Earth and knew—no, hoped—there was another kingdom, a kingdom of justice, kindness, and yes, love. Love so good it was worth dying for; it was worth dying for this kingdom not seen, only imagined.

All his people were dreamers, knowing something was wrong with reality when everyone else said it was right. They sensed the wrongness, the willfulness in humankind, the deceits of Satan, and they staked their futures on Christ. That took something, and even though He was the Christ, He had all that God, his father, had in intelligence and discernment. He wondered how they had known, known enough to give all to Him. Why should He wonder? The Holy Ghost had made the invisible visible. He had taught them well and fought for them all their lives. Amazing. Life was amazing. Jesus began to laugh. Yes, amazing.

He saw the love upon their countenances, the quiet deference in their movements, the absence of speech, whispers, shushes. Jesus stood, a glass in his hand. They all looked down at their hands, and they instantly had a glass filled with wine or grape juice, whichever their preference. In the other hand, a freshly pinched morsel of bread. He spoke. "Take, eat; this is my body." He himself took as they all did. He held his cup high, and they too raised theirs. He said, "This is my blood of the covenant, which was poured out for you. We are partaking anew in the Kingdom of God, and His Kingdom will have no end." He drank, and they drank. "Amen, my children. I love you with all that I am and with all I have. The Father loves you; the Spirit loves you. I thank you for working for Our Kingdom, for saving lives."

The owner, Jesus's friend, said, "I speak for all. We love You, the Father, the Holy Spirit, with all that we are, forever."

"Thank you," Jesus said. "Come and shake my hand, all of you."

All remained, many shook hands, some wept as they hugged Him, others spoke, telling of their conversions, or of hard times that were conquered by His presence, His words, their faith in Him. When the last person had been greeted, Jesus spoke to Andy, John, and Diana. "I do this at least three times a day with groups. In between, there is always the lone person who approaches me. I never tire of it. It energizes me. Many people say that my life gives their lives meaning, but I can equally say their lives give my life meaning, satisfaction, peace." He began walking toward the door, waving to Lev and his daughter, exchanging parting words in Hebrew. All the people had glowing peace on their faces. His party stepped out into the bright light of eternal day.

"Are you going home tonight or waiting for the morning of the world outside the New Jerusalem?" asked Jesus.

John laughed. "We had planned to stay the night, but now, as beautiful as the city is…I could leave now. I miss my river, the mountains, my routine, my friends. As much as I like the history I'd find in this city, the present and the future call me forward."

Andy had caught John's intent. "I feel that also, more so than at any time in my life. There are interesting facets of history to explore, but they will always be here. I'll look them up on some lazy, rainy day. We have entered a new dimension, a new world—the heavens stretch out to us. With you, with eternal life, we are complete. No need to search for who we were, we as individuals or as humankind. The exploring of our Father's world has been planned to happen at this time, and it is the right time in history."

Jesus looked into Diana's eyes. She answered his quizzical gaze. "Yes, forward. We know who we are in you. The past has lost its hold; all the wrongs have been righted, and I yearn to explore all of life's possibilities."

"Well spoken, all of you. I would like to visit you, fish your river with rod and reel—just a man's view of the water, knowing what the fish are eating gives me the advantage. Still, the tug on the end of the line delights me—the runs and jumps, the digging deep, the race to obstacles to break my line."

John spoke. "Visit us. We will give you space to be with your thoughts, and when you are with us, we will ask for nothing."

Jesus answered, "May I give you a flight pass, so you will arrive home more quickly?"

"We have the funds." John spoke with appreciation in his tone.

"Why spend what you don't need to spend? Besides, it could function as compensation for my upcoming stay."

Andy entered the conversation upon John's perplexed silence. "Yes, we will take the pass, and we will be expecting you."

Jesus's eyes sparkled in appreciation of Andy's grasp of their interaction. By taking the pass as compensation, they had entered a deal, and a deal needed to be sealed by completing the terms. The three shook Jesus's hand, even as one of Jesus's aides returned to him with flight passes in hand.

***

Andy sat in an Adirondack chair, alone on the riverbank landing, only feet from the water. A few fish were still rising to the surface, some jumping, but the heavy feed of the early morning had slowed as the sun was fully upon the waters. The New Jerusalem trip was still playing through his mind after three days of being home. He was having a difficult time imagining himself moving through a star scape within a sophisticated vessel. He had easily taken to the age of machines and technology; he, with depth, understood the fundamentals of atomic power, lasers, the forces of space. Still, he wondered if he had jumped too quickly into this space program. He was growing bored with life along the river—to a point. Eternal time had to be filled with something worth doing, a new frontier. Life could be stale, empty when Jesus was not being actively served. He envisioned that decades and centuries would be needed to explore the tiniest part of the vast universe. Well, he had eternal life, and the lecturers had said anyone could opt out at any point in the process.

An angel presence came into his mind gently, then expanded its presence and message. An ancient one was coming today, a man or woman who had lived prior to the coming of Jesus. Even greater was this one's status, as he or she had lived before Moses declared the laws of God. Very few of these men and women existed, such was Satan's hold on humanity in those days, and they were revered by all. Abraham's friend Melchizedek, king of Salem, was such a man. Andy stood and went up the bank, thinking he would retrieve another chair to place beside his own. The ancient one was at the top of the grade among the collection of chairs and small tables. He wore the tunic of ancient Israel and a prayer shawl. His face was bearded, but he wore no side ringlets. The man smiled. "Free of the law. A little of this, a little of that. Don't ask for rhyme or reason."

Andy laughed at his guest's explanation of his clothing and appearance and responded, "I am the same—a coating of bear grease on my skin, under my modern fabrics."

The ancient one laughed freely before speaking. "I am Melchizedek. You may call me Mel or Chizz…whatever is your pleasure. I know you as Andy."

He wondered which name would be chosen for him and why; he guessed that Andy wouldn't mention his name, but if he did, he would use Mel—more formal than Chizz. "Let us sit here. I like the elevation for a more comprehensive view." The ancient one had read Andy's thoughts as to seating and had given an answer.

Andy extended his hand toward the chairs in deference to his guest's request. "Are you hungry or thirsty, Mel?" asked Andy.

Mel answered, "Good, thank you. To business. You have been chosen as a ship's captain. Training will take place in Florida. You may assemble your own crew, full or partial, or you may have one given you. You have a month to make the very first training cycle. You think this is all casual, but it is not. People will quickly find what positions they are most suited for or may realize they are no longer interested. No shame in dropping out. However, know that a special upgrade is coming, like the upgrades of the past years, and it will be of great benefit.

"A salient point: one quality has merit of great importance and is not found in everyone, and it cannot be upgraded. It is the ability to work quickly under pressure and without the niceties of consultation or collaboration, immediate respect, or manners. This quality is well represented in the population. God's people just don't take offense and hold grudges. On the other hand, they aren't challenged in harsh tones or with disrespect. Nor do they daily make snap decisions on which people's lives depend. They are patient and have confidence in their decision-making and keenness of mind when there is no pressure.

A corollary to this line of thought is: only success counts. Why some people have a high percentage of right decisions, made in a timely fashion, and others do not is still a mystery. But it seems that knowing what facts are crucial and the relative dependability of such facts may be the key. Having the ability to shut out the influences of others is also key to good decisions. A personality that needs "others" for validity and love or acquiesces to "others" in time of stress, can't make clean decisions based on facts. We let captains pick their people—friendship, teamwork, and knowing the actions and thought process of your team will dominate any adversity."

Andy spoke. "The world we grew up in, during Satan's kingdom, will provide the highest percentage of successful people during times of stress. People born in the Millennium will produce fewer, I fear."

Mel nodded his head in agreement. "Yes, the Millennials were born into a world where good was the norm and snap decisions were rare. Except at the very end, during Satan's rebellion." The happy eyes of Mel turned serious, as did his words. "But the rest of us did live in times of stress. Snap decisions that could bring, death, failure—punishment. Harsh words, demotions, gloating men of rank. Enemies, seething with hatred, wishing to inflict pain physically and mentally. That was Satan's world. Our Christian forces will be like family, of that you can be assured. We may very well enter Satan's world again. It will be separate from us, outside of us, and we must not let it in. I am about to give you information that you cannot tell anyone. It is being shared only among captains, and even captain candidates cannot discuss it with others of the same rank."

Andy's tone held a gravitas. "I understand and will not divulge to anyone what you share with me."

Mel spoke. "Lucifer had decided to rebel long before the advent of mankind upon Earth. Angels participated in the creation of the cosmos, as did Lucifer, who, as a ranking angel, had angels under his authority. Lucifer tricked the angels into creating the image of God and of living things, not specifically on Earth but through the cosmos. God allowed the deceit to take place, knowing that far in the future history of mankind, He would make it yield glory to His name and Kingdom. What I am telling you is, there is life on other planets. Some of this life may be partially or entirely in the image of our Creator, and I mean soulfully and spiritually: cognizant life-forms that have the awareness or capability to know God exists and is our Creator."

Andy studied Mel's eyes and spoke. "God's creative word was pure. Satan simply lied, misdirected it."

"Yes. He was the deceiver. A liar from his birth," Mel said in a tone of loathing. "He lied to his subordinates."

"So…conflict is certain," stated Andy.

Mel did not answer; he seemed to place the ancient mantle upon himself. A silence of peace descended. In time, he said, "You may eventually mention that cognizant life-forms may exist, when appropriate. Allow all other information to flow naturally into awareness. Be the passenger in the new world coming, not the driver. In other words, don't suggest, don't espouse negativity. Let the unfolding reality drive events." The ancient one looked Andy in the eyes and said, "You understand."

Andy answered, "Yes. Clearly understood."

"Good. Many people can't comprehend my words." The ancient one smiled. "You have a beautiful home and grounds. I live in New Jerusalem. Abraham is doing well, of course. He is deeply excited about our new mission."

Andy returned a wide smile. Mel had read his mind.

Mel stood and said, "Good day to you." He took a step toward the river and then spoke again. "Soldiering men would be of worth. Praise be to God." The ancient one faded away.

CHAPTER 4

Andy had mulled the words of the ancient one for a week, alternately pondering, then tasting, grinding, and finally digesting, until he was on the verge of knowing whether to accept or reject the training program for captaincy of a vessel for deep-space exploration. He needed to be all in, assured that the Lord, indeed, needed him and that he had something to offer in return. He logically concluded that he had a weakness and he had a strength. His perceived weaknesses were in the sciences, mathematics, chemistry, physics. Most of these tasks were performed by AI computers. Still, he needed a strong overall grasp of these subjects—as well as of AI functioning and weaknesses—so that he could recognize glitches, errors in the systems and actual processes. Mel had mentioned an upgrade and inferred it was to be beneficial to space exploration.

Upgrades had begun at the Millennium's end, when Satan was consigned to eternal Hell. An upgrade every ten years, first with the physical body and then with the mind. All God's chosen were affected, all benefitted, if they wished; nothing was forced. Those with pre-existing strengths in the upgraded area gained more strength, on average. That is, an individual's pre-existing strength kept him ahead of the average. The physical routing of neurons within the brain were affected, as was blood flow in the targeted areas. Blood levels of oxygen, hormones, minerals, amino acids, and vitamins changed. The latest monitoring equipment showed the enhancements.

The moment an upgrade began was clearly defined as supernatural by the participant. Everyone felt the presence of the God force—the Holy Spirit—upon and around them, much like their initial conversion state of mind, when the Holy Spirit entered their minds and became their teacher and friend. They felt loved and blessed by His presence. The Spirit seemed to hover and brood upon the participant as He did upon the waters of creation. An impelling urge came to them, a loving prod, to continue as the Spirit had led Jesus to his temptations upon the mountaintop. Then slowly the upgrade began to take hold, and within days or weeks, it was firmly established. The gift came complete from the beginning—no trial and error; it just manifested in repetition upon repetition. Success, even if unearned and not understood, brought confidence, assurance, trust. Through time and repetition, the God force seemed to be less noticeable, and the mechanics of movement and muscular control or mental logic and processes were understood and controlled more by the person. Even when the person felt in control, the safety net of the Spirit was always present and quick to correct and rescue attempts gone wrong. The gifts of the mind entered and followed the same process.

Andy remembered when the visual-artistic upgrade had allowed him to draw, freehand, any scene, from complex equipment to the human face or landscapes. He could pick up a pencil or charcoal and, without hesitation or thought, he could draw as well as the most noted artists of history. Previously, he had been limited to an average ability in landscapes. The same had occurred to humanity when the musical upgrade occurred. Andy could sit down at a piano and play, hesitantly and slowly at first, but within an hour, he was remembering tunes he had heard and reproducing them faithfully. He began to understand the written language of music and could express textually the music he heard within his mind. Another upgrade had allowed him to add and subtract huge numbers. The very first upgrade had allowed a clear understanding of God's storage of knowledge in the vaults of life. Everyone had learned how to operate his or her mind within the system of stored universal knowledge.

Whatever skills those formally labeled idiot/savant possessed, all of humanity had tapped into. Their God had been showing humanity His latent power and capabilities placed within Adam at the beginning. He had blessed the poor of spirit, the seemingly useless souls, to validate His care, concern, and love for them, reveal humanity's potential, and to mock man's carnal pride. To many, the physical adaptations, which were the first upgrades to be initiated, were the most miraculous, affecting motor skills of bodily movement. Everyone was now capable of a standing front flip, a handstand, a cartwheel, and leaps of distance and height equal to Olympic records of the past. He would trust the upgrade coming.

Andy believed his past life, lived in Satan's kingdom, was his strength. His life had been rooted in war, in single combat, raids, skirmishes, ambushes, in full-scale battle, in tactical and strategic capabilities. He had been convinced by the Ancient One there would be conflict with cognizant life-forms that would create anger and hostility toward the presence of God's people. Andy was a man who intimately knew conflict, the emotional, soulful side of destruction and loss. He had experienced more hostility than most. He could think, function in periods of great stress and achieve success. He would be needed by his Lord.

With this thought in mind, he sent a reminder card to his new acquaintances from Jerusalem, Paternus, Seth, and Woden. It could not have been a chance meeting of three soldiers—God had arranged it. Andy thought it would be natural and polite for his invited guests to require a firm invitation separate from the chance meeting and spontaneity of a quick friendship. No one wished to impose on another on a whim of the moment, however delightful the whim. They were men who had come of age in a world of conflict. They had adjusted and conquered with the Lord's intervening guidance. Although the meeting was fortuitous, *was* it God's plan? A proving needed to happen. Questions needed to be asked. Could Paternus, Seth, and Woden play a role in the opening of space? Would they wish to? How would they relate to his other potential cadre members? In the end, would the talk of past conflicts in their lives expose something within his own motives as to intention and desire? His newfound friends accepted the invitation to visit.

***

Andy keenly observed the river from the highest bank, where tables, chairs, picnic tables were scattered. The gentle slope down the bank led to beached kayaks; two floating, flat-bottomed, wooden, johnboats; and a docked pontoon boat minus a canopy. A few deer were grazing in the nearest island's pebbly shallows of river grasses. A bald eagle soared overhead. Andy heard a vehicle enter the back approach to his home on the loose limestone that had been spread just the day before atop the existing stone embedded in the soil. He liked that sound of tire-pressed stones grating, crunching against each other, telling of visitors approaching. Robin and Tuck, in separate wheeled vehicles, had picked up his guests at Harrisburg International. Wheeled vehicles had made a resurgence over the newer air-lift systems.

He was about to turn and walk around his home to greet his guests when he saw the vehicles coming to him across the lawn. He smiled. His boys always delighted in leaving roads behind, and his guests could exit, flop into a seat with a river view, or walk the river trail, if legs needed stretching.

He knew Leaf and Diana, in the kitchen, had decided that outdoor eating would be the lunch plan.

Paternus, Seth, and Woden waved immediately upon exiting as Andy approached. None showed signs of travel wear and tear, and their eyes were beaming in delight. Seth had already turned and viewed the looming green mountain ridge behind, and other guests were stretching their eyes to see the treeless area—the obvious course of the river. The handful of women were pointing at features of the expansive home, especially the flat roof sporting shade umbrellas, trellises, flagpoles, and wind indicators. Andy, through past photographs, recognized the women: Helen, Woden's former wife, was tall, thin, and had the dark-black hair of her Greek ancestry. He knew Paternus's former wife, Agnella, immediately. She was tall, muscular, and fair—a radiant queen, at one time, of countless harvest festivals. The shortest of the three, petite but wiry, had to be Seth's wife, Sara, of the original forest people. He noted a relaxed quickness in her movements.

The strong hands of the guests embraced Andy's hands. John materialized from the river entrance to the home and strode over to support Andy in greeting. Tuck and Robin were by the vans, getting instructions from the now-gathered women, including Leaf and Diana, as to who would sleep where and the baggage consigned to each.

The principals exchanged travel information concerning flight times, smoothness of connections, traffic conditions, the scenery. The group began to stroll as Andy gave an informal orientation tour; the beauty of the home and land were commented upon. The thickness and greenness of vegetation on the steep mountainside, the blue sky with numerous vultures circling, the fecundity of the vegetable gardens, the numerous wild turkeys on the lawn, and the relaxed fox family spread out in the grass were all noted and enjoyed. They strolled to the riverbank, commented upon the clarity of the river's water and the abundance of fish seen, even from the riverbank vantage. The once-soaring eagle came down within inches of the river and made a snatch into the water, snagging a long fish, and settled in the top of a dead tree on an adjacent island. Squirrels chattered high in the massive river oaks. The Baltimore oriole nests hanging from the great river trees over the water provided oriole sightings of oohs and aahs.

Ten more recently arrived guests were introduced—children, grandchildren, great-grandchildren (called "children," though they now were perpetual adults)—whoever had been free of commitments at the time and wanted to see the United States, Pennsylvania, and the people who lived there. Food and drinks appeared, and a fire was started. Some people went to the river to wade and cool themselves on this hot day. Others went to see their lodging arrangements. Then the Pennsylvania friends, in their homes nearby, began to collect and mingle with the foreign guests. The Burnells were a mild surprise to the guests, as they had had very little contact with Africans and none with African-Americans. Before the evening was gone, the Burnells were beloved. Homes and properties were toured, prized plants, flowers, pools, domesticated pets, and livestock shown. All had Christ in the center of their lives, and they shared and became the deepest of friends by the time the sun was near its setting across the river. All sat quietly and began their supper of corn and buffalo steaks. Seth commented that buffalo herds, which Seth, Woden, and Paternus had seen and even hunted in their youth, had been returned to eastern Europe.

The grass became dewy and the air cooled, and buffalo robes, Afghans, and plaid blankets appeared for the people who had arrived in shorts. The firelight danced upon the trees, the nighthawks cheeped, the big fish jumped and slapped back into their homes of wetness. Some people catnapped, and others remained alert and talking into the predawn. They ate fresh pancakes, eggs, and hashbrowns or a sandwich from the offerings of the day before. Ten desired and were given fishing rods, and Tuck's private bait setup offered live minnows, earthworms, and crayfish. Into the cool waters, ankle to knee high, went the guests. Tuck kept track of the "keepers" and the guests who caught them. He would send remittance to the fish and game department to pay for further upkeep of the Pennsylvania waterways and aquatic life, as well as the salaries of fish-and-game employees.

By midmorning, fish were frying and being eaten. Everyone was up, some playing volleyball on the spacious lawns. Some hiked to John and Diana's home on the mountaintop (they would transport from the summit back to Andy's home). By afternoon, the sun was hot, the sky hazy with humidity, and most people were in the swimming pools of various homes or gathered at a natural soaking hole within the river.

****

Andy, Tuck, Robin, Dan and Emily, John and Diana, Tim, Mat, Pete and Grace, Jack, Tom Jr., and Tom Sr. were at the archery and shooting areas held in common by all in the little settlement. At Andy's insistence, Woden, Seth, and Paternus had brought replicas of their 800 AD weapons and armaments and were explaining usage, tactics. Recreations of past wars and lifestyles were immensely popular, and replica villages and towns for every period existed, delighting tourists with the oddities of culture and life. The three Byzantines jointly owned a recreated village in their home nation. Andy believed that primitive weapons might be seen in the universe, and the knowledge was important. Plus, this bonding moment was insightful—and downright fun.

Andy brought out his replica muzzle-loaders—matchlock and flintlock—a stone-headed war club, English-made tomahawks, and his long bow and arrows. The males were shirtless with sunblock applied; all wore shorts. It was obvious by musculature that Woden, Seth, and Paturnus had greater bodily mass. Their lives of physical labor, with few machines to help, and unlike most people of their time, plentiful food, plus genetics had shaped them. Wars in those days were fought with muscles pounding opponents with heavy objects, not the hand-and-eye coordination used for bullets and laser bursts. They pointed out where physical scars had been numerous—on heads and necks and near armpits and waists, where gaps in armor were common. They left their resurrected bodies for a moment to show the location of the tortured flesh of battle.

***

Woden, the teacher of the moment, spoke to his armed audience. "I separated the weapons. One group holds the stabbers; the other, the beaters. Stabbers: short swords, long daggers—almost a mini sword. Even an arrow or a bolt can be considered a stabber. A javelin, held or thrown, is a stabber, as well as a lance used on horseback. Even giant arrows thrown by tension bows are stabbers.

"The best course for survival against a stabber is to incapacitate the enemy first—before they attempt an attack. The second is concealment behind barriers—a shield or fortified works. The third defense is disrupting their aim by movement, and the fourth is wearing body armor.

"Body armor forces the enemy to use beaters—for example, the mace—either bladed or a swinging ball. The long sword, because of its weight, falls more into the category of beater, even though it has a sharp edge. A sword thrust with a long blade usually lacks speed and can be deflected. Sling shots and all the mechanical throwing machines send beaters, as well. War hammers? Beaters. War axes? Beaters.

"Both weapon systems demand time to deliver, and this is why group tactics are important—the nagging little movements and thrusts coming from a thousand different directions to deflect and weaken a blow and the enemy's strategy. The pike can be a disrupter weapon. My half-brother, Little John, and I held back an army's assault on a fortress wall, at a choke point, of course, with a pike and sword and sometimes a battle-ax. With his pike,

Little John jabbed and poked the few bodies that could face me in a narrow opening, keeping them off balance, vulnerable, defensive, and not advancing. I had the chance to swing the broad sword or axe or finesse a thrust. He cleared the body as it was falling with a hook and a sweeping motion.

"To liken it to your American football, we were the linemen, sometimes offense, sometimes defense. We sometimes liked tall tight ends with pikes or short swords behind us. We would pull down an opponent's shield—" Woden held up a battle-ax with a significant and purposely forged indent—like a can opener. This latches onto the top of a shield. A quick pull down. The enemy exposed sends a thrust toward me. I block as the tall man behind me gives a quick thrust with his pike into the head of the enemy, who then can be hooked and pulled closer or discarded. Once a momentum was created, a wedge formation would go in." Woden stopped, as memories of the dying and falling swept across his mind. He studied the faces of his audience, then spoke. "That was the world without Christ, remember." His sad eyes sought their confirmation.

Amens came from the gathered.

Woden continued, "So let's all try these weapons. Crossbows, archery, javelins first. Paternus is setting up some of the heavy artillery of our day in miniature—catapults and bolt-throwing ballistae." He paused. "Before the weapons, try on the body armor, the helmets. Feel the weight and know we sometimes fought in humid weather just like this central Pennsylvania summer day. While armored, take a few swings at the chopping post so as to understand the strength needed to carry the armor and to fight. Understand how the body was forced to work with the armor." He searched his audience's eyes. "Any questions?"

Emily raised her hand. "When did Christ become real? When did He walk into your heart and you knew it was forever?"

Woden smiled. "Thank you for asking. I love the telling of this story." He paused to gather his thoughts. "In my teens, I only wanted a wife and to work the forest soil, downing trees, raising crops, hunting. Perfect life. Then my grandfather said that I needed a guardian spirit, gods or a God, to seek power from. Within days I was traveling to the great city to scout for a wife. Just by chance..." Woden chuckled. "Just by chance." He stopped. All gathered saw the humor, as all knew there were no chances in life; just their Lord working through the foolish thoughts of prideful men and women. "Just by chance, I met a traveling priest, Peter, who told me of the Christ, His Kingdom. We parted ways and met again, just by chance, outside the city, as a pagan funeral ceremony was upon the road. Peter wished to save a wife of the dead man, as she had given her life to Christ. The pagan custom was for her to die with her husband, follow him into the afterlife. Some force took ahold of me—I now know the Holy Spirit had come to me. I backed Peter's request; the girl was temporarily saved. Then, my life as I had known it fell apart. My land was conquered, my people—the true people, who loved freedom—fought and lost. Dispossessed, I struggled with the Lord, fought the truth, yet clung to Him."

"When did it come together?" asked Emily.

Woden laughed. "A year and a half later, in a dry desert theme. In combat, trying to carry a wounded man to safety, with dust a pall about me and a horseman searching for me to kill me. Anger at God came to me. I tried to harness that anger at God, but no power came. It came to my mind that praise was the power of the redeemed, the power I sought. 'Trust in God,' the Spirit said. 'The power of rage and hatred of God is Satan's power.' I stepped into the power of the Kingdom of God. I said to Satan, 'I'd rather be a slave to my King than a prince in your house. I'd rather be dead than use your power.' Satan fled, never to return, and God's power was secured in my heart. Finally, the inner battle had stopped, and it's been praise ever since. My source of strength comes not from my flesh but from the living God, and His power never quits."

All gathered began to clap. Praise came, and a quiet, contented peace followed the gathered as they spread to their stations on the lawns.

***

In the evening, those interested in conversation had gone to Tim's home (hosting rotated daily), and specifically, to his flat rooftop of comfortable outdoor furniture, telescopes, chiminea, fire boxes, and refrigerators stocked with food and drink. The mountain ridge seemed to be closer, more looming than at Andy's. The river view was from higher ground and was nearer to the river's bank, giving a slightly more open view of a wider swath of river. Those who still had energy had gone to Tim's pool, which had increased in size in the last hundred years. The underwater lighting was excellent, as was the lighting on overhead poles. A water volleyball game had many participants. More of Tom's clan, the Burnells, had come, as well as Tim's family; and more of Woden, Seth, and Paternus's relatives and friends had arrived. Ling, a former Chinese army officer, had come, bringing a son. Ling had happened to be near Mat on the final day of the final battle of Armageddon, when Christ arrived in the clouds. Ling, one of the few Chinese Christians of that time, had been directed to go with Mat, and so the connection was made, and it had lasted. The acres of yards were lit by balloons, the invention of Dan. The balloons festooned walkways, and many had been hung on trees surrounding the vast lawns so that night creatures could be seen—the highlights being a panther and her two young cubs, who had come down from the mountain, and a pack of frolicsome coyote pups.

Andy was sitting on Tim's roof, looking out at the river, enjoying the difference in the view and more so, the sense of guest status at Tim's home. There was a slightly exotic feel to looking into someone's refrigerator and trying something new and to analyzing the layout of lighting, open fires, furniture, and improvements that he might wish to have. It was a far cry from huddling around a fire of sticks with bear hides as covers as he and his family had done the year their bark longhouse burned down. Mat, Jack, and Tom Jr. had come to the rooftop slightly wet from four hours of diving, volleyball, and just sitting in the heated pool, feeling their muscles unwind. Andy spoke. "Are you carrying the party tomorrow night, Tom?"

"You got that right," Tom said. "Dad's all stocked with food and drink; pools are cleaned, all extra beds, cots, and air mattresses are out. Jack and I will be facilitating the event."

"Good. A staff of helpers is needed for this many people." Andy saw Ling on the roof and jumped up. "Ling, over here!" He met Ling with an embrace. "My brother in Christ and Asiatic cousin." Ling laughed heartedly at the native American connection with Asia before written history. Andy continued, "Sit. And enjoy. Need food or a drink? Tim's fridge is well stocked."

"In time." Ling's voice held anticipation.

John and Diana, Emily and Dan, Pete and Grace popped up from the stairway, saw Andy's waving hand, and joined the group. Andy counted his people. He needed his boys, Tuck and Robin, as well as Tim and Mary, Woden, Seth, and Paternus. They were his picks for his crew. He had approached each individually and hinted at space travel, then exploration, and gathered their opinions as to their interest—in general, for a new adventure—in space. Many embraced the idea in theory. None knew Andy had the opportunity for a captaincy. Following the realization there was no force called "chance" for those in God's will, Andy understood he should present his invitation, this very night, to space travel and their possible role in the endeavor.

"Could I bother anyone to round up my boys, and Tim and Mary, Woden, Seth, and Paternus, as the rest of us remain here as a group? I want to announce something."

The youngest men stood—Jack, Mat, Tom Jr.—no words spoken between them. Mat addressed Andy. "We're on our way."

When all requested had gathered in silence, no one guessing at Andy's intended conversation but understanding that the Spirit present was at peace, and so Andy's thoughts would be good, Andy spoke. "I took a trip to New Jerusalem, as you know. John and Diana accompanied me as traveling companions. We met Woden, Seth, and Paternus, seemingly a chance encounter, when John asked for directions. What good friends they are, and what a unique time in history they lived in, when an empire had professed to be Christian and the world's greatest political and religious threat to the Lord—Islam—was practiced unchecked and weaponized.

"All those dangers are gone from Earth now. In a way, this leads to another topic. Why did I go to Jerusalem? I was invited, informed, tested, and sent home with a question I was to answer: Did I wish to participate in space exploration?"

Soft whispers of surprise rose from the gathered. Andy continued, "I have decided my answer is yes, and I will participate in training for captaincy of a space vessel—me, a once-ignorant savage, who hunted daily for meat for my family and had no liking or understanding of the Lord of the universe. When I succeed, I will be allowed to pick my crew, who will also have been trained. I believe you are my crew. Think upon that and only that. And the fact we may meet cognizant life-forms that need to know Christ. Do you want to be a part of this endeavor?

"Approach me at any time during the next week to talk. I will give a more detailed list of possible crew positions and the training for them tomorrow. Do not be daunted by any consideration. You can leave training at any time. An update to our skills inventory is promised. The volunteer list is projected to be immense, do not feel obligated to participate—someone will take your place. For this evening, relax, let the thought caress the mind gently, and let us continue to bond with old and new faces."

The gathered applauded, then hesitantly broke into small groups and headed for refrigerators or a table of food downstairs in the living room, with homemade root beer and birch beer offered. Some put on sweaters and light jackets, changed to long pants, and reassembled on the deck, gathering by the three telescopes to view the distant stars, which were shining brightly, no haze in the sky. Groups of people and single souls were walking by the river's edge, through woods and planted tree rows, on paths and roads, experiencing a summer's night. Unnecessary lights went out as the food was eaten, and even the night creatures on the lawns faded back into the woods.

When stargazing had been satisfied, the group settled around the one remaining active fire box. Sofas, chairs, and chaise longues had been brought to the fire's light. In the silence, it was Emily whose voice was heard. "Seth, tell us of your walk with the Lord. Anything like Woden's?"

Seth smiled. He was deeply tanned, had been born with olive skin and dark hair; he blended into the shadows. Only of average height, he exuded tamed power in a broad body, heavily muscled. "We are two different studies; contrasts abound. I was born and baptized, raised in the Church, knew the catechism, knew the law, knew the saints, but had the same rebellious, warring spirit that all flesh gives their allegiance to. I went into the armed services as a lark, seeking adventure and a reputation, and I found I was not hero material. A backward theme of untamed souls showed me what Hell could be like, and it mirrored my own soul. But I had a Captain Lucian. I watched him die, but he is eternally alive. I visit him once a month, when my schedule has regularity. He showed me the error in my thinking. The Spirit set the world in order within my mind and dared me to believe in God's plan and make it mine. Only through the indwelling Holy Spirit could that happen. The Lord saved me, burst my chains and burdens. I renounced sin and legalism and my confusion for the Spirit and God's ownership. I saw that a soldier's work was of utmost importance in a fallen world. He took away my fears of death and mutilation, He gave me daring and boldness…" The tears began to stream as Sara, beside him, wrapped herself around his arm.

Paternus watched Seth's tears, wanted to divert attention from his friend so that he could recover. Paternus's voice boomed, "Well, dearest Emily, I know I'm next, so I might as well get it over with."

"How astute you are, Paternus. I was gunning for you next. Give it up." Shy Emily laughed at her boldness, as did her audience.

Everyone was chuckling, including Paternus, until he began speaking. His solemnity, the depth of his emotion, held them spellbound. "I cracked apart under the stress of constant combat. I feared death and mutilation. Feared my manhood was not enough to save my wife and children, or our theme of constant conflict and sorrow. I'd be darned if I'd give up my good life of control and what I wanted for some wimpy Christ. I ran away from what I loved best—my wife and family. I found peace in wine, women not my wife, and avoiding military duty. I found regret, sorrow, and shame in that peace I controlled. Man's peace and control is Satan's greatest lie. At the depth of my despair, not knowing the way home or to victory over myself, the Holy Spirit had a general—on horseback, mind you, going to war—stop when he was diverted by a blocked street. He saw me. He had only seen me once before, many years in the past. He got down off that horse and made me his priority. Me, covered in white flour, fat and slovenly—a baker's helper. Told me he was going to my hometown to free my wife and kids and that I should come along as his aide. I couldn't have marched; I would need the horse given an aide. I hesitated, and he left me for the ship. A voice from Heaven said, 'Go!' and my feet moved, my legs reached out, and it wasn't me who moved them. That's the God I'm talking about—that's the God we follow and obey. Praise his Holy Name.

"I went back to the front, gaining strength every day, the excess weight melting from my body, the clear mind returning, the strength to resist temptations completely fulfilled. I was dead to sin. I went back and I heartily killed the enemy and freed my family. Oh, what joy to have my children in my arms and my Agnella by my side." Now the tears were streaming down his cheeks. He said, "You exchanged one teary face for another." Agnella hugged him around the waist.

Emily's eyes were streaming tears. "Look around you. We're all taking the same bath." So it was that in tears, they remembered their salvation. Through their tears, they remembered God's goodness, and they knew that if space held one hurting soul, one being who was not cognizant of God, their maker, or of His character of unfailing love, they should find that one soul and proclaim the wonders of their Father God.

CHAPTER 5

Andy stood at the helm, watched the stars in the black void of space through the Explorer 7's clear window—a narrow window that ran three-quarters of the way around the oval-shaped command center deck. Occasionally the segmented window shutters would blink—partially or even fully close—when space debris seemed headed for a strike. An antigravity shield, invisible, protected the entire craft, as did a repulsing force shield that reached out and pushed objects aside. The craft had reduced speed for a debris field. He had no reason to desire speed; the vessel was not in danger, was not behind in scheduled mileage. Admittedly, he'd enjoyed the speed of minutes before, simply because it matched the tempo of excitement, of space exploration.

They were one month into their adventure. All had been routine, the Explorer 7 had no known problems and was textbook-perfect in design and handling. The crew was performing flawlessly. It was seven months since they had all gathered at the river settlement to welcome Woden, Seth, and Paternus to Pennsylvania and had been invited to participate in the adventure. With the new mental upgrade, six months of training was all that had been needed.

Dan "the man" sat in his navigational command console of electronic screens, which were all movable simply by silent mind control, if he wished. In front of Dan, only feet away, and a head length below him, sat Emily, his lifelong friend, the helmsman (the term kept from ancient times). She had charge of speed, fuel consumption, the antigravity shield, the repulsing force field, and close support laser weapons. Dan had oversight of nuclear propulsion, the fission reactor for the thermal system, the cryogenic system for the liquid hydrogen. Dan's priority was to take the ship where the captain wanted to go, in the time and manner he wished to arrive. Dan was charged with creating maps of the Explorer 7's journey, including atmospheric conditions and space highways. He also surveyed their surroundings both near and far for hazards to the ship, including the likely ambience of planets, gathered through drone readings. Dan's secondary duty during combat was to assist the helmsman with all duties, exclusive of real-time weapons-fire control. Dan had been trained to be a shooter of long-range weapons, such as torpedoes, drones, and sometimes massed artillery, if necessary. In essence, the helmsman could concentrate on weapons control in times of close-quarters combat.

Tom Jr. was in the captain's seat when Andy was not. Two captains for Explorer-class ships, working alternate shifts. Tom had grown bored with business and inventions; he loved his children, now adults, and extended family, but they could manage without him for a time as he explored the universe. Besides, his great-grandson, Jack, was along. He couldn't die, so what was there to lose? Certainly not eternal life. He had strengthened his most salient weakness—his inability to grasp the emotions, the workings of the minds of others. Time had brought maturity in the understanding of the logical processes of others.

When Emily was not at the helm, Tuck (Andy's son) was. He had always dreamed of space exploration during the Millennium and had consumed every scrap of knowledge written. Had he had greater natural math skills, he would have been considered for the navigator position. He did achieve greater spatial and object-in-motion acuity more quickly than his brother, Robin had. In the time difference between instinctual and calculated, Tuck had the advantage. His brother, Robin, the banker, who had a calculator mind for numbers, had expanded his math knowledge at centers of higher learning to qualify as a navigator. The teams were considered equal, and both captains felt secure with either team on deck.

Pete (the grandson of Mat) and Grace (Pete's former spouse), were the psychological/spiritual counselors for the crew and would profile any aliens encountered. Ling held the physician title. Though sickness and ill health were currently unknown on Earth, it was believed that other planets might test God's chosen. Alien populations assuredly would need assistance, as well. Various diagnostic apparatus were included on the vessel. Tim and Diana held the dual positions of geologists and biologists for the investigation of new planets. Uranium 235 was particularly sought after, as the new class of vessels labeled Explorer class (superseding the Probe class) used thermal nuclear power for the heating of hydrogen fuel. Tim had been a geologist on Earth. Diana had no science background but had taken courses to qualify for flight status as a biologist. She had attempted physics because it seemed interesting and had done so well that some considered her a prodigy. Her aptitude surprised even her.

The Explorer-class vessels were armed with torpedoes, cannon, lasers, and mines, and crew members manned these weapons. These crew members served as internal security as well as a possible security force for planets with hostile animal life or cognizant beings. They were also considered the muscle of the expedition. On board, they routinely cooked, kept sanitary order as well as neatness, performed routine checks for air quality, water quality, and systems maintenance. In their tool shop, they tinkered, invented, and repaired. John and his nephew, Mat (Tim's son), Jack (Tom Jr.'s great-grandson), and Woden filled the security positions. It was believed that Woden's Earth period, circa 800 A.D., held advantages for the understanding of primitive weapons and rudimentary farming and food storage. Woden's friend Paternus and half-brother, Seth, had been selected for another ship, Explorer 8. Andy had badly wanted the two men for his crew, but crew size seemed to be nonnegotiable. The eternal people of God were independent and did not have the need to cling to familiar others for support as in the old world, as they clung to God. Seth and Paternus humbly joined Explorer 8, knowing God's will would work this problem for them. They had the friendship and support of the Holy Spirit within them and the knowledge that Explorer 8's eternal people had open hearts and souls to their fellow citizens, even when strangers; and with eternal life ahead, the two men would eventually return to close friends with the bonus of having stories to tell.

Woden was the only relatively new member of the group of friends. He and his former wife's presence at Andy's summer meeting and his long security-training period in a class with Mat, John, and Jack had solidified his oneness with the group. He was more quiet than talkative, but he was known, in his quiet, to be in communication with their God. From the beginning, all had known his story and his walk with God. Raised in the forests of eastern Europe, his adulthood found him fleeing his homeland with a tattered band of refugees from the barbarian wars. Andy and Woden had the primitive forest world, war, and displacement of their people as common themes in their lives, as well as meeting Christ in times of great trouble. Tim and Mat had the combat bond and survival experiences from the Tribulation that Woden understood and appreciated. John had been a veteran prior to the Rapture and, along with Diana, Jack, Dan, Emily, Pete and Grace, and Tuck and Robin, who had fought in the last uprising of Satan, shared that combat experience with Woden. The crewmates had left many people behind, and all these people had willingly remained on Earth, but were extremely support-ive of their loved ones who had gone to space.

The tight-knit group of fourteen onboard Explorer 7 was supported by an Earth-based facility of two hundred workers, who were diagnostic trou-bleshooters for the vessel, and another group for the preplanned course of the exploration journey. At two-thirds of the journey's predicted distance, a facility was being built, ahead of Explorer 7, as an emergency station for the offloading of crew, if necessary; or an electronic post office for any parts or supplies suddenly needed from Earth.

Last of all, the ten thousand angels assigned to Explorer 7 ran contingency scenarios in which resources outside the Explorer 7's manifest would be need-ed. Andy and the crew knew these forces were about, scouting ahead, but had no say in their command and control structure. Captains could request help or directions or scouting reports, if needed. Angels could inherently move in and out of sight and dimension in space as the resurrected could do to a limited de-gree. Angelic beings could also board their special craft for space flight when space environments were hostile to their natural bodies.

Angelic beings knew that their former comrades who had chosen to fol-low Satan had not all ended up in the Lake of Fire—or that was the rumor. The Trinity had not chosen to clarify this rumor. The angels who had had contact with their fallen brethren in space through actual armed encounters or sightings were sworn to secrecy. The rumor was that many fallen angels (now demons) had fled into the far reaches of space, even before the open-ing hostilities began in the garden of Eden. They may have bound them-selves to other cognizant beings, either through genetic hijackings pass-ing as reproduction, or by occupation, either peacefully or through force. Rumors were that hastily erected camps, discarded body armor, scraps of fabric, tools, and other debris of life had been found scattered throughout the galaxy—even discarded space vessels and space tracks through cosmic dust leading into the unknown zones. These facts gave an edge to space exploration for angels.

As Paradise (the first planet colonized after the Millennium) and Ha-des (repurposed as Hell) had been located on actual planets, so, too, did angels have four planets of origin in the Milky Way Galaxy. They were aligned with four cardinal points that were unchanging in the cosmos of myriad galaxies, suns, planets, debris clouds, black holes, and stars. On these planets, angelic leaders were keenly attuned to the threat from fallen angels to their resurrected comrades and themselves. The Godhead had no fear; the fallen angels were created beings, and if they lived, it was because of the forbearance of God.

Humanity believed any life-forms discovered in space would have technology less or equal to their own. God, through the Spirit, would be the Explorer crew's helper, imparting the wisdom of understanding to all situations. He certainly wouldn't send them out to fail. Earth's space travelers counteracted the feeling of being tourists with the knowledge that demons—sworn enemies of humanity—could be lurking; cognizant beings, if existing, might not know the Savior or might be in active rebellion to Him.

***

Andy turned from the window to Dan, his navigator. "Are we still in the vein?" The vein was the terminology for the newly discovered channels within space not seen by the naked eye. Three separate diagnostic machines for gravitational forces, objects of mass, and gaseous formations were overlayed to present a three-dimensional map of veinlike avenues or clear channels in which, in the simplest terms, a current flowed.

Dan answered, "Yes, and clear sailing at this rate of speed for one hour." Time was in Earth units, and nautical phrases alluded to a sailing-ship past.

Andy's eyes went back to the window. He saw a shadow pass by ahead, a mere blur due to speed; evidently delineated by passing before a gaseous cloud of unknown density. The density of the cloud appeared random and scattered. "What does that moving shadow across the gaseous cloud directly ahead consist of?" Andy asked as he squinted into space.

"No shadow registering," said Dan. "Only the gaseous cloud."

"Full stop," commanded Andy, without emotion.

"Full stop," Emily said immediately, even as all seated members on the deck were pushed against their seat belts, and, as shoulder harnesses were not being worn, some slapped their heads into soft consoles. Ling and Woden, sitting in the guest seats, had come to the helm in their free time to observe. They reacted most severely to the full stop.

Andy spoke as soon as the stop was complete. "What does the gaseous cloud consist of?"

Dan answered quickly, "Vapor from a propulsion system of unknown type or origin."

Andy spoke rapidly; the crew heard emotion in the voice. "Helmsman, reverse course by backing up. Slide fifteen degrees to port. At top speed."

Emily's left hand pulled the course back even as her right hand traversed to the left of center. "Orders completed." The decision to back up meant time was short—a turning of the ship took minutes. She guessed Andy thought they were under someone's gun eye. Her mind entered what she called her "mechanical stage," a keen, sharp mind operating by the book of rules.

"Stop at fifteen nautical miles," Andy ordered.

"Fifteen nautical miles complete. Full stop," Emily answered within seconds.

Andy, holding the command rail tightly, was able to stop his legs from buckling and his body being thrown onto the deck. "Battle stations. Battle stations," Andy announced dryly to the ship through his intercom. The claxon was sounding throughout the ship. From the corner of his eye, he saw Ling and Woden rushing from the deck. Only under the battle-stations command could crew leave the deck without a formal request to the captain. He knew Ling, chief medical officer, was already receiving status reports that were automatically requested when a full stop at speed was initiated. Woden was receiving alerts on his wrist communicator to man his battle station.

Andy stood erect, alert, a deep concentration in his eyes. He thought of the captain of the unknown ship and the meaning of the gaseous exhaust cloud. Had the cloud been formed by a sudden leap into full throttle when another ship was seen approaching? Or had the alien captain stopped and the exhaust cloud held by currents caught up to the ship? Either way, that captain had been reacting to the Explorer 7. Why so wary? Why not an attempt at communications? The alien captain viewed Explorer 7 as possibly hostile. Was the alien ship on war status, or did this alien people have a paranoia, or were they of a pirate nation?

He should be broadcasting the identity of Explorer 7's home planet and a statement that they had no hostile intent. They were new to this quadrant of space. Then, whatever happened, Explorer 7 would be absolved of guilt. Yes, absolved of guilt and blown from space into a thousand million fragments—it would be months before they would be reconstituted whole and back to space exploration. But the alien vessel should and would know Explorer 7 was alien by vapor trail, by aerodynamic size and shape, by the language being spoken within Explorer 7. Perhaps the alien could not monitor the shipboard chatter. Andy spoke. "Navigator."

"Yes, Captain?" said Dan.

"Send out to Earth headquarters this message: 'Alien vessel sighted' and give coordinates. Just keep repeating for three minutes or until you are certain the alien vessel has homed into our message. Diffuse the origin point of the communication. Scramble our internal communications. At the same time, direct our standard peace message to our alien contact."

"Yes, sir." Dan's voice held a succinctness and a tone of assurance that all was proper.

Andy wished to put his shields up, power up the antigravity screen, but the sudden power surge might be detected and believed hostile in nature. His command panel alerted him to all battle stations ready. The claxon had silenced as each unit had reported. Andy addressed the ship under dialogue scramble. "Unknown object passed across our projected path, moving to our port; as it was undetected by our instruments, a full stop was ordered and a reverse and slide maneuver to port initiated."

Andy nodded at Emily. She barely smiled. Her captain was being wary beyond protocol—he was assuming the alien was hostile. He was assuming the alien could not visually or instrumentally "see" the Explorer. Her captain was intuitive and clever. He sensed trouble. If the unknown object was a spacecraft of hostile origin, the sighting could be a prelude to ambush, with a torpedo already launched to meet Explorer 7's projected course. That torpedo may be cruising through space now. A good enemy gunner would have fired at the last position of the stopped Explorer 7. Or would have assumed a reverse of the target on the previous course. Andy had been ahead of both likely assumptions of the enemy, audaciously sliding to port, closer to the enemy.

To her horror, the energy sensors on the Explorer showed an object trailing back along the course of the alien ship, then turning right—as if on a road or rail—onto the projected path of Explorer 7. "Captain!" Emily's voice had risen in volume and deepness.

"I see the enemy torpedo," said Andy calmly. "All shields up."

Emily responded, "All shields up."

Andy saw another object following the course of the first. He calmly watched the first torpedo follow the path of the Explorer prior to the fifteen-degree course alteration. Why hadn't the alien captain just cut the angle with his rounds? To create confusion? Or to hide the torpedo in the exhaust? Or was the technology so low-level in that craft that they could not locate the Explorer 7? The deck crew watched the torpedo explode in space; saw the shock waves expanding out, coming their way. Andy spoke calmly. "Brace for impact." Andy felt the shudder in his bones—a robust blast—nothing substandard in their weapons technology.

Emily automatically pressed the warning siren. The warning sound brought chills to her skin.

Andy realized the enemy torpedo had exploded purposely to cover the probable radius of the location of the Explorer if it had continued on course or reversed course at operational speed. Either the torpedo technology was poor with no onboard sensors, or the enemy, knowing they were firing blind, hoped the quarry would move in fright, rendering itself locatable. Was that the purpose of the second torpedo? Just to follow up? Or was it all a ruse to hide their superiority? "Torpedo room."

"Here, Captain," answered Mat.

"Ready firing of bow torpedo on our previous course, the fifteen-degree slide."

"Yes, sir," Mat said. "Ready, sir."

"Stand by." Andy looked at Dan. "Has our peace message been picked up by the alien vessel?"

Dan answered, "Yes, sir."

Andy spoke. "Scan space by plotting a torpedo course from our present position to the straight-line projected course position of the enemy ship at its last contact."

"Yes, sir." Dan's voice held an urgency; his hands moved swiftly over the keyboard. "Enemy approaching at high speed—range 20,000 nautical miles and closing. With another vessel behind by 40,000 nautical miles from the first ship."

"Odds two-to-one now," Andy announced as he smiled wryly to deck and gun crews through ship-to-ship communications viewing screens. He continued, "Helmsman, sound off if their torpedo takes a fifteen-degree slide course." Andy realized the enemy had used torpedoes to distract and buy time to distance itself by twenty thousand miles and team up with its hunting buddy. Smart captain. Fast ship. Faster than any Earth model by much. He knew every strength had a corresponding weakness. The weakness was the enemy captain who had run for support—unless he wanted numbers before stopping Explorer 7 and boarding. The enemy captain should have blasted the Explorer at first sighting.

"Enemy torpedo has taken the fifteen-degree course," said Emily. She, like her captain, knew the enemy torpedo was smelling its quarry by the exhaust track of Explorer 7.

"Torpedo room, fire bow torpedo on fifteen-degree slide course."

"Torpedo launched," Mat stated dryly.

"Navigator, I want a straight-line course to approaching second alien vessel."

"Done, Captain," answered Dan. Then, "Captain!" Dan's voice held alarm. Andy answered. "Make it quick."

"Second enemy vessel 35,000 nautical miles behind first ship," said Dan.

"Okay," answered Andy. He was aware that time was compressing. He wanted both ships in the same line of fire. Odds were when the second ship reached the first, one or both ships would begin flanking maneuvers. He called out, "Navigator, initiate course to the alien vessel at battle speed ten."

"Course set at battle speed ten and initiated," said Dan.

Emily spoke, per protocol, as the navigator had initiated the speed. "Noted by Helm." All knew that was the speed limit of the Explorer. No one knew how long it could be maintained.

The Explorer canted to port, shook at the increase in speed, and righted itself; and the crew, noting the pull in their guts, knew they were in a zone of speed never felt before.

"Gun room," Andy demanded sharply, as he glanced at the gravitational-force charts. He knew no one on his ship expected a change from torpedoes. The gun room consisted of six nuclear-propelled guns—actual barrels would be inserted through gunports on port and starboard, above and below. Multiple warheads, four to be exact, could be fired from the main propellent charge, then assume the power of their own charges for propulsion, if that option was chosen.

"Yes, sir," said Jack crisply and forcefully.

"Send a starburst down our new course at our first target, the nearer alien ship, with a proximity fuse." Andy was painfully aware that he had now engaged in offensive actions. Christ's forces had become the aggressor. Simply put, they could not assume another cheek to turn would exist if they remained passive.

"Yes, sir." Jack had already punched the course into the fire-control computer, where the speed of the enemy ship, the speed of the firing ship, the starburst grouping, and atmospheric conditions were tallied and gun barrels adjusted. What was their captain's strategy? A starburst was a four-shot group fired within a second from one gun. In this instance, an exploding pattern was created with a north and south group and an east and west group, designated a, b, c, d, per clockwise order. The pattern covered an immense center of total destruction. Proximity fuses were rarely used, as the shell's guidance system seemed never to fail homing in on a target. The captain did not want four bullets aimed at the target, but rather, a shotgun spread encompassing the target.

"Fire first burst with proximity fuses," Andy commanded.

"First burst fired with pf," said Jack.

"Fire second burst five degrees higher and a third burst five degrees lower with proximity fuses. Now."

"Second and third bursts with pf fired."

"On the horizontal axis of burst one, fire the fourth burst five degrees to port and fire the fifth burst five degrees to starboard with proximity fuses. Now."

"On the horizontal axis of burst one, bursts four and five at five degrees from center, port and starboard fired with pf."

The Explorer 7 shuddered as the momentarily forgotten torpedo initially entered on the fifteen-degree slide struck the enemy torpedo. Emily spoke. "Enemy torpedo destroyed."

Stillness and quiet filled the deck area. All crew members had been receiving the communications audio. Jack entered communications with his captain. "Countdown to strike: ten, nine, eight, seven, six, five, four, three, two, one." They heard Jack suck in air. "First starburst shredded target. No movement. Electrical pulses on board indicate life still sustainable." The blast was apparent on the deck screens before Dan and Emily and Andy, and it affirmed Jack's communication.

Andy waited patiently. The second enemy vessel would see the damaged ship before he would. The enemy radar, or radar like devices would be showing shrapnel from bursts two and three, a vast vertical linear grouping, coming toward him. He, likely, was unaware of bursts four and five, on the horizontal, which were waiting to meet him as he took a sufficiently wide course around the shrapnel he could see. Those bursts, fired last, were not yet on his radar. Hopefully, the enemy captain would have no time to react to the deflection groupings. Andy's mind explored possible future scenarios for the second alien ship. He thought the ship would veer to port, the Explorer's starboard. The shrapnel was being pulled by gravitational forces to the enemy's starboard. For the enemy captain to go to his starboard, he would fly into the shrapnel or be forced to go wider, away from his enemy, placing his ship on the outside of unlimited space, with nowhere to hide and no ability to send a successful round through the storm of metal. The enemy's port would be preferred.

Jack entered comms. "B shell of fifth starburst caught the alien ship approaching at high speed. Second enemy vessel shredded—moderate to heavy damage, mass casualties on board, speed decreased to a crawl. Attempting a turn around."

Andy addressed the crew. "One shell from twenty individual shells fired. The burst on the tail end. Had he cleared that, we would still be fighting. His near success was due to his reckless use of his speed. They are aggressive, willing to gamble. Keep that in mind for the future."

Dan spoke. "It seems we have the advantage now."

"Give thanks to the Lord," said Andy, knowing that all onboard had done that very thing in the first breath after the enemy was destroyed.

Andy's eyes gleamed; he rubbed his sweaty hands together in the hope of dispersing the moisture. "Our work is not yet finished. The opportunity exists to save two crews and two junked ships, but also to destroy two crews and their ships. Navigator, I assume our language systems were tuned in on conversations in the vessels, and the computers are trying to establish a vocabulary. Send communications to the second vessel, in their language. Copy: 'You have assumed our hostility. Our intentions have always been peaceful. Let us work together to save your damaged ship and crew.'"

As Andy waited, he noticed his shirt was soaked in sweat, now cooling. The shirt fabric hid the moisture, not that it mattered, except for the coldness. His ship family knew his peculiarities. He studied the faces of Dan and Emily. "We're not out of danger yet, but you two performed magnificently."

Dan responded, "We thank you and that perfect deflection shot." His head tilted as his earpiece filled with chatter. "Sir, Captain Tom and the language group say there is no word for 'peaceful.'"

"Try 'not destructive.'" Andy waited, "Does that work?"

"Yes, sir."

Andy sat on the edge of the captain's chair and toweled his face and hands dry with the cloth he kept handy for just such moments. He sipped an energy drink, which clogged momentarily in his parched throat. He could not yet release his crew from battle stations or commend them for their actions through the course of combat. For all he knew, an enemy armada could be bearing down on them at this very moment. He thought back to his first years in Paradise and his readings on John Paul Jones, the American navy captain during the American Revolution, and a follower of Jones's 136 years later, Ernest Evans, an American Indian, who served as captain of a destroyer during World War II. Were they now in resurrected bodies? Jones was an original thinker and a man who took chances with bold actions, and Evans was his protege. As it is with bureaucracies tainted with self-serving souls, Jones was always stifled for promotions. Ernest Evans fought aggressively, with cunning, and could have left his ship alive. His body went down with his ship in the Leyte Gulf. Only Heaven knew he had remained with the unmovable dying, giving them the peace of his confident voice and presence.

"Sir, the reply is back."

"Put it up on the screen. All screens aboard our ship."

"From the commander of Halcyon Forces: Nothing is wanted from you but your immediate surrender and admission from you, your crew, and your nation as to our right of conquest. A state of war exists until that time your nation is destroyed or made a vassal state."

Andy opened the intercom. "Crew, you handled yourselves well in combat, and it appears, against experienced crews on both vessels. We, of course, could make them a pile of flotsam in space for eternity. But at this time, this course would not be God's way. Perhaps we are talking to one bitter leader, ashamed of his crew's performance or his own. Perhaps the leaders of the Halcyon Forces do not convey the thoughts of the crews or of their people. We will contact our leaders and Christ in Jerusalem at this instant, as well as use the angelic messenger service. They may have information we do not. They may advise on war. At this time, we will withdraw, rest, and wait.

Thank you again for your conduct. We could be at battle stations again, so plan your activities with this in mind."

Andy looked at Dan. "Dan, send this reply back. Copy: 'From the commander of Christian Forces. We offered our hand in peace to fellow warriors, who know the turns, twists of war are most unpredictable, and victories and defeats come to all participants. We give you time to leave the emotion of combat and hope the future holds a time when we may talk in sincerity as to future shared aspirations.'"

Andy said, "Navigator, send that out to our crew also. I didn't want to say too much or too little. And I am assuming our enemy has humanlike thought processes and emotions."

"Yes, sir," said Dan.

Andy spoke again. "Scan space for a place to rest, behind a planet or star, with tricky approaches. Keep me informed. If your see none here, set a course, at highest possible speed, for a new search area."

"Yes, sir," answered Dan, his voice strong and positive. Dan sensed Andy needed that voice. Their captain had just trashed two alien space vessels and likely killed hundreds. The first-ever cognizant life-forms contacted in an historical meeting of civilizations, during the exploration of space, had been rendered dead, dying, or helpless in decimated spacecraft.

"Also, begin watch protocol," said Andy.

"Will do," answered Dan, as he smiled wryly at his captain's faith. He clearly saw his captain's sense of grit and duty overcome the gravity of a possible error. Who better to trust in than Christ, who took the defeat of hanging upon the cross as the catalyst for a revolution and victory.

CHAPTER 6

Andy stood on the deck, hands on the railing, his eyes searching, through the unshuttered window, every corner of the scene before him. An unknown planet! Quick measurements gave dimensions as two-thirds the size of Earth. The round form of the planet was encased in roiling clouds. Flashes of lightning revealed heaped and twisting cumulous clouds of gray and copper colors. A mist hung above the cloud formations and molded itself into a semitransparent sphere that surrounded the planet. The crewmen not on deck were gathered at the second observation window in the room below the deck. A planet with water! Dan had sent out drones, and the data sent back indicated chlorophyl-based plants, breathable air, and life-forms. No advanced civilizations were currently discernable by energy concentrations or pollution detectors.

Andy allowed his crew this brief time of awe—the delight of discovery. It had been Tom's gamble to wander far from their preplanned course with the assumption that their computer log's security systems could have been compromised during their interactions with the alien vessels. A drawing down of electric capacity had been noticed at that time. With a subsequent burst of speed and hidden by intervening planets and stars, the Explorer 7 had left their motionless and almost powerless foe in damaged ships. Then, the wet planet had been detected far in the distance, in their left quadrant. Discovered not by drones but by human sight through telescopic lenses.

Days of travel had been needed to reach the wet planet. Explorer 7 maintained communications with Earth through a scrambling, dissected, misdirected covert system that they hoped an enemy could not trace. A messenger angel had also been dispatched to Earth. Not till a directive from New

Jerusalem concerning the recent hostile incident could the Explorer 7, in good conscience, continue space exploration. Tom believed that odds were, a hostile craft would eventually arrive at the wet planet, searching for its enemy and redemption from defeat. Two days previously, Tom had been dispatched in Explorer 7's small shuttle craft to hide behind a moon and stand guard for the possible sighting of pursuing enemy ships. Now, Tom was back. He strode into the deck room, smiling widely, rubbing his hands together, eyes turned toward the window, as if the portal was a meal long needed and desired. Andy caught Tom's excitement and smiled as broadly, as did Emily and Dan, and Tuck and Robin, their waiting replacements.

The Earth dwellers' bodies vibrated, hummed with anticipation at walking upon a new planet, enlivened by the promise of discovery. Still, trepidation clung to their thoughts. The damaged alien ships might be on the way, patched and wishing to destroy them—or new ships of greater firepower and with top-notch crews. Crew members reminded themselves that they could not die, but wounds, grievous wounds, could leave them recuperating and immobile for weeks, if not months, as their bodies underwent regrowth. They could be taken from this adventure; they could fail to complete it all, taken when the excitement was at its peak. In the past world, failure brought ridicule, disgust, self-justification, supporters and detractors. The world of the resurrected only knew applause, satisfaction, a cheering Christ, and supporters. Setbacks were bound to come, but God's people could only learn from the past, overcome, and advance.

Tom came up beside Andy and slapped him upon the shoulder, then gave him a jolting little push. "The real fun is soon to begin," said Tom.

Andy turned to Tom and placed his arm around him—to settle his giddiness by example. "Let's descend and hide our craft in the clouds and rain. Cutting power to a mere fraction. Crew on battle alert." This had been previously discussed and accepted but not officially decided.

Tom spoke. "If there are mountains or high ground, let us take it. Better to be shooting down on them if it comes to that."

A seriousness came to Andy. "Shooting" was a word from the past, surrounded by bad times. Tom's tone hinted that he knew there would be conflict on this planet. Andy inquired, "What do you know?"

"A small alien craft is headed to this planet. It is still on the other side of a blocking moon. But this planet seems to be the destination. The outer hull resembles the engineering of our recent foe. It does not appear to be of military bearing—no guns or portals visible. It may not belong to the hostiles."

And it might be hostile, thought Andy. Andy's eyes, deep within his mind, returned to Tom's gaze. "We should receive a message by tomorrow from New Jerusalem. In the meantime?"

Tom knew Andy thought uncertainty was the most undesirable form of the cognizant state of mind. He knew this came from Andy's protective past, his desire to shield his boys from the cruelties of life. Tom spoke. "In the meantime, let's surveil the craft if it lands. Maybe there is a civilization here, either of the Halcyon Empire, or a vassal state, or a land still free with its own culture. Let us simply trust in the Lord till that time we know the path we should take."

Andy absorbed Tom's words. "Spoken like the captain you are."

Tom laughed. "Or we could skedaddle out of here without trying to monitor our visitors. Wait in hiding at another location. I am not averse to other options. Your call as senior commander."

"We will proceed. We will abort the mission at any stage necessary to save our ship. We will value caution above knowledge of our alien contacts."

"I agree," said Tom. "Let us move now before they can pick us up on their scanners."

Andy looked back at Emily. "Helmsman, descend at safety speed."

"Yes, sir," said Emily. "All detection units working." Emily and Andy switched their gaze from the broad window to the screens of individual cameras spaced along the bottom of Explorer 7. The formations of hills and mountains became distinct, and a topographical representation appeared upon their instruments. Relatively low mountains, ridged, eight-hundred– to fifteen-hundred–feet high, marked the edges of a great, flat plain stretching beyond sight. Trees covered the high ground and clutched shrouds of mist tendrils within their branches. Falling waters, some from great heights, tumbled off the edges of rocky cliffs, and the mist hung from the waters. The map began to be overlayed with concentrations of energy roughly every twenty miles, which could only be interpreted as towns. A sprawling, vast plain before the mountains was dotted with towns. The collections of energy were weak, and the onlookers assumed the sources were fire lamps or some equivalent, such as a type of solar panel. The only evidence of sunlight was the radiant heat coming from the rock and soil.

The Explorer settled upon hard ground, tucked into a ravine of steep sides. The reactors were lowered to pulse. The craft was at rest. Captain of the deck, Andy, relinquished command to second captain, Tom, with a salute. Tom returned the salute and in a formal command voice said, "Second captain assumes command." Turning to Tuck and Robin, he said, "Second helmsman and navigator, man your stations." He watched Tuck and Robin settle into their seats one at a time, as Dan and Emily, one at a time vacated their positions. Tom gave time to his crew to read and interpret their screens of data, then spoke. "All secure and in order?" Both responded with "confirmed." Tom continued, "Send out additional probes for environmental factors and human life viability immediately. Summon Ling, Tim, Diana to the deck." The gathered knew these three would interpret the data for human-life sustainability.

The deck crew monitored the approaching alien craft. Emily and Dan had gone to the galley, where Pete and Grace had prepared hot soup and warm biscuits. Pete and Grace assumed they would eventually be called onto the deck, as towns or villages meant cognizant life had been found on the planet. As spiritual and psychological counselors, they had cross-trained in alien cultures and life-forms. They were also valued members of the linguistics team. Andy had retreated to the captain's room adjacent to the deck. The room was more a nap and relaxation area, with a tension-reliever of AI massage hands and heat or cold applications for muscles or sinuses. The designers of the ship, knowing the sparsity of crew capacity and complexities of duties, understood that two captains needed to be able to meet emergency situations without the distractions of physical ailments and stress.

At this moment, the need for a rethinking of crew responsibilities was apparent to Andy. As a captain in a war situation, his mind had been cluttered with decisions that would have been better passed to a second. Managing the movement of the ship and armaments was responsibility enough for a captain when an enemy was nearby or situations were unknown on a planet. He sat in the massage seat, took a sip of a protein drink—chocolate—punched in the massage type and location, set it for five minutes, and began to relax. He purposely emptied his mind of a hundred questions and duties that were looming. His duty was to serve Tom when needed, conform to Tom's thought processes first, then layer on his own thoughts, so they could reach consensus.

Tom summoned Andy when Ling, Tim, and Diana had gathered on the deck. All had understood from the preliminary readings of the probes that the planet and atmosphere were earthlike; had a narrow band of what was air. More in-depth readings quietly printed on the view screen verified the atmosphere was earthlike, though currently, moisture was high. Habitations were plentiful but scattered over the surface, and electronic communications came from distinct sources at fifty-mile radii. The probes had not picked up signals consistent with image projection, such as TV.

"Oh!" Diana blurted in surprise as data for the water samples were posted. Tom, too, had a look of surprise as he reviewed the data. "I see what you see, Diana. This is not water like Earth water, not in the angle of bonding between oxygen and hydrogen. And three unattached molecules, not two. And what is that unknown, misshapen molecule?"

Diana spoke. "I think it's a mineral so light, so small, and so highly absorbent in water that it may cause problems for humans if we're not careful."

"Careful? How so?" Andy interjected. Diana glanced at Tim; he was the mineral authority, and with his squinting eyes, he envisioned the problem.

Tim spoke. "This is an agrarian planet with cities or government facilities every fifty miles. The substrata of rock has this mineral as yet to be named—nothing like it on Earth, except maybe asbestos fibers. I believe the constant tilling of the soil has pulverized it, in addition to the natural effects of erosion, sun exposure, and temperature changes. Likely, it is found in the bones of the inhabitants, if they have bones; or in their lung fiber, if they have lungs. It could clog our lungs and lead to suffocation. At the least, we may develop stomach issues. They probably use this substance in their electrical generating and therefore lighting and communications."

"Can we produce a scrubber that will pull out this mineral before inhalation?" asked Ling, who, at a glance, thought current filters might not work.

"It would take time and testing," said Tim. "Our existing air filters may work." He added, "We can postpone the issue of drinking, as we have plentiful water reserves onboard."

Tom spoke. "Right now, we just need to anticipate the ship approaching. They may not be inhabitants of this planet. They may have a device that cleanses the air. We need to follow them and learn from their interactions on this planet. Any theories on where they might land and what they might do while here?"

Robin, the navigator on deck, spoke to the gathered think-tank members. "Captain, the vessel is communicating in the Halcyon language with beings on the planet, and they are returning conversation in Halcyon."

Tom spoke. "Place the recordings in the language bank—for interpretation, of course. What's the content of the messages?"

Emily, in the linguistics room below the deck room, chimed in. "Linguistics. Dan is with me. The aliens are discussing the upcoming taking and shipping of the planet's harvest, which occurs every three months and has for decades. They call the inhabitants *slaves* or *thralls* and have established them as sub-Halcyon in all respects. Really quite degrading language. It appears the Halcyons, at this harvest time, engage in mass rape of sub-Halcyons, of any sex. We have yet to determine what 'any sex' means. A mass humiliation has been customary every harvest."

"They call it a mass humiliation?" asked Andy, "or is that your interpretation?"

Emily answered, "It is a derogatory event based upon the words used, and the emotional delight of those describing the event."

Tom spoke. "Thanks, linguistics team." He looked at his gathering on deck and studied each person before speaking. "Our course of action will be to place more surveillance devices, hearing and vision, and observe the upcoming harvest. Eventually, we'll send out exploratory parties with self-contained air in the stealth mode of invisibility. Let's see where this vessel lands and target that area for our surveillance priority.

"Start assembling the spyware in the main bay. Reinspect space suits and internal oxygen systems. Bring our security team in and share the mission. Meeting dismissed." Tom paused. "No, not dismissed. Top priority—ship safety. Are we sitting among a network of trails for foot traffic or herding or hiking? Can we be seen from distant points when the rain and fog lifts? Where are the nearest homes? If that fog lifts and a village has a clear view of us? John and Woden, need to get on this problem quickly." Tom shook his head. The next words would be difficult to speak. "No action to disrupt the mass humiliation at this time. However, keep it in your thought processes. Now dismissed."

***

Explorer 7 was silent. Tom remained on the deck, still at his duty station, as all discussion of the future moved into the below-deck conference room of sound containment. The Halcyon vessel was tagged, by an infrared beam, into the computer system marking real-time interstellar space. An actual mark was scratched onto the outer hull with a laser beam without the knowledge of that ship's crew. The ship penetrated the atmosphere over the town nearest Explorer 7 and immediately landed. The onboard communications continued to be monitored by the Explorer linguistics crew, Ling, Diana, Emily, Dan, and an interested Andy. The cryptic language was analyzed, understood, translated into English. The conversations in a nearby Halcyon-occupied building were also recorded, as were the conversations in a slave domicile. Appearances were that the Halcyon personnel (now beings called "Hals") felt completely safe. They had no air assets buzzing over the planet, nor were they sending any traceable beams from surveillance satellites planetward. It appeared the crew of the Explorer 7 was undetected for the moment. A drone had verified a spacious security zone around the Explorer, but there were known buildings miles away that would offer glimpses of the Explorer. Drones had cast camouflaged nets over the Explorer, and this was effective. Was it just a coincidence the alien ship had landed only twenty-five miles from the Explorer?

A sudden voluminous mass of linguistics data entered their storage system to be digested by AI. The source of the data was unknown, but it had come a vast distance and had credible security clearances. AI estimated 90 percent of the Hal language was now in their possession. The data probably had started its journey yesterday morning, thought Emily. For she was analyzing the importunity of the data arriving now—creating a notable noise and a jump in the electrical field, as if warning the Hals. Had the security walls of Christian Forces been overloaded purposely by enemies within?

Ling had the first notable reaction; his head canted to his right—this ear above the norm for sensitivity—and he pursed his lips. Andy moved from a chart table to Ling, understanding the importance of Ling's head tilt. Emily too heard, and her eyes went to Ling for an unspoken affirmation. Ling nodded his head as they listened in on an official aboard the alien vessel castigating someone stationed on the planet. "Aliens…ship…defeat…ambush" were surrounded by unintelligible sounds, words. Explorer 7's AI program was scrambling to find English words to accurately reflect the filth and anger of the Hal words. Assumptions had to be made by AI, because no one knew the physical structure or functions of the alien bodies, nor what was considered gross and despicable. What was the import of this dressing down? Was Explorer 7 involved?

Andy said nothing, even as apprehension gripped his mind. He saw the precariousness of their position in a real and political sense. The Earth dwellers had landed on a planet not their own and which clearly had a civilization, without first having announced their intentions or requesting permission—even though the enemy, the Halcyon Empire, claimed dominion. Becoming hostages would not be good. A shootout on someone else's planet did not bode well, either. The best of intentions had gotten them to this point, and that was worth nothing. Maybe the Hals already knew the earthlings had landed. Maybe the earthlings had been led to this place. Maybe the trap was soon to be sprung.

Andy had been watching the faces of his crew as he had reached the conclusion of his thoughts. His very look had silenced them, and they stared back. He spoke. "Crew, I think we need to leave this planet and distance ourselves from the alien craft. Then, by distant communications, make contact. We are in a precarious situation. Show of hands of those who agree."

Every hand was raised instantly. Andy pressed the intercom. "Deck." He knew Robin, as navigator, handled incoming calls to the deck.

"Yes."

Andy said, "Access to the captain, please."

"Patched in," said Robin.

"This is Tom, Andy."

"Tom, we overheard the complete dressing down of a Hal subordinate by a high-ranking commander. We think it has to do with us. All gathered believe we should leave as quickly as possible in stealth mode and, if possible, wait to see if a reaction is forthcoming."

"Done," Tom said, as he cut off Andy and raised the silent battle-stations alarm of flashing lights and flashing screen messages.

They felt the electromagnetic whine within their ears as the ion thrusters fully ignited. The ship was lifting easily from the planet.

Then, heaviness, silence, a sinking in the stomach as the ship fell heavily back to the surface mere feet into rising. By the quietness, the crew knew all defensive weapons, including force shields and the destabilizing shield, a paralyzing force field, were down.

A metallic voice penetrated the hull, entered the halls and rooms of Explorer 7.

"YOU HAVE BEEN CAPTURED BY THE HALCYON EMPIRE. EXIT YOUR CRAFT OR BE TERMINATED."

****

In the armory room, where Woden, Mat, John, and Jack had finished checking the Explorer's weapons and were suited up in body armor and external-environmental suits for testing, the jolting crash and enemy announcement sent a blank and foreboding spirit into their hearts. They had heard the degrading, filth-filled conversation of the enemy ship with the vassals of the planet. They remembered the torpedoes that were fired at their ship and the subsequent combat. They were the security crew of their ship. They loved their crewmates, their Emily, Diana, Grace of soft voices, kind thoughts, razor wits, who always brought them to memories of their former wives. The entire crew were their spiritual companions, soulmates for eternal life. None had experienced a situation of strife or war where degradation, physical discomfort and pain were not part of the experience. This new, and as yet unseen, enemy talked hate. The security detail had shared their thoughts on war, combat, confrontation in private and group conversations since they first met. Each man knew that the others, for as long as their bodies were whole and functioning, would resist and escape.

Woden, who had fought barbarians in eastern European forests and barbarian Muslims on barren plains and rocky heights, and lastly the legions of Satan during the last harvest, blurted out the intent of his passion. "I'm going out in stealth mode." He stepped over to the weapons locker, grabbed a laser pistol and rifle, rechecked all closed external openings, tested breathing internally, and strode resolutely to the external hatch.

"As am I," stated Mat.

"And me," said John.

"And I too," said Jack. In a very short time, with immaculate patience and attention to detail, external checks were complete. Weapons in hand, Woden messaged to Tom and Andy, "Security detail exiting the ship."

Tom, without hesitation, replied, "Go."

Woden held his thumb up before his men. They returned the gesture. In an instant they were gone.

CHAPTER 7

The team chose to go free flight, though they knew nothing of the conditions—gravity, winds, electromagnetic fields, the tugs and pulls of the planet's sun or suns and moons. They only had experience under Earth conditions. A flight-supporting rocket-pack system would have given security but also weight and bulkiness when visibility and substance were reentered. They went invisible, within the natural body of the resurrected—not a cloaking device cast over their forms but a molecular disruption that displaced solids with gasses, which, they hoped, then blended into the natural atmosphere of the host planet. Each had, attached to his mouth and nose, a portable supply of air, which, if breathing were slow and steady, would repurify for twenty-four hours. After twenty-four hours, their devices would begin to collect noticeable amounts of the minerals floating in the air. No studies had been done as to life expectancy, years or hours, if they breathed the unpurified air. Woden had aimed his direction setter at what appeared to be an enemy vessel or troop carrier that might carry five human-sized life-forms. He quickly reviewed an assessment of threat level and a preplanned scenario and plan of actions developed by the captains.

To the surprise of the band of warrior earthlings, they had landed among an enemy crew of four dispersing from the carrier vessel. The overwhelming size and strange body contours, weapons, and clothing of the enemy created a panic that was quickly subdued by the Spirit within them. A wry smile came to their faces as their laser rifle barrels chose targets. Targeting beams were not used. They withheld a trigger touch. Did the hulking forms have an awareness of aliens among their group? Could their presence be felt? Heard? The answer seemed to be that Woden's men were invisible.

The enemy were two to three feet taller than humans, lanky, and seemed to wear a jumpsuit-type covering of black. Their arms were doubled up before them, as the forearms were longer than the upper arms. The hands were gloved, long, and bony, twice to three times larger than human hands. The torsos were long and slim but not supple. Were these beings human or another species or mechanical? Their skulls seemed triangular, or did they wear triangular helmets? They had deep-set eyes with a seeming visor projecting over the forehead, so the eye sockets were immersed in darkness. Various small lights flickered on and off on the suits.

The Hals moved with a strange grace, lanky, long movements that ended in a shortened stop, then into another lanky movement. He sensed by the form and fit of their clothing that their outer skin, if any, was more a hardened shell. Or was this shell manufactured body armor? Their thin waists seemed naturally bent forward, and the waist jerked with bends and twists and with risings and falling of the torso from the flexion of their upper leg muscles. Their legs were thin and did not show the muscular bulk of the human body. The thighs were shorter than the legs below the knees—knees that seemed able to flex forward and backward. The feet were long and shod to the ankle. The aliens had a smell like a deep licorice that was not offensive to the earthlings but perplexing. Was this some mechanical lubricating oil? Or was it a hormone produced by stress, excitement, or wariness?

The Halcyons favored the insect species more than the human. Praying mantis came to Woden's mind. He was amazed at how quickly he had adjusted to their appearance and distorted body type. Hands were hands, legs were legs, regardless of appearance, and hard, shell-like skin was skin. He had reached a place of acceptance with their appearance, though he thought wings would not be out of place under the uniform.

The earthlings adjusted to the jerky and quirky movements of the enemy, realizing this was their natural state, perhaps tinged with fear and wariness. Woden adjusted his height estimation to a foot taller than first surmised. He searched for strengths and weaknesses in their forms. The enemy was focused on dispersing and approaching the Earth vessel. The voice heard within the Explorer 7 seemed to have been transmitted by a box of electronics attached to the Explorer's hull, the box likely shot onto the fuselage. He believed one alien had a satchel of explosives upon his back. A forced entry of the Explorer made sense as a next move. He could not allow the outer hull to suffer a breach. A breached hull meant the Explorer would be trapped on the planet.

Woden's men had looked beyond the alien crew and their carrier to a second, larger ship—the vessel tracked while approaching the planet. A sizeable contingent of armed aliens had erected portable barriers, and they now stood behind the barriers with rifle-like weapons aimed. The sudden course change of one of the dispersing aliens brought a near contact with Mat. White light flashed along the alien's combat wear and the assumed location of the backbone. The entire alien party of four froze, as weapons extended from the sleeves of their clothing. He had not noticed the absence of weapons until he saw weapons appear. The three unlit uniforms were now flashing.

The earthlings noticed the weapons were not aimed at them. If the weapons would be aimed specifically at humans, invisibility would be discarded and lasers would be fired without hesitation. The earthlings were communicating in the sentience of the resurrected, that quiet reading of the thoughts. They noticed a sound, or sounds, coming from the helmeted heads in the same location that corresponded with the human mouth. An ingress and egress of hissing, smelling, breathing. Conversation? The earthlings began to distance and separate themselves from the enemy without being bumped or tramped upon by the long and rather wide feet—an amphibious capability or the response to a marshland environment? Perhaps a platform for increased load bearing.

An alien taller than the others separated from the contingent of enemy soldiers by the larger ship and was followed by two of lesser height. These beings were dressed in tunics consisting of laminar bands, with a dull bronze, metallic luster. The headgear was of the same material with distinctive emblems above their foreheads. The actual helmet was of the same make, with visor, as those of the advance team. The leader seemed to be reacting to the flashing uniforms, which appeared to have picked up some noteworthy new data: the presence of an enemy? A command decision was needed, no doubt.

A small, naturally armored animal, resembling Earth's armadillos, had been hiding behind the erected barricades and suddenly burst into sight, trotting toward the tall commander. The animal had been fitted with a vest, which had been loaded with sensing detectors. The animal, as soon as passing the commander, began spraying air and ground with a natural and clear liquid that carried the deep licorice smell. The animal seemed to be sniffing. Woden, with a quick motion of his hand, told the men to gather with him, as he further separated himself from the aliens to a place beside them with unobstructed fields of fire. If this animal were a doglike creature with superior detecting skills, it would follow the human scent trails to their present position. Then, the animal would be killed, and the firefight would start. The Earth men tensed, and laser rifles were grasped more firmly, and safety straps to holstered pistols released. Jack understood the new positioning and the reason; the entire crew knew. Following Jack's lead, they had all activated their wrist-computer language programs. Would the wrist computer startup be detected? Or could they have the Hals' language translated before they reacted to the animal's warnings?

Woden understood the complexity of the ways in which a hostile interaction would impact the future of Earth explorations of the universe and the interactions of the two worlds represented by the participants. More dead Hals would be a larger barrier to peace. He had explored the subject in depth after the initial destruction of the Hals' warships. These aliens appeared, from conversations about the past with the planet's inhabitants they dominated, to be indigenous life-forms and not artificial intelligence personnel (AIPs). But who knew if AIPs in other worlds did have the status of indigenous life-forms (ILFs)? Perhaps death wasn't even considered a provocative act by the Hals, as their intent was to conquer and prevail over any life-forms, peaceful or hostile. It appeared likely that they had no moral system of right and wrong.

The complexity, the right decision, deepened when the eternal-life quality of all earthlings was understood. The aliens could destroy the entire crew—scatter their atoms throughout the universe—and most Holy God, Father of creation, through angelic beings, would gather up the pieces and bring life back, even thoughts and memories, as if nothing had happened. The path of patience, nonretaliation, even nonresistance, lay with God's people, if it was God's will. This all assumed that the beings discovered could understand that peaceful coexistence was better than war.

One had to be born with a moral sense, placed within humans by God through conscience and then revelation. Even then, a life-form had to believe or experience the penalty for ignoring morality. Beings who obeyed only out of fear of punishment were never acceptable by God for eternal life. They never became His children, and the fruit of the Spirit, which showed the true essence of God's character, could never be implanted, because the first great attribute—love—would be missing. Through love, which was the essence of God, did all other attributes have birth and presence: joy, peace, patience, kindness, goodness, faithfulness, gentleness, self-control. For love to even be seen in the heart, the being had to love God, who gave it life. These thoughts ran through the minds of God's warriors in a flash and then subsided into the essence of the soul from which they had come.

The armadillo-like creature seemed to sniff around the mantis beings of the advance party, still locked in the position of their last footsteps before the flashing lights had appeared. Woden saw the enemy's mistake of not continuing the process of planting the explosive devices. The three enemy commanders stopped yards away from the advance party. The armadillo-like creature lifted its head and stared back at the three. Then it lowered its head and began to examine the ground. Woden had his laser aimed at the dog; the others had chosen their targets among the advance crew. When the advance crew were dead, the three leaders had been chosen next for death, and beyond these events, the Earth soldiers had planned to cast death into the barricaded aliens.

The little armadillo slowly began to follow the trail of the Earth soldiers' gathering place. Woden did not shoot, for the enemy had not shifted a weapon to the course of the dog. The creature was at the earthling's feet, sniffing. The creature seemed to become playful and was lifting both front paws simultaneously, creating little hops. It went between the Earth men, following a scent. Woden sensed an unseen wind, carrying the human scent of the initial pent-up odor burst from the original recombining of their molecular structure. At this moment, their standing scent was so little and so diffused that the creature could not categorize it or call it dangerous. The burst of human scent traveling and slowly dispersing on the wind was evidently pleasing to the creature. The creature ran into the terrain of sand, rock, and scrubby plants. Woden knew it would return rapidly when the scent disintegrated.

Quickly, Woden silently called Jack and Mat even as he strode, invisible, toward the leaders, aiming his laser at the tallest figure's head. John remained to cover the advance party and the explosives-carrying soldier. Woden opened communications to the Explorer. He pressed the number 1: status report. A prerecorded narrative should have been activated, but instead Andy's voice, live, came through. "Guessing you want to know when flight is possible here."

Woden clicked three times for "yes."

"We are ready for flight, and force fields are up," answered Andy.

Woden had always known in his heart that the Hals would kill his materializing men immediately; there would be no wait-and-see period, no "let's parley" interaction. He knew, by protocol and civility, it was necessary for him to offer talk to them. He had developed a plan and presented it to the captains, who'd agreed. Woden had worked it out with Andy, Tom, and John yesterday. Now was the time. Woden pressed the number 7 on his wrist communicator.

"Roger that," Andy answered in a voice absent of emotion.

A hologram appeared before all the gathered soldiers, spaced well away from the Explorer 7, yet visible to all. On a slight ridge, the same that extended past the Explorer, fifty Earth men appeared to rise. They were dressed in robes, weaponless, and held open palms toward their adversaries. A wide banner behind and over them said "nondestructive" in the Halcyon language. One of the Earth men spoke in Halcyon. "We wish to talk. Tell your people to lower their weapons. We are from Earth. We come in neutrality."

The armadillo-like creature had turned to face the hologram and began running to the assemblage of Earth men. The alien advance party pointed their weapons reflexively at the fifty men. Loud whooping sounds came from their weapons in rapid succession, even as the barricaded forces at the main ship were turning to the assemblage. The tallest leader began to yell and, it seemed, curse, waving his hands. Something extended from the hands; Woden thought it was a pointer or a knife. Men in the hologram assemblage were falling, calling out in pain, begging for mercy. The tall leader's frenzied arm-waving gathered all eyes to him. The firing only stopped when the hologram earthlings were down and silent. The armadillo-like creature had been killed, and no one seemed the wiser. Woden hadn't expected the leader to stop the assault. Did the leader believe the value of hostages far outweighed the value of a dead enemy? Woden had not expected that finesse, that realization. But he had planned and was prepared for the scenario.

From the low ridge, within the fallen group of bodies, streaming blood and movements were seen. A leg was drawn up, a torso rocked from side to side in pain. Then an arm went up, then a blood-choked cry of pain. A man lifted himself to his elbows and looked toward the shooters. All four shooters took a hurried glance back at their leader. A loud, quick command came from his mouth, a piercing, shrill command. Almost instantly, the four blasted the lying bodies with their weapons. The earthlings heard laughter. Even the tall commander and his subordinates laughed. It was apparent to the Explorer 7 crew that live earthlings had no value when they were the survivors and, therefore, witnesses of an unprovoked massacre.

Woden, Mat, and Jack materialized within the leader's group with weapons drawn. John, by the ship, materialized, shot the four enemy soldiers nearest the ship, and returned to invisibility in seconds. Woden was beside the leader. The earthlings grabbed the three hostages by the scruffs of their tunic collars. Woden's laser-rifle barrel was pressed against the back of the skull, where the spinal column entered; Jack and Mat had their weapons pointed at the base of the spinal columns of their hostages. Woden spoke into the language interpreter on his wrist. "Tell your men to put down their weapons, and we will do the same. We wish to talk."

Almost in unison the three captives dropped their full weight toward the ground as they unsheathed long daggers. Woden knew peace had lost. The enemy soldiers at the barricades, seeing their leaders resist, would resist as well. Woden's laser burst caught his assailant at the top of the head, even as he felt a sharp and searing cold on his left thigh as the skin was exposed to the air. The alien crumpled, lifeless, to the ground. Jack and Mat, in what appeared a quick jig, avoided knife thrusts and kicks to their legs and with two shots apiece to the pelvic area, rendered their assailants useless but momentarily alive. Woden stole a glance at the enemy explosives team, saw them all upon the ground, motionless, dead; John materialized, on the flank of Woden, standing, shooting laser bursts, aiming toward the barricaded enemy at the larger vessel. Woden fired at the smaller vehicle of the explosives team, and it erupted in flames. He then joined John's stream of laser bursts at the large vessel and barricades.

Jack and Mat retreated to Woden, then turned to fire on the enemy, as Woden ran to John. The Explorer's door opened as Jack and Mat ran to join John and Woden. Their wounded prisoners appeared dead, with self-inflicted dagger thrusts to the neck. Their bursts at the enemy ship were opening a hole in the vessel's skin, and then success came with an explosion of fire and smoke. A large-caliber round came from the enemy vessel, whoomphed into the Explorer's force field, and ricochetted downward into the ground, which caught fire. Immediately a round came from the Explorer's starboard cannon and struck the alien ship attempting to rise and slip away. The aliens behind the barricades were scorched by the space-ship explosion. The survivors could manage only to return inaccurate, fitful fire. The horizon bust into yellow-orange flame as the alien ship debris spread into the air and fell, piercing Hals, earthbound debris, the ground. All the alien personnel were dead.

The Earth crew entered their craft, tumbling through the door as Andy pulled them through. Tim, leaving his forward gun location, no targets to engage, pulled them to their feet. Mat was already bandaging Woden's leg from the knife-swipe wound. The Explorer sent a second nuclear round into the barricades, courtesy of Ling. The round struck, and from the barricade, body parts and debris flew into the air. The Explorer 7 rose slowly, then slipped across the surface of the planet, barely clearing trees, homes, hills, and peaks, till launching up through the planet's atmosphere and into the darkness of space.

***

John, Mat, Jack, and Woden sat in the armaments room, peeling their gear and clothing from their bodies. Ling eased back Woden's bandage, quickly pulled out his vacuum suction, and slowly worked it across the wound. Woden tensed in extreme pain. Ling spoke. "This resembles a snake-venom wound. I will run a test. For now, here's a shot into the leg to counteract possible bacterial or viral threats."

Mat looked at Jack. "The daggers into the necks may have held poison." Mat and Jack's hostages had stabbed each other with long, wood-like daggers.

Ling heard and took note, wishing an alien body had been brought on board. Woden smiled. "Never easy." They all had a tiredness not of physical exertion but of intense mental alertness over a prolonged period of uncertainty. They had accomplished their tasks of avoiding a major injury or making a mistake that harmed the mission or others, and of accomplishing the mission, and killing those who wished to kill them. They had thin smiles on their faces—not the big-tooth smiles of victory over overwhelming foes, not the turned-up corner-of-the-mouth smiles of happiness to have survived. They had yet to assess victory over forces of an unknown civilization.

God had brought them through again; another day at work. They were deeply thankful, knowing what could have transpired, how it all could have been a tragedy—the margin of error so slight. The crew members coming down to the armaments room and thanking them, wanting to hear of their mission and of the enemy, telling of their experiences aboard ship, inviting them up to the dining room, where supposedly someone might be baking a cake—their friendship and their godly faces gleaming in pride were all the reward these soldiers needed. They knew they had started God's Kingdom down the pathway of war, and it was likely to be long, and less-than-desirable events would occur. They had trusted in Him on a foreign planet with an alien climate and an untried and unpredictable foe, and He had brought them through. They did not fear the future because He always brought them through.

Andy came down, congratulated them, and asked how the hologram charade had worked. He received advice on the presentation of the imaging and kudos for being wise enough to program in the "nondestructive" Earth party members being shot and writhing in agony. Andy asked Woden, "What did you think when their leader called his men off?"

Woden answered, "It surprised me, but I knew we had our second play to show their real intent."

Andy shook his head. "They wanted no living witnesses to their massacre. That tells us they know the rules of war—or perhaps they just read up on our rules of war. Whichever it is, life has no value to them."

Woden answered, "Or maybe it was a cultural rule: the life of foreigners has no worth." Woden studied Andy's eyes. "It was interesting that the would-be hostages decided to resist. Decided victory or death, nothing between—no draw. They believed they could not be subdued in hand-to-hand combat."

Andy smiled. "Look at it from their eyes. They outweighed you by likely a hundred pounds apiece, their reaches were longer by feet, and they moved much more quickly than their mass suggested. And they have seen a lifetime of combat. Maybe they have a hubris and can't conceive of any alien people being their equals."

Woden spoke his truth. "Our Lord will change that attitude."

Andy's eyes showed a gleam as he said, "Our Lord will make His will known—who is the Creator and who is the created. All-powerful is He."

Woden felt his body tingling with the presence of the Spirit, and he added, "Amen." Woden thanked God that Andy had been introduced to him and that he had followed up on that invitation to visit Andy's river home. Andy was thinking, too, as he settled into the Spirit's company. He commended Woden to the Spirit and to a God who created such good men—capable and with servants' hearts. He and the Spirit settled into thankfulness.

Robin popped up behind Andy's shoulder. "We've got news from New Jerusalem."

Mat interjected, "Do they know about this current event just completed?"

"Yes, they know the complete picture from our first encounter through today's event. The Lord said, and I paraphrase, 'Well done.' He said that we played these situations correctly, and we brought honor to the Kingdom and to Him."

The four men cheered and were thankful. Three—Woden, John, and Mat—had begun their military careers in the "world" and had had leaders who might not comment, who might distance themselves till the political correctness of the action was validated, or who might walk away from the men who so valiantly carried out their orders. All the gathered, including Jack, said, "Amen."

Robin spoke. "There is one more thing."

"What?" asked Jack.

"Our King has sent his orders for dealing with the Halcyon Empire."

"Well, what are they?" John said, not impatiently but knowing Robin was purposely building suspense, and it had worked.

"Find out in the conference room in half an hour," said Robin as he turned to leave.

***

The deck crew on duty, Andy, Emily, and Dan, were the only members not in the conference room. Tom, as second captain, chaired the meeting. He looked upon his crew as he rested his arms on a thin podium with a supporting base of steel so thin that it appeared almost invisible. Food was still being eaten, and the favorite—coffee—dispersed in countless personal mugs, gifts from crew members and family, was sipped. They had yet to learn that a daunting task lay before them. They would like it, and he was eager to share it.

Tom spoke. "Our King, along with trusted experts and leaders on Earth, has issued a policy statement concerning the Halcyon Empire and our intended relationship. We have it on the screen, and I will read it, commenting where necessary. Hold your thoughts, even to my comments, until the end." Tom looked down. He had the speech printed out; he preferred a printed text because it was easier to manage, notes could be scribbled quickly, and he could lift his eyes and then get back to the written word without losing his continuity. "Our Lord says the following:"

Recent space explorations have led to contact with an alien culture, which we have mistakenly named the Halcyon Empire. The word 'halcyon' does not fit the individual or national personality. *Halcyon*, in our language, means calm, peaceful, prosperous, affluent times and derives from an ancient Greek legend of seabirds that calmed the rough seas of winter for the incubation of their young. Now, having a greater volume of language and a historical context for the Halcyon nation, we know that a ravaging seabird species on their home planet viewed the native population as a food source. It was revered for its ferocity and lustful appetite. In the philosophy of "if it doesn't kill you, it can only make you stronger," the native mantis inhabitants overcame these giant birds through ferocity and unrelenting drive. The mantis inhabitants now have an orderly, affluent, existence—at the expense of all other life forms of their known world. The new official designation of the mantis civilization is the Predator Nation.

The individuals of the Predator Nation are of an unknown species. Their general body configuration matches human criteria, consisting of a head, torso, arms, legs, and feet. The head is smaller; the arms and torso, longer. An opposable thumb is present. They are up to three feet taller than the average human. They do have characteristics that remind us Earth dwellers of the mantis species of insects. They have intelligence, as proven by their space vessels and weapons. Spiritually and morally, they worship the creature and not the Creator God of Christianity.

The Predator Nation has consistently attacked our peaceful exploration vessels. They desire no communication and do not warn of their attacks. They may feign interest in talks for the purpose of taking hostages. From intercepted communications, we know degradation and torture can be expected if you are unfortunate enough to be taken prisoner. Angelic rescue forces are roaming near all Earth forces. A full list of attacks on our exploratory vessels and personnel throughout the galaxy will be afforded you.

We are not interested in the prolonged futility of attempting coexistence with such a civilization. Provocations, assaults, thefts, and hostage-taking have been proven to be the normal warm-up for full war. Therefore, we are in a state of war with the Predator Nation. New space vessels with the sole purpose of destroying their ships, their resources are even now being produced. This war is one of the extermination of the Predator Nation and will be waged until they unconditionally surrender or until there is nothing left to surrender.

We will prevail. We will suffer temporary losses. No one will lose eternal life. At some time in the future, all that has been created will bow in submission to our Father, God-the Creator of all that is. Thank you.

The screen projecting Christ's announcement went blank, and the text appeared, to give the opportunity for study. Tom continued the presentation in his own words. "We know the Lord's intent." He studied the faces; some were sad, as they thought back to past conflicts waged in the human flesh. The new mind-set, the spirit of the resurrected, would soon cast off the memory of weakness. Others had a keenness in their eyes, realizing their new state of being, wanting to begin the task as soon as possible.

"We have been given specific instructions for Explorer 7, as to our immediate goals." Tom wondered if they were ready for his words. Here it comes, he thought. "We are to return to the planet of our shootout. The planet is called Thermador by the natives—those enslaved. They are of the same race as the Predator Nation. We will initiate a desire for rebellion among the indigenous population, called Thermadorians. We will create an army and a democratic form of government, if possible. We will reallocate the bounty of the land to those who produce it; we will establish laws. Christ will be introduced to the population. Then, we will follow the trail of the Predator

Nation's tribute convoys, and the process will begin again. Furloughs to Earth will be granted at any time and for any length of time, dependent only on the availability of replacements."

Tom studied his audience; they were lost in their thoughts but not weighed down with worry or sorrow. He would let them digest the new information and talk among themselves. "I am open for questions and speculation, even as you are now formally dismissed."

CHAPTER 8

Woden watched his team members, who were running in a crouch and then jumping onto the air platform. Stray laser blasts hummed above their heads. Huddled groups of native civilians, dressed in torn rags, were scattered on the flat field before their squalid mud-and-thatch homes, which now were smoking ruins. Slave collars, cut cleanly or hacked deliriously, littered the flatness. Woden and his men had, at the war's beginning four weeks ago, called the Thermadorians "grasshoppers" then "praying mantises" shortened to "PMs"—distinguishing labels that were necessary and hastily contrived. The living resembled insects: their dead bodies, mutilated by weapon strikes and their enemy's rage, seemed like debris before a garden bug zapper. The monikers struck the Christians as lacking dignity, and so use of those terms stopped, not by orders or debate but by the goodness of the Spirit within each soldier. The crowds kept their heads low as stray rounds hummed. One citizen forgot the new protocol, and Woden watched the head explode into thin wood-like fragments and yellow mist; the body crumbled on the ground. The wounded and the forlorn grunted and cried in their unearthly, inhuman tones. Somehow, through their suffering, an emotion, a chord of divine empathy, arose in the sound and said, "These beings belong to me, God."

John and Mat (uncle and nephew) situated themselves in the bow of the air platform, laser rifles moving, bound to their searching eyes. They made not a sound when moving—from their rucksacks, attached knives, war axes, laser pistols, or combat-slung laser rifles. The sky hung low, and the humidity was pulling out the sweat in rivulets that could not evaporate within air-tight suits. The planet should have been called Humid Tour, thought Mat.

Seismic activity had played a significant role in the making of the planet, but it was only coincidence that the English word, "Thermador," fit the phonetics of the planet's name. Abe and Donkey, two recently liberated Thermadorians, followed John and Mat onto the air platform. Abe and Donkey were the nicknames given by the Explorer 7 crew. The Thermadorians were of the same species as the "Pins," the new moniker for the Predator Nation enemy. Pins were at least a foot taller than Thermadorians, thanks to the plentiful harvests on their vassal planets, including Thermador. Last, Jack and Woden deftly jumped onto the platform.

Woden took one last look into the distant hilly terrain, where they were destined to penetrate and traverse. Pins were in the hills; how many, he did not know. He did know they had Thermadorian captives, and perhaps they held earthlings, too. That info was from the comms chatter. No one of rank had ordered his squad to go. He and his band fought, subdued, or conquered, and then moved to another fight on the assessment of the moment. This flowing, waterlike quality of their advance was working: the Pins were running for their lives.

The four weeks of warfare on Thermador had been sparked by the spontaneous eruption of an angry populace. The idea of freedom had been seething in their hearts from the moment they had first been conquered. Every man and woman—and even children—had been raped by the warriors of the Predator Nation. Their thrall necklaces had been cut, in covert actions, by Earth liberators, both angelic and human. Simple weapons had been handed out, but truly, the large hands and quick, muscled arms and legs of this alien race could easily kill. The middle finger of males was fully fifteen inches long—five inches longer than their other fingers and capped by a conical nail as hard as steel. A deadly toxin seeped or squirted from the apex of the cone. Initially, in his first encounter with the Pins, Woden had thought a knife had swept past his legs. Luckily, Ling had discovered the poisonous nature of the injury, made an antiserum, and healed the wound. Every Earth resource in the vicinity had been rushed in to support the uprising. Explorer vessels 7 through 12 had added their manpower and firepower. The academies of space exploration on Earth had recruited volunteers, who had received weapons training on the voyage to Thermador. The security crew of Explorer 7 had been operating independently of their vessel, with only sporadic contact and help.

The indigenous males formed bands, fought independently; some adhered to the earthlings, obeyed orders and directions, and received weapons. Abe and Donkey had shown aggressiveness. They grasped knowledge quickly and were anxious to learn English; they were given laser rifles and incorporated into the unit.

John, a history buff, said Abe looked like Abe Lincoln, a former president of the United States, because of his great height and his antiquated Thermadorian helmet, which had the shape and high crown of a stovepipe hat. Donkey was wider than the average Thermadorian, and, with his strong legs, carried heavy gear upon his back with ease and seemed proud of his strength. He became the unit's donkey. The name closely approximated the sound of his Thermadorian name. For brevity, they called him Don, using Key as his last name. Sometimes they called him "Francis," as in Francis Scott Key of "The Star-Spangled Banner" fame, for Don Key liked to sing (badly, to Earth ears). Don and Abe were tireless, savage, loyal, and had already saved the earthlings from maiming and temporary immobility countless times.

Woden had become the squad leader by unanimous vote and handled the duties of a sergeant. He blamed his promotion on his age—he was born circa 800 AD—and his sixty years of military service during his first lifetime on Earth. No one retired from war on the frontier region in the times in which he lived. Men fought until they died or could not hold a weapon, regardless of kingly proclamations and prescribed retirement ages. John may have said it best. "There isn't anything you haven't experienced in combat."

Or, as Jack said, "You've done it all."

John was considered the lieutenant, as all his experience had been in the modern period of lasers. He was better with fire coordinates and plotting courses. He knew the intricacies of weapons systems, the strategies of large units of combined arms, and the protocols and methods of military forces.

The rotors whined, and the platform's undercarriage rotors lifted the air platform. Woden had learned to drive an air platform during Satan's last hurrah at the end of the Millennium. The movement created a breeze that struck the sweat-wicking clothing. Even with no exposed skin, a coolness was felt and appreciated. Their clothing blocked large pollens, sand, and soil particles, and a thin, crusty mud began to accumulate. The sandy dust was tapping and shushing on his plastic face shield. He caught a glint of metal in the hills to his left.

Abe saw it too. "Chiuck! Chiuck!" he called out in the guttural voice of his species. *Chiuck* meant *enemy*—one of the first lessons learned by earthlings.

Woden turned down the speed of the platform with his left hand on a dial and pulled into a straight, deep-sided, rock-lined water canal that intersected his straight-line path to the hills. He held his position and hovered softly (by closing baffles to narrowest point) over the currentless water, barely agitated by the rotors. His craft was hidden from the hills by the canal embankment. He rotated the platform half a turn to face left. He would use the canal to outflank and surprise the enemy.

He pushed the lever to full throttle as he opened the baffles. He kept the craft inches from the water, and from his perspective, the hills remained hidden. Then, solely by intuition, he rose for a second to catch sight of the highest hilltop in the range; that height would be his marker. "Get those heavy packs off and be ready to disembark quickly and pursue," he said into his throat comm. They signaled with their thumbs-up sign. Don knew to keep his squad's war supplies on his back—grenades, Bangalore strips, claymore mines, thrall cutters, battle-ax, medical supplies, water bladders.

Woden pulled up and out of the canal when his men had completed their tasks, and on a straight course to the hills, he skimmed over the flat and barren agricultural fields. He knew he was out of sight and range of the glint that told of enemies. He saw nothing but barren hills and a draw that led into the heart of the terrain. He knew every Pin in those hills was lined up at the top of the draw in ambush. Any feeder ravines probably were covered as well. He veered to his left, went past the draw as he looked back and up. From the top, coming down the draw, a power burst had been fired at his platform, the shock wave appearing and then disappearing. The platform had passed; the power burst exploded onto the empty fields.

Suddenly, he slowed the craft, flew slowly up the side of a hill as his men searched the terrain for sniper holes, manned trenches. A fleeing form was seen, a Pin, lost or on an errand, or a messenger. Jack's laser crumpled the soldier before he could gather himself for a hop. At the top of the hill, Woden tilted the bow to give an angle downward, so every laser in the craft could fire simultaneously upon the reverse slope. They saw swarms of enemy platoons, sitting in formation, resting; and foxholes crammed with troops. The platform spewed bursts of heavy fire, and the formations began to crumble.

Then, because of the bold actions of a few, the warriors began to reunite, regain their senses, and return fire. Woden slipped back over the hill's top to silence and a motionless terrain. "Give them grenades." His voice blasted over his squad's throat comms. When he saw all hands holding grenades, he moved the platform to his left, around the hill. Abe and Don had four grenades in each hand. This was allowed, as they had demonstrated through fifty practice throws that no grenade was ever dropped or fell early or failed to have a ring pulled. His squad turned the corner at the base of the slope's rear, at eye level. The grenades were tossed into the enemy that was now facing uphill, waiting for an assault from the hilltop. He saw elements ahead, far away: fleeing civilians, hostages, and Earth men in military attire, bound in agricultural binding twine, yanked along by their Pin captors.

He made two passes over the confused enemy ranks before breaking contact and moving to the fleeing enemy with their captives. The platform overcame stragglers moving up a wide, ascending flatness; the hills had thinned. They easily sniped from their platform at Pins, in groups of twos or threes, who were distracted with keeping their weakening hostages on their feet. The method was to keep the platform centered on the enemy's back, turn when the enemy turned, pull up quietly, and without a sound, send a burst into the nexus of legs and spine. When a Pin crumbled, a blast to the nexus of neck and skull finished the job. Many times when the second shot needed was of distance, or the line of sight cluttered, Abe and Don would hop off the platform, and in a few bounds, lop off the heads of the prostrate with battle axes. John once suggested the Thermadorians should be called "hoppers" for their unearthly jumps. On their backs were rigid wings of insect material that did not flap but extended and functioned as a stabilizer. The happiness of killing their enemies lit up the eyes of Abe and Don; the subdued, twisted laughter added a perspective.

The enemy targets demanded precise shots—the tall, thin arms and legs never seemed to be still, and the jerky movements of their torsos made heart shots difficult. Their outer skin and musculature were so dense it seemed more like leather stretched over wooden chitin. Even the heads were compact, with thick, semitriangular, chitin skulls. The helmets fitted tightly, and the underlining of shock-resistant material was state of the art. The traditional weapon of the species had been the battle-ax fitted to a strong and lengthy handle. The method to victory was to hack off an arm and severe the neck. Usually, two arms needed to be immobilized or severed. The Pins weren't "bleeders." Oxygen entered their bodies through many small pores in their hard skin. Their greenish-yellow blood carried only nutrients to the body and waste out of the body. A severed arm or leg could jerk reflexively for hours.

Near the top of the grade and the end of the hill terrain, a ridge ran for miles. The dropped clothing articles, the bandages, the footprint trails crossed the ridge's exposed core of rock of barely six feet in height. Woden stopped the platform fifty yards to the left of the trail and ridge crest. The men disembarked. The ridge was the perfect ambush site for Pins on the other side. The squad crawled to the edge of the ridge, peeked over the top, and saw the straggling column of bodies far across the sandy plain. In the distance were high, barren, volcanic-rock mountains, perhaps a half-day's march. Near the ridge top, they saw the movement of Pins into freshly dug gun emplacements. An assault would waste time—time enough for the non-combatants to be murdered. Woden signaled Jack, at the end of the squad line along the ridge. Jack moved to Woden's side in a crouched, one-armed ape shuffle. He sat.

Woden spoke. "Tell Don he will remain here and snipe and pressure the enemy at the ridge. Tell him John will be near the stragglers on the far side, but he will be sniping toward Don at any exposed enemy. Make certain you click on Don's blinker."

Jack had picked up the Thermadorian language quickly, more deeply than the others, and had become their interpreter. The invisible blinker would identify Don to John. Woden thought again. "Bring Don here and let me see you tell him," Woden said. They had time to communicate, to assure that all was understood. A mistake could mean death or immobility. Jack turned to look down the line; all heads swiveled to Jack and Woden. Jack made a sign with his hands that represented a Thermadorian beast of burden, followed by a cupped hand being gathered in. Don moved down the hill to hide his height and trotted to the men.

Woden watched and listened as Jack spoke. He watched Don nod his head in understanding, a gesture taught to him. Woden spoke. "He will be alone with his blinker on." Jack repeated the phrase. The head nodded in affirmation. Woden said, "John will have his blinker on." Jack repeated the phrase. Don nodded in affirmation.

"Okay, saddle up." All but Don ran down to the platform and jumped aboard. Woden walked with John to the platform, and said, "Ride with me in the back and pick your spot on the far slope."

John answered, "I've already picked it. Stay far to the left, and I'll signal when you should cut straight over to the trail."

Woden smiled at an expression he had learned in the Millennium: John had his 'head in the game.' Woden said, "Okay." All were aboard. They traveled to the left as a feint to anyone watching, then, at top speed, to the right, out onto the sandy plain. The speed was exhilarating, even as Woden watched for an incoming blast from the enemy ambush barely discernable on the far slope. John tapped Woden. Woden slowed the craft. John touched him again; the rough hand remained on Woden's forearm, then tightened and pulled. This was the place. The platform was severely slowed but not stopped. John rolled out, off the side, into loose sand, and Woden turned to the stragglers ahead at full speed as John began setting up his hole.

Ahead, Woden had his first close look at the earthling soldiers in captivity. They were at the front of the column. They still had strength in their movements, a calmness of movement and demeanor. In contrast, their captors seemed more fidgety and unpredictable in movement than was normal for their species. Yes, the immortal body had outperformed the enemy on the battlefield. A familiarity, a sense of déjà vu was eerily in Woden's mind. Who were they? Black hair on the one of large size. The other was short, with wide shoulders, thick chest and neck muscles, a buzz cut of dark hair. He knew them! Paternus and Seth, his comrades from his early manhood and wars past. He had just seen them months ago in basic training for the explorations. They had been assigned to Explorer 8. They were his lifelong friends, from his early adulthood and his old age, till his death; they had been battle companions during the eastern invasions of the forest land and the Muslim wars. They were his Paradise buddies, his Millennium neighbors. He smiled at the volume of memories and the eerie quality of his remembrances. Four weeks of constant fighting had seemed a millennium.

He turned the platform away from the rear of the column of stragglers, all Thermadorian civilians. His captive friends, as soldiers, were a force multiplier, and they had the most worth to the captors, who would use them as bargaining chips if given the chance or kill them without hesitation. Fast and surgically, he piloted the platform on the flank of the column. He spoke into his throat comm. "Paternus and Seth ahead. Be ready for stop." He paused; something he forgot? "Jack, make Abe aware."

All but Abe knew the two men, and in the confusion and dust of battle…. He saw his men stiffen bodily, their heads went forward as they watched with a businesslike eagerness and cunning, planning their moves on the enemy. Jack was face-to-face with Abe, speaking through the throat comm. Abe listened, nodding his head. Suddenly, Abe was yelling into the throat comm, "Chuick! Chuick!" as he pointed at the civilian stragglers and their captors.

Woden had a momentary confusion. Was Abe angry that the squad was not dealing with the captors of his people but rather with the earthlings? Abe knew the worth of soldiers over civilians. No, Abe was saying the civilians were not civilians but soldiers dressed as civilians. This was a trap. Woden searched his mind for Thermadorian words to verify his thoughts. No time. "The civilians may be soldiers. Kill them." What was he forgetting? "Watch for captured lasers!" The enemy weapons were just as effective as lasers but noisy and with a lesser rate of fire.

"Remember Paternus and Seth are in the mix! Do not fire upon them." Woden prayed his words. Thumbs-up signals were coming from the crew.

The "civilians" began pulling their weapons from their robes. Abe was the first to recognize the movement and the first to fire. Woden ran the platform into the end of the largest group; near the head of the column, the rotors jammed up on body parts. The men dismounted, shooting their way through to the head of the column, where Paternus and Seth were located. Mat and Jack had fought clear of the mass of fallen, wounded, fighting Pins, moved swiftly toward the head of the column. Woden and Abe buddied up and waded through the center.

Mat was the first with a clear sighting of the captives and their assigned guards. He knelt; the guards were distracted by the mass of moving figures and ignored the lone figure, likely wounded and hunched up on the desert alone. He fired four times, and four captors fell. Jack appeared at a run, moving toward Paternus and Seth and a lone Pin guard, who was struggling to his feet. Seth jumped up to use the captivity ropes to garrot the guard. Paternus grabbed the guard's ankles and pulled the feet out from under him. Jack ran up, placed his barrel into the recessed eye portal, and shot him dead.

"Grenades!" called Woden, as he and Abe separated from the mass of living, wounded, and dead, and began heaving grenades into the mass. Jack and Mat joined in the grenade tossing, until there was silence. As they stood reviewing the carnage, Don and John were seen coming up the trail of bodies.

Woden called out, "I could have given you a ride."

"You were busy," said John. "Don killed nearly all of them, once they turned to face my shooting."

"Well done," said Jack.

"And I second that," said Mat, who added, "Look who we have here."

Seth and Paternus had found a knife and were cutting their bindings, as well as dusting themselves and each other. Seth was motioning with his hands. "Cutters," he said. The squad now noticed they had thrall collars around their necks.

Jack and Mat were the first to approach their friends, then, Woden and John, Abe and Don. Abe stood erect before the two human strangers and spoke. "Why you come, fight?" Jack was quickly by Paternus's side, and Paternus answered, "All God's creation should be treated with respect." Jack interpreted the English into Thermadorian.

Seth quickly added, "All God's creation should be free to rule their own lives." Jack interpreted with passion in his voice.

Don spoke. "You like *semach*?" He pointed to both men.

Jack spoke quickly, "*Semach* is *thrall collar* to us."

Seth spoke. "We grieve with you for your people's sufferings." He placed his open hand on his heart as Jack translated. Don bowed his head in confusion. Who were these foreign creatures who shared his people's shame and hurt? Abe, too, was confused, as no Thermadorian had ever heard such words from foreigners. He placed his open palm on his heart, then touched Seth's heart.

Quick handshakes, a rub of the back or shoulder, quick praises to their God, began among the crew. A hallelujah boomed from Mat. Abe and Don mimicked Mat's praise, for in their language, the sound was a near proximity to happiness and lightness of heart. All were aware the battlefield was still active, and a throng of men made a rich target. The feeling of gratitude within their souls continued. All the earthlings saw that within the recessed helmets, the red eyes of Don and Abe held thankfulness and mirth. The Thermadorians had human emotions.

***

From the distant mountains, an air platform came directly toward them, an Earth vessel, trim, armored. Pin air platforms had armored bows that resembled a beak and stubby wing extensions for lift. The vessel set down within twenty yards of the squad; dust and debris was almost nonexistent. The rotors functioned as a vacuum, collecting the sand and debris into a funnel that emptied away from the vessel. The rotors remained on ready, as four helmeted, Red Cross-badged people, two women and two men, stepped out and began walking to the squad of soldiers. One of the women waved. Grace! The second woman smiled but did not wave. Pete was one of the men, and it was Ling bringing up the rear. Grace began giving out hugs, and Pete gave handshakes, as Ling spoke. "Anyone injured?"

Ling saw the "no" shake of the heads. He spoke. "Well, then, let's run some monitors over you and get vitals. Probably all of you are dehydrated." Ling saw Seth and Paternus of Explorer 8, and said, "Your squad made it out of the caverns alive, but two are wounded—maybe a month recovery time is needed." Ling's voice trailed the pleasant surprise of seeing Seth and Paternus alive. Seth raised his hand to Ling, and said, "Thanks."

"What's happening on the battlefield?" asked John of Ling.

Ling answered, "The Pins have been pushed out of the population centers and are forting up in those mountains." Ling pointed where his vessel had traveled from, and then added, "Many are fleeing under the agricultural lands, in vast tunnels, funnels, and caves from past mining projects and volcanic activity millions of years ago. There's chatter that the Pins are sending a relief fleet."

Pete and Grace were busy testing blood, heart rate, and eyes, and passing scanners over bodies. Particular care was given to the rate of infiltration of the airy mineral that was found in air and water. Mat watched the unknown woman, who avoided the squad and went directly to the bodies of the dead. Her reason for being here was unknown, and he was a curious soul. She was studying the dead, had a short pointer that she used to expose wounds from the almost-weightless veil of clothing. Pin women were difficult to distinguish from men, as they were of the same size and build. Hips were not wider, and breasts existed under the hard skin and muscle and did not protrude. She found no Pin women; only Pin men dressed as women.

A living contingent of true Thermadorian women, children, and oldsters had gathered in the rear. Abe and Don engaged in conversation with them. Mat continued to watch. The woman approached and began talking to the gathered in their own language. Abe and Don seemed agitated by her talk.

Mat quietly approached Grace, squeezed her arm, and said, "I need a diplomat."

"Certainly," said Grace, not following Mat's gaze into the distance. Only when they had cleared the squad and she wondered why the quick pace, did she notice her partner, Ava, being misunderstood. It had to be that, for Ava was a kind soul. Ava knew Andy from New Jerusalem and the officer's academy. Her field was linguistics; she had arranged the Predator Nation's language study and had presented their dictionary and cultural history study just before war broke out. Evidently, Ava had hit a sore spot on the collective conscience. Grace thought violent action was imminent. She raised her arm and began waving while calling, "Ava! Ava!"

Ava turned and waved and began to walk toward Grace. As they met, they continued to walk toward the group. Thermadorians could smell indecision and fear, and, like a predator seeing a running animal, would take up the chase and kill. "Where'd it go wrong?" Grace spoke in a whisper as Mat stepped in front and led the two.

Ava spoke quietly. "I mentioned the sacred graves in the mountain region and Thermadorian history. They have a deep secret they want kept secret, and I was getting close."

The earthlings were upon the group of natives. Grace immediately went to Abe, whose eyes seemed to burn with hate. She took his large, baseball-glove hand into her small, slender hand, and she felt the presence of her soul and her God pass to Abe, even as his slashing finger innocently wrapped around her hand.

She spoke to Ava. "Apologize now." A torrent of sound came from Ava. Whatever she said elicited a low, soothing tone, almost a songlike quality from certain women in the group. Eventually, the whole group assumed the soothing tone. They watched Abe and Don's eyes go from fiery red to the orange-red beauty of a rising sun. Ava knew how to soothe, thought Mat. That was a gift of the Spirit.

Mat spoke. "Ling needs to test Abe's and Don's vitals, as well as the vitals of these civilians. Are they hungry or thirsty?"

"Yes," said Ava, "and we have Thermadorian water and food on our vessel."

Grace said happily, "By all means." She raised her arm and made a gathering motion to the crowd as Ava announced the availability of food and water.

CHAPTER 9

By late afternoon, when the first sun was near to exiting the sky and the first moon was appearing yellow-orange and reflecting warmth and light, the day's battlefield trail had been revisited. All wounded had been gathered, fed, rehydrated, and treated; all corpses had been piled and marked for evacuation to tribal burial sites. The children of God had a deep peace that the day's events marked a turning point in the war. The road to victory had begun.

A portable, hard-shelled troop restorer had been dropped from an air platform, providing a living and sleeping space where earthlings could unmask, remove their suits, towelette the sweat of the day from their bodies, and communicate with home or friends in the field. They would sleep on soft mattresses and have clean blankets over them. They would eat solid foods, not the sucked-in liquids of fighting and marching in airtight masks and uniforms. The troop restorer had windows for observation and a sensor system to warn of approaching life-forms, a hard shell that deflected laser fire, and a defensive force field that repelled rockets. Abe and Don had been allowed to enter and partake of Earth food, then they left to be with their people. This unsolicited, voluntary leaving saved face for the Christians, who could not allow aliens to sleep inside, due to the possibility of betrayal. No one knew what this species was truly feeling for their allies.

The squad and medical crew were relaxing in the restorer pod. All had cleaned, all had full stomachs, all had been rehydrated, and their eyes washed with salve. Although not near to exhaustion from six weeks of 24/7 combat, they did have a mellowness of mind and body that created a desire to speak and share their thoughts and experiences. Mat's voice broke the stillness as he spoke to Ava. "Can you enlighten us on the talk you had this afternoon with the natives?"

Before Ava could respond, Grace said, "Yes, we all need to know their touchy places, so that we can avoid them—or at least prepare ourselves for a reaction."

Ling, in his deep and introspective voice, added, "How were you chosen for this task of linguistic and cultural exploration? You know how to probe— ask tough questions—and soothe and heal, as well."

Ava smiled at the kind thoughts. It was only right for them to know. Still, her apprehension in presenting her "cover story" seized her with terror. "I agree your questions should be answered. I am Ava Rodriguez, born in the Tribulation, from parents who survived that ordeal in Mexico. I was serving on Explorer 12 when this war came to us. I am the psych/spiritual adviser on my vessel. My fields of study are anything ethnocultural and all aspects of psychology and sociology. My second major is language. The big push initially was to understand the Predator Nation's language, and this, of course, took us into literature and history, the only way words have context and relevance to a culture. I had a big advantage, as Explorer 12 had discovered and was studying the Predator Nation language a full two months before any incident had taken place." She realized she needed to add her 'rapport' information. She changed the direction of subject matter and added, "By the way, I know Andy, Tom, and Grace from courses offered at training in Florida. Andy goes way back to the first New Jerusalem testing."

"How did that come about? Studying the Predator Nation's language early," asked Jack.

"We stumbled across a well-traveled tribute route, with plenty of chatter between ships and planets, and we parked behind a moon, out of sight. We also picked up personal messages to the home planet from crew members of their fleet. We didn't want to announce ourselves till we could speak their language. We quickly understood what their nation was about and so never announced ourselves."

Mat's eyes lit in recognition of a possible connect-the-dots moment. "Were you responsible for the data dump, the dictionary, and the book on Pin culture?"

"Yes, I helped in that work." Ava smiled; being appreciated felt good, even if it was unwarranted and unwanted. Her apprehension level dropped. Her cover was secure. She would have exposed all Earth forces with that data dump had their security systems not been extraordinary. Might have turned the course of battle. She then realized these people might be dead, or if you believed them, severely disrupted for months. She, suddenly and with a start, realized what pain that would have caused her—and guilt. She was fond of all of them—hadn't met a crude or cruel person since she began her interactions. She continued, "We now have a firm grasp on their language and their history and political setup, and even on their morality. This is a first-of-its-kind situation—unique, to us earthlings. Imagine: a group of indigenous beings of another species whose babies are placed into group nursing centers at birth and are raised as a group by surrogate staff. They live relatively long lives of two hundred years. They have no concept of a god; they do not fear death; they have no empathy or compassion for others; they live for the moment and enjoy sex, food, the emptying of their bowels, and belching. They enjoy clothing and signs of rank. They enjoy inflicting pain on others—these others must not be of their ethnicity—which, in effect, means their home planet, twice the size of Earth. Having the good opinion of their peers means nothing. If they seek rank, it is only because of the inducements to their fleshly selves.

"There is no conflict between good and bad behavior or thoughts. There is no 'love thy neighbor as thyself,' nor is there 'love God with all your heart, soul, mind, and strength.' If you want an analogy, they are like giant praying mantises. They are indeed nearer to insect life, morally. If you would tell them the Creator of all things loves them and wants the best for them, they would not be able to comprehend." Had she oversold her personality? Love God with all your heart, soul, mind, and strength: Why did that sentence seem glued upon her conscience?

Mat spoke up. "Your assessment may tilt to the extreme. Earth cultures that rejected God's truths tended toward cruelty, selfishness, and pleasures of the body and were animallike in behavior."

John added, "Do you see how the Thermadorian females have taken in their young and are mothering them, now that the nurseries have been destroyed by the Pins? Same species."

Jack commented, "Abe and Don express thankfulness and appreciation for the weapons we provide."

Ava spoke. "Weapons to kill…and I recognize the Thermadorians are different than the Predator Nation individuals I was studying. The Pin's home planet is named Rau-toon, 'the vicious land.'"

Jack shrugged his shoulders. "Most weapons do kill, righteously or unrighteously. Thankfulness is thankfulness. It is not for the ability to kill *better*, is it? Or is it for the ability to better defend what they love? They love each other, they love their freedom and autonomy, they love their people."

Ava, desirous of softening her position, readily spoke. "You all raised good arguments. I must add that the Thermadorians suffered the worst kind of moral degradation—rape at the individual level and societal level. They have a reason to hate. But perhaps they, like the Rau-toons, have an innate ability to enjoy killing beyond the external factors we use to justify that act."

John answered, "I see your point. Only time will tell us whether they are genetically amoral or whether amorality is a learned behavior."

Ava's facial expression held a reluctance. "I haven't shared everything with you. The Pin species may have made a radical departure from human history and had a different corrupting influence. On Earth, God breathed His life into man, and this human race was corrupted by external powers—Satan, his demons, the world, and the internal power of the flesh. God gave us new life through the death of Christ, and so our deaths and our souls have been changed—like yanking the space engine from a ship and replacing it with the same engine but better, as it was formed pure and is impervious to all degrading factors." She paused, scanning her listeners' faces. "It is rumored, in old manuscripts, that species of both these nations experienced a radically different event than earthlings: they had to leave their bodies for a hardier body, that of an insect species of their planet. A praying mantis-type form offered the hardiest body for surviving the changing environmental factors confronting their world."

"What form were they naturally born within, before the insect body?" Grace's voice held amazement.

"We don't know. We believe they don't know. We believe there is subterfuge involved."

"By whom?" asked Ling.

"Perhaps by their intelligentsia, perhaps by an outside power." Ava stopped her flow, prepared her mind for the words that would follow. "It is believed by the few scholars on Earth studying this history that the Predator Nation could not genetically alter the praying mantis species to its specifications. But more radically and incomprehensibly, they discovered what we call the 'soul' and implanted the souls of their dying individuals into the praying mantis bodies. And this is the larger secret that cannot even be alluded to. I'm not certain as to why that is."

Ling spoke up. "The concept of the human soul has always been seen as being of a spiritual nature, not measurable, not seeable, there but not there, transcending flesh. Many Earth cultures thought they could see the soul leave bodies upon death. In reality, they were seeing the angels who transported the soul. Only late in Earth's history did scientists believe that the soul consisted of matter that could neither be created nor destroyed nor separated into parts; but even greater, the matter held immutable properties, and it was eternal."

Ava spoke. "Somehow the Pins learned how to pull the soul from their dying, original shells and place them in alien shells of greater physical hardiness."

"It seems that would be painful and never-ending torment," Jack said.

"I agree," said Mat. "The soul, to me, is the collected experience of an individual gathered from the body, through the spirit, mixed with emotion and knowledge, and soaked into—or I should say, stored—in that material substance that has eternal being. To then be placed into a form that had not collected the life experience and was not of the same spirit as the life-form would be trauma enough. To live in an inferior body, with one's mind, spirit, and perhaps even a contending soul fighting your soul…that would hurt."

Pete's mind was working. "Pain can be masked by drugs, by hypnosis, by a greater pain. Maybe that is the secret they need to hide." He didn't verbalize the end of his train of thought, that if an enemy knew how to unleash the pain, expose the raw nerve of the secret to a conscious mind, that enemy could destroy the species.

Ava, listening, analyzing, was amazed at the wisdom revealed. She spoke. "Let us keep these thoughts to ourselves. The entire subject." She had spread confusion. Goal met.

Ling spoke. "Are we certain they are not artificial intelligence personnel, AIPs?"

"Mothers give birth," stated Grace. "We call them mantis, but they aren't fully insect as we know insects on Earth. Live births, no eggs. Mothers have breasts and suckle their young—the breasts are hidden under the leathery skin and dense muscle. Males aren't eaten after reproducing."

Ling asked, "What if they were to raise their own offspring, families, as John alluded to? Would this spark something? Paternal, maternal instincts? A greater inclusive kindness?"

"Perhaps the original life-form had a superior culture before being transferred to an insect/mammal body," said Woden.

"Perhaps they were exactly like us before the transfer to the alien body," ventured Paternus.

Seth joined the speculation. "Perhaps they are human, of the stock of Adam and of Eve, kidnapped from Earth by Satan's fallen angels or transported by God's angels for safety reasons."

"Well, there is only one Creator of the universe, our God. Of that we are certain," said John.

Ava spoke again. "That is why I want to respect them, not hate them. Perhaps we can uncover the secret and heal them." She was becoming good at lying.

Ling spoke. "We will respect the Thermadorians; they were dominated and abused by their captors. It is the Pins I wish to destroy because they would destroy us. Even so, I can envision for the Pins a planet all their own, if safeguards are in place to keep them there."

John added, "There is the possibility they are human and made in the likeness of our Father, his Son, and the Holy Spirit. Or they could simply be creations of God. We are here to subdue the Pins and respect all life-forms."

Ava spoke. "He has certainly given us an exciting new world." That was true; a year ago she had never heard of Earth or of their god-myth concept.

"Amen," said the chorus of voices. Only John lingered in his thoughts. Ava had mentioned rumors. Rumors could turn to gossip easily, and gossip turned to slander even in the purest soul when the word "possibilities" was added to the computation.

***

Jack and Don had volunteered for the external night guard—the boots upon the dirt, sitting or lying upon the rocks in the cold, their eyes searching a bleak and desolate landscape for trouble. The first moon gave light; the heat reflection was gone. The second moon was just a sliver in the distance of space. The internal night guard consisted of watching the monitor screens, the control panels of all shields, and the environmental monitors that detected everything from life-forms to rainstorms. This internal night guard was centered on a ship, with satellites and drones slowly circling the perimeters of countless assets and encampments, and was staffed by another command structure. The soldiers of the external night guard knew that human and Thermadorian eyes were important for catching movement and the trickery of an enemy long versed—over thousands of years—in the stratagems of war. This external night guard, of Don and Jack, heard the wails of a nocturnal predator species of reptilian origin, which moved as quickly as Earth's wolves, had no dragging tails, and whose howl was shrill and syncopated. This night guard smelled the scented breeze, saw flitting movement among the rocks, and searched the star-filled sky. They patrolled the piece of ground they found themselves upon.

Jack looked across at Don, on his left, and said, "Don."

Don answered, "Ya."

"What do you think of Jesus and our God?" Jack asked.

Don smiled. "God is good. Jesus is good." Silence.

Jack inquired, "Have you given yourself to Jesus, for Him to lead you and love you?"

Don shook his head. "Don too bitta. Too old ta change. Bittaness go away when bad guys all dead."

Jack understood the directness. "Jesus sent us to help you kill the bad guys. You help Jesus by seeking Jesus to kill *your* bad guy."

Don turned his head toward Jack. "Who dat? Bad guy?"

Jack answered, "The bad guy inside of you who holds onto your life and won't let you give it to Jesus."

Don was silent. He knew what was being asked, what was required, and yet he wanted no change. He was weary, he told himself. He sighed, then spoke. "Be quiet. Enjoy peace." The quiet became minutes and then an hour.

Jack spoke again. "You could be dead before you choose. Then it is too late to belong to Jesus forever."

Silence. Fifteen minutes passed.

Don said, "No forever. Just now."

Another quarter hour passed in silence before Jack said, "I am forever. I live forever."

Don thought upon this fact, which every Thermadorian knew—the earthlings said they had eternal life given to them by the father God. They had all died and come back in new and better bodies. It seemed impossible to dispute. How could you know they lied, unless one of them would be killed before your eyes and never came back? Trickery could still exist; they could have gone somewhere else. Better proof would be if an earthling would die before his eyes and *did* come back. Don said to Jack, "Be quiet, enjoy peace." Silence stretched on.

Don was first to see a band of creatures pierce the silhouette line of a distant ridge. Don pointed and said, "Chiuck."

Jack followed the pointing killing finger and saw the band of wolflike reptiles. Jack wondered why Don would call them chiuck, for enemy, instead of their name, *chioonzi*. Pesty or dangerous animals always seemed to start with "*chi*." Jack inquired, "Chiuck?"

Don responded "Chiuck."

Jack asked, "Shoot?"

Don answered, "Ya," which was as near as he came to pronouncing "yes."

Jack slid to the right, where a large boulder sat, and removed the sheath from his laser, clicked the generator button on, and heard the start-up hum of the engine. He popped up the scope lens protectors and sighted in where he had last seen the gang of reptiles. He assumed they were hidden in the depression at the bottom of the slope, a common feature on slopes on this planet. Don had readied his weapon, even as he had moved farther to his left, probably fearing the reptiles would outflank their position. Jack saw a flash in the sky; a satellite or drone had exploded. Odd, but within normal probability of accident per use, considering the huge number of spy craft that must be above them.

Another explosion in the sky. He picked up the forms of the reptilian pack, which was beginning to split to either side, as if they saw the two shooters in the center. Keen eyes, Jack thought. Or was it scent? How many of the objects in the stratosphere belonged to the Pins? Was this a coordinated attack? An ear-ringing explosion blinded Jack with light, even as the concussion bounced off the overhead force field. He quieted his mind to everything outside of him; life was in the lens of the scope.

The reptiles seemed to have picked up speed. The veer to outflank gave him a larger target, but it was one that required a leading shot. He placed the laser on full power; the generator now sung in a tenor's key. His bead was on the long head of the first reptile. He unleashed a burst two feet ahead; the head exploded, the beast kept running. He aimed at the neck, pulled; the beast stopped as the neck and decimated head were planted in the ground. He had struck midbody, sending a praying-mantis body cartwheeling. He began his systematic firing of four torso shots to the running forms. His concentration was on his aim, even as he was aware that he was firing at vehicles with Pin operators, not a species of native predators. He now understood Don's "chiuck." Above, the heavenly light show was equal to a meteor shower; more explosions were hitting the protective shields.

One reptile had veered from the flanking movement and was coming for him at incredible speed. He moved to his left just as a burst of concussive force pulverized the rock where he had been. He fired, watched the cartwheel of the body. Who had shot at him?

Personnel were leaving the restorer pod, crawling, slinking out. Woden, Seth, Paternus were outside; the first two had shoulder-held rockets. Paternus carried extras strapped to his back and two in his hands. Don was waving his arm to his friends to come to him. Rocket fire was pouring in from the distant ridge across from Don's position, and the volume of fire was able to penetrate the overstrained force field. The pod was hit. Abe was seen, launching a rocket.

Above the planet, the heavens were shaking, and huge shadows passed at lightning speed. Clearly, two armadas were engaged in battle. Every earthling knew the enemy had a greater number of warships. Six Earth ships, at most, against an interplanetary empire.

Mat had grabbed the arm of Ava as she awakened from her sleeping-bag cocoon at the first sounds of explosions. Her eyes held awareness, and she grabbed her outer suit and had it on before he had readied his weapon and bound his boots with the Velcro binders. Her boots were on. Grace was scrambling out the door with John. John wondered if it made sense to leave, as the pod had a high ordnance rating. Yet, hiding in the rock formations directly behind the pod had merit too. He always preferred seeing his enemy, seeing where the shells were coming from. Digging into the ground was preferrable to trusting a factory-stamped rating on a pod. Too many variables in a rating and in the ordnance being fired.

Mat was out the door. He saw John and Grace before him, running. He saw Don and Abe from across the perimeter, running toward him and the other fleeing humans. Jack remained on the perimeter. Ava, holding Mat's hand, followed. Ava was petrified. She wasn't invincible; she did not have eternal life; when she died, she died. She cursed her decision to become an operative in this struggle. She liked her earthling friends. He shouted, "Stick close behind me!" Just as their hands broke apart, she glanced at Abe and Don. Mat shouted a phrase unintelligible over the noise, reestablished his grip on Ava's hand, and was turning to round the back end of the pod, when a blast caught him in the back and flung him into a high boulder wall, fifteen feet from where he stood. His helmet's earplug shields had reacted quickly enough to shield his ears from 75 percent of the noise. Now his ears were simply ringing. He threw up, as his stomach had been violently twisted, and his brain rattled. He felt his hands in the dirt through his gloves. Where is Ava? Where is Ava?

He turned, still prone, and saw no one behind him. His mask had been blown off his head. Don and Abe were crawling toward him. He saw Grace and John on the ground, maskless, intact but disoriented. He crawled to them. "Where is Ava?" Their eyes were disoriented; dirt clung to their eye lashes. Don and Abe, even on hands and knees, towered over the group. Their eyes were dumb with fear. Grace's eyes were first to focus. She spoke. "Get the containment kit." She was telling him that Ava had disintegrated.

Protocol was to find as many pieces of the dead as possible for the angel who would soon arrive, conduct his own search, and whisk the remains away to the renewal site. Ava's body would be remade using her original DNA. The more of her they could find, the less time would be needed to bring her back. Her soul, spirit, and human memory were safe, never touched by the blast.

He found the kit, strapped in a box under the pod. Grace administered eye drops to his and John's eyes, and John to hers. Don and Abe, who possessed recessed eyes, could see clearly. They started at the blast center, even picking up shreds of her clothing, as these held microscopic bits of her. Abe and Don understood what was to be done, though they believed it was part of the burial ritual. Mat found her pelvis, attached to a femur, attached to the backbone. Grace found both arms, and John found her bowels staining the front of her uniform. Abe and Don's big, scooping, clawlike fingers picked up slime, blood, body parts, even wet sand. They worked as they ducked the sound of explosions, the whizzing of shells. The angel was among them, using a hand-held vacuum to suck up bloodied dirt, clothing bits, helmet, hair and scalp pieces. Another angel came who wasn't assigned but came because of what angels were: fearless and compassionate.

The angel, as tall as the two Thermadorians, ran his vacuum over Abe and Don's hands. They seemed in awe of their giant partner. "Bury," said Abe.

The angel smiled and said to the two mantids, in Thermadorian, "She will live again," then was gone.

***

Andy was the captain on deck that night, responsible for fully half of the airspace of Thermador, when he saw the small drones emanating from extinct volcanic cones, fissures upon the surface, cave entrances. He saw in deep space an armada of Predator Nation ships converging on his position from the north and the south. The crew had planned for the attack, knew drones would be a factor. Tom captained the shuttle craft, and Tuck manned the weapons system, a jury-rigged artillery gun under the hull, welded into place, with no swivel capability. It would fire where the shuttle was pointed. The breech, the loading mechanism, had been turned upside down so that it could be manned inside and reloaded. Lasers had also been installed for bringing down drones. The lasers had a more precise aim and were virtually unlimited in firing capacity. Finally, torpedoes hung from the underbelly of the shuttle craft, four in number. Here Tuck sat, waiting for his chance to destroy drones and incoming missiles.

Soon, they were engaged in shooting down drones and missiles aimed at ground targets. As Andy watched over his independent command, he saw Thermador burst into specks of light as the enemy upon the ground fought against his ground crewmen and the crews of other vessels upon the ground. Armada missiles added their destructive force.

Andy waited patiently as the armadas came. He watched as the enemy in space flooded his zone. He swore to God, the Almighty One, that he would push every fiber of plastic and metal, every electron beam and laser weld, every moving member of the propulsion system to its highest tolerance. Not one torpedo, one artillery round, not one laser charge would be left if the enemy remained before him. He would grind the nose of the Predator Nation's exalted fleet on the hard, cold reality of defeat. He would make them know they were second best and the God of all Creation, the God of the universe, had no more tolerance for their bestial, hateful behavior.

CHAPTER 10

Andy called the shuttle craft back from the drone-destroying mission as the Predator Nation armadas neared and the shuttle's laser generators were close to maximum heat levels. Tom had wisely refrained from using the cannon, saving that ordnance for an eventual attempt at larger, more significant targets. Andy had scouted, via his control panel, a space-debris field produced from a scarred moon. An asteroid had hit the moon, skimming the surface, creating a gouge of over one hundred miles in length before regaining its freedom of trajectory at the moon's curve and being pulled into a larger moon's gravitational force. The debris was a mixture of solid pieces miles in diameter, small rocks, boulders, and soil. In this debris field, he would have the shuttle hide behind a large chunk of the moon.

In front of the debris field and the shuttle, Explorer 7 would wait, facing the debris field as if inoperable, scant miles from the field's safety. It would appear to be a fortuitous gift, perhaps even an intact prize, for the overly confident Predator Nation combat vessels. The fastest enemy vessel, or the vessel with the highest rank onboard, would lose all caution and race ahead to secure the victory and recognition. The Explorer 7 would limp toward the debris field as if incapacitated and fleeing, enter the debris field, and find refuge behind the largest debris rock. Tom, in the shuttle, behind his own protective piece of space debris, would fire head-on at the alien vessel seeking the Explorer 7.

The trick was to wiggle the Explorer 7 like a lure before a Susquehanna bass and its schoolmates. Andy watched the view screen as Tom closed within sight of the debris field. Andy spoke into the communication computer, "See where I want you to hide?" He used the computer's pointer on the shared map. "Release your cannon fire as soon as I turn for the larger debris piece on your left quadrant." Andy moved his pointer. The words were scrambled into a numeric code, picked up by Tom's computer and deciphered.

Tom answered, "The Pins, just as a precaution, may shoot up the debris field and me with it, prior to firing upon you."

Andy responded, "I see your point. Suppressing fire. Would they do the same if they were interested in taking my vessel intact and, therefore, interested in sending a boarding party?"

"Yes," Tom said, "motivated by caution." Tom signaled he was coming on board. Andy answered, "Make it quick; they're moving fast."

Tom materialized on the deck, right at the chart table. He instantly began speaking. "Stay at a safe distance from the debris field. If the enemy ship lines up directly behind you, I will launch a torpedo at you. Power off all systems and free drop through space, using the gravitational pull of the moon below, and your topside thrusters on low, so their glow won't be seen."

Andy held up his hand. Tom's words stopped. Andy spoke. "I may send a visible blast upward if the gravitational pull is slow to act."

Tom measured Andy's idea. Tom spoke. "Yes, only if needed, of course. My torpedo will pick up the enemy vessel before it has a chance to begin evasive action." Tom stared straight into Andy's eyes and pounded a fist into his palm as he said, "Then, you enter the debris field, and in the few remaining seconds we have left, we will launch our last three torpedoes and run to the far side of the moon."

Andy laughed. "Wonder if we'll make it? Perhaps it would be better for the Explorer to go straight for the enemy, with artillery blazing. We would see you again in a few months."

Tom answered, "Probably half a year, so weigh if it's worth it, and I'll do the same." Tom offered his hand.

Andy shook it and placed his left hand over the extended hands. "You and Tuck come back to Explorer 7 once your rounds are fired, if it is feasible. The shuttle isn't needed."

Tom answered, "Sure thing." In a second, Tom was gone.

Emily and Dan had heard the two captains make their plans. Emily pivoted her rearview mirror at the helmsman seat to look back at Dan, in the navigator's seat, and smiled as he listened to her unspoken thoughts. "I hope it's quick."

Dan responded in thought to her. "No pain, just the emotional fear of pain." Both believed a temporary end was imminent and assured.

***

With lightning speed the armadas came, coalesced; their onboard lights, the heat and light of their thrusters made the darkness of space light. The earthling forces raced to scatter within the enemy fleet so that every weapon fired at them had the potential to inflict damage to the dense numbers of the Predator fleet that formed the backdrop of the fight. Only Explorer 7 limped away from the approaching enemy and seemed to stall in space. This intrigued the commander of the northern armada. He moved his ship of three thousand personnel, a ship of torpedo tubes, rocket ports, and concussion artillery cannons, directly to the insignificant scrap of metal that was the earthling spaceship.

Some underling brought the Pin commander's attention to the number 7 on the craft. There had been a bounty on the destruction of this craft since the beginning, when it had destroyed two top-of-the-line star cruisers. The commander thought it would be great sport to land with his staff and his boarding crew, within the vessel, and torture the earthlings in their little home away from home. Torture was best when done in the victim's safe and familiar surroundings. His warcraft scientists had done studies on this—the shame of unawareness, of befouling the sanctity of home with the innocents' screams, their blood, their body parts, while familiar faces looked on. Shame mingled with horror always twisted on the faces of the dying. He involuntarily laughed aloud at the memories. A Predator Nation ship would never be captured; a Predator Nation ship would unleash all weapons and hurtle itself into the nearest enemy ship before surrendering. These earthlings deserved the torture they would receive.

Andy listened to the Pin flagship's intercom chatter on the deck, the computer quickly translating and filling the screen with words. He resolutely banked his thrusters to maximum when boarding was being discussed. He watched behind as the enemy fleet grew larger in size and increased its speed. The enemy flagship had not lined up directly behind him, yet it seemed ready to open its mouth and swallow him. He saw Tom's full spread of four torpedoes coming at him. The plan of one torpedo followed by three had been abandoned.

Andy waited only a second, knowing that Tom saw an immediacy he could not see…and then he cut power, fired his upward thrusters at full. His crew left their stomachs on the ceiling as they dropped suddenly, and the torpedoes passed overhead. Then, the engines raced to full horizontal thrust, pushed his crew against their harnesses and seats. He turned his ship, overriding the helmsman, to save the seconds needed for communication. He saw the shuttle heading toward the enemy ship at full speed. Lasers were streaming bolts of light toward the enemy. The lone artillery piece, the barrel methodically recoiling, was spewing out rounds. Andy, aware of a presence, sensed that Tom and Tuck were off the vessel and onboard Explorer 7.

The shuttle vaporized into a cloud of debris from the enemy's fire. Tom and Tuck materialized on the deck. The enemy flagship was just contemplating evasive action when the torpedoes hit; programmed to find openings in the hull or unusually high heat sources pulsing through the vessel's skin. Andy released all of his torpedoes, even as the enemy ship seemed to be convulsing and fire was seen coming out of openings. Rau-toon hulls consisted of one solid tubular construction. Flames had blown out the tail, propelling the flaming vessel at incredible speed as the missing nose sucked in all debris before it. The flaming vessel was coming to engulf them in death. Andy had maneuverability; he juked behind a large moon fragment, and the moon created darkness behind him. He wanted his crew and Explorer 7 to live and fight again. His thrusters braked, then reversed—he was speeding backward into the dark moon, when the awesome light of the exploding enemy ships came roaring over the silhouette of the blocking moon.

The great flagship of the northern armada had exploded, casting debris into other ships of the armada, which had waived combat protocol of ship placement to be nearer to the humiliation of the enemy. The debris cast out created a chain reaction of exploding ships, fireballs, more debris, and greater losses to adjoining craft. The debris shredded through the natural debris field of moon rock and propelled this through space. The Explorer 7 crew was silent. Internal lights had been turned off, and they continued to move backward into the protective shelter of the moon fragment. No one had experienced a blast of the magnitude now upon them. It would not end. It even increased in vibration and loudness, changing pitch so much that the ship was shaking and the metal was twisting as it was designed to do. Welds did not break; few bolts had been used, and they did not pop. The crew was forced to put on emergency G-suit coverings; the suit pressure allayed the fear of disrupting their internal organs and skeletons.

Debris began to fall on the dark side of the moon. He saw huge chunks falling through space, even as small jolts were felt as the antigravity and force field reacted against the falling debris. Andy decided it was time to leave. An ongoing scan was taking place, intending to find and contact Earth-force vessels. Their ships had fought and were destroyed, and some had left, without operable weapons, to ports of safety. By a roundabout route through debris-filled space (Andy sought out natural debris fields) he returned to Thermadorian space. He had just entered the Thermadorian atmosphere when a missile, one of hundreds in a barrage, hit the Explorer's tail. He had staged his crew in their ejection pods, knowing that ground fire was likely. The force of the hit automatically triggered the pods' release. All were safely gone. He entered his pod quickly, his mind at ease, knowing God was in control, and ejected just as Explorer 7 fell apart in silent disarray.

***

John and Woden lay with Ling, Pete, and Grace within the perimeter's center, their eyes heavenward, watching the great armada of vessels, many exploding. Mat, Jack, Paternus, and Seth guarded the perimeter, but mainly their eyes looked upward. They had enough electronics around them to warn of any possible enemy attack. Abe and Don were with their own people in an encampment just over the ridge. The earthlings could hear the Thermadorians oohing and awing in their native tongue of songlike hums.

The crewmates had quickly rid themselves of the emotional turmoil over the absence of Ava. The quick response of the angels had been substantial proof of their faith in the battlefield protocols of first aid and bodily repair of the resurrected. Eternal life had been promised, and eternal life procedures were working. They knew Ava had felt no pain. Ava's revelation concerning the Thermadorians and Pins was a topic of conversation still. It had the effect of creating greater warmth and sympathy for the state of the "mantis people." This was Ava's temporary legacy.

The explosions dotting the heavenlies seemed to be increasing. The onlookers thought there was some irrationality, strangeness in the phenomena, as they knew their new war vessels were few, and most of the older ships had rather unmuscular armaments—the Explorer class had not been designed for war, but for exploration. Debris was falling so heavily that Thermador's stratosphere was lit by streaking, seemingly unending flames.

John spoke first. "Maybe we should seek cover." He rose, and others began to follow his example. A buzzer began sounding from his forearm computer. This sound quickened the standing and gathering of blankets, rucksacks, weapons. Astonished, he announced, "That's the call signal of the Explorer 7." All noted John's words and prayed the best for their ship. Immediate concerns were upon those who needed attention.

Woden thought it prudent to check on Abe and Don's people. "I'm going to check on our charges."

John addressed Woden. "Have them dig into the ledge overhang for shelter. We'll dig in under these rocks." He pointed to the massive boulders behind the cracked and dented restorer pod. Woden nodded and was gone.

In the shelter of their newly dug holes, roofed by a massive boulder, John studied the message associated with the buzzing. Ejection pods had been launched, and the Explorer 7 had crashed. Direction coordinates had been provided. The coordinates belonged to the north, close to the northern pole, a mountainous region but of like climate with the entirety of the planet. The signal was for crew members. It was possible that whoever at headquarters on Earth was responsible for the Explorer 7 might not be aware of the ejection and crash or might have been reassigned in this fast-evolving war. The chain of continuity and responsibility could be broken. The angel contingent would be aware; angels were always on point. Nothing was ever lost to them. He would assume that in the human world, only the crewmates knew of the Explorer 7's destruction, and only his people would be responsible for a rescue mission. It would be good to have Abe or Don along; better to have both. His mind engaged in planning the mission.

Burning debris was raining from the sky. It was falling everywhere. What had happened up there? Whatever it was, it spoke of, as Jack just said, "the burning debris of victory." Early tomorrow, in a few hours, really, they would choose a route to the Explorer 7, determine what food was needed, and find more rockets. They would find vehicles, or hitch a ride, and go. Someone could be seriously compromised in health or besieged by hostile Pins. John stood. He would begin massing the items needed. He would let the others catch a few hours of sleep, then they would go.

***

Woden found Don and Abe and their extended families securely dug into the soil under the ledge overhang. Don and Abe had not gone fully into the recess, as they wished to watch the falling debris. A few children were with them, only allowed to be inches behind the adult frontal position. One child repeatedly and purposefully slipped out farther, and in frustration and anger, Abe reached out his long arm and hand and snatched the child aggressively to the safe position. Woden always marveled at the quickness of the Thermadorian reflexes. He and his team had studied the movements and had recognized "tells" in premuscle movements through body positioning, muscle flexions, and twitches of hands and shoulders to aid them in combat with the Predator Nation. These "tells" were never mentioned to the Thermadorians.

Woden spoke, as he pointed to the heavens. "That is how fast Satan can take your souls to death, unless Jesus is there for you."

Abe laughed. "What Jesus do, Wotten?"

Woden smiled. "He slows Satan down so you have a chance to win, or speeds you up, or carries you to eternal life."

"Don't believe," said Abe.

Woden shook his head. "All the earthlings have died, me included, and yet here we are. We cannot die. We can be badly injured, and it would take moons to come back, but we would be back. Ava was blown apart and is gone, but she will be back."

Don answered excitedly, "We see Ava juice. Angel took. Say she return."

Woden asked Don, "Do you believe angel?"

Don answered, "Ya, he no can lie. I believe angel know Jesus."

Abe waived his hand in disgust. "I believe when Ava come back."

Woden spoke. "You may be dead by then—too late."

Don excitedly interjected, "I believe now."

Woden reached over, shook his hand, looked into the small, orange-red eyes, and was compelled to hug Don. "Do you accept Jesus as your Savior? Will you listen to the voice of the Holy Spirt? Will you honor God?"

Don became animated. "Ya, yas, yas. I believe."

Woden, tears in his eyes, said, "Welcome, brother, to eternal life."

A shuddering ran through the ground into the seated men and children; eyes jumped, and double and triple images were seen; teeth chattered. A white light fell over the ledge. They heard the women in the deep recess scream and moan. Woden had started to roll out of the sheltered overhang and was free when heavy, pulverized soil fell upon him.

He became cognizant. He was digging with a short-handled shovel into the mass of dirt. Abe and Don were digging with their massive hands and throwing flat, sedimentary rocks behind them. Woden hit the crease of the recess, where the ledge had fallen intact, creating a long pocket of shelter. Thermadorian women, young children, older adults began emerging from the darkness, and Abe and Don pulled, tugged, and righted the crawling Thermadorians. The debris falling from the sky was now landing in the desert.

Woden studied Abe's face when all the refugees were declared alive. He spoke. "Jesus saved their lives, Abe. Had they died, they would be in Hell in eternal torment."

Abe shook his head. "No Hell, nothin'."

***

Andy and Tom had gathered their crew, Dan and Emily, Tuck and Robin, Tim and Diana. All were well, except for a few sprains. The Explorer 7 frame had been found, and its stores of food, water, medical supplies, bedding, and any other thing needed for survival had been salvaged and temporarily hidden. Tomorrow they would scout and find a better overnight campsite, one with defensive strengths. They would camouflage the Explorer and attempt contact with their missing crew members—they had been automatically signaled when their host ship went down. The heavenlies were now stable, the enemy gone. The destruction seen was far greater than could have been expected from such a puny opposing force—unless some incredibly destructive malware had been activated. The nerds on Earth were capable of such a feat—*nerd* no longer a pejorative in the English language, ever since the Millennium had begun. God's legions of angels also could have tipped the inequality between the forces, either by spreading the malware or by direct military force.

Andy looked at the circle of friends—every mind was in the game; they had confidence in the future. Humor bubbled below the surface of each person, and there was vigor within their movements. Andy spoke. "Paraphrasing Diana's favorite insight, this has been the unending adventure that is eternal life." He waited for the groans and the confident cheers. The redeemed replied with vigor. Andy continued. "The captains will take this night's watch. We've done well this day for our Lord. We punched the Pins square in the jaw. It's unfortunate that His created beings only cease from their rebellion when they are physically stopped. Earth's history bears this lesson out. We've learned much about our enemy. Now we will survive. John's crew has been notified of where we are and no doubt will come to us. Emily, busy with her testing gear, found that the debilitating mineral that plagues most of the planet is nonexistent in this northern-pole region. It's missing from the soil and rock, and the winds circulating from the top of this planet's stratosphere have no particulates. No sign of Thermadorians, and no sign of Pins. But sleep with your weapons in reach. On the tourist side of life, the visuals here are absorbing."

Andy stopped and viewed the semidark sky of moons and half-moons and quarter moons, of planets near and far, some ringed, and some blurred by colorful mists. The northern pole's geology was stunning, with weird rock formations from huge boulder piles of immense and rounded rocks to sedimentary river layers, and from jagged pinnacle spires to artistic lava flows. The scarce, grubby, dirt-clinging vegetation had the scent of lilac. Around them, the hum of lava-flow falls, hanging from the heights above, hardened in their falling, and with delicate spray projections, caught the wind, moaning and laughing their siren sounds.

His crewmates had followed his eyes as they viewed their new world.

Andy spoke. "God is good."

Tom added, "Good, indeed."

"Everlasting goodness," Tim said, stating a familiar refrain.

Diana, Dan and Emily, and Tuck and Robin chorused, "Hallelujah and amen."

***

Outside their circle, the air lit to an intense whiteness in the shape of a sphere. The suddenness of the light jolted their peace. The crew instinctively dove for cover, grasped their weapons. The sphere appeared to be six feet from the surface and twenty feet in circumference. The sphere pulsed once in a brilliant increase in whiteness. Human eyes automatically closed. Eyes opened when the light lost its white brilliance and smoothed to a dull yellow-white. A man was within the light; he was lowered to the ground within the sphere and stood. The sphere seemed to dissipate. The earthlings had weapons at the ready and nonchalantly pointed in his direction.

"No need of weapons," said the man. He appeared to be in his thirties, with brown hair, normal proportions, and better-than-average musculature. He had the shadow of a beard and piercing blue eyes. A pleasant, "let's become friends" statement seemed to glow on his skin and smile. He wore trousers and a long-sleeved shirt, both black and lightweight, of rugged quality, and having numerous pockets. Ankle-high, black boots with thick-treaded soles were on his feet. The belt around the waist was wide, with no apparent buckle, and had many slip-in pouches holding thin electronic devices of rectangular shape. "My name is Or. May we engage in conversation?"

"Yes," said Andy in a pleased tone that held no surprise. Andy knew the name "Or" was of Middle Eastern origin, Hebraic, and meant "light" or "brilliance." He decided not to mention that knowledge. "Sit with us."

"You are certain this is a good time for you?" Or's voice was strong, manly; his words held a graciousness in their tone.

"Yes, a good time to begin, although it is possible we may need to continue our discourse at another time." Andy spoke sincerely, even as he addressed the possibility of a break. Or thought that statement a clever idea, allowing a gracious exit if the talk was not to Andy's liking.

"Certainly." Or walked nearer to the group, sat on the flat rock Diana had been using as a table.

"Where are you from?" Emily asked innocently, as he clearly was human or a human projection. Perhaps, Or could appear as a duplicate to whatever life forms were before him.

Or looked at Andy for only an instant, and answered, "I do not mind conversing with each individual. I am from the ruler of this quadrant, our great Creator God. He wishes you to leave. He understands this will be against your desires, but he has great patience, and eventually you will understand his case."

"Case?" said Andy, feigning an affront in his tone, reconfirming to himself that only One God ruled the universe, and "case" was of the vocabulary of doctors and lawyers. Was this a translation gap or an intentional pivot to confrontation? Could this projection or being register the emotion of indignance? Andy continued, "We are a humble people and love truth. We would like to hear his truth. Perhaps, we will be eager to obey."

"That is refreshingly optimistic but unlikely." Or looked over the humans. He could read their emotions and thoughts; they should know of his ability. "Your collective thoughts and emotions went to the same defensive stance when I said, 'My Creator God.' My God is not your god, who you thought was unique. The universe has many gods, all with overwhelming powers, each with his own created world, his kingdom. These gods were not created, but rather, they separated from the great father/mother god of one substance and essence. They were not born; they are not children. You belong to the god of the planet Earth realm, the first god to conquer his realm and to expand into the universe. He was not to do this—expand—but to continue in the cyclic harmony."

Dan surmised the tactics being employed. Evil always accused man, and evil was truly more cunning and clever than the pure in heart. Mankind was never meant to debate with evil but simply to interpose the champion of mankind, Christ. All the gathered earthlings knew this; all had their individual stories of revelation of this great truth. Dan stood, faced Or, approached to a conversational distance, and addressed Or. "I am Dan, a disciple of our God, who includes within His being—His essence—His son, Jesus, and His Spirit. Our God's earthly representative, Jesus, sits on the throne of our home planet, Earth. Have you thought to contact Him? Did you not know He reigns? Tell Him what He is and is not supposed to do. This would be more efficient than contacting us, don't you think?"

The earthlings pronounced deep and heartfelt, "Amens."

Or's posture and demeanor reacted; he was startled. Andy spoke. "Dan is quite right. Go to Earth and talk to someone your equal, who has real power. You will get speedier results. What say you to this proposal?"

Or disappeared. The earthlings smiled within their minds.

Tom was first to speak. "A hologram made before the fall of Satan and his imprisonment in the lake of fire?"

"Maybe," said Tim. "But to what purpose, other than a momentary disturbance in our peace?"

Tuck added his thoughts. "Perhaps, now he feels free to use brute force and intimidation—he, meaning the Pins or whatever force the hologram represents."

"Do the Pins have a higher civilization pushing their hate buttons?" asked Robin, who added, "The name 'Or' is Hebrew, which suggests the Middle East."

"Fascinating," said Emily. The gathered thought deeply on the possibilities.

Tim spoke. "Perhaps it is coincidence and the spelling is different and means something else in this yet-to-be-known language."

"You believe that?" asked Diana.

"No," said Tim, smiling.

"Not knowing their degree of sophistication in weaponry, let's move to a new location," said Diana, "just in case the hologram was simply targeting our position."

"I second that," said Andy. "All in favor?" As one, within seconds, they rose, gathered their belongings, and were gone.

***

Within an hour, encamped at a new location higher up the ravine, they heard explosions at the old site, and shook their heads in wonder and gratitude as they stood watch on their perimeter, or lay in their sleeping cocoons, or sat resting against a supporting rock, looking at the wonders of the night sky. Everyone shared a persistent thought: the time between Or's leaving and the explosions was significant and spoke of incompetence or poor technology. Andy felt the need to mine this vein of thought and spoke in a normal, conversational tone. "Or coming to us in a sphere, or ball of light from the sky, was a common literary and cinematic technique during the Age of Man upon the Earth."

Dan and Emily, sitting beside each other, shared glances. Emily spoke. "Dan and I, toward the beginning of the Millennium, watched scores of movies and television series from Earth's not-too-distant past, and this hologram did seem to represent that time frame."

Diana, beside Emily, joined in the conversation. "The alien beings who produced the hologram likely used human experiences represented on visual entertainment platforms that took decades or centuries to reach them."

Tuck spoke. "That may be true, but it's less important than the fact that we were all momentarily stunned, thus being unfocused on a sleight-of-hand trick."

Andy added, "And that trick was to implant in us or recognize a marker within us, so as to track our movements."

Robin added, "Maybe the bombing of our old position was simply to place the thought within us that the danger had ended."

All eyes turned to Tom, approaching from the perimeter, where he had been monitoring the surveillance devices. He spoke. "So, let's try to find out how they are marking us."

With that comment, all rose and began to apply the surveillance equipment and possible strategies to the question at hand.

CHAPTER 11

John, pilot of his airborne platform, glanced back to his second-in-flight platform, just made available early that morning. Weather conditions were good: clear, with clean-appearing air. No wind, bright sunlight. His altitude was thirty feet and allowed him an easy traverse, with only slight adjustments, over the flat farmlands. The second air platform had been recommended to him by Abe, who had seen it sitting alone near an outcrop of rocks. Thermadorian civilians had reported to Abe that the two earthlings on board had purposely parked the machine, and another platform had picked them up. John pursued the information and had been given permission to take the fully flight-ready platform.

After a stop at a resupply depot for food, water, and shoulder-held rockets, they were on their way to Andy and his crew. Even with the temporary loss of Ava, everyone was in good spirits, meaning one with the Spirit, whose history was to meet all obstacles and overcome. The vast farmland fields were stubble from the last harvest. Replanting had not begun, and the small villages of mud-and-thatched homes had been destroyed. Little movement on the surface of Thermador was seen, except at resupply depots, maintenance shops for air platforms and armaments, and sites for surface-to-space missiles. Thermadorians worked at these stations, were taught skilled and semiskilled jobs. Money was earned. The tents of their extended families spread over the surrounding acreage. In these makeshift villages, daily life found its rhythm once again. Earthling teachers were holding classes in all aspects of Christianity, social deportment, Christian capitalism, life expectations, the nature of the heavenly Father, and the meaning of Christ's work upon the cross. Attendance earned cash. No forced participation, no dogged determination to pit cultures against each other. Hospitals bound up wounds and explored Thermadorian hygiene and the Thermadorian body, both mentally and physically.

Freedom was in the heart of every Thermadorian. Everyone debated and talked of the future and the political system with which they hoped to guide their nation, the economic engine that could bring prosperity to this new land of opportunity, the laws and morality they wished to live and use as a guide for all citizens. The centuries of mass rape and degradation were over. Any enemy captured usually had been tortured till a time came when even the need for revenge began to die. Their newly found self-respect, given to them through Christ, lifted them up from Predator Nation behavior. They wished to be better than the evil nation that had subjugated them. They sensed a moral soul to their people and their new nation rising.

But the Pins were not gone from Thermador. The battle for Thermador had become subterranean and was being savagely fought in grottoes, on lakes, seas, along rivers, in abandoned mine shafts, and among ancient city ruins and dried-up lava courses and funnels. Explosions rumbled over the surface, cracks and canyons formed, and flames and steam and dust blew out from fissures, man-made entrances, and caves, as massive expanses of soil subsided. The surface of the planet was littered with broken machinery, sometimes in large, recognizable form, but mostly as indefinable litter, stationary or blowing in the winds. The battle for space above the planet had added tons of debris, ranging from hollowed-out space vessels to unexploded ordnance and body parts. Gathering the litter for recycling, or discovering finds of rations, ammunition, and weapons was profitable. Thermadorian bodies were still plentiful, as the Pins had delighted in mass executions and tortures. Thermadorian vultures, their reptilian ancestors' genetics still visible on their scaly wings and toothful grins, swarmed as black clouds in the sky.

Occasionally, a single Pin-manned craft would whiz overhead, the pilot so fearful of attracting missiles that scant attention was paid to the planet's surface. Abe and Don had both received communication devices, strapped to their wrists, which had combat applications but were also authorized for civilian calls. Like kids with new toys, Abe and Don were chattering happily with others as they rode the air platform, even as their eyes scanned the terrain. John thought upon the two. He was more secure in their presence, their intentions, and their level of loyalty and had held an informal meeting with his crew every night when Abe and Don were on guard duty. Most were relaxed with the aliens and attributed human emotions and logic to their every action, much like earthlings at home did to their pets.

The word and translation dictionary may have encouraged this sameness, sacrificing precision for immediacy. John had been trained to keep a mental distance from this logic of like needs and desires and even from the interpretation of events or words that could lead to an Earthlike evaluation that was easy to digest and harmless. Yes, two plus two equaled four. But it was possible that the Thermadorian *two* was really a prolonged and complicated equation in and of itself, which, if broken down and readded, might be something greater than four. Just as the first mention of God in Genesis is a plural noun in form but singular in meaning when it refers to the true God. Just as one cluster of grapes is not one grape but many. Misinterpretations were possible with this language of clicks and tonal ranges and the odd life experiences and history of this people.

John gazed over the land and wondered what this new nation would become in a hundred years. He wished Abe and Don the best in their futures. Overall, Thermadorians and earthlings had a common goal—to destroy the Predator Nation's hold on Thermador. This was the bottom line. When this tie was no longer necessary, would Christ reign? Would the Thermadorians see the value, individually, of knowing Christ and living in Christ? Don seemed rooted in Christ. Abe's defiance was deep and bitter, but the bitterness wasn't toward Christ directly; it flowed from his own life experience. John studied his two men, humphing as he called them *men*. They were mantis, but it certainly was obvious they had every emotion that humans possessed. Still, their emotion differed in application and intensity and how it was culturally expressed. God had allowed the mantis to possess cognizant life and a soul life, even if given through Satan's initial actions. Satan's role was all conjecture, supposition, just a lurking possibility. Yet, the fact was readily grasped: the mantis could become the children of God.

John came out of his reverie, studied Abe, as Abe seemed to be in an emotional crisis at this very time. Abe dropped the arm that had held his communication device to his ear and began an excited conversation with Don, who immediately turned away from his own conversation on the phone. Abe was gesticulating with his arms, in utter rage. Don attempted to grasp Abe's wildly moving hands. Abe, in anger at the attempt to control his hands, slapped Don upon the side of the face, and continued to push him down and over the side of the platform. John immediately slowed speed and lowered the vehicle, as Don clung to the vehicle, pleading for help.

Mat, beside Abe, had been alerted from the outset and was attempting to place his body between the two, with his back toward the aggressor, Abe. Abe pushed Mat in the back, in the same direction as the falling Don. Jack, beside Don, had first attempted to distract Abe by a hard grab to

Abe's shoulder. The hold did little to move the eight-foot alien, who easily outweighed earthlings by hundreds of pounds. Jack received a push that nearly knocked him over the side of the platform. Protocol was clear; an earthling could not be touched with violence, and Jack and Mat had been pushed hard. Jack had locked his feet under the seat apparatus behind him, and his powerful ab muscles allowed him to spring up with his rifle in his hands. Jack's rifle butt went onto Abe's helmeted head. Abe began to crumple, even as he withdrew his killing finger from the neck of convulsing Don. Paternus, beside John and behind Abe, sent a kick into Abe's head and neck that sent him tumbling over the side of the platform, now only five feet from the ground.

In seconds, both platforms had landed; Seth and Woden, from the second platform, established a perimeter. Pete and Grace remained in the craft as Ling went to the first platform. Ling pronounced Don dead from asphyxiation caused by the coagulating effect of a poison. Ling turned his attention to Abe, now surrounded by John, Mat, Jack, and Paternus. Abe had already been tied and a stun collar placed on his neck. Angry hisses issued from his mouth; his eyes were bright-red, his slowly moving arms seeming ready to block any and all blows. Mat and Jack had their rifles aimed, the barrels outside the massive reach of Abe's arms. Paternus could only shrug his shoulders and shake his head as he queried John. "What made him snap?"

John shrugged. John had found his large computer screen in his rucksack aboard the platform. He readied the translation app and said, "I'm going to find out."

He typed, "Explain," on the screen and with two hands, in deference to Abe's reach, held the screen toward Abe's eyes. The feeling of loss was growing among the earthlings. Don had been a good soldier and companion, who was already missed. Abe's right hand went out with speed and vehemence, the fist in a tight ball, except for the long claw finger, still wet with Don's blood. "Chiuck! Chuick! *Eardlins* chiuck!" he said, as a shock pulse entered his neck.

John spoke almost inaudibly, "Enemy, enemy earthlings. Enemy."

Paternus weakly smiled. "Thanks."

Mat smiled sadly, and Jack chortled. Everyone knew those simple words. And yet, to be spoken by a soul they thought their friend was chilling. An outside source, beings, had won the confidence of their trusted ally. Or was it simply paranoid chitin responding?

Abe pointed to the screen, and with both arms outstretched, made a gathering motion. John thought it worth the risk and with only one arm extended, tossed the screen under the outstretched hands onto Abe's chest. Abe sneered at John's caution. He wrote quickly, revealed the screen, and pronounced, slowly in his tortured English, "Torture me now?" Abe tossed the screen back.

John wrote, "We love you like a brother. No."

Abe's sudden jerk of his head and eye contact revealed his puzzlement. Then, the hardness of heart returned. "Liar," he wrote, and tossed the screen back.

"Where does this come from?" asked John, with a screen toss back, as the sentence was enunciated.

"From my brain." Abe showed the screen to the men, then tossed it far and high in the air. Using the distraction to ball up his left fist and jab under his neck collar with the claw on that hand. He hissed as the airway slowly closed. John administered a hard and prolonged pulse into the collar, and Abe passed out. Abe had tried to bleed himself into death, as all gathered knew that a mantis could not kill himself with his own venom. Ling quickly packed the neck wound with coagulant and stapled the sides together.

John spoke slowly and sadly. "Load up the body, gents. We will take Don to a morgue. Perhaps a medical inquiry can be performed on Abe. Maybe Abe's use of the term *brain* instead of *mind* meant something more than confusion with English vocabulary."

"Aye, aye, sir," said Paternus as the reorganizing of the platform's content, the blood cleanup, and the wrapping and bagging of the body had already begun.

"Almost forgot," said John. "Ling, take both communication devices. Find out what these two were arguing about, please. And Paternus, you're in charge of Abe. Here's the shock wand."

"Love to," said Ling as he gathered up the phones. "My curiosity is up."

"Aye, aye," said Paternus as he took the wand from John's extended hand.

***

An hour of flight passed; the altitude was under a hundred feet. Vast farm-lands, irrigated, with new crops taking hold, the lime-green crops brilliant in the sun, the canals sparkling, not a soul to be seen, filled their vision. Only the ever-present debris from the defeat of the armadas reminded them of war. Then, desert lands, barren soil, rock and sedimentary layers twisting within dry river beds or thrust upended, forming ridges. A wide river was seen snaking across the land, the banks green with tall bamboo-like forests and brakes. As the two air platforms crossed the river, passengers saw a great sprawl of thousands of Thermadorians and their hastily constructed shelters; saw the earthling constructions of designated morgue center, hospital, and barracks surrounded by dirt embankments. The Thermadorian shelters of windproof and waterproof fabric rectangles and squares, supplied by the earthlings, rippled in the breeze. Portable troop restorers, like giant boulder clusters, or a nest of oversized eggs, their hard shells gleaming in the sun, lay scattered on the brown sand, beyond the barracks. The restorers had been given to the most wounded and destitute of the Thermadorians in the hope that the sanitary and safe homes would aid in healing and restoration.

As the platforms closed the distance to the makeshift city, the earthlings on board could feel the tension emanating from the Thermadorian camps, roughly four great camps at the cardinal points, with trailings of shelters, and cognizant beings moving between them. Real, palpable, crackling air, supercharged by the unknown yearnings of the masses, was measurable on electronic monitoring devices. They saw massive spreads of bodies in disarray, unmoving or limp movements of arms and legs, the dead and the dying. Clearly a riot, a confrontation, a battle had taken place. Other masses were standing, the Thermadorians jumping, bobbing rigidly in the tight, jerky movements that characterized their rigid muscles and stiff, leathery skin. The long arms were raised, holding rifles, axes, and shoulder-fired missiles. The licorice odor seemed like a haze over the sprawling town. The ground pattern coalesced in the minds of the air-platformed earthlings: the remaining earthlings on the ground had collected, were armed, and were barricaded in a circular pattern. Within the center, an air platform was being loaded.

The veterans among the encircled earthlings on the ground were first to understand that a massacre was about to be unleased. The air-platform warriors read the signs, as well. John calmly spoke into his throat comm. "We are descending to aid our people. Ready yourself for combat and to load up noncombatants." That was the best he could do; to remain airborne in the hopes of providing air-to-ground fire was simply a poor gamble. Hundreds of rockets would be fired from a hundred directions, all heat seeking. The platforms would be blasted out of the sky in seconds. He thought they were experiencing the last sensations of life in their bodies. Perhaps in months, their mangled bodies would be rebuilt, and they would come back whole. He asked of God that no Thermadorian would desecrate his body, gloat over his temporary death, in the intervening time till angels carried his body away.

In a split second, the first of the enemy missiles came streaking toward them, even as the dive for the friendly perimeter had begun. He remembered his platform's return fire; he remembered missiles bursting in the air. He remembered quickly finding empty ground and setting down the platform. Then a supernatural light roiled above them and a dark cloud came across the flat, empty fields from the direction of the Thermadorians. As if his eyes had disconnected from his body, he rose into the air and saw the masses of Thermadorians pushed to the ground, tumbling backward till they were ground into the soil. A huge, billowing blackness rose above them, and the white light that had crushed the Thermadorians rose toward the blackness and the ensuing clash. The white light became angelic hosts, and the black mass became demon angels, and the blackness was in death throes as it was carried north across the flatness.

Complete and utter silence pervaded the circle of humans, who thought their last cognitive moments, for months, had been upon them. Not one standing Thermadorian broke the level horizon. Whole and healthy, touching their bodies and the bodies of their friends and loved ones, the humans smiled. They began to cry, "Holy! Holy! Holy!" Hands went into the air in praise; voices strained with disbelief, with thankfulness, with praise.

Grace, standing in front of John and Woden, said, "Our angels came. They saved us! We were promised ten thousand angels, and they came!"

Woden looked at John and said, "That was a first."

John answered, "Same for me. But certainly not our last."

John's eyes scanned and found two soldiers, their hands upon each other's shoulders. They were jumping up and down, yelling praises.

John, with a questioning in his voice, said, "Those two look familiar."

Woden laughed and answered, "Mat and Jack." He pointed. "Look over there."

John's eyes followed Woden's extended hand, and answered, "Seth, Pete, Ling."

Woden stood in awe, unsure of what to do next. He just wanted to get down on his knees in thankfulness. No, he wanted to remain standing, jumping as high as the heavens with arms raised, praising his God.

John's eyes were scanning, with intensity, then he saw Paternus sitting on the ground with a compliant and remorseful Abe sitting near him. John smiled at Woden's unspoken thoughts of praise. "Me too," he answered, "Gather up our people. Let us sit and rest in His love and give Him thanks." As Woden left him, John wondered how it had gone so wrong—a friend dead, killed by his friend; and a people who had loved their partners in freedom, now the enemy.

***

Andy turned his eyes from the narrowing ravine and the sheer, cliff-faced sides before him to look behind. He was forced to turn his body around completely. Below him, coming up the rugged stone steps leading to ever-increasing height, was his column, consisting of Diana, Dan and Emily, Tom, followed by Tim, Tuck, Robin. He had placed his boys at the end, searching the flanks and rear for an enemy that might be there or might not be. Dan had never found a marker on the crew that would indicate a hostile power was tracking their movement. Their chemical compositions and their heat signatures were sufficient for tracking through unlimited space, with the right detection unit. Andy had placed Tom in the middle to act as leader of his trailing squad if trouble came and a flanking maneuver was needed.

Tim enjoyed the hike, even with possible enemies lurking. The scenery was spectacular. Canyons, chasms, waterfalls trailing into vapor; clear-blue skies and sparse, deep-green trees, scoured and wind whipped; twisted, whistling lava rock and sedimentary rock layers of various colors. It all clamored for attention. The ancient stone steps of the trail had been marked with stone columns to tell the visitors, past and present, how far they had come. A rushing brook intertwined with the stones, and small stone bridges were scattered among bamboos and pines. Flowering plants of all kinds broke the vista of hard, barren stone. He sensed they were on a trek to something; some place or object that the ancient Thermadorians may have called holy, or at least, was worthy of veneration. Would they find tombs or a natural feature of rarity at the end? Perhaps this was a nature walk, as many of the stone carvings had representations of animals that were likely extinct—reptilian fish, birds, predators, bearlike creatures, cattlelike grazers with heavy mammary organs.

Diana turned completely around when she saw Andy turn. She looked out into the horizon. She could see the vast plain beyond the hill country, where they had crashed. She could see the rugged uplift where the steps of stone had begun. This route had been some type of pilgrimage, no doubt. What she found odd was the size of the steps—perfect for human feet. Now that she thought of it, the height of the steps was perfect for human legs and cardiovascular function. She wondered if the steps predated that time in ancient history when the Thermadorians and Pins had changed their native bodies for the hardier insect form. Ava, still not back from medical leave, had introduced that thought to them a day or weeks ago. Time had been a jumble since war started.

Diana's thoughts upon the steps had been heard by everyone in the column, and they all began to wonder where this trail led and if Thermadorians would be happy they were upon it.

All had gathered around Andy. Tom inflated the helium balloon; the cable, as thin as fishing line, was attached, and operated as an antenna. It unspooled and soon was out of sight. The electric motor was turned on, and a small propeller was activated to oppose the slight breeze that was pulling the ballon into the mountain peak. A signal was sent out, a human operator answered, directed the call to rescue headquarters, and soon the downed crewmen of Explorer 7 were told a repair crew was on its way, with an ETA of two days. It would either make the Explorer 7 flyable to a maintenance shop or prepare it for towing by air platform to the repair center. John and his two air platforms were notified, with John sending his ETA as late the next day.

Andy turned his phone off, smiled at the peaceful faces staring at him. "Mission accomplished. Our missing crewmates should arrive late tomorrow; and a repair crew, within two days. We could start back down now or continue onward until late morning tomorrow. Whatever we decide, I think we should remain together, no splitting of our numbers."

Emily spoke. "By all means, let's find the end of this trail. We've only hiked for two hours, and the end must be near, as it seems we are coming to a solid rock face."

Andy spoke. "Show of hands for Emily's suggestion." All hands went up.

CHAPTER 12

John and Woden were smiling, as was all their crew, at their temporary rest stop under weathered pines. The call from Andy had reunited them. As much as every person was Christ centered, they realized through absence how much they needed their family—their Spirit-led family, their shipmates, their exploring and combat buddies, their friends at so many different levels. They were the world to each other, through constancy of presence, and shared experiences, thoughts, hopes. They delighted in each individual; they loved doing for their friends—elevating their spirits, smoothing their realities, encouraging their efforts; they leaned on them and found solace in them. They thanked the Lord for these friends, who did so much to brighten their days. Without friends, daily life experiences would have seemed so meaningless. For within the daily life experiences, their Lord was present and desiring to be shared, to elevate the mundane to the supernatural. All had learned through the passage of time that life was supernatural.

John studied Abe, sitting alone dejectedly. Paternus was close by, and "one eye never left him," as Paternus was wont to say. Don was in a body bag aboard air platform 2. Their haste to leave the massacre site had precluded contacting Andy and crew; the medical facility, the morgue, the jailhouse had been forgotten. That was the only reason Abe had been brought along. What would God say to Abe, a man who had killed his best friend, who had rejected the Light of the World, and turned upon the power, the planet, the people who were helping him and his country with everything they had?

The heart of God said, "Speak to that man, plumb his depths, and lift him into the light."

A moment before, John had felt remorse for not leaving Abe at the destroyed villages with the military police unit. Now he moved to Paternus's side, and to his astonishment he heard Paternus, in a quiet, almost whispered voice, reading the Psalms from a pocket-sized book. He was nodding as he aimed the words into the computer's audio/visual translator screen and into the heart of Abe. John recognized phrases from Psalm 51—"cleanse me from my sin," and "Against you, you only, have I sinned and done what is evil in your sight."

John sat and began to pray for Abe. The dejection on Abe's face, such utter desolation, brought tears to John's eyes. He heard lines from Psalm 52, "Behold the man who would not make God his refuge." John saw the defiance break and the tears welling from Abe's eyes. Psalm 53, "The fool has said in his heart, 'There is no God.'" And "Is there anyone who understands." Paternus raised his right hand, and the hand fell and was lifted, fell and was lifted repeatedly as praise to God, for God to descend upon this lonely mantis creature. A being with a soul—a being cognizant of his sin. Abe fell on his side and lay in a ball, weeping.

Paternus looked at John and spoke. "This is why we are here. To open the doors of God's Kingdom. All the soldiering, all the skill with weapons and tactics is for this: to save and restore. Centuries in the past, someone prayed for me, showed me the way, and here I am with eternal life, doing the same. Stay with Abe, I am going to eat. I think he will talk to you." Paternus rose, handed over the control stick of the collar, and moved to the food being offered by Pete and Grace from their air platform.

Ling came to John, bent down beside him. "The phones were interesting. Don was talking to a relative about Christ and his new life and how his depression had been lifted. Abe was talking to an unidentified person. This person said humans had been found on Thermador spreading lies about the Thermadorian people, that they were soulless, mere insects, whom ancient humans had inhabited because their bodies could not take the extremes in weather. The humans claimed they had been modifying the mantis species for a thousand years without their knowledge, and what little mental acuity the mantis has had been accomplished through them. Abe's caller said there were thousands of humans living within mantis bodies. They were helping the Earth humans destroy the mantis people. There is video of humans operating on mantis bodies."

"I see," said John. "A painful realization, if true. Why no measured confrontation? Why rage? Why assume you were being told the truth?" John shook his head in disappointment.

Ling responded, "At first appearance, it does not speak well for the Thermadorians, unless there is more to the story."

"What could it possibly be? I cannot envision more to the story," said John.

"Perhaps it is time to just trust God and His wisdom and wait," said Ling.

"Yes, keep moving forward and wait for revelation." John stood, tightened his body, raised his stiffened arm and rotated his shoulder quickly as he loudly bellowed in command voice, "Time to go. Load up. Let's move out."

***

Andy's group came to the solid rock face hidden in the darkest of shadows. The temperature in the shade was at least ten degrees cooler than the world of shining sun. The water source was now just wet dirt and stone by the base of the rock wall. A tunnel entrance, tall enough to accommodate the height of the mantis people, penetrated the rock, and at the far end, a point of daylight could be seen. They entered the tunnel in a staggered sequence, fearing a trap or roof cave-in, and used their forearm computers for light. An air was blowing into their faces, traced with water, warmth, plants, the scents of flowering life.

At the end of the tunnel, they entered sunlight, open sky surrounded by lava extrusions eroded into delicate, wispy monuments. The lacy-appearing monuments caught the breeze and whistled and hummed, produced notes that mimicked the mantis voice in song. An immense lake lay at their feet, filling an inactive caldera. A small island, with trees, had formed in the center. Tom was slowly moving his detectors through the air. He spoke. "Benign, no harmful odors or gasses, long ago extinct." He moved down to the shoreline, stuck a probe into the water. "High mineral content. Nice to look at, but don't drink it or swim in it." Just as he finished flicking water from the probe and began to turn, they saw the long, snaky back of a reptilian fish break the surface and bend on the journey to deeper waters.

Dan commented, "Let's hope that creature has no legs."

Tim laughed. "Or doesn't know how to slither upon the earth." Tuck and Robin had put a bead on the creature before it disappeared. They had rechecked and readied their weapons when they had first entered the tunnel. Upon entry into the open space, the barrels and sights had been continuously searching.

Tim noted, "All the flora seems to be chosen from a horticulturist's list. Just not kept in order for many years—no weeding, no thinning, perhaps for hundreds of years. The work of upkeep by Thermadorians forbidden by the Pins? A slight to this holy place?"

Diana and Emily had their ocular devices scanning soon after arriving, concentrating on the mountain heights surrounding them, the far shore of the lake, and the distinct rim that gave the appearance of loose lava cinders. "I see a large, cave-like opening under an expansive rock ledge, and what appears to be masonry work," said Diana. Emily took note of the direction of Diana's gaze and homed in on the area. "I see them too. That should bear further exploration."

Andy was already studying the topography and putting together a route, knowing a trail already existed to the masonry location. Probably a trail around the circumference of the lake and likely a trail around the rim of the crater, and a steep trail on the far side of the crater, leading straight up to the massive cave and masonry work. Andy spoke. "Tuck and Robin. Transport to the cave and secure the surrounding area. Overwatch us. We will be there soon. Just want to walk the intervening space."

Tuck and Robin each gave a salute of respect and lifted off. They soon realized the difference between the natural forces on Thermador and those on Earth. The wind patterns of the rugged terrain had their peculiarities as well. But with study and patience, they began to read the forces of the planet and landed upon the surprisingly pristine tile work of a piazza before the mammoth rock overhang and cave opening. Robin reported in. "At cave site. Transporting forces on this planet are tricky—don't recommend to amateurs. Over."

Andy answered, "Roger that."

Tuck was scanning with his DNA/life-signs detector and seemed to have a trail. He turned suddenly and began heading the opposite way. "Brother, I've got human signs, recent. Laid on top of old mantis activity."

Robin reported back to Andy immediately. "Recent human presence noted and being tracked." He and his brother could be gone, severely disrupted by a sniper in seconds, leaving their friends open for ambush.

Andy answered, "Roger that. Over."

Tuck was moving quickly to the far corner of the rock overhang, where a cave seemed to exist. He stopped before it. Human excrement, hours old. Seems the person had stepped on a corner of it, and that was being carried by his boot. The person had backtracked his trail. The size of the boot print spoke of a male. Tuck scanned the vast cave—more like an open auditorium—with long stone benches, tables, a stage of stone in the rear of the cave, and wooden posts for the hanging of hammocks, the preferred mantis sleep method. Thousands could be accommodated under the massive stone overhang. Two sets of human prints came from this sleeping area and joined a third set. Robin moved quickly into the sleep area and then back out just as quickly. "They slept back there, cleaned everything up. Doesn't look like they're planning to return."

They sensed danger. No earthlings had been reported in the area. But this did not preclude special-ops people on long-range reconnaissance or tracking leads to possible safe areas for Pin warriors or Thermadorian civilians. It was possible, due to the caldera, that deep and extensive subterranean shafts, tunnels, and living quarters existed here; those networks had been found in numerous locations on the planet. But now, the Thermadorians seemed to have become the enemy of the earthling forces, opening up a greater list of possibilities. Robin and Tuck thought back to the man named Or. *Was* he a hologram—or real in the present, with countless followers?

The brothers moved fast, quickly coming to the end of the overhang and following a wide, ancient trail that entered an area of loosely spaced, single boulders before the mountain slope. Then down a crevasse along the seam of the mountain structure proper and the new land of the caldera upthrust. Recently set-up surveillance cameras shaped as rocks and even plants were spotted and confirmed by a spyware app on their computers. Robin called in, "Spy cameras scattered about."

Andy was tracking their real-time location on his map. He realized they should coalesce behind his two scouts in the event of conflict. Robin and Tuck slowed as the trail narrowed and began to descend. They saw a tunnel entrance, fortified with stonework, and with two large doors, side by side, closed, wooden, and ancient. They stopped. It seemed foolish to enter an enclosed area beneath the surface, knowing they likely were being watched and this might be the point of no return. Their equipment was giving no life readings, not even air quality. Andy messaged, "Wait." They took a break, drank water, opened a packet of dried fruit and flat bread, and spread peanut butter and a jam.

As they finished their meal and waited, Tuck located the nearest cameras and placed them down in the rocks to neutralize the advantage of sight. Andy arrived with the remainder of the crew. He peered down the descent to the doors, studied the faces of his sons, and asked, "Got any ideas?"

Tuck answered quickly, "Let's go in and say hello."

"And what's up?" added Robin.

Emily and Diana, who were beside Andy, sniggered softly, and Emily spoke. "Let's keep two people here so we are assured of getting out."

Tom came to the group and spoke. "Yes, on the return, a climb up a narrow trail leads to a nice corridor of fire."

Emily added, "Let's blow those doors off their hinges, so we can't be locked in."

Tim, behind the women, added, "We have enough time for a half hour in the tunnel, then we need to head back, at least out of the caldera, before nightfall. Who knows how many are in the tunnel or responding to our presence here?"

Andy looked at Dan, behind Tim.

"I agree," said Dan.

Andy knew Tom's mind; he wanted to enter. Andy spoke. "Tuck and Diana, remain on guard. Order of descent: Tom, Robin, Tim, Dan, Emily, me." So simple, after all the years, to choose. Tuck and Diana were great shots, had tenacity; Tuck was protective, especially of women, and Diana read the actions of men and anticipated to another level of oneness. Tom could process a new scene more quickly than anyone and make the right call. Robin could do the same with targets—he was quick at target acquisition, and the targets were always hostile. Tim was a good shot, but like Dan and Emily, he was also a deep thinker, who could see beyond immediacy. Andy knew that the deep thinkers needed to be by him for a command to be issued and stick.

Tom stood at the heavy, closed, oak doors, his eyes and hands running over the latch, the hinges. He spoke. "We need a major charge."

Emily came from the rear, her demolition bag slung before her, resting at waist level. She pulled the latch trigger quietly, pushed the door in, only a quarter of an inch, and then opened the door. Light streamed out. She ran a thin plastic rod in and felt no obstructions. The rod was tipped with a camera. She placed her dark goggles upon her eyes and searched. "We're good," she declared in a whisper. She retracted the rod and closed the door. All had expected her to open the door but waited in curiosity as to her next action. She reached into her bag and pulled out two coin-sized charges, which she placed on each of the massive bolts that aligned the hinges to the doors. She thought it odd that earthling and mantis would both have hinges and bolts. Independent inventions? she wondered. She spoke. "Turn your heads." They obeyed. She held up a lightweight blast board before the top bolt and touched the fire button. A muffled snap was heard; she repeated the process at the bottom.

She left the snapped bolts in place, explaining, "No reason to advertise our presence. We can leave when we want to." She quietly, gently opened the door. If an enemy regained the door from Tuck and Diana, the bolt halves could easily be removed, and the door would fall. Tom slithered like a snake through the doorway, his head moving side to side, neck and eyes following. The squad of earthlings all mimicked the snake in their movements.

Luminescent rock lit the wide, high, and level corridor of tiled floor, ornately etched with scenes from Thermadorian life. The walls, floor, ceiling were searched with piercing eyes for hidden gates or barriers that could descend or slide to capture travelers unawares. The squad maintained combat distance and moved soundlessly. In this quiet, they heard the strong hum of a generator or a pulse-power unit vibrating from behind a pair of doors at the corridor's end. In single file, they stood at the doors. Robin had reached up instantly and covered a peering camera with a squirt of slime. Tom, by hand motion, communicated to Emily and Andy to remain at the doors, as he touched Tim and Robin, designating them as the entry team. Dan remained with Tom.

Tom had his hand on the left door, and Dan had his hand on the door on the right. No time for the wand probe—speed was everything now. They choreographed a quiet probing opening, not knowing if the doors were locked, as Tim and Robin entered, barrels first. Bright lights, too bright to gaze upon for very long, hung down from the ceiling on jointed arms. Earthlike appearing men in white lab coats were gathered around unseen objects. The men wore eyepieces with telescoping lenses, surgical masks, and white caps. Large-wheeled, gray, plastic carts surrounded them, filled with dead or dying mantids. Tom's people assumed Thermadorians were on the operating table. The licorice smell was so heavy that it nauseated them. Gasses seemed to be hazing the air above the carts.

"Hands up." Tom's command voice echoed over the twenty or more humans surrounding the tables. He repeated the phrase and realized he had spoken in English. Were these humans earthlings? Perhaps they were Thermadorians or Pins cloaked in holographic projections of earthlings. He remembered the first night's visitor, Or. Had Or been real or simply a projection of a human? Were these Or's men?

The hands went up. The mystery deepened.

"Who are you people? What is your place of origin? What are you doing here?" Tom's voice demanded an answer and promised an unpromising future for failure to comply.

One man turned and faced Tom, taking off his ocular devices, his mask. "I am Dr. Fromen, from Earth. Switzerland is my native land. We are working under the auspices of the War Commission and a subordinate branch of Central Intelligence Special Operations, bi/psy."

"What is bi/psy?" asked Andy, who knew the answer, and who had easily heard Fromen's words from the doorway position.

"Biology/psychology," stated Fromen.

Andy said, "Your secrecy could have led to temporary immobilization."

"A small price for the secrecy we need," said Fromen, who added, "May we resume?"

"When you adequately prove by documentation what you have stated," said Andy.

Fromen appeared agitated and indignant. He straightened, almost standing on his toes; chin and chest were thrust at Andy. "No documents were issued. Our computers state who we are." The voice, arrogant in tone, invited combativeness.

Andy moved to Tom as Dan immediately moved back to Emily at the door. Andy sensed Tom's unease, and the shared statement ran between them that computers were dream worlds. Anything could be created and passed as legitimate.

Tom's tone to Fromen was demanding. "What is the work before you this day? Explain these bodies."

"Certainly. The Thermadorians seemed to be in crisis, a mass dying, an extermination. Paranoia, hallucinations leading to destructive and reckless acts. Just when they seemed to be winning their war of independence. We are performing autopsies, hoping to find the reason and then, hopefully, the cure."

Tom turned to Andy, then approached closely, his back to the surgical teams. Tom spoke in a whisper. "Let's get in touch with John and his crew. He witnessed the Thermadorians becoming unhinged. We might want to consider that our communication channels have been compromised over the whole range of the command structure. John, we can trust."

Andy studied Tom's face. Andy blocked the vision of Fromen by using Tom as a shield. Andy whispered inaudibly, their soul minds would hear. "Wise decision. Let's not try a broadcast from within this building within a rock fortress. Who knows what these people are capable of? I'll dispatch Robin to Diana and Tuck, have Diana call John—she knows his voice and his vocabulary better than anyone else. She will come back to us to report. Also, I will establish a fixed time for John's arrival."

Tom smiled. "I concur. Let's get it done."

Andy gave an affirmative nod to Tom's can-do, confident spirit. Andy whispered, "On my way." He touched Robin's arm, who then followed his father. As Andy moved back to Emily at the door, Robin continued out the door. Dan was again one of the forward three, with Tom and Tim. Dan took a comfortable sitting, shooting position. If shooting occurred, the white-robed men on the far sides of the tables would duck right into his spray of floor hugging laser blasts.

Tim, who had remained with Tom from first entry and was the nearest to Fromen and the white-robed humans, looked at Tom. They made eye contact. Tom looked into Tim's eyes; Tom sensed Tim's thoughts: to be silent and communicate telepathically. Tom searched the eyes of Fromen and the others. All of their internal senses were probing him and Tim. Tim could hear the telepathic conversation of Fromen's men—actual words and sentences, in a foreign language of Middle Eastern origin, he guessed. Logic said these earthmen did not have Christian values; who had a problem verifying their credentials in the Christian world? Such a person did not exist—till now. The language of Earth was English, even through to the subconscious. Therefore, logic said, "These are humans but not Christian." Earth had no such type of person. Tim, knowing Andy heard the same language and had reached the same conclusion, silently spoke. "Let's be cautious."

Tom answered, "I agree." He watched Fromen's eyebrows rise as one of Fromen's cohorts turned his head to Fromen, just for an instant. Tom's command voice sounded through the room. "I am going to separate you and your workers until we have clarity as to who you are and what your business here is."

Fromen answered in a resolute tone of finality. "We will not comply."

"Then we will force you to comply," said Tom, as Tim turned his rifle barrel on Fromen.

"So be it." Fromen spoke defiantly.

Dan stood, calmly watching every move of the foreigners.

Andy understood Fromen had gained advantage by Tom's hasty threat to use force. Three men to subdue more than twenty. Diana and Tuck were at the first door, with Robin on the way on messenger duty. Andy and Emily must keep the second door closed, with no escapees allowed. That left Tom, Tim, and Dan to subdue the captives.

Emily, at the door, felt the emotional tension between her people and the frocked men. She had heard the conversation between Tim and Tom. From her vantage, she could see more clearly the subtle movements of the men on the far side of the tables. Their minds were being pulled to double doors at the rear of the operating room, no doubt, an extension of the hallway she guarded. They were expecting help and readying their actions for when that help came. She willed this awareness to her comrades. In response, Dan had moved to the side in a position to better surveil the doors. He sat. She understood why: to keep his head under the table, the field of fire. She heard running footfalls coming down her hallway, one individual. Robin returning?

Total darkness suddenly possessed the room and hallway. She aimed her laser where she had just seen the doors to what she presumed was the far hallway. The doors through which the aliens expected help to arrive. She pulled the trigger. Nothing, no generator, no whine. Bodies were upon her;

the licorice smell thick on their frocks. She began clubbing, with the stock of her laser, whatever was within her reach. The laser was immobile, grasped tightly by the enemy. In a moment, her combat knife was unsheathed. She began stabbing, pulling lab coats by collars, belts, any loose fabric, and stabbing. She heard curses in a foreign tongue; jumbled, rushing words; orders, unknown words—just sounds—whose brutality was from the vehemence of the soul. Then someone grabbed at her foot with both hands, and her other foot was caught and pulled out from under her. Anger flooded over her. She was screaming the name *Jesus*, not as a plea, but as a summons for help in her rage. Her comrades were calling His name. Kicking, stabbing, punching. A force was over her, and bodies were flying through the air, crashing into walls and tables. Men were moaning.

"Jesus!" Emily screamed.

CHAPTER 13

The room suddenly crackled with brilliant light—for a pair of seconds. It seemed the room would explode, the pressure pushed upon eardrums, eyes, skin. A dazzling white mass of angels burst the far doors from their hinges and roared down the hallway. The faint shouts of dying humans were heard, and the light, the pressure went with the angels. All was clarity, all was quiet in the darkness of the departing angels.

With a click, a fizz, electricity filled the wiring; the operating-room light returned. Robin stood guard over Emily. Andy, Tom, Tim, and Dan were standing or kneeling in a wedge formation. Their uniforms were wet with the red blood of their foes. Individual, white-frocked men lay on the white-tile floor, their bodies twisted, bones broken, feet facing backward, heads facing all sides. This had been the work of the angels.

Robin, standing, turned and offered Emily, propped on her right hip by her right arm, a hand up. He spoke as she grasped his hand, and he pulled her up. "What happened here?" He had evidently missed the showdown.

Emily spoke concisely. "Light had disappeared from the room, and lasers were useless. It got basic. It seemed forever. A band of angry angels cleared the room." Emily was bent over, her left arm on Robin's shoulder, as she checked her lower body and legs for wounds. Robin grabbed her head, turned it to him, and was suddenly rummaging in his first aid pouch, cramming "no-bleed" powder into a long gash that ran down the left side of her face. "Couldn't you feel that?" he asked.

"No," she answered as she felt the wound becoming puffy with the no-bleed powder.

"You should have the healing wand applied," he said as his eyes scanned for a standard, emergency first-aid kit.

One of the angels had reappeared and was in conversation with her crewmates, when he noticed Emily. He approached, eyeing the wound for the length of his walk to the victim. He had a deep-healer wand in his hand and ran it the length of the wound, inside the crevice. No pain occurred, as the wand anesthetized the wound as it moved. The deep healer was replaced by the skin wand, which repaired skin and capillaries. "Thanks," said Emily as she looked up at the ten-foot-tall angel.

He answered, "Your call to Jesus sent shivers through my heart. Your passionate faith will resonate within my soul forever. It is I who thank you."

Emily blushed as her eyes held the amazing confusion of God's overwhelming love. She spoke. "He saved me once from myself, and He never stops…never stops…saving me." The angel laughed in commendation for and with her joyous heart. Her voice had been slow with wonder and gratitude. Her God had saved her from brutal men and women when she was a child. He had saved her from hopelessness and despair and had given her the Johnsons during the Tribulation. He had resurrected her body from a clash with an avalanche boulder. He had protected her from combat harm during the time of the last harvest, and now, again, He had saved her for all eternity. She saw her crewmates gathered around Andy, who was conversing with two angels. Her angel touched her shoulder in good-bye and joined his teammates. The short conversation ended, and the angels vanished.

"Gather round," said Andy as he moved toward the doors through which they had first entered the operating room. They would be leaving shortly, and the corridor out was the primary route, with Diana and Tuck still guarding the entrance. Suddenly, striding down the hallway, came Diana and Tuck, and behind them, John, Woden, Seth, Ling, Pete, and Grace. Paternus held a leash to a constrained Abe. John, hearing Andy's unspoken question, answered, "Jack's at the far door, as is Mat, and they know that the door hinges are compromised."

As the two crowds comingled in handshakes and embraces, Tim, Diana, Ling, Pete, and Grace went directly to the operating tables, the diagnostic machines, and data computers to explore the contents. Emily and Dan followed, knowing a trail had been found leading to someplace stimulating. Pete perused the bins of Thermadorian bodies. He called Dan and Emily over to help him. All the corpses were wounded in various ways, the results of combat strikes—bullets, bombs, mines, heat, fire, or stabs and gash wounds from knives or swords or axes—or amputations, flying debris, falls. All the skulls had been surgically entered and probed. The dense chitin that was the equivalent of bone in humans had been lasered open. Small, natural openings in the chitin, almost invisible to human eyes, were breathing access and exhalation ports. All the heads were triangular, but the angles softened by a roundness, including the apex angle—the place of a human chin, the location of the mouth. Eyes had a slightly peripheral tilt on the broad surface of the two base angles. Nostrils were equidistant from eyes and mouth. Unlike the praying mantis on planet Earth, they did have ear openings under and behind the eyes.

The skulls had been tagged with an identifying number; the tag fastened to the leathery chitin-based skin. All skulls were hairless; there were not even bristles. Pete was calling out the numbers, and Diana had found on the nearest computer the data associated with each. Ling, on another computer, was able to bring up corresponding info age, sex, and a sensory rating as well as a dosage chart. The ultimate reason for the data collection was uncertain.

Paternus had pulled Abe to the white-frocked corpses, heavily stained in deep-red earthling blood. Paternus spoke. "We killed these human types. These are your enemies."

Abe spoke. "Why they here?"

Paternus answered, "To cause trouble of some type. Didn't your phone have recordings of humans performing surgery? Perhaps these were the beings."

Abe said nothing, his brow was furrowed in deep, painful thought.

Those crew members not engaged in the research sat with their backs against the wall, eating combat rations and making coffee with confiscated Bunsen burners from Fromen's lifeless lab technicians' work stations. Andy engaged in small talk. Andy and Tom kept their eyes and ears on their research party, not wishing to break their concentration, yet wanting to follow the discovery process.

Ling's piercing exclamation, "I'll be darned!" brought the eyes of his research party to focus on him.

"What?" inquired Diana with intense puzzlement.

Ling's voice bellowed over his crew. "All Thermadorians received a cleansing every six months, a vibrating hum sent through their bodies to clear their breathing portals of dust and the mineral we first discovered in the water. The minerals from these cleansings were then given to the Predator Nation overlords for sale to a chemical factory. Every Thermidorian's blood was filtered at a six-month interval for this mineral. Fiscally, a very efficient return on their efforts, I would imagine." Ling's eyes were running along the walls of the room. "Over there, by the back doors, corrugated paper barrels of the minerals."

Pete asked, "But that had nothing to do with the current mass mental instability?"

"No, but it was an opportune time to hide nefarious probings of their bodies. Search for a chip or even a glandlike structure in the brains or perhaps collected in a container somewhere nearby," said Ling. He paused, realizing that Dan, Emily, and the ever-watchful Andy and Tom were missing information. "Listen up," said Ling. "I analyzed the phones of Abe and Don. Don, prior to his conversion, was being affected by dark, depressing thoughts about his own self-worth and that of his fellow mantises. Of course, we need to remember that they had been systematically raped, both sexes, all their lives, and degraded by their overlords. But in addition to this, a device—either manufactured and electronic or a glandular-disruptive chemical cloned and inserted—heightened their sense of worthlessness on cue from another master. I found a computer tracking system for the devices, showing when they were boxed and distributed. Never saw one in person or a picture or diagram of one. Their minds became physically painful to use, and they just wanted a cessation of thought. Their kill instinct became aroused—to kill the source of their pain. Any external sound, especially speech, was unbearable, and no doubt triggered paranoia and psychosis as well. That is what Abe felt; he wanted to kill Don to shut him up." Ling studied Abe, who had been listening intently. "Is that what you felt, Abe?"

John heard a leading question.

Abe answered, a startled, emotional, self-revelation in his voice. "Ya, ya."

A leading question, but mantises, especially Abe, were not adept at projecting false emotion. John knew Abe was telling the truth.

"Who are these humans lying dead on the floor?" asked Andy of Ling.

Ling answered, "I suspect they are the bad guys, manipulating the mantis people against each other and against us through false rumors. They are using physical means to control the Thermadorians—implants and perhaps long-term genetic alterations. The best bet is these earthlings broke away from Earth soon after the creation of Adam and Eve and up to and perhaps including the time of the flood. Satan, a fallen angel, and his demon crew were the likely source. These earthlings may be scattered throughout the heavens. No doubt, genetic testing will reveal much more as to the origin and time of the migration. Or they could be humans from another world unknown to us, independently created directly by God."

Diana's mind wandered onto the topic of mantis death. How she missed Ava, whose knowledge had been deep on the subject. Ava had told her that mantis people lived up to two hundred years. Then they succumbed to neurological disease or simply the breakdown of the actual physical components. Ava said predators killed mantis people and ate them. Mantises were cannibals—the Predator Nation ate Thermadorians but not their own citizens, a fact not widely known to earthlings. This was, oddly, not done by the Pins to taunt or humiliate Thermadorians or celebrate their deaths. When their usefulness as thralls were gone, they simply were considered food like any other food. The dead from disease were burned, their ashes scattered with no rites, no marking of their having lived and contributed to some worthy goal.

Diana wondered if, maybe, they had not been dead. Maybe they were just broken parts, for the mantis body was simple in construction, design, function. For all the dead mantises she had studied, the smell of putrefaction seemed to only concentrate within the spilt blood. Put the pieces back together, flush and cleanse the arteries of old blood, and if desiccated, moisten with a simple infusion of their blood, even synthetic blood, and send a current through it. What would happen? Would there be a retention of what the individual had been? A self-awareness of the past? Or did the brain dissipate and lose potency? What was the soul but the collection of what a cognizant being had lived and processed? How indestructible was the hard drive of a cognizant nonhuman being? Was it still waiting, in storage, to be revived? The mantis people's souls would have remained in their bodies, as they had never been promised Heaven or Hell.

Diana spoke. "Ling, I assume you would like to search Abe's brain for a transmitter or glandular implant."

Ling answered, "First order of business, if he accepts."

Diana asked, "Where is the body of Don?"

John answered, "Wrapped tight aboard air platform 2."

Ling spoke. "Yes, retrieve Don, please."

"You know where I am going with this," Diana said. "Do the cranial procedure on Don as Abe watches. The simplicity of the operation may give him confidence. God knows we may be able to revive Don."

Ling laughed happily to himself as Diana's thought flooded his consciousness. "Yes, we may. Simply constructed, add the blood, the electric shock. The entire chemical mix of the brain may just be dried, awaiting to be reconstituted. Good to go. Like sending electricity into a turned-off computer."

"Or water and heat to freeze-dried soup," said Diana.

The entire crew, having listened to the conversation, was now standing, clapping, cheering Ling and Diana with encouragement. Even Abe caught their cheer and stood. Secretly, he prayed to the foreign god Jesus that Don would live again. Then there would be no guilt for Don's murder. Abe hoped to have his own mind returned to him, clean and hopeful…he was embarrassed to ask for himself.

***

John, Mat, Jack, Woden, Seth, and Paternus sat on the edge of the parked air platform 1. Both platforms were parked on the tile floor of the outdoor piazza before the vast rock overhang before the caldera. They had carried the bagged and wrapped body of their comrade, Don, into the operating room, where Andy and Tom loosely commanded the operating and support team. Dan and Pete were the guardians of Abe, who appeared calm, resigned, and ashamed. But everyone, including Abe, realized that his flashes of anger and confusion may have been generated by an alien presence within his brain, which, in theory, could be revived at any time. He did realize that he could assert his will against its power now with a new truth.

Ling, Diana, and Tim were the chief surgeons, with a supporting cast of Dan and Emily, Grace, and Pete. Tuck and Robin provided security in both corridors leading into the room.

Dan, Emily, Pete, and Grace had prepped the body of Don, washing external surfaces, rinsing internal conduits, clearing air openings, repairing all wounds, rehydrating the body with fresh mantis blood from the mantis stockpile amassed by Fromen's staff. Ling, Diana, and Tim became familiar with their instruments, rehearsed the cuts and procedures they would use in the surgery.

The security detail of the expedition, John, Mat, Jack, Woden, Seth, and Paternus, had left the immediacy of the operating room because they could only sit and watch as two cognizant beings they had worked with twenty-four hours a day, seven days a week, for weeks—who had saved them countless times from wounds and temporary, lengthy impairments—would be part of an experiment with an unknown outcome. John spoke. "Hope, however small, beats death any day."

"Amen," said Mat.

Jack laughed. "Remember how proud Don looked when he was told we needed him to carry all our heavy gear of ammunition and weapons systems?" Woden, Seth, and Paternus began chuckling.

Woden spoke. "You would have thought he had been promoted to general of Earth Forces."

Paternus added, "And how he was honored to have the last name of *Key* and how enraptured he had been to hear of 'the rockets bursting in air.'"

Seth interjected, "And the flag still flying in the morning. He took it all to heart."

"That's because we three Americans had the story embedded in our hearts," John said.

Seth spoke. "Yes, you are correct. You guys made him an American, somehow, through your stories."

"The land of the free and the home of the brave is no story," said Mat, "Abe was a good guy before he snapped. Finding out he was named for a United States president gave him satisfaction—a president responsible for freeing a people; he saw the parallels."

"How could these insect-appearing beings *not* have souls?" said Jack.

Mat spoke. "The Lord does not view life as mankind does. Man looks at the outward appearance and attitude, but the Lord looks at the heart and the steadfastness of the same." After a pause, Mat added, "Samuel 16:7."

Paternus nodded solemnly. "Let us pray for Don and Abe."

Woden said, "Go for it."

Paternus began, "Oh, Holy God, God of eternity who holds eternal life in His hands. Judge the hearts of Abe and Don, consider their circumstances, where they were and how far they have come by hearing of your greatness and walking in simple faith. Open their eyes to your presence. Renew their lives so that they may finish the course they are to run. In your mercy, gather them into the recesses of your love and teach them the knowledge of the heart."

"Amen," intoned the gathered in solemn hope.

***

Abe was first on the operating table. He was to go second, but he asked to go first, stating it would be good practice for Don's operation. The staff knew why—Abe had given God control over his life or death by being first. The surgeon's hand might more readily fail during the first operation. He'd had the mental breakdown that had caused Don to die. Abe knew the abnormality would be present in his brain. His brain could give the surgeons the map for destroying that object of death.

None of the operating crew had any doubts the operation would be successful. The surgical instruments had bonded with their minds and hands, as if they had completed thousands of successful surgeries in the past. In this familiarity, they recognized the presence of God, either in person or through the many updates He had given to His chosen. A problem did appear. Ling had first attempted to cut open the skull with a scalpel, thinking the blade would be less intrusive, and found the procedure impossible. All the skulls had been lasered open by Fromen's people not because lasering was fast, but because it was the only method that worked. The laser was used, and success was had, even as they noted there were two layers of transversing chitin. To no one's surprise, there it sat: a piece of hardware, made by a cognizant being, yet absorbed into a chitinlike gelatinous mass.

"Don't destroy it," warned Tim. "We may want to reattach it or study it."

Diana spoke softly. "Just lift the entire mass."

Ling pursed his lips. "I can't. Something is anchoring it to the entirety of the brain, either a body substance or a contrived, nonfleshy anchor."

Tim spoke. "Likely a metallic anchor, acting as an antenna, a conductive rod. You must cut around it."

Ling turned up the power on his operating lenses. "At max resolution," he said.

Diana and Tim turned up their magnifications.

Diana spoke. "Just a cut on the side. Yes, pivot the mass. A T-shaped anchor." He cleared a sticking membrane by cutting. The small mass was lifted out and placed in a container of preserving fluid. He asked, "Is that all we need to do?"

Diana answered, "Yes. See the scarring? They went in through the nose. See the slight disturbance where their probe hit the front of the brain, then they backed off, bent their apparatus upward, and gained the top of the brain in the crease that runs along the top. That's all they did. Simple and fast, which it needed to be, when so many operations had to be performed. May have been done by AI."

Tim spoke. "Just recheck where the mass sat; make sure there is no contact point going deeper into the brain."

Ling probed and reported, "No. There is nothing. No protuberance or change in suppleness of the brain."

Diana answered, "Okay, we're done."

Tim spoke. "How about packing the newly made depression with some material that may keep the brain from shaking—a snug fit, just like it was."

"Good thought," Diana said. "I concur."

Ling spoke. "Okay. Present the packing."

Diana produced a petri dish container with a man-made gelatin. "This is the stuff."

Ling's probe, with suction grasp, picked it from the dish, and then packed it, really laid it in the depression—the missing piece of cranium would secure it. "Close."

He stepped away. Diana reseated the skull section. Tim drilled small holes. Diana inserted the screws. Tim seated the screws, and Diana rechecked the seal.

"Is anything happening?" asked Tim.

Diana answered, "Heart beat steady, light painkiller added. Wheel him aside. Let's get to Don." Abe was wheeled aside and a blanket was placed upon him as the three surgeons collected around the dead body of Don.

Ling, speaking as the lead surgeon, an authority in his voice, said, "Implant removal first, then neck-wound repair. Lastly, blood infusion to flush the poison, and then an electric jolt." Ling looked at his crew and felt urgency should be communicated. "Quickly, my children, while the Creator's healing presence is upon us." A sudden infusion of energy and cognizance coursed through the huddled figures as they began the transformation, the journey from death into—Lord willing, and certainly, He was—life.

***

On the piazza after the silence and meditation of prayer, John reengaged the conversation. "Where are we at in our guessing? I understand the science. Abe and Don are relatively simply made life-forms, designed for hardiness and survivability. But their souls, their thoughts, aren't simple. Are they really stored in the brain like a computer, the drive not wiped clean when the power goes off? Is this the soul? The true hard drive? The soul is God's possession—perhaps of His very substance, which He sends to Paradise or Hades. What of life-forms that have heard of neither?"

Mat answered, "Let's assume the Thermadorians and humanity both had a like soul, in function, and physical/spiritual make up. Meaning the soul separate from the host body has eternal life-maybe eternal function is a better word. The difference is that God promised man eternal life through His son, Jesus—if Jesus, in all that entails, was accepted by man. Historically, no promise was made to the Thermadorians. Their souls would remain with the bodies even at death, and when the bodies turned to dust, the souls would be sitting, still intact, alone, and having no sensory apparatus. They would be in a peculiar state."

Woden picked up on Mat's narrative. "In humanity's case, because God has engaged man, taken a special interest, a contract is in play. The soul never just sits, forgotten for eternity. The soul is given a destination: either Hades and then Hell—eternal death—or Paradise and then Heaven—eternal life, the very life we are now living."

Jack continued the thread of logic aloud. "We are living because God allowed us to retain our senses, our bodies, our cognitive state."

Seth entered the conversation, "Will God allow Thermadorians to enter into the existing contract that He has with humanity? Will they be grafted into this contract through their acceptance of Christ? Could they then have eternal life. What Will God do? Does He love these Thermadorians?"

John injected his thoughts. "Well, brothers, the Jewish Christians—newly converted from Judaism into the fulfillment of Judaism's hope, the Messiah—faced this problem with the gentiles. Would they be accepted? The Holy Spirit answered the question by falling upon, inhabiting the gentile believers."

Paternus sighed contentedly. "John has given us the answer: God decides, through the presence of His Holy Spirit, who becomes His and who does not. The Thermadorians have free will, they are cognizant beings. Many already appear to know the Spirit. Don appears to know Christ."

John spoke. "The real questions are, is it required of all cognizant life forms to taste death once before returning in their resurrected bodies? Does there need to be an apocalyptic end to their planet before they return? Does there need to be a Paradise—a temporary holding place till that time? Or a Hades and Hell?"

Mat said, "Would Don need to live if he is already the chosen of God? If he returns to us, will he then live forever or will he die? To reappear in the future?"

Jack spoke. "All these questions will, at their appointed time, be answered. As it has been said before, 'We are on the eternal adventure of life unending.' Diana's observation." Jack looked across the faces of his gathered crewmates. "Explain to me again why Fromen's people are here and how these Mediterranean types came into being."

John answered, "If it happened as Ling believes, and Fromen's men are descendants of humans who were transported to the galaxies from Earth soon after the deaths of Adam and Eve, then Satan had planned it all while he was still an angel known as Lucifer. He had angels loyal to him carry out the plan, or perhaps the plan was unknown to them, and they were simply in the chain of authority, never suspecting that one of their own, higher in authority, was a deceiver. When Adam fell, all humans fell from grace, even if separated by vast distances. The lie was clever; it was the same as the Earth lie: Satan's kingdom was better. Their ancestors bought the lie, and they were trained to be administrators of planets possessed by Satan and his demons. Satan, an administrator of God on Earth, had simply corrupted God's pronouncements for Earth and distributed the same throughout the universe."

"Satan controlled the communications," stated John.

"Yes, and when God spoke, the universe obeyed," Seth said. "And so there is a counter universe in disarray."

"Why was this allowed?" asked Paternus.

"You know the answer," Mat said. "God allowed the lie because He knew He would turn the lie into something good. 'All things work together for good to them who love God, to them who are called according to His purpose.' Romans 8:28. God's people, us, will now perform the miracle that was performed on Earth. We will destroy Satan's kingdom, destroy the unredeemable wicked, and find, nurture, and lead to redemption those chosen who exist within this travesty." Amens came from the gathered.

Jack reentered the talk. "Fromen's people were killing Thermadorians by the thousands by activating a chip they had planted in their brains. Not a chip, so much as a glandular organism. The glandular organisms were interconnected in real time by something akin to sound waves. It is rumored that this gland allowed the mantis species to take on the functions of cognizant life, and it raises their emotions, intellect to a higher realm. It allowed them to have souls. Genetically, the mantis could never reproduce this gland. It was inserted at birth."

Mat spoke. "That's all hearsay, unsubstantiated rumor probably disseminated by the earthlings of Fromen's type. Probably just a 'last resort' kill button to wipe out cognizant beings, who, at some point in time, would wish to be free."

Seth nodded. "The soul produced was eternal, and yet it had no place to spend eternity, for Satan never had this control and could not lie it into existence. The souls of all cognizant life-forms simply remain with the flesh. Or they float in the cosmos—no Hades or Paradise. Perhaps, Satan had set in place a transferring of souls in the mantis people."

"What of the rumor about Fromen's type? That their souls were being placed in mantis bodies?" asked Mat.

"Probably just a ruse to confuse the Thermadorians," John theorized. "Transplanting a soul into an alien's body would kill the soul, drive it insane. We talked about this the first day Ava mentioned it."

"And yet," Mat said, "think of Fromen's type. They were of the race of Adam. They had enough within them at birth to know that God existed, as Romans 1:18–20 indicates. They must have a discomfort, a realization of incompleteness and wrongdoing within, an awareness of an inability to do what is right. A vague or pronounced guilt. Deep in their hearts, right and wrong exist. Satan could only pervert those feelings, twist truth to fit his lies. The harvest field is ripe, gentlemen, and we are just the disciples of Christ needed to introduce the Savior."

John's wrist computer chimed. Andy was calling. "Yes, Captain," answered John, placing the phone on speaker.

Andy spoke. "We've got the chips removed from Don's and Abe's bodies. Their wounds have been patched. A low voltage is being applied.

Come, help pray these two to life." The squad was on their feet before the sentence had finished.

***

The entire crew of Explorer 7 gathered around the operating tables. The bright overhead lights had been dimmed. They could hear the low-voltage hum of electricity flowing into the gigantic nine-foot bodies, mantis bodies, with triangular heads capable of stereo and unilateral vision, eyes of great keenness—more so when the slightest movement enters their orbs. In combat, they had proven their ability to solve problems, be creative; they were capable of mathematics—addition, subtraction, multiplication, division, geometric rules—of remembering fire coordinates and ranges. They had shown emotion when the enemy was defeated, and when the enemy had temporarily stymied them. They had shown tenderness toward the female and children of their species, and anger and rage toward their enemy. They had taken correction and reproof from their trainers without offering retaliation or anger. Somehow, these winged, insect-looking forms of long legs and arms, with a spike on each massive hand, and cooing, singing, chirping words must have a soul. There must be a repository for all that they had lived, seen, experienced. Their very lives must be imprinted within the mind, and the mind within the soul. That was the hard drive that could never be destroyed or erased, as it was imbued with that medium—half substance and half spirit (whatever you deemed spirit to be. Only God knew, even at this late date in the history of cognizant beings).

Anyone who had ever looked into their eyes knew they were thinking, emotional beings. Could they not have a soul? The assembled watched the exhalations of their air ports, not one large rising and falling of lungs but of individual portals, as many as sweat glands on a human, so that a pulsing was seen in various collections and separations. No veins were seen in the necks or along the craniums; they simply lay on and under the leathery skin of arms, legs, hands.

Then, the sheer membrane covering Abe's eyes moved up and down. Suddenly, Don's facial skin seemed to rise, as if the brain were forming a question and wished to speak. The prayers of the people were audible and whispering, seeking the will of God. The prayers borne of what was good in Don and Abe were cast up into heavens, even though they knew their God was right beside them, standing shoulder to shoulder with them. He knew exactly what was to come. He always knew and always gave them what was true, even if their wishes just weren't to be. He never lied, He never falsely encouraged, never changed an outcome to fit a temporary plan of human invention. The truth was written into Him, and He had written it.

Mumblings and cooing and cries of delight and pain became a cacophony from the creatures, Don and Abe. So much so that a momentary fright passed over God's children. Laser generators were turned on, rifles moved to a position of freedom of movement, and the assemblage moved back three steps. Was God's glory coming? Or the wrath of Hell?

Don became subdued as the orange-red light in his eyes slowly grew in potency. He had entered life, seeming to be within his mind, seeing something, exploring his condition. Abe was screaming in pain, his body attempting to burst the restraints. Then he gave up. Grace stepped out of the crowd and took him by the hand. "Wake up, Abe." She rubbed her free hand over his grasped hand. She could feel his life force within, sensed his confusion; and then he touched her, and it was of warmth and familiarity. "You're alive again, Abe."

Still looking at the ceiling, he said, "Why?"

She said, "Because it is not yet your time to die—not till you know Him and make your choice."

His eyes turned red, his head turned to face her and the assembled. He let go of her hand. "Choice?" he said, the *ch* pronounced with the Thermadorian accent, the letter combo commonplace in the language.

Jack approached; he still retained the superior vocabulary among the earthlings speaking Thermadorian. He had bonded most closely with the two warriors. "Where were you, Abe?"

Abe looked confused, then he uttered, "It is to come. To come."

The gathered imagined a prophecy to be spoken. Jack sensed this idea in the minds of others, and he spoke. "That's his way of communicating. He needs time to find the words. There's no prophecy coming."

Ling was loosening Don's restraints. Ling and Tim lifted Don to a sitting position. Don's eyes began to engage the faces of the assembled. His stare was frightening, as they could tell he knew them yet could not place them within his life.

"Up," said Abe. Jack knew Abe was sound and at rest—enough so that he wasn't violent. But he hated restraints, a reminder of his slavery, and restraints could provoke him. Jack lessened the set of restraints on his side of the table while Paternus loosened the set on the opposite side. Abe sat up. "Was nowhere. Empty…empty…ness. Food…army."

Seth pulled a ready-to-eat meal from a thigh cargo pocket and handed it to Abe, who said, "Good friend." The soldiers laughed, and Abe laughed in the happiness of receiving his wished-for food and also for having made them laugh.

Don saw the food packet and could even smell the meal. Don spoke. "Pork chops, me."

"I got that," said Woden, and handed it to Don, who grunted and said, "Buddy."

Woden responded, "My pleasure." The he thought to ask, "Did you see anything, Don?"

"Nowhere," said Don.

Andy spoke in his command voice. "I suggest we move to the outdoors, the piazza by our air platforms. We will allow Don and Abe to decide when they wish to come up. Mat and Jack, watch over them and realize their memories could come back at any time. That may lead places we don't want to go." He referred to the death struggle that had occurred between Abe and Don. "Tom, Ling, anything to add?"

Ling spoke. "We really don't know yet if they were in a state of nothingness, so watch for and analyze any mention of memories."

Tom spoke. "On a different note, a compromise may have occurred. Perhaps the old is gone and something new has arrived." The earthlings read the unspoken: that Don and Abe could now be free agents, either by tampering or assent.

***

As Andy began the gentle, upward walk through the corridors to the air platforms on the piazza, a foreboding, like a throbbing tumor, seemed to possess his thoughts. He thought of the alien bodies of Abe and Don, crowned with earthly names; two gigantic insects, who now were thought to possess souls and have minds of compassion, fair play, and love of freedom. What perfectly human men they were. Andy pulled Ling into him by a brotherly arm around his shoulders as he called out, "Tom, come to me by my free side." Tom obeyed without hesitation. Andy was an affectionate man on those occasions when his heart had been touched and when he felt weak and faint of emotional stamina. Tom sensed this happening now. The beloved strong man, who had led them through so many crises in the past and had always shown himself full of grace and grit, determined to serve the King, needed human help. Tom came willfully and placed his arm around the shoulder of their beloved leader, saying, "Speak your heart. I feel a burden overwhelming you."

Andy said, "Between us three, secret thoughts to be shared: Ling to Tim, Pete and Grace, and Dan and Emily. Tom to John and Diana, Mat, and Jack. Me to Tuck, Robin, Woden, Seth, and Paternus. I sense the bewitching of us earthlings by Satan's feminine demons. We believe insects to be men, capable of all that men are capable of. It is so outrageous that we consumed the poison, and it will kill us if we continue in our slumber. So hungry are we to believe in the attributes of God that we see life through a beautiful filter of inclusion. How easy it is to be used in such a state. Fromen and his colleagues' bodies are still below. What can they tell us—their DNA strands? Perhaps we are related; some of us, at least. What would that tell us? How did they ingratiate themselves into the workings of these catastrophes? What is their connection to the Predator Nation, to the Thermadorians? Where is their home planet? What are their real capabilities? Was Or a part of their nation? Are they the puppet masters who deceive us with the mantis people? To what ends?"

Tom knew Andy, and he was not hearing Andy's thinking. He knew "feminine demons" were probably from Andy's past fascination with Shakespeare's plays. Perhaps from Macbeth's three witches—sisters who foretold a false fate to Macbeth. Andy seemed to believe these demons were hiding the truth of the drama from his world, his military, his crew. Tom spoke, hoping to temper Andy's thoughts. "Hardened veterans of war who have seen the peaks and valleys of emotions have vetted Abe and Don. Scientific and dispassionate reasoning by our trained crew has seen virtue in them. The soul is everything, and the body is nothing. When God made men in His likeness, He was not speaking of the flesh, the outer shell, but of the inner soul. Perhaps we are not fooled. But your approach is sound, and we must be sure to the core of our beings."

"Yes, be sure. I hope my thoughts are wrong," said Andy.

Tom thought the Shakespeare play, written when witches and witchcraft mesmerized and perverted common sense and Satan roamed free, held the key to Andy's unease—a Satanic remembrance embedded as if it were scripture within the mind. The words were already dead, destroyed at the cross where the flesh died and the Spirit of God lived. The power of the indwelling Holy Spirit would destroy again what was false.

Ling whispered to his friends, "I will go back to the lab for autopsies and DNA of Fromen's crew—gut samples, pollen samples, trace elements on skin, in lungs, upon clothing, extensive tissue samples. I will track their trail through time and space."

Tom added, "And I will form a polygraph test to be administered secretly and in small portions to the minds of Abe and Don. We are living in preposterous times, and our conclusions have slipped upon us so naturally."

Ling had the final word. "Let us take our time. Let us pray to our Lord for wisdom and not force our efforts to a preferred conclusion."

"All will be well," said Andy, now overwhelmed in the peace of his supportive friends. "The ranking angel gave me a heads-up: the war will move to Rau-toon, the vicious land, the massive planet twice the size of Earth, the home of the Predator Nation. Ava is soon to return. We are to track the ancient earthlings of Satan's kingdom.

CHAPTER 14

John studied the rugged desert and mountainous terrain on the small planet, named Kimberlee, through the intense heat of shimmering mirages. Five-hundred– to six-hundred–foot hills before a range twice to three times that height. Pans of salts and minerals scattered before, within, beside the higher ground. Many of the mirages were the inventions of Satan's people—Fromen's race of Earth-dwellers—and were meant to hide structures or at the least, confuse any searching enemy as to coordinates. Huge, manufactured hills, fake salt pans of mirrors and shimmering glasslike material replicated existing features. He and his crew had reconnoitered three times before they solved the riddle of deceit.

The Explorer 7 was parked and camouflaged miles away. The air platforms were hidden a mile from these structures, on overwatch, with heavy guns pointed toward the narrow doorways to the internal chambers of a false hill—a building shaped like a hill, covered in unmovable sand and rock. The scattered stones on the desert floor were observation cameras or small gun emplacements with dug-in chambers beneath, holding thousands of pounds of belted ammunition. Old powder cartridges were ideally suited for ambush weapons, due to their inexpensive cost and their ruggedness. Personnel and vehicle mines had also been placed. These weapons were of Earth manufacture before the Millennium—stolen or bought from arms dealers at least 1,500 years ago. Who had visited Earth and secured the weapons?

Ling's initial exploration of Fromen and his people's corpses had pointed to Kimberlee (named for the first astronaut to be reconstituted during space explorations) as the place of last notable habitation. Soil samples on clothing, lung biometrics as to last breathed air and pollen types all matched perfectly. Confirmation from the satellite security tape of the planet's surface activities left no doubt. Two vehicles had come from this area, proceeded to Thermador and the northern caldera two weeks ago, and had not left. Meaning Andy's crew had not found the two vehicles they presumed were still in that vicinity. No activity had been recorded around this hill during the two-week interval. Was anyone inside?

Tests had revealed that Fromen's scientists had the pure genetics of the first Middle Eastern humans; no other humans existed on Earth. They were of the first humans created, taken from Earth before the flood, perhaps; before the tower of Babel. Their initial hardiness had been eroded over intermittent years of breathing machine-purified air, of moving in near-weightless environments, of living through protective suits that stole the strength-enhancing contact with pathogens, bacteria, germs. Only recently had this race found permanent home planets, where they could live more naturally and rely on muscular exertion, fibrous foods, animal flesh, and germs.

At some point during Earth's ancient past, estimated as within the four hundred years of Hebrew servitude in Egypt, an influx of Earth genetics had mingled with Satan's pilgrims and strengthened the waning genetic pool. The assumption was that slaves were bought in Egypt and transported into space to join their cousins. A standard name had been given the Satan-manipulated wandering travelers by the higher echelons of the space program: pilgrims. These people, the original travelers and the later additions, belonged to the newly designated Pilgrim Alliance. No formal announcement had been made, but it was believed the Pilgrim Alliance had responded to diplomatic outreaches from New Jerusalem.

John, seeing no movement around his position and no movement or electrical impulses recorded from the artificial hill, spoke into his throat comm to the forces of Explorer 7, who were dressed in combat gear and armed. "It's a go."

He, Tom, Seth, Mat, Jack, Abe, and Don—fully cognizant and healthy—watched a speck come from the top of a peak in the mountain range behind the hills. This speck was Woden, strapped into artificial wings and sporting the thin tail of one of the native reptilian vultures. He circled five times, high above the land, then slowly made a wide corkscrew descent onto the top of the man-made hill. The hope being that any enemy surveillance cameras would misidentify Woden as a vulture.

John and Tom studied the reactions of Abe and Don, respectively. They had oohed when they saw the speck and gave sounds of cooing approbation when the speck landed. They had regained most of their memories, repossessed their equanimity and steady good-naturedness. Abe vaguely remembered his killing of Don and had asked for forgiveness, and the two men had hugged. The act appeared to be genuine. It was made more palatable by the fact it had been Fromen's men who had caused the death. Both Abe's and Don's personalities had changed; they talked more—about everyday occurrences, their families, politics, and Jesus, and how Jesus would perceive their world and lives. They laughed at themselves and at life. They read their new translations of the New Testament. (The Old Testament translation was still in progress.) The joy in Abe was that he had not killed his friend, and he saw the hand of God in this, for it was God's men and their belief in God that had even made them try to save a dead insect.

Woden appeared to be roosting on the sandy peak and had waddled around the sand in typical vulture fashion. Once he was in position on the peak, he lowered a drill from a holster on his belt and began drilling. The outer shell was pierced without incident. A probe was inserted, and Woden explored within. With the retraction of the camera, an explosive was packed into the opening. The explosive's top side was thermal, and it immediately began burning upward through the shell material. Woden took off in flight and met a circling Paternus vulture in the air. Far above the hill, Woden detonated the charge. A weak-sounding *whoomph* was heard, and visually, the mound rose a foot.

In a short time, Woden and Paternus were on the hilltop, descending into the hill, stripping off their wings and tails, and slowly working their way down to ground level. They discovered bunks, personal lockers, kitchen, pantry, dining table and chairs, an extensive work area filled with computers, an extensive electrical-generating system. No personnel, no security devices in the temperature-controlled rooms. The outside security devices—mines and miniguns shown on an electronic map—were on. Woden, by cutting wires, turned them off, even though "on" was made to register upon all surveilling systems. The Explorer's security crew entered at the base of the hill, through doors opened by their inside crew, and established a protocol of defense. Soon, Ling, Andy, Tim, Diana, Dan and Emily, and Pete and Grace had grasped the significance of the huge data cache; they had established its perimeters, delineated the topics and the intended thrusts and goals; and sent all information to the Department of Space/War Studies located in the United States.

By nightfall, all relevant data had been retrieved, and it was determined that sleeping outside suited Explorer 7's crew, as sleeping in a small space, perhaps to be surrounded by enemy forces, was deemed imprudent. Seth volunteered to remain in the Pilgrim Alliance's mountain fortress to monitor possible enemy communications with the fortress or the arrival of enemy personnel for records retrieval or destruction. As the Explorer 7 was secure, but a tempting target, the crew opted for an encampment by the air platforms. It was determined that in the first light of morning, the miniguns would be made harmless, or taken along, and the mines would be marked but not unearthed. The mines had been deactivated through the central control panel within the building. A preliminary study revealed many mines were carrying secondary explosives to kill hapless deactivating personnel. Robotic deactivators with thick-metal coats were preferred for future disarming.

No campfires, lights, or sounds were permitted in the camp, and individual sleeping spots were spaciously arrayed between the two air platforms. Tuck and Robin manned the platforms' guns and had oculars trained on the alien headquarters. Only one moon cast dull-yellow light onto Kimberlee that night. The wind was still, and only the smell of sandy soil was in the air. The exploratory team had uncovered significant knowledge of the Thermadorian past, and Andy thought it best to share it with Abe and Don and the entire crew the next day, when sound volume would be less of a concern.

***

Andy, John, Jack, and Mat approached Abe and Don. John, Jack, and Mat had been comrades-in-arms with the two aliens from the beginning. Seth, Woden, and Paternus had guard duty, as did Tuck and Robin. Andy and the others approached in a crouch, not wishing to break the skyline and horizon. As was his fatherly way, Andy grasped their shoulders with his hands and squeezed. "News for you two. Good and great discoveries were made today, and I wanted to share."

"Ya, share," said Don in a low voice.

"Medo," said Abe, which was pidgin English for *Me too.*

"We, all those who entered the pilgrims' headquarters yesterday, agree there is proof that Thermador's ancient inhabitants, the builders of the shrines, the nature walks, and the historic sites, were of the mantis race, but of a lesser height and weight—comparable to earthlings five to six feet tall. Without conscious effort, the genes of the far range of weight and height began to prevail, and within two thousand years, the recessive genes no longer had impact. This shift is being studied, but it appears to have happened naturally," Andy said.

"The pilgrims saw the opportunity to insert a lie into this naturally occurring event—many lies to undermine the mantis people's sense of history, of importance, uniqueness, and individuality. They wished to destroy the collective soul of your people, and as such, the individual self-worth of every male, female, child. They claimed you were genetically soulless and what soul you did possess was not your own. The Rau-toon were informed. A lie they could use to control you.

"The Rau-toon mantis people, of course, were delighted in the new discovery that they had souls. You Thermadorians were the only weak ones—weak culture, weak souls, substandard." Andy saw Abe and Don drifting off in thought, into their personal experiences. Perhaps he had given too much information at once. It was time to let them be. One last fact needed to be known. "We, before you and all of Earth, worship the God who gave you—and us—life. This same God is offering you His Son, Jesus, who rescued us, redeemed us, and told us the truth about ourselves, so that your people may know the truth and be rescued and redeemed. We will become one family, united and strong."

"Amen." Abe raised his arms and moved his massive hands as if wishing to grasp the hand of God.

"Amen me," said Don with joy. Then, in mental weariness, he added, "You splain *redeemed* anudder time."

The gathered crew laughed, including Andy and Don and Abe.

As an afterthought, Don spoke to the gathered. "I live Jesus." In a lower tone, to himself, he said, "I live Him good."

Jack laughed lovingly, so poetic were the words. Mat smiled broadly. "To love Him is to live Him."

John spoke solemnly. "Amen. Brothers forever."

***

Ava awoke from the induced coma. Her throat felt dry. The lighting in the small room was subdued. She wiggled her fingers, then her toes. She moved her eyes up and down, sideways, then rolled her eyes clockwise and counterclockwise. She saw a cup marked "water" on the bedside tray. Her arm pivoted on her elbow and swung to the cup. Her hand picked up the cup and brought it to her lips. She drank. She was alive, whatever that meant. Was her whole body intact? Did she have unlimited movement? What did her body look like? Was it mangled and scarred? She should not even be cognizant—shouldn't be able to ask herself such questions. She was supposed to be dead, annihilated, nonexistent, noncognizant, or perhaps, in tortured flesh, in a tortured place.

In her spy-craft training with her handler, she was taught that the Christians believed they couldn't die, that their God resurrected them from death just once, and thereafter they could sustain life forever, no matter how destroyed the human body became. Apparently, that was a lie, for she was not a Christian. She knew the Christian beliefs, mind-set, culture; knew the Christian history. Now that she knew Christians, she liked them. It was all part of her cover, but never did she believe, nor *want* to believe, that she was one with their God concept. Evidently, all life—or perhaps all human life—had this innate ability to never die. Why had no one come back to say as much? "Shit!" she said loudly. "I'm alive, but the world I once was in, I am not in."

She noticed a light blanket upon her form, and a light tunic was upon her body as clothing. Tubes dispensing fluid were hooked to her left forearm. The room in design, décor, lighting was a room of her former world—that of the Christians. She rolled onto her left side. No pain in movement. She moved her legs to the side of the bed so that her feet hung out and the blanket remained on the bed. The feet looked like her feet; they were not bandaged or mangled. Using her arms, she pushed herself up, sat up on the side of the bed. No dizziness. She heard noise outside the closed door.

She steeled herself; no doubt a creature would be entering, as a force of intelligence must have been monitoring the room. The door slid open. An Earth human, female, identified as such by dress and mannerisms, had entered. "Good afternoon," she said in a friendly but businesslike voice. "My name is Angie." Ava saw "nurse's aide" on her nametag. Angie anticipated her patient's thoughts. "You are at the trauma-recovery/renewed-life complex on planet Earth. Others will be coming to explain the next stage—"

Ava interrupted hurriedly, "Of my recovery?"

Angie smiled. "No, you are complete. Recovery has already been undergone. No physical therapy even needed in the process. We need to send you back to your last assignment, or to leave time, if you wish."

Why did they not know she was not one of them? Was her cover so deep that her very DNA had been entered into their files? On her final day of spycraft training, she had been told the DNA vaults were impossible to enter, so this aspect of her cover was always to be ambiguous. Only the supreme God and His highest angel had knowledge and access. Did God have His concentration upon her? How had her side entered the vaults? She thought of a large lens collecting the rays of the sun, and an intense beam of light upon an ant. She was the ant. He had healed her to destroy her—unless they wanted information or to use her as an agent for their side?

Angie heard her patient's thoughts, as the sedation opened Ava's mind, even though, technically, she was not redeemed, but rather, simply alive in the body she'd had before. Ava had not yet given herself to the Lord. Angie knew she was a pilgrim. Her DNA was marked "present" in the roll book of human creation. As a covert operations officer, Angie had authority to open a dialogue. Angie spoke. "I lived on Earth before Christ ruled from New Jerusalem. In that time, many people who had dismissed their decision to choose Christ or Satan, had, when death seemed near, confessed internally or audibly a desire for Christ. They understood they had nothing to lose and everything to gain. Some, not many, were accepted. Do you know why?"

"Either because God is not all-knowing or they were exceptionally good actors?" she said without humor or guile.

"Just the opposite. God knew they had reached their tipping point and were balanced on one shaking leg, on an unsteady rock, and they had been forced to decide on a direction to leap: Toward God, with His open arms; or toward self and, they thought, a solid piece of ground. The decision decides everything. Is God good? Will He catch you, though you don't deserve it, or will He let you fall? The thoughts racing within their minds either condemn or rescue them. Of course, there are those who try to think of nothing, but there is no such thing as 'nothing.'" Angie knew Ava would continue to hold back; she would not answer Him now. Soon she would answer, and the consequences would be forever. Angie spoke. "Perhaps you made the choice already, before you were turned to vapor. Perhaps your memory has not caught up to the present."

Ava realized what a clever woman this supposed nurse's aide was, and yet she had left a way out. But even this "way out," she likely had presented purposely. Ava spoke. "That must have been it." Immediately, she realized she had stepped into the trap. She had admitted to not being in Christ, originally. Which Angie seemed to already know. Ava continued, "Okay, you got me. DNA would have told you I'm a pilgrim and the enemy. My confession of not being in Christ was just 'icing on the cake' for you." She liked that Earth idiom.

Angie spoke. "We have known from the beginning—from the time you and Enrique traveled to New Jerusalem. Really, God has known since your birth. Now, you have the opportunity to convince God that you love Him and wish to follow Him, the God who actually sees the brain's ruminations in real time and identifies truth from lies before you can." Angie studied Ava's face and listened to her thoughts, and there were none. "You have from this moment until your fixed and known death date. Death dates can be lengthened or shortened by you, but God already knew what you would choose before you even came into life."

"How can anyone convince God, Secret Agent Nurse?" Ava smiled. "'Convince' is a word for 'selling' and does not imply belief."

Angie understood the narrow validity of her remark and answered, "Then you can only live Him. Live Christ: there is no actor alive who can portray Him. Live Him through His Spirit, Ava, and know what all His people know: He is God, He is good, He shares His eternal life with His children. Then health, peace, and truth will be yours."

"Right. Maybe I will do just that," she said. "I bet you don't send me back to where I was."

Angie laughed, not from disdain or mockery as she looked at Ava's discharge papers on her hand-held computer. Angie spoke as she presented the computer screen to Ava. "Take a look, Ava. Right under my finger. Let me highlight it." Angie dragged her finger across the screen, and read aloud, "Return to duty with Explorer 7, Captain Andrew Springs, currently enroute to planet T-24, as intelligence officer in sector 4. Isn't that where you came from?"

"Why, yes!" Ava said in mocking disbelief. Deep down, she was surprised. Yet, perhaps in seconds, a listening system had written her desires on the screen.

"Get dressed and meet me at the nursing station," said Angie, as she began detaching the tubes from her patient's arms.

***

Upon immediate entry into the Earth ship bound for the outer reaches of known space, Ava stopped at the viewing window within the corridor leading to seating. Perhaps this would be her last view of Earth–home of the human race! She fondly remembered her journey to New Jerusalem with Enrique and her time in training in Florida. The Earth's human inhabitants, they were so open, so friendly. It was strange that they were the enemy. It just didn't add up—except they had sold out their individuality, their minds, to their version of god. Dread came to her, invaded her body in a cold, enervating chill. She believed she had made Him angry. She thought He was saddened, not angry. Why was she thinking about Him…who didn't exist? Why did she say, "He" so easily, naturally? "They," "them," "it," and "she" had all been in her vocabulary at one time.

When the 'Be Seated' sign flashed, she went to her seat, against the side of the ship, a windowless hull. An old man was in the seat next to hers. His age was startling to her, as all Earthlings stopped aging at fifty, then recycled to their midtwenties and slowly entered the cyclic scheme of regeneration. For a moment, she thought he could be one of her people, a pilgrim hundreds of years old. A regimen of treatments could keep them appearing and feeling young into their hundreds. But when the treatments were denied, pilgrims aged rapidly and died. He could be one of the dying. Sleep was invading her mind. The nurse's aide, Angie, had said this would be common for up to a month—the desire to sleep, the need for sleep. She slept.

She awoke in dimness; only small floor lights were on. She saw her breath, realized her fingers were cold. She looked over at the man beside her. He was sleepily awake; she saw his breath in the air, and a smile was on his face. She sensed he had been awaiting her awakening. She noticed he wore a thick, tunic-looking coat; the sleeves touched his palms, and the garment reached easily to his shoes, even with his legs bent. He can't feel the cold, she thought. He had a windbreaker-type jacket over the tunic. "Why is it so cold and still?" she asked him. He turned his head to her, looked down upon her—clearly, he was a tall man. His head was covered in a wooly, sheepskin cap.

He spoke. "My dear child, the sleep, our stillness, is prearranged—we have so far to go. But the cold is not. It's a malfunction, not very common in our world today, when people and our machines are very near perfect. Take my coat; give me the opportunity to do good. A splendid coat, the exact type of coat that Jacob gave Joseph."

"Where are the ornaments and the colors?" She had had extensive training in the Bible. She had parried the thrust, and now she would attack. First strike: "Are you of the Pilgrim Alliance? You do not show your age well." She saw love and kindness enter his eyes; these were the *last* emotions she expected to see.

"The tunic has two sides. I wear the colors on the inside. The color side has tabs for ornaments so that people can choose their own—almost like a charm bracelet. Yes, I am one of yours, genetically. I am near death. I have given myself to Christ, so spiritually, I am not like you. The Lord placed me here to tell you about your father—your real father, the father you have always wanted to know."

"Okay." She shrugged her shoulders. "I'm game." She wondered if what he told her would be the truth. Why were they trying so hard to turn her? How did they know about her love for her dad? She had never written a journal. She had never discussed him with a single soul. He had only filled her heart and her prayers of yearning. He was a part of every free moment of her life. He had kept her sane. She wasn't very important in the scheme of things. She would not challenge the "I'm one of yours" statement; she believed the old man was telling the truth. She shuddered. He saw the beginnings of hypothermia—her operations, her rebirth, had depleted body fats and caused disruptions; hypothermia susceptibility was real.

He stood, peeled his jacket off, unbuttoned the wool garment from neck to above the knees. He kindly asked, "Colors out?"

She answered, "Yes, please."

He reversed the coat.

She spoke. "Astonished. Not as bright, not as many-colored as I had been led to believe."

He laughed. "They knew what 'garish' meant, and no one wanted to be a walking target to thieves and robbers."

She responded, "Tasteful, blending colors."

"Stand," he said softly, then quietly suggested, "keep that heavy sweater on."

"Yes, of course," she said. She stood, and he placed her hands within the sleeves, shrugged the coat up her arms, seated it upon her shoulders, buttoned it completely. As he faced her, inches apart, she looked up at his face. Where did she know him from? He hugged her with an overwhelming tightness of warmth that penetrated into the coat and lay trapped within the layers of fibers. She felt no fear. No, it was impossible. It couldn't be. He placed the sheepskin cap upon her head. He pulled out a wooly beanie for his own head. He spoke. "Sit, daughter of Zion."

She answered, "Thank you, my prince." Acting was a part of her; she liked being another, liked little adventures of self-creation. She saw him lose himself in an emotion.

"Just call me Daddy, my princess, and lean against my breast so that I may sustain my life within your aura of warmth."

"So be it," she said. When she was a child, her daddy would play along, encouraging her dream world. They settled down into the seats, and he pulled up the dividing armrest. His emotions, she noticed, were of love and yearning. She suddenly realized a presence. The presence said, "Behold your father." With unshakable certainty, she knew the man was her daddy, gone from her life when she had turned seven.

His eyes were wet with tears. He spoke. "How life moves on, rushing us to a destination we know not, and yet we go anyway, like dumb sheep panicked by a wolf." He studied her face, saw the little girl, dark of hair, olive complexion. He saw her mother, the same black hair and olive skin, beside her, smiling but not happy in heart. She was just a shell of a woman, scheming behind the smile. How had the witch tricked him into believing that they had found love?

He turned in his seat to fully face Ava and said, "I loved you, little girl, from the beginning, when you were in your mother's womb. I wish I could have hugged you more, kissed your cheeks more, said, 'I love you' more. I should have told you how patient, kind, intelligent, and just plain good you were." His sentence ended in tears and choked voice.

Her heart was breaking. She sobbed. "Oh, Daddy, I knew, I knew, I knew you loved me because you stayed when Mommy was so mean to you. You stayed for me."

"And I left for you, to find work, to make the money to pay the courts that could free you. I did not give in. How hard I fought for you. I spent all I had and even what I didn't have. I fought men for you, those men who came for your mother, but were after you. I prayed to a god I knew existed but knew not where. I planted flowers for you, and built a pool and bought a trampoline, and a little dog for you, hoping for that day you would come to me. When she died, I thought certainly you would come….I'm so, so sorry I didn't win." His soul slumped within his chest.

"You did win, Daddy, because you fought, and because I know now how hard you fought." Her tears ran on his windbreaker. She clutched him tightly with her fingers.

"I was an old daddy when you were born, and soon I will die. The Christians are here. They are good; our race is just a collection of liars, connivers, schemers, and not one is capable of love. Christ is in my heart, and He knows how to love. I know my Redeemer lives, He listened to me, my appeal, in the courts of Jerusalem. And when I die, I will return, just like you have returned from death. He did that for me! Jesus Christ in Jerusalem did that for me—allowed you to have a renewed life, a loan till you declare your life for Him. You should be dead. Do you know that? He bestowed life upon you. He's betting on your goodness. I told Him what a precious heart you had. He and I, we should never have had this meeting, but He allowed it. Just because He loves, He needs to love us because we need Him. God loved His son, and His son loved me and you, so forever we can live. Our lives are not broken but repaired."

She buried her head into his chest and spoke as she cried. "Yes, Daddy, we can live forever together—houses side by side."

"Promise me you will love Him. He knows love. He is the champion of love. Be one with Him as I am one with Him and you."

The years of suppressed yearning for his presence, his love, ached and found release. She wept till no tears were left. He cried with her and held her tight.

***

The white light of angels shone about her. Their faces were so kind. One lifted her head and hands from her daddy's cold form. The angel placed his hands upon her neck and face, lifted her head to meet his, and he whispered,

"Your daddy has eternal life. He is bound for the Renewed Life Complex on Earth for a resurrected body. A very brief stay. You must hand over your life to Jesus to receive eternal life. There is no other way, no other means for eternal life. For it is written in the Holy Book, in the book called John, in the fourteenth chapter, sixth verse, 'I am the way, and the truth, and the life; no one comes to the Father except through Me.'"

The angel and the soul of Ava's daddy were gone. The flight attendant and copilot came, reassuring her that her daddy would come back, this time for eternity. They placed her daddy's body in a wheelchair and pushed the empty fleshly vessel to a quiet place within the ship. Those passengers who were awake were praising God in silent whispers.

***

Early in the morning, the comms equipment in the encampment was flashing lights of various colors, white on wrist computers, blue for satellite phones, red on two of the interstellar devices. Andy was the first up; he always wore his earbud at night, attached to the interstellar phone. Dan had the same practice, a carryover from being head navigator.

The message said the invasion of Rau-toon had begun. All Thermadorians were to report to their base camps. Starship commanders on Thermador were to initiate an attached list of individual vessel assignments immediately.

Andy saw Dan looking at him from across the encampment. Andy waved him over. The blinking lights had gone unseen by the majority of the crew. Only John, Woden, Ling, and Tom seemed to have awakened.

Dan quietly approached Andy and whispered, "I have already accessed our code and found our assignment."

Andy spoke. "It is?"

"To proceed to a small planet—T-24—within half a day of our present location," Dan said. "We will be joined by Ava Rodriguez, with further instructions. In addition, we have been explicitly ordered to drop Abe and Don off at this planet. They are not to accompany us in the future."

Andy nodded slowly.

"I wondered when we'd get Ava back," Dan said, "and I wonder why we are losing our Thermadorians."

Andy saw Dan's eyes leaping into future scenarios and said, "Don't guess. I have enough real info to worry about."

Dan smiled at Andy's calm acceptance of the burdens of leadership. Truly, he was the perfect captain.

CHAPTER 15

Ava watched the skies from the airport observation platform, a bolted metal frame with a metal-lattice flooring and a slanted roof of corrugated metal. The Explorer wasn't due for another fifteen minutes, but she chose to be outside, where there was sun, wind, people moving, and great space vessels coming and going, their engines thrusting on lift-off and reversing, pulling back on landing. Her mind was clear and untroubled for the first time in her life. She had grown up in a world of suspicion, of plots, schemes, actors, and dissimulators. That was pilgrim society. The goal in their world was happiness, which, simply spoken, was what you wanted from life. And you defined what that meant for you. She had quietly, within her own mind, given her life to Christ. She would listen for His voice and she would obey. It was simple. She had not interpreted the meeting with her dad as a bribe to switch sides. She knew that God knew she had no wealth of spy information to give. He knew all. He did not need her. In a sense, she did not need Him. But she wanted Him; she had found a being of pure kindness and goodness.

She had been introduced to this Christian civilization of simplicity—not of technology or processes, but within the thinking mind, the being in and of life, of aliveness. She guessed those words defined it best. Life was not a great deception, a trap that one had to decipher to live. She simply had to love her daddy, God; and her brothers and sisters who loved their daddy, God. She laughed at how stupid and moronic it sounded—and would sound to her past culture. What horror and disgust it might arouse. The fact that she was anticipating with happiness seeing her teammates was a revelation that defined her newly found life. She had never heard them utter a negative word about anyone. They loved, and so she could love. No defenses were needed to protect her worth, her standing in the group; there was no need to hide weaknesses or exult in her good traits and accomplishments. Her friends had given their lives to this idea of God—that a loving relationship was the key—and it was satisfying to be around them, to be a part of their lives. Everything they produced, even their civilization, was good.

Look what their God had done for her. He had treated her as one of His own, even as she had plotted against Him and His people. He had given her a reprieve from death by His largess, His love. He was breaking His own rules to do so. He had taken the supplications of her father, a man of no standing in life, and acted upon them. God had found a father, a run-of-the-mill, ordinary, common man, who loved his child extraordinarily. There it was: love and grit, a resolution to love! God cared about Ava's Earth daddy. He listened to the ordinary man's prayers, heard his anguish, hurt, and took action. God cared about her. Daddy God had sent His own son to suffer on a cross of shame and pain. It was all about love, and she understood.

She looked up into the sky at a slowing space vessel, Explorer 7. Already! She checked her watch—right on time—as the Explorer 7 slowly set itself on the paved disembarking area. She watched the entire crew come down the steps, move into the crowd that had gathered, then coalesce around the towering, hulking forms of Abe and Don. Strange that just a day ago, she thought of them all as the enemy, and yet at that time she could not think of one person in the group she did not have the warmest personal relationship with. She had done great harm to Abe and Don and their people. She had helped spread the lies of Thermadorian inferiority, of their not having souls, not having intellect. They would hate her if they knew. She watched the two Thermadorians through high-powered field binoculars. She had reread their files, their histories, the updates since she left—the murder, the reviving, the incident with her former people, Froman and his scientists. Both Abe and Don had left the pagan life for Christ. There had been reports that Thermadorian warriors seemed different after the mass suicide event, as did the entirety of the population, even the unsaved. She had gleaned from their files that her death of gore and finality had touched their beliefs and that Abe had been particularly hesitant to believe she would return.

She wondered why their God had sent her back to her old position—a highly sensitive position, one that could cause great harm if she'd persisted as the old Ava. He knew all along she would invite Him into her life; that was the answer. He knew she could never turn on the God who had set her free.

She had begun to believe the official reports about the Thermadorians before she had given her own life to the Lord, though nothing had been proven scientifically, by numbers—charts, tests, interviews. Many proclaimed they had given their allegiance to Christ and were living by the Spirit. They were not carrying themselves the same; there was a seriousness in the walk, a lessening of their nervous bobbing and genuflecting. Their heads seemed different in movement, less precise, less quick. She knew from her spy-training readings and studying histories of personal Christian experiences through the historical age that transferring allegiance from self and the world to Christ and entering God's Kingdom had a very personal and deep effect. The convert experienced a death of his old body, self, and interests, and then a new nature, a new spirit arose within. Below, every crew member either hugged, shook hands, or spoke to the two Thermadorian team members. Then Abe and Don were gone, walking to a waiting transport to be united with their families.

She had liked Abe and Don; cognizant forms like those two had made it difficult to support her people's practices of domination and manipulation. She remembered thinking, Why couldn't life-forms respect each other, treat each other the way they would like to be treated? There it was again, rising in her consciousness: the teachings of their—her—holy book, uttered by their—her—fully God, fully human figure, Jesus. Yes, God, through the Holy Spirit, had been preparing her for her conversion.

She knew that the "old" Ava, by hiding herself from the two, could weaken Don and Abe's belief in God's resurrection power. If she were not seen, they would always wonder if He had raised her. That would be a lie, and it would be against a God who had allowed her to walk away free, without condemnation or punishment for being "the enemy." A God who had waived the rules for her, healed her from catastrophic injuries without the prerequisite "I will follow you. I am yours" statement. He did it for her daddy soon to die. Her daddy had beckoned her to Jesus. The thought of His goodness overwhelmed her; she knew she would not have done the same for one of her enemies.

Ava knew she could not allow Abe and Don to walk away to their destinies without seeing her. What kind of woman would she be if she returned hate for the goodness given to her by God? She knew she had to hug them, welcome them to the family of their God. To do anything else would be morally dishonest, for God had given her life. Spiritually and emotionally, she had to greet them. They had seen her leave life as blood and mangled tissue, more goo than anything. She had to show them, prove to them, what their God had done and could do again. She bolted for the steps, mapping the chase that she must take through the buildings and walkways.

"Abe! Don!" she called. Then she understood that the weakness of her voice could not catch them. Deep within, in the desire of her mind, she called their names, saying, "Turn! Look! See me!" She burst out of the doors of one building, looking far ahead to the next building, when she saw them right before her eyes, two hulking forms standing silently, waiting for her.

She leaped upward into Don's chest. His arms caught her, and she gushed her words. "See! I'm whole, alive! Your gooey mess is alive. God is good, Don. He can do anything." She turned to Abe. "See, Abe?"

His outstretched arm and hand touched her luxuriant dark hair. Her flowery scent covered him. Ava hugged him with the strength of a Thermadorian. Truly, Ava was back from death. He remembered his bitter heart that could not believe such a thing were possible. He had been a fool, unable to believe the humans who fought for his people, thinking they could lie such a huge lie to his face. He had bet against God; had said he would only believe when he saw Ava alive. Now, he saw Ava alive. Now, he couldn't argue within his mind that God did not live and love His people. God loved him, Abe, one unimportant creature among millions of mantis creatures. Truly, Jesus was the son of the forever God, the all-powerful God, and Abe surrendered his heart, soul, mind, and strength completely to forever God.

"I don't have much time." She was shaking Abe's hand. "We're brother and sister now. Grow in Our Lord, you two; teach your wives and children of His goodness. Promise me!"

They both said, "Promise."

She laughed and turned to leave. Abe's long arm reached out and held her arm. "Thanch you," he said as he released her.

She smiled wistfully; the *ch* had always given him problems, even where it wasn't in play. "My pleasure, good mantis."

Ava walked down into the terminal to a hangar. The joy she just had experienced overwhelmed her and in a small way was admission and vindication of her prejudice against the mantid creatures-cognizant beings-people! She moved behind the hangar. She sat in a corner, under a stairway, and cried. She couldn't lie, she couldn't be hateful, she couldn't have denied hope to two good souls just needing a break. Why had she been so hateful in the past? God, it felt so good to do good, to *be* good. She had been trained to see her culture, her people, as truth. Now, only God was truth. Now she was officially an outcast, an enemy of her people's goals. What would the Christians do to her when they found out about her duplicitous past? Could they forgive her?

Why did God love her? Why did He care for her? Why? Why? Why? She cried until she realized she just had to accept His love, even though she could not comprehend it. She submitted to His will. She spoke to Him. "I don't know why You wanted me. You're a crazy God. I give you all that I am, and I know that is not much." She wiped away her tears, blew her nose three times, and left the corner under the stairs. She walked outside to a tent, in which a podium stood before three rows of bleachers. She stood behind the podium, preparing her notes, still smiling from her meeting with Abe and Don, when she realized that tears were still upon her cheeks. The scientific mind had cried. Well, she couldn't think of a better reason for those tears. She quickly wiped her face clean. She had work to do.

Into the tent came the Explorer 7 crew, led by Andy. They were utterly surprised to see Ava, her long dark hair, her form as perfect as it had been before the catastrophic-seeming annihilation. She was beaming beyond the radiance of the immortal; it seemed her glistening white teeth had run out of face. All rushed to her, and everyone had to touch the woman they had left as vapor, stains, and chewed pieces of flesh, dashed against dirt and rock walls. The praise was for God, who could do such a thing and who wanted with all His being to do so. He loved them. He loved her, her tears, her joy at seeing them. Her complete love for her God was so strong that she had to be held up by the crew, who passed her on to others like a rag doll. All knew by the intensity of emotion that Ava had not been but was truly now with her brothers and sisters. Death had no sting.

Ling marveled, for he had studied the human body more closely than the others and knew the intricacies, knew the chemical compositions, the nervous system, the miracle of the brain that even in his day had yet to be fully understood. "What a God! What a God…" He continued to mumble under his breath. He laughed to himself in the end, for if God put man together once, why would man marvel when God did it again?

In time, Ava recovered and greeted, calmed, and seated her friends. They looked upon her tear-stained face and knew that their faces glistened too, every man's and woman's. They sensed a newness about her, not just of body but of her spirit. She spoke. "Thank you for your love. As you see, our God has no limitations. I felt no pain during the entire process. I awoke in a hospital room on Earth, remembering nothing. I was told later that my soul had been stored in the vaults of Heaven, awaiting my body. The body, on Earth, was back together within weeks—not with miracles as such, like a ball of spiritual white light wrapping around the pieces, but by men and women who have been taught the science of regeneration. The Lord is our teacher. He can now trust us with everything." She looked down at her notes and flicked the first page of information upon the canopied screen. She looked at her people. "Now, I was to brief you and I will, but first I must make a deep confession.

"I was never one of you. I am a pilgrim, sent undercover to destroy you and your political and spiritual influences. But our Lord has won. I hope in the weeks to come, you will learn to trust me, forgive me—"

Mat stood up, and his deep voice rolled across the concrete. "Hush, girl! We have aways loved you…we have already forgiven you…we've all taken the plunge, bathed in His mercy. We have all cried till we could cry no more, wondering at His love."

Jack stood up and spoke. "What Mat's trying to say is, 'Carry on, Ava.' Give us the briefing, then we can adjourn to the crew lounge and have a welcome-home party." The crew stood and cheered.

Ava shook her head in disbelief: such no-nonsense people! Or was it that they trusted God so completely that they truly understood "there is a time for everything, and a season for every activity under heaven." The wisdom of Solomon. The cheering waned; her crewmates sat.

She spoke. "Thank you." A deep breath, a new beginning. "To the business at hand. We must conquer the Rau-toon of the Predator Nation Empire. To do this, we must know our enemy at a basic level and all the way up through their higher musings, thoughts, goals. To facilitate this, we have, in a prison, recreated a Predator Nation town or factory—the terms are interchangeable. They seem perfectly happy to live there, as all their basic needs are met. To you, they will seem arrogant, confident, happy. And they are. There is no one plotting to break out, as far as we can tell. The common Pins have no aspirational goals concerning societal or national interests, only personal goals of pleasure. We will talk more about this. Right now, I want to take you into their world, literally. We will be protected by force fields. We will hear their language in real time translated into English. We will observe them at rest, eating, fighting, arguing, even copulating—privacy isn't important to them; they like the attention.

"They are different than what we are now, but not too different from what Earth's people were like while living in and through the flesh and the carnal spirit. Remember, they have no concept of 'love God with all your heart and soul' or 'love thy neighbor as thyself.'" She moved away from the podium. "Let the tour begin."

***

The class saw themselves on the screen—projections of their faces and body types fitted into electric-shock overalls and helmets with face guards. A column of twos was formed. The class entered the forbidding prison gate, set within overlooking towers manned by armed mechanical sniper rifles.

They immediately drew the attention of a group of Pins policing the grounds in a long line that stretched across the width of athletic fields. Ava turned to her class. "Notice they are staring at us with a purpose. They know what fear looks like, the subtle nuances in movement and even standing posture. They also have studied the human body and know what a healthy walk and posture are. If you have a limp, or favor one arm over another, or barely move your head, they are interested in your weakness and hope to exploit it. To be dominant over another is to have access to that other for sex, degradation, and any material possession they have."

The Pins were calling, and the language program translated. "Look at the flat chest on that one. What does baby suckle? At least two transgenders there. Look at the slant-eyed one. Some are wearing body paint." All of the Pins were laughing.

The entire class of Explorer 7 was laughing as well. Not one of God's people was self-conscious. They were beautiful in the Creator's eyes; they could do all things through the Creator's power. They were so esteemed that He had sent his only Son to save them from Hell. The Son, who had no sin, hurt beyond hurt to bring them to the Father. The Pins were momentarily shocked at their enemy's laughter. The Pins' body movements tightened, their faces scowled, and aggressive hands signs were thrust in the direction of the tour group.

Woden asked Ava, "How would they respond if we taunted them?"

Ava turned and faced her class. She spoke loudly. "Do not taunt them, and cease laughing without appearing humble or cowered as you do so, or a barrage of feces will be coming your way." By her crewmates' expressions, she knew they had understood.

"Your laughter was good to a point. In their culture, not to respond to provocation is to admit weakness. But too much response, and you will have entered their world, and they will pull you ever deeper."

"We can't win at their game," stated Woden, "without losing what makes us godly."

Ava answered, "You have to split the difference between your affirmation of self-worth and provocation, which quickly leads to aggression. They love flattery. If you must use force, be extremely decisive, with no qualms or quibbles. They are almost indestructible, as you know, so don't worry about damage to them. If you kill one, so be it." She thought before continuing. "I know that sounds callous, but your life is more important, more worthy than theirs are."

The class turned in a wide arc, anticipating the corner of a building ahead. They wished to avoid a hiding enemy behind the corner. A line of Pins was waiting for a turn with a rape victim, on all fours, who was howling.

"I think I've seen enough," said Emily.

"I, as well," said Dan.

A force field descended on the participants of the rape and paralyzed their bodies as they slumped to the ground in a semiconscious state.

"This is your enemy," said Ava. "They do have peace in their drug rooms; eventually, they all pass out. The only reason they work in the shops is that they earn meal tickets; otherwise they don't eat." Ava paused and studied the faces of her students, then spoke. "We will access from another vantage."

Ava saw herself on the security screen, her class behind, making her way up an outdoor staircase and entering the top floor of the building. A staircase into the room below had been removed for security reasons. The room was a part of a hangar. It was draped with wall curtains, and three-tiered bleachers and individual chairs filled the rectangular space. A camera hung down from the ceiling of metal rafters and roof. A tube beside the camera and extending upward to a tank, shot a heavy mist down into the draped room. The large room on screen was relatively quiet, smokey. The licorice scent from the mantis bodies seemed a vapor in the air. All the mantis were in some state of euphoria, which released the licorice hormones in greater quantities. Their long forms seemed draped over chairs, the floor, each other. One mantis had his arm raised, and his claw finger rose above the fisted hand. John commented, "One swipe from that claw can cut flesh to the bone." The sound of hissing from hundreds of mouths and noses filled the room. Occasionally, the red eyes would open, seeing nothing, lost in a state of euphoria. "Okay, I've smelled enough," said Diana.

Ava looked over her students, who seemed stuporous and uninterested. Ava spoke. "Back to the classroom."

***

The class sat on their bleacher seats in a hangar outside the prison walls. They'd had little physical exertion that day, and many of them wondered at their tiredness.

"You feel that draining, that tiredness?" Ava looked at their faces. "It is real and has quantitative measurements attached. Fear and vulnerability can be unleashed in mantis prey by the mantis body—the licorice smell. They have a charismatic power that drains energy from others. Your helplessness feeds their desire to consume you. They have eaten humans! It is real! And they are overpowering when in groups numbering ten or more. Keep them dispersed and dodging laser blasts, and their power is almost nonexistent. Don't ever allow any number to sit before you and brood."

The drooping class was now straight-backed on their seats. John spoke. "My security crew experienced the Thermadorians' mood effect when we flew into an evolving massacre scenario. Violence was palpable in the air and was caught on our meters. Crew, raise your hands." The members raised their hands, thus verifying John's words. John continued, "A question I believe we all have: How has this nation of misfits become a force to be reckoned with in this part of space? They have no qualities of teamwork, strategy, or selfless giving. No sense of duty. Really, no goals, no patriotism. They seem to have a national identity of superiority…but that's it."

Ava smiled; the smile drifted over the class. "John is correct, and the puzzle is real. How do we account for the vigor of the Rau-toon—mantis—yet motivated? Hands of those who wondered at this very same issue." All hands went up. "Simply put, the mantis species is enlivened by the hunt. The hunt is triggered by weakness, mental and/or physical, in other life forms; and this stimulates a part of their mind, produces chemicals, vitamins, hormones, mental thoughts, and physical actions. They become focused, energetic, purposeful. It is played out like a script. There is an elite class on Rau-toon, of humans, as you know, taken from Earth before the time of Noah. They are of greater evil intellectual ability and greater vision of the future. They know how to use the mantis predator/prey personality.

"Back to Explorer 7 and a new destination on Rau-toon, which I will share in flight, for security reasons."

The crew rose as one and gathered by their Ava.

CHAPTER 16

Tom had just taken command of the ship, stood upon the foredeck, looking through the wide forward window at the array of stars, moons, planets cast before him. Tuck sat in the helmsman's seat, and directly behind and a head above Tuck was Robin in the navigator's seat. Andy had been in command for the last twelve hours and had exited the command and control room, headed for the galley.

Tom's thoughts randomly focused on Ava. The party held for Ava's return had ended with a baptism. She had shared her life as a pilgrim, including her life with her father, and her life as an operative. She had never gotten the chance to hurt the Christian cause. She had only two marks against her, the data surge on the language and history of Rau-toon, which had been sent during the beginning of hostilities, and the spreading of wild rumors about the history of the Thermadorians. The surge had not been detected by the Pins, and the rumors had soon been proven false. In fact, her espionage training in Christianity had been so thorough—her actions and thought patterns had become so Christlike—that she hadn't noticed the conversion from the darkness of pilgrim culture into the light of Christ till that day she had embraced her pilgrim father.

Ava had never announced their destination; she just promised them they would soon know. Security concerns were a logical assumption at the time, thought Tom. But what were they waiting for now? This waiting seemed odd. The Explorer had been secure, its radar signature wiped clean; it was literally invisible. Tom had been in Andy's presence when Ava had presented her authority documents, requesting permission to come onboard. Andy had accepted the documents as legitimate. As Tom was thinking these thoughts, Ava came into the room.

A wariness came to Tom. Nothing in God's world was random. Why would he be forewarned that Ava would appear? Was he being paranoid? Was it just chance that he was thinking of Ava, and she appeared? "Permission to approach," said Ava in a formal tone that was proper to custom.

"Approach," said Tom. She approached him; he was aware of a perfume, feminine and woodsy as opposed to flowery; a pine and sandal-wood scent. Had she always been a user of scents? She presented a document and spoke. "New coordinates, which have already been entered in the directional navigating system." Tom looked at Robin nervously; this was all out of protocol.

Robin, who had been listening, said, "New directional coordinates have been entered into the system…without my input?" Robin's voice had raised with the last word in puzzlement and panic. Only the captains had the authority to enter new coordinates.

Ava spoke in a cool tone of complete confidence. "And within a minute, countdown will be acknowledged by the ship's directional control." Robin's facial expression held confusion and fear.

"Abort! Abort! Helmsman, full stop!" Tom yelled at Tuck.

Tuck yelled back, "Control taken away from me! The system won't allow!"

Tom commanded, "Contact first captain." Tom had left his laser pistol in the execs' room, located beside the deck. It should have been strapped on his belt. His dagger was pulled as he lunged toward Ava, who had already pulled a pocket pistol of cartridge vintage and was aiming at Tom. A hidden laser weapon would have been picked up by the security system.

She commanded, "Cease resistance." He noticed her composure was without fear or alarm.

Tom suddenly realized the deed had been done, and killing Ava, even if that were possible, would not change the coordinates locked into the system.

Tom spoke. "Tuck, call your dad or physically retrieve him. Robin, sound the alert throughout the ship. Then, see if emergency channels are open to Earth, which I doubt." The emergency alarm sounded through the ship.

Ava pointed her pistol at the rising Tuck. She spoke slyly, "No, no, no… stay seated." He complied. Still, there was hope, thought Tom, as angels were always nearby, and likely even now the message was going up the angelic chain of command.

Ava saw the hope in Tom's eyes. Only one source for that: angels. She studied Tuck and Tom; they had loyalty to their ship and pursed lips for her. She spoke. "Even the angels are unaware and will remain so for quite some time. This is only a security check but keep the alarm going a few more minutes. Andy will verify once he is here." She knew that if a crewmate were a spy, that person would be reporting the emergency signal to his or her handlers right now.

She saw anger on Tom's face—highly appropriate. He began to speak. "Lady—"

Just then Andy walked into the command and control center. Andy noticed that Tom stood by the seated Robin and Tuck; they appeared agitated. Ava knew that Andy had already discovered that any access to navigation equipment or engines had been blocked through the computers and manually by electroshock systems. He had culpability in the crew's failure to discover the tampering and for his crew missing the devices on their preflight inspections. They had lost their sharpness and disrespected the cunning of their adversaries. Or, trusting in angelic backup, had they become lax?

Andy saw Ava on the foredeck, waved his hand, and in a friendly voice of command strength, spoke. "Ava, may I approach?"

"Approach." Her voice held an admiration for his relaxed tone and posture.

He spoke as he approached her. "My guess is you are of the lineage of Satan's earthlings taken after the fall. You never were a Tribulation saint. You were not of the Millennial period on Earth. You showed up in New Jerusalem with your fellow foreigner, your husband," he said, sneering.

"So?" she answered defiantly. That was the truth she had revealed to them all, yet the mention of it hurt. She wished to chuckle but she could not.

"So, you do not have eternal life. Christ doesn't live within you. You are bound for Hell," he said. He watched her face carefully, watched a change in the eyes, the set of the mouth, a change in the brow, the cant of her head. A messenger angel had told him three hours ago to watch her carefully. He suddenly realized that she was as much a part of the test as anyone. The angel had wanted him to recognize her innocence, not her duplicity.

"Enough." She mockingly raised her hands and waved them as if erasing all he had said. She had played the crew to perfection, and then had been played herself, thinking Andy had been played as well. In this invented scenario, she had been tested too, for her loyalty. Andy's head tilted; he realized the prearranged dialogue, given to him by angels, had hurt her deeply. The angelic messenger had not told him that his ship would momentarily be taken from him. He understood the lesson being taught: Trust no one, not even angels; only trust the rational path to what was truth. No assuming.

"What's going on here?" an insulted and shocked Tom queried.

Andy spoke. "This was all preplanned. A ruse to free Explorer 7 for a special assignment. On Thermador, we presented our training film outside to make spying easier. We gave the impression we were headed to Rau-toon to fight the Predator Nation. Even now, visible on the tracking screen, anyone viewing us will see on their instrumentation panels that we are headed to Rau-toon."

Ava spoke. "But we are not. And to assure ourselves that no listening devices were installed, no data theft was occurring, we had to stage this little row." She looked at her wrist computer. "And no such security breach has happened. We are 100 percent the good guys."

Andy smiled as he faced Ava. He saluted in respect for her and to remind her of protocol.

Ava straightened her posture, placed her feet together, and returned the salute. She spoke to Andy. "Permission to leave the bridge."

He answered, "Permission granted."

She lowered her salute.

They were no longer the center of attention. He whispered to her, "I apologize. Anytime you wish to talk privately."

She answered, "Thank you, sir. Perhaps in time, I will."

Tom thought back to Andy's "feminine wiles" comment. Had he known then of this coming test and sowed doubt that would add authenticity to this moment? That seemed a stretch. He would not ask Andy. Tom would think it through; he had always thought things through, that was his nature.

***

Their destination, the unnamed and unexplored planet below, was less than Earth's size. The planet would only be known as PA 1. The gravitational pull was stronger than upon Earth, but the sun, the predominant feature of Quadrant B, had a counter pull that matched almost perfectly, so that the Explorer 7 was in a very slow and secure orbit. The Explorer had disguised itself with panels that created the illusion of a rough-surfaced asteroid of solidity. A minimum of energy was being used to keep navigation and air-quality systems operating.

The planet was the home of a sizable colony of pilgrims. As the planet did not rotate, the side exposed to the sun was baked desert. On the fringes of the sphere, the rays were less intense, and many were deflected by the curvature. Here, life was sustainable. The dark side of the planet had been interlaced with reflective panels mounted upon high towers of interlocking girders and trestles. The panels moved with the sun's rays, casting the sunlight onto the cold ground, and so forming a circular pattern of human and plant life. Water was present, welling up internally from the depths of the planet, until it met the freeze line in the soil. Solar panels reflected heat, warmed the soil and water. Condensation was a secondary water source, due to the sun's heat on one side and the planet's natural coolness on the other.

This pilgrim colony was the home planet of those who had a stealthy but steely hold on the Predator Nation Empire. The colony was two thousand years old and had, from its founding, been manipulating Rau-toon. Other pilgrim colonies had been seeded throughout the galaxies, and only the God of creation knew how many. Satan, who had created the seedings, was locked in eternal Hell forever, where his power had been so degraded that if it were possible he could be freed, he would be speechless and without will, a powerless entity, incapable of action. The knowledgeable people of Earth believed he had been the only Satan. It was believed that while he held power, he had taught his pilgrims and their children to continue in their bondage to his being and his ideals. Now, in eternal Hell, without power, his people had defaulted to their carnal nature. The founding father had been discarded.

The Pilgrim Alliance still had a system that worked. They were in charge, and they reaped the benefits of their manipulations of less technologically advanced beings. They would be dealt with separately from the Predator Nation Empire. Once all pertinent information had been gathered on their culture, politics, and manipulations, a case for Christ would be presented. Those who accepted Him would be brought into the fold. Those who rejected Him would lose their military power and see their clandestine operations destroyed. They would be arrested, imprisoned, perhaps executed for any new actions occurring as part of their affiliation with their past political allies and enterprises. It was thought that once the pilgrims learned and had proof of eternal life and saw the good lives of Christ's people, they would all wish to convert. The Christian people's dreams were tempered, however, by their remembrance of Earth history and of all the fathers, mothers, brothers, sisters, and friends who weren't beside them now, enjoying eternal life. More had been left behind than came along.

Being in oneself, being a god, had great advantages, pleasures, and the pilgrim culture had rules for such a life. Eternal life? On their own, through science, they could achieve eight hundred years of life for individuals. Eternal life wouldn't be worth the cost—being under someone else's control, not having your way in sexual tastes or rules, not being able to con, cheat, and lie your way to riches. The present worked fine. Why change?

There would be people who would change the outer self and pretend to be of Christ, while inwardly following the rules of life embedded in their flesh. This dilemma Earth had known till Christ came for His people: carnal-minded people wanting Christ for worldly reasons—health, careers, status, high standards of living, wealth, eternal life. These people lived in their own tainted, sin-infested bodies and minds, never giving up their spirit of lust for His Spirit of righteousness. Spirit-led people had only wanted Him—His leadership, His companionship, His understanding and help as they did His work. That had been their focus. Christ's people wondered how that problem of sorting goats from sheep would be resolved.

Like on Earth, would God assign a time when the harvest of Christian souls had reached a zenith and the fields of weeds should burn. Would cognizant life-forms, at each individual death, be immediately separated to Hades or Paradise to await their world's end? Would God simply read the inner motivations of the new converts' hearts and decide their fates immediately at death? Or would He give them the status of trainees, withholding good until they had proven themselves through the inner workings of their minds. Would it not then be works? How could you *earn* salvation and call it salvation? How long would the undecided have to make their decision?

This was the reality of why God had allowed evil to exist on Earth; and why life continued generation after generation, seemingly within endless time; and why humankind had walked by faith. For free will to exist, at least two choices had to be present. Humankind had been given a lifetime to choose, by their free will, the kingdom of Satan or the Kingdom of God, upon a planet that had an expiration date, forgotten even by believers, a judgment date known only by God. That is why humans had cursed and adored their God and either had become bitter at His missing hand of justice and fair play and gifts; or had become gentle and kind and humble at the unworthiness of any scrap of God's favor or presence in their lives. Holy God had wanted a relationship with His created beings as deep as that of a father with his children. He wanted the relationship to be more valuable than the material gifts He could bestow. He had wanted a relationship of family, togetherness, shared experience and purpose—of love. True and eternal love.

***

The strategy to win the pilgrims was called Plan 96. Four days to win the hearts of the people. The entire crew had been given written copies of the twenty-page list of objectives and reasons and desired outcomes. The crew had been given six hours to read and, if they wished, to discuss it with others. Then they would meet, with Andy and Tom as debate hosts. It was unknown how much of the plan was inviolate and what was open to changes.

The physical setting was the planet, with focus on the two main population centers on the dark side of the planet, both beneath the ground and joined by one long tunnel. The northern population center held captured Thermadorians and Rau-toon, each in their own prison camps. Between were laboratories, cells, surgical centers, and propaganda centers, where the native populations were induced or coerced to follow the plans of the pilgrims. The pilgrims were scientists, guards, and administrators in the north.

The southern population center was largely the agricultural and livestock center for food production or production of any needed product for the pilgrims of the planet. The mantis peoples' agricultural production had always been used in trade with other mantis people and was not consumed by the pilgrims.

It was hoped the southern town would have pilgrims of less loyalty and fierceness—less dogmatic people, who could be presented with the Word of God. The first twenty-four hours would see a blitz of written tracts, pamphlets, messages on audio equipment, and visual means of communication. An invitation would be extended to a mass meeting in the town's major auditorium. If all went well, a message from Christ, via hologram, would be presented. Electronics of great sophistication could detect the audience's reactions, through gathered sounds, good and bad exclamations; by body movements, postures, facial expressions; even from heat signatures. The corridor to the southern town would be blocked during this event.

While this meeting was taking place, Christian forces would enter the northern town and surveil the activities directed against the imprisoned population. It was thought that experiments in mind control were creating undercover operatives who would wreak havoc on Rau-toon. Once this surveillance was completed, Explorer 7's operatives would remove the barriers between the two towns and surveil the flow of information.

CHAPTER 17

Andy sat in his small room, both a living space and office, with desk and chairs. His feet were elevated, moccasins on, as well as a soft, thick sweater. He had been reviewing within his mind the plans for the future. Ava came into his mind. Ava had never requested a meeting. He thought she was ashamed of her role as an operative for her people, and that was understandable. Another element was apparent but subtle; she had been hurt emotionally by the belief that the sabotage ploy aboard the Explorer 7 was partially to assess her loyalty. But the possibility that she was a double agent and still loyal to the pilgrim world might be real to high-ranking people. But who was higher than the Lord, who knew her heart? Why had He not cleared her pathway to assimilation?

She was slated to be in the first delegation of Christians to meet with the pilgrims. The obvious problem: What if they recognized her or she, them? He could take her off the list—a simple solution. She could watch the recording of the meeting and comment, which could allow her, if she wished, to lie without consequences. She could lie about knowing Mr. X or Miss Y Pilgrim. But by withholding her presence, she could hide who she truly was in pilgrim society. She could be a top commander, or royalty, or have the reputation as a knave or scoundrel. He didn't believe any of those scenarios; and he could be, at this moment, duped—completely fooled—by her persona. He knew she knew the possibilities he had just thought, or she would think of them soon.

Then, again, she could admit to the pilgrims that she was a pilgrim who had met Christ and given her life to Him. Would she ever be more than a traitor to her pilgrim people, to be shunned, hated, or perhaps played in schemes of intrigue?

She had just contacted him, no matter which Ava she truly was. He heard a knock at his door, and his intercom click on. "Ava, at the door, Commander." Her voice was soft and friendly.

He spoke happily for having known she would come and knowing there would soon be resolution. "Enter, Ava." He fully trusted his Lord that truth would be revealed, and whatever the outcome, he would have peace.

She came in; he sensed apprehensiveness. He spoke. "Have the free chair. Water, coffee, tea?"

"No thank you, sir." She heard her own voice sound like a child's compared with her captain's voice.

"Andy," he said, thinking that anyone was more likely to lie to a superior than to a friend.

"Yes, Andy." She smiled.

Andy spoke. "You have not changed since our first meeting in New Jerusalem. You and Enrique, placed by chance beside me, being presented with a new world before us." Andy was engrossed in thought. "For me, it was a new world. You and Enrique were already space travelers. I was given no insights into that, only that I mistakenly thought you had American Indian blood within you even before you mentioned Mexico. That was a good choice, Mexico. Was that spur-of-the-moment thinking based on my heritage? Or was it no accident you two were sitting next to me?"

"No, it was coincidental. We had decided on our deep-cover stories here, in space—quite deep and involved life stories, memorized forward and backward. Our Middle Eastern ancestry, we wished to keep far away and hidden, in case of future discoveries by your side. Plus, Mexico had a small harvest of redeemed from our chosen time period of life, and they were mostly poor, uneducated campesinos, who lived apart from society. The odds were low that someone would know who we truly were. Now, during our training in Florida, I purposely entered a class with you, hearing that you were showing promise and definitely would be a ship's captain."

"Someone tell you that? Who was that person? A part of your spy team?"

"No, throughout this experience, we, and then, I, alone, found that the redeemed could not be compromised and were so sentient and intuitive that we ran the risk of ruining our covers by reaching out, even for the smallest, most benign bit of information."

"Good to hear," he said with a forthrightness in his tone, as he thought, If it is true. He asked, "What about Enrique?"

"We returned to Mexico and waited, together, for the letters of acceptance or nonacceptance. I was accepted, and he was not. The next day, I arose, and

Enrique was gone. Haven't heard from him since. No one in the agency ever came to me with an explanation. That scares me."

"Why?"

"He was a pilgrim patriot and a man who wanted public laurels. I'm sure they reassigned him, probably changed his cover story completely. I don't want to accidentally bump into him."

"Where do you stand with Jesus at this time?" Andy decided to abruptly cut to the chase.

She stated, "I stand *because* of Jesus. I have my life through Him. Because of Jesus, my pilgrim father gave his life to Christ. My pilgrim father, redeemed, petitioned Christ for me. God allowed me to not taste death, though it was my time; He allowed me to meet my father and allowed me time to make my choice. He broke the rules for me. He loved my father and me before we knew Him. He loved me so much that He gave me a chance at life. From vapor, mist, and goo, I lived again, and now for eternity I live. Think of that love. And I get a second chance to know my pilgrim daddy—forever."

He saw her tears and knew they were real. He spoke. "We all share that born-again story, and I am so glad to hear of yours."

"He did it for *me*," she said appreciatively. "I'm nothing, never was; certainly no scholar of the faith. Even in my world, I was nothing."

"Why have you waited to tell me of this deeper you? Why haven't you confided in greater detail to others about your past?" he asked.

"That was my original plan, but I realized I didn't want to *tell* people about the past. Jesus is the present. I wanted to *show* people. I wanted to do good. Words are cheap; acts have consequences. In not telling, in hiding the past, I may do a greater good in helping to topple pilgrim ideology and end the violence we created with the Rau-toon and with the Thermadorians. What we did to them was pure evil."

He knew about her meeting with Don and Abe. He had seen the surveillance video, and Don and Abe had corroborated the event when contacted. He wondered why she had not told him of Don and Abe and the love she expressed to them. Why had she not mentioned the aspects of God's Kingdom and personality that she had revealed to them? She could have held that up to him as proof of her change of heart. Was that a calculated act? Or was it modesty, like praying in secret in one's closet? Wherever she truly was with Christ, the Holy Spirit and angels had a tight rein upon her and would not allow her to do evil, even to her death. Why couldn't Andy give in to what his heart told him: that Ava was the truest of Christ's followers, so full of love for His created beings and Love for Him?

He spoke. "What do we do with you now? Can you mingle with pilgrims and not be known? Or would they hide knowledge of who you are? Would they accept you as Ava from Christ's Kingdom? What would we gain from having you in public?"

"Pilgrim society is scattered across the vastness of space in isolated communities, exploiting whatever they find, rarely interconnecting. There are at least fifteen tribes. I admit the Rau-toon and Thermidorian scam had us gather like vultures on a kill. I was not a part of it. I'm unknown. I grew up on an isolated planet with my father, till he was forced to leave the family. My mother and sister are both dead now. We gathered a mineral of rarity from the planet's surface. There was only one other family, thousands of miles away, on the other side of the planet. I met them maybe twice. That was one of the reasons I was chosen for this assignment. I only had one trainer, and he used material from computers, holograms." She took a breath. "Besides, pilgrim culture is based on the scam and stealth. No one says, 'Don't I know you?' even if they do. Everyone assumes a scam is in progress, and if you're not part of it, you should keep silent, and maybe you can pick up a morsel. That is what pilgrims are."

Andy heard the disgust in her tone. He asked, "Space academy?"

"None with the pilgrims. My handler knew my strength was my background of isolation. He kept me pure. I saw no pilgrim operatives at the United States Space Academy—no pilgrims whatsoever."

"What of your handler?"

"I do not know. I only know his face, though I believe he wore a disguise. He did not give his name."

"Let's have you sit out this first meeting. You scan all the faces of pilgrims we have recorded, both dead and alive. Then, get a new hairstyle and dye your hair blond. We'll give you a facial/eye hypnosis treatment to fool the facial/eye scanner ID technology, and new fingerprints. Sound fair?"

"Yes," she said. "Thank you."

Andy spoke. "I agree with you that you should tell no one who you were. I will instruct the crew that you don't exist outside of Explorer 7. Think you can keep the secret?"

"Yes," she said.

Andy stood, offered her his hand. The Spirit prolonged the touch and melded their souls in united purpose. Ava had walked out the door when a realization came, and he understood the panic that had overcome him when Abe and Don received life. A nonearthly, intergalactic demon had projected the Macbeth witches into his mind that day. The demon had been sent to destroy his trust in Ava.

***

Andy, Ling, Tim, Dan and Emily, and Diana were carried by the shuttle to a location outside the southern town of PA 1. Just hours ago, a mass meeting of the population of the town had been held, though the presentations had been given by hologram. The audience had been attentive if not enthusiastic, especially when viewing planet Earth and the lives of the Christian inhabitants. A smaller meeting was scheduled between the leaders of PA 1 and Explorer 7 representatives. Discussion and debate would then decide a future course of action. The Explorer delegation transported, invisibly, to the classroom where they had been told to report. The invitation had appeared to be given with great honor and delight. The pilgrims of ancient Earth were excited to establish contact with their long-lost cousins and were curious about this new way of life their cousins espoused in the media barrage of the past days. To the Explorer 7 crew monitoring space communications, all talk seemed genuine and without guile. A sticking point in overheard remarks was the killing of Fromen's men—many believed compensation should be paid, while others said it had been war, and Fromen had chosen to die as a martyr.

The Explorer 7 delegates entered the classroom occupied by seven seated pilgrims, four men and three women. The Christians momentarily remained invisible, studying the pilgrims, who were shorter in height and thinner, yet with defined musculature. All hair was dark, from black to dark-brown, from wavy to curled; the skin was olive-toned to varying degrees. The three women, by posture and demeanor, seated between male counterparts, seemed independent, perhaps unmarried. The women wore long, one-piece dresses, black or dark-blue in color, fitting closely to the form, with pendants or necklaces upon the chest. The men wore long jackets, extending below the belt to midthigh. Below the belt, the jacket was slit, and the segmented fabric covered thigh and groin. High collars seemed to frame their personalities in attentiveness. Trousers were baggy and of the same loose volume as the jackets. Black was the color of the fabric and medallions of merit upon both sides of the chest. Black shoes were likely ankle-high for the men; the women wore black sandals.

The Explorer 7 contingent appeared before the guests. "Greetings," said Andy, attempting to create the right tone of volume and friendliness, a timbre of depth and strength of resolve, while remaining polite, yet formal. The seated pilgrims had arisen. They had knowledge of clapping as a form of welcome and approval and were engaged heartedly, thinking this was a custom they would like to appropriate. The Explorer 7 crew bowed graciously. All wore dress uniforms, jackets and pants of blue, scarves of gold. The "Christ's Kingdom" emblem, a patch, was sewn upon their right chest.

Depicted was a globe of the Earth and myriad stars, extending from Christ's opened arms. Angels in white clustered behind Christ's shoulders. The Holy Spirit moved as a wind around all, culminating in celestial fire as an aura around Christ's head. All depicted were cradled within the hand of God. On the upper arms was the flag of the United States, the nation that had led the way to Christ and funded space exploration.

All present knew they were making history, and wall and table cams were recording. "Speak more," said Sarah, a pilgrim woman—the computer screen at the table before her translated. Sarah appeared to be in her forties; and by Earth standards, she had great beauty. The Explorer 7 crew agreed, in quiet consent, that she resembled Tim's former wife and partner, Mary—the clear-blue, sparkling eyes and unblemished skin; the firm jaw and the understated fullness of the lower lip; the black lashes and eyebrows, made darker against the skin; and the thick, black mane of hair hiding her delicate ears. Sarah had the lightest shade of Mediterranean skin, whereas Mary had ivory skin of the whitest hue. Sarah had been captivated by the foreign language— so clean and uncomplicated.

"Yes, of course," said Andy. My name is Captain Andrew Springs, a native of the central eastern area of North America. The State of Pennsylvania, to be precise. I, we, represent Christ's Kingdom."

Diana had engaged a hologram that showed the globe of Earth and Andy's place of birth upon it. As members of the delegation spoke their names and described their locations, their birthplaces were added to the hologram globe. Andy continued the narrative. "And we assume the Middle East was your place of origin." The globe location appeared. All the standing ancients applauded and gave words of approbation, their words appearing on their computer screens.

"Sit, please," said the male host, standing next to Sarah, the woman of beauty. He spoke the sentence in English with his own voice. The Explorer crew sat.

He was the tallest of the seven, the only bearded one among the male pilgrims. He spoke. "My name is Kenan, and my position would be comparable to your secretary of state. We represent the Pilgrim Alliance. Seated before you are Sarah, Jemima, and Keturah. Followed by Jared, Enoch, and Noah." The computer screens of the introduced, facing the guests, presented their names written in English. The Hebraic names perfectly matching their alleged history was the first thought to enter the minds of the Explorer 7's crew. That no other names were represented suggested there had been no contact, or rather no friendly contact, with any other civilizations. Diana thought it would be rude to ask for their surnames, and this politeness seemed to be in agreement with her crewmates. The members stood as their names appeared. "All of the panel hold positions in our nation of the highest level," Kenan said. The host committee sat.

The Explorer 7 crew had their computer screens up. The lady of beauty's title was secretary of resources. Sarah spoke. "Your skin tones and hair are of many shades. Perhaps, in time, we will take from you and you, from us in marriage."

"Perhaps," said Andy. "All things are possible through Christ, if it is of His will." He saw a smile form on Sarah's face, just for a second, and then fade.

Sarah knew that this Andrew Springs had conveniently not mentioned their current abstention from procreation. Yet, he had not told a lie.

Kenan, not keen on the topic of religion, realized the foreign leader had just introduced the topic. He spoke. "The decanters and glasses are for you, if you wish—a weak alcohol in one and water in the other." These words were spoken in his own language and appeared onscreen as a translation.

Ling, as crew doctor, had been designated to address food concerns. Ling spoke. "We will drink our own water. We do not know if our digestive tracts have the same bacterial qualities. Do not take offense."

Graciousness of tone came from Kenan, who said, "Yes, of course. Fascinating. All so fascinating. The possibilities are endless. And our histories are so different." Then, Kenan faced the topic he disliked. "Please tell us about your god and what you hope to accomplish here, in this first meeting of our two cultures."

Tim spoke. "This subject is my portion of the presentation. We represent the living God, the only God of the galaxies of the universe, the creator of all that was, is, or ever will be. He has given us eternal life, eternal purpose, and eternal love. He desires that you join our ranks and partake of His love. He asks nothing but that you allow Him to proclaim His offer. No one is forced to believe, and the reality is, few are likely to join us. The people who exist on Earth now chose Him and He, us. We are just a fraction of the human life that had existed on our planet. The great majority were consumed by their choice to follow their flesh, the world system, and your benefactor and founder, Satan."

Kenan held up his hand for a halt. "You will by necessity speak against Satan, our founder?" He amazed himself at the lack of disgust in his voice.

Tim answered forthrightly. "Only in a historical sense, as he is eternally in Hell and will never reign again." All of the Christians waited for the response to Tim's prickly comment.

Kenan looked over his people. "Can we live with that?" His voice had risen in tone by his last word—in irritation but not anger; he was a pragmatic man.

Sarah spoke. "Why not? Satan has never been a presence here, and the word throughout the galaxy is that he is, indeed, gone. Equally, he is welcome to come back and say it isn't so and present his case as these people are doing." The Christians remained stoic of face, even as their hearts cheered Sarah's common sense.

"I agree," said Jared, who sat beside Kenan, which confirmed his rank as the second-highest of the delegation, as secretary of security. His tone was positive and unequivocal, his voice deep. The man beside him, Enoch, loudly proclaimed, "And I agree."

The Christian delegation could only attribute this desire or openness to Christ and Christianity to their media blitz. Perhaps the openness should acknowledge skepticism. Had these people really considered the ramifications and the price that was demanded?

Keturah had worry in her eyes, and an anger, as she said, "Wouldn't acquiescing to the false fact of our founder's death and punishment affect our national and ethnic identity, our very concept of ourselves?"

The second-ranked female, Jemima, answered, "Do we have a concept of ourselves, other than to enjoy the moment, to live and to love and to take from the world and life what we can?"

"You could have eternal life," Tim said.

Sarah laughed. "That is large on the plus side of your package, you believe. No one here wants to live forever—it would take the poignancy from life. And…what is life without sex? Who could bear it? We have all read your literature and know what you offer and at what price."

Ling laughed in delight at Sarah's appraisal, her honesty so pure, so unbeguiled. He looked directly into her sparkling eyes. Sarah was puzzled by the one who had laughed, without mocking, at her words. Ling believed that in that moment, he witnessed the Spirit of God claim her for His Kingdom. Tim answered Sarah. "As our Captain Springs stated, most of Earth's population wanted nothing to do with Him."

Andy spoke. "At this time, there is no reason to present the upside or the downside of life after death—that once He is rejected, the soul of the unbelieving faces eternal cognizance in a hellish existence."

Keturah, third among the women in rank, quickly rejoined, "Which means nothing at the moment, as we do not believe Hell exists." Her face reddened and tightened in anger as she continued. "I wonder if your words don't fall under the category of manipulation and pressure."

Andy was not offended and had enjoyed her retort. He answered, "Please excuse my boldness and provocative words. I have few skills as a diplomat. I am just a soldier, who has seen much suffering. My heart wants only the best for your people and you. I realize only your people can make that decision."

"This is all so confusing," said Kenan as he slowly stroked his beard. "Maybe it isn't worth the confusion." He had entered the conversation to douse a fire, but he enjoyed projecting confusion, a wait-and-see approach to their meeting.

Diana quickly interjected, "Many of your people may conclude that is true—it's best to avoid the confusion. But in fairness and in sound political judgment, it is best to let the people decide their own fate, remembering that we offer products of consumption, technological knowledge, and medical advances you may not have. It is possible to be on terms of friendship. We just wanted to offer the best of what we have first—Christ."

Sarah spoke. "Let us say your people are allowed to present your God concept freely, like any other topic is presented. Do you intend to stop us from conquering other nations and prevent us from using the Predator Nation and Thermador for our purposes?"

Dan understood by Sarah's statement the depth of her understanding that the Christ concept was not an exercise of the mind for inner peace or a social grouping for friendship and belonging. She knew this Christ bond would affect all of life, in every area. Dan raised his hand, and his screen flashed the recognition logo. He was given the floor. He stood, calmly studied the eyes of the pilgrim group, and answered, "We believe every nation should be independent, as should every citizen. Nations can agree on treaties with other nations if force and coercion are not used. Positive, fair, equal transactions bring peace. Our Lord declares that you should 'do onto others as you would want them to do onto you.' This applies to nations as well."

Dan watched the lady of beauty's facial expression as the words of God entered her mind. One could see the digestion of the thought and a peace enter. She was about to speak and then remained silent, her question having been answered by the Spirit before it was spoken.

Kenan said, "You have not fully answered our question. You believe one thing about foreign relations, and we believe the opposite."

"That is true," said Tim, "as there is a concept missing between the two positions."

"What concept?" demanded, Keturah in a tone of disbelief.

The Earth representatives clearly saw Jared, Enoch, and Noah wince in disgust and anger. Was it her tone or her forgetting her lesser rank that caused the wince? Or had it been Tim's comment?

"Reciprocity, the idea that two opposing sides both can get what they lack without either feeling cheated," stated a calm-voiced Tim.

Andy spoke. "Would you be willing to halt your economic plans if another means was found to supply you with what you hoped to gain–just this one time—until we can find a lasting solution, such as reciprocity?" Andy knew the resources of Earth were abundant, extravagant. Food, raw resources, machines, and technology could easily meet the demands of empires, as gifts.

Kenan answered, "Plans are set. Have been for hundreds of years."

Andy heard the dismissiveness in the tone of voice. *Not even interested,* it said.

Emily spoke. She had wished to remain silent, simply observing this first meeting of two different worlds. "Do you know the pain, sadness, and grief you cause the Thermadorians at a personal level? Your manipulation of them has caused a war against us, even as they fight your allies, the Predator Nation, for their freedom."

Kenan spoke dismissively. "They are insects, not humans. War is their way of life. I know your people step on bugs on your home planet."

Tim, realizing Emily's pain for the downtrodden and knowing the possibility of undiplomatic words, quickly engaged Kenan in a soothing voice. "It is a complicated situation, but we can find a solution working together. How wonderful to have all human life, ours and yours, in peace and agreement. Even the mantis beings knowing peace would add to our serenity."

Sarah and Jemima heard the cleverness; aside from insects, human life in agreement and peace. Keturah heard and sneered. Kenan had a flashback to the Christian hologram seen earlier. They were a rich nation, if the media had been accurate, and his people could benefit from a closer relationship.

Kenan answered, "I will pass this along to others with more authority. But your hope for humanity, our nation and yours, and peace for the mantis beings, is captivating."

Andy spoke. "A good beginning. Let us enjoy each other's company and share our two different cultures and beliefs in simple conversation about our lives."

Kenan rose. "You may learn too much of us and use it to your advantage. This meeting is over."

The quick dismissal and lack of courtesy toward the leader of Christ's Kingdom greatly annoyed Andy. He rose quickly, settled his outstretched hand over the delegations, "Stay yourselves for a moment, please." His voice was calm and soothing.

Kenan remained standing; none of his party had risen.

Andy spoke. "We thank you for hosting this meeting. I believe our talks were productive. Sitting before our cousins, whom we never knew existed, is exciting and offers so much hope—a family reunited. We should meet again, if not simply to know each other as friends."

Kenan sat peacefully.

Andy continued, "Our King, Jesus, loves you, wants the best for you, and thanks you for your presence at this meeting. And now, we too realize that many thoughts and plans must be sorted out through contemplation, research, and discussions. We take our leave from you, only wishing for the chance to meet again soon. Let us shake hands and say good-bye." Christ's people rose, extended their hands, and warmly embraced their counterparts' hands.

Collecting together, the crew of Explorer 7 departed, disappeared before their hosts.

***

"Not one mention of the death of Fromen and his entourage," said Andy to his diplomats, gathered around him in the mess hall for their post-mission summary.

Ling spoke. "Not one mention of our probings of their defenses."

Emily added, "They just wanted to see us, watch our mannerisms, our speech choices. They were just curious, as we were of them. Perhaps something was accomplished. I felt them analyzing every second."

Diana asked, "Do you think they honestly portrayed a leaning to our way?"

Tim answered, "Yes, most definitely, and Kenan's, Keturah's, and even Sarah's negative observations were real."

Dan smiled as he spoke. "Nothing ventured, nothing gained."

Andy posed a question. "How many think we stopped a war?" No hands were raised. "What did we accomplish?" Andy asked.

Emily answered. "We softened some hearts; the course ahead may show results because of this."

Andy spoke softly. "Amen."

CHAPTER 18

The security- and intelligence-gathering forces of Explorer 7 had fallen behind on their timetable estimations. They had been dropped outside their target location, the northern town of PA 1, and entered, within their invisible state, only to find empty rooms and hallways that had not, it appeared, been used for years. Their thermal locating equipment was being jammed, and it was quickly turned off. Two squads went out in transporting mode, through the miles of hallways and corridors. The first squad leader, John, had Mat, Seth, Robin, and Tom, the force commander. The second squad leader, Woden, had Jack, Paternus, Tuck, and medical/intelligence specialists Pete and Grace. John and Woden were considered the savviest soldiers—experts at small-unit tactics, bold and clever, and the best at making their decisions happen. Mat went with John, as he was the best shooter—he had quick reactions and he was an excellent sniper. He was to protect John and Tom, whose energies were directed at leading. Tom and Jack had been separated, because they were heads above the others in speaking the mantis language. Old soldiers Seth and Paternus were divided so that each squad had someone with their physical strength, combat fighting skills, and unique perspective. The brothers, Tuck and Robin, were split for the same reason. Pete and Grace had a synergy of thought and action that needed to be preserved.

Hours later, the first squad found the prisoners, through the heavy mist of licorice and the hanging emotional energy of doom. The second squad joined the first squad in a room within the abandoned area of underground offices. Tom reminded all that no pilgrim deaths should occur, and prisoner taking was not an option. He told them the meeting of the two sides had gone well but with no major breakthrough. He directed squad 2 to infiltrate the holding areas of the approximately two thousand Rau-toon and Therma-dorian prisoners and make observations and assessments as to their ability to move to embarkment points for transport to safety. Squad 1 would enter the medical facilities and see what plan was being carried out in the name of thralldom and manipulation. The two squads would return to the meeting point and discuss options.

***

Woden's squad was first to return to the meeting point. Half an hour after this, John's squad returned. Members of John's squad looked upon their comrades, trying to determine what they had seen. They saw calm faces but sensed emotional disturbance or perhaps worry. As he attempted to gauge the emotion on Woden's visage, John asked, "What do you have to report?"

Woden answered, "The report is this: Of the approximately two thousand prisoners, five hundred are Rau-toon, fresh and fit fighters; and fifteen hundred are Thermadorians, consisting of walking wounded and worn but able fighters.

"The two groups are separated by strong fencing. Both sides are highly intoxicated. The pilgrim guards are refereeing war games consisting of hand-to-hand combat between pairs of healthy Rau-toons against one wounded and one healthy Thermadorian." Woden shifted his eyes to Pete, who wished to speak.

Woden assented, and Pete said, "Prisoners and guards are betting on outcomes. The Rau-toons are ahead, as they rush both players either to the wounded or the healthy Thermadorian, whichever is considered the weaker one of the pair, usually the injured one. The participants are so drugged that they believe the drug is not affecting their reaction times. It is really a game of extermination." Pete, stopped his conversation, seeing John gesture his wish to speak.

John spoke. "What is the demeanor of the pilgrims—specifically, those you believe are officers?"

Woden thought momentarily. "They all seemed more interested in the payouts and getting their money. I think they see the participants as insects, not with feelings, families, and souls. The blood spilled does not look human, the appendages lying in the cage are not human limbs. The pilgrims have found a simple way to dispose of the unneeded enemy in a monetarily rewarding way."

Tom, who had been silent since the two squads had rejoined, asked, "If these games were Christians against pilgrims?"

Woden smiled. "You mean human against human? Some, it might bother. But they would not interfere with their friends' fun."

Tom spoke. "Thanks for that report. I will let John tell you what we witnessed."

All eyes turned to John. John spoke. "The operating tables look like an assembly line at a parts factory. Thermadorians are being repaired to return to the fight against the Rau-toon Empire. Trackers are being embedded, as well as that organ within the brain that produces the paranoia that we witnessed between Don and Abe.

"The Rau-toons are receiving trackers also, and brain implants. More importantly, their bodies are being turned into bombs. Pilgrims seem to be injecting the chitin with explosive-absorbing chemicals. Something is being added to their blood, too, and electrical detonators are being dispersed throughout their bodies. This species doesn't have an immune system, so these foreign chemicals and objects are not rejected.

"We don't know what kind of power these bombs can produce. Certainly, vests or other shrapnel protection will have to be worn. I don't know what impact these suicide bombers will have. At the least, they'll add to the tension for frontline soldiers, and they'll cause more deaths. If they're deployed against specific, high-value targets, either structures, equipment, or high-ranking officers, more impact may be felt. It would be best if these fighters did not reach the battlefield."

John paused and studied the faces before him. "I suppose you have picked up the salient points, the obvious, that prisoners are being executed because the quota of suicide individuals or teams has been met. More importantly, the pilgrims have openly changed course. Once, they backed Rau-toon and allowed Thermador to suffer. Now they are arming both sides. They want chaos. They now see both sides as their enemy. Either the pilgrims wish to generate chaos to hide their departure, or they wish to destroy both peoples and rule over the remnants directly."

Tom looked John in the eyes. "How do the pilgrims view us? Our place in this conflict?"

John answered, "We are the dominant power. We are beating Rau-toon's finest—their star fleet. We have armed Thermador, and Thermador is winning. The pilgrims will seek another planet to exploit. They know they don't have the military capability to win against us."

Pete returned to the conversation. "Their leaving is consistent with pilgrim culture. They began as drifters, explorers, simply looking for a home planet. They are looking for a new scam. They learned to use other life-forms—animals, subhumans, but cognizant life-forms. They are parasitic. They take as much as the host can endure. Now, they simply want to make a huge mess—as cover for their escape."

Woden spoke. "Or that is what they want us to think."

The team members stifled their laughter. Woden had given the tag line at every briefing they'd ever had during this conflict.

The room went silent as each individual quietly assessed the reports. Then, on the viewing screens within the room, red, blinking warning signals appeared. The signals came from the hidden security cameras the squads had stationed within the laboratories and prison complex. Tom immediately projected the feeds from the live-streaming cameras to the alert-faced squads.

What they saw was shocking. The prison was in full riot—mantis against pilgrim, and the carnage was graphic. Human blood, red and viscous, was pouring like paint upon the cement floors as body parts were strewn about. When no living pilgrim could be found, Thermadorians turned against Rau-toons. To their horror, cameras in the laboratories showed pilgrims igniting entire rooms with "cling" fire, which stuck to the living, dead, and wounded mantis—and to the panicked living pilgrims. Mantis were grabbing hold of their enemies to share the flames of death.

Suddenly, the speaker and monitor from the command deck of the Explorer 7 was open and broadcasting the voice of Andy, urgent and deep. "Security forces, return to ship. I repeat, return to Explorer 7 immediately."

With alacrity, everyone stood and gathered their gear, packing quickly. Captain Springs, the most placid, calm individual in God's Kingdom, was alarmed. His voice pulsed with energy and excitement. "Something ominous is occurring on Thermador and Rau-toon, seismic readings increasing. Get to me now!" he ordered. "I am directly above your coordinates."

Tom held up his hands, and in his command voice, said, "Gather up equipment and go, each when you're ready. Go!"

They obeyed, not waiting for friends or to help another; no one would break protocol and ask for help. Better to leave a person behind than for the mission to fail. They were ordered to leave, and the mission depended on their obedience. All were obedient, and all would leave; and if a problem arose, Tom would help. That was his duty, for he would be last to leave the place of rendezvous. Tom counted them—gone in groups and singly, till he was alone. The little war occurring in laboratories and the prison would end on its own. So many souls lost. A shame. He pulled into his invisibility, his spirit being, and he flew through mortar and stone, steel and chitin wood, and entered Explorer 7. He had no sooner entered his material body, smelled, seen, touched the crowded main deck hall of Explorer 7, when thrusters pounded him into a wall. The humble starship that appeared to be an asteroid blew off the camouflage of space rock and gained the speed of a fighting craft.

Tom regained his balance, cleared his head, and rushed to the command deck.

Andy's voice boomed, "Good to see you, Tom. Our ambassador friends' vessel has taken on more pilgrims and is moving at top speed away from here. We are locked in on their every move. Hopefully, we can establish contact and meet to discuss this turn of events."

Tom spoke. "You heard John's assessment a few minutes ago—"

Andy broke in. "We heard. We've been thinking along those lines in higher command for some time. John likely has it right."

Tom noticed that Pete, Grace, Tim, Diana, and Ling were in the small waiting area by the captain's quarters, off the command deck. Andy spoke to Tom. "Join them. One scenario is that I board the pilgrim ship alone. Will they fight if we come in peace? A consensus, please." Tom moved quickly past Dan and Emily, who were consumed in their navigator and helmsman duties, to join his group.

***

Andy noticed the digital clock at the bottom of the computer screen, delineating the course of the vessel of the pilgrim ambassadorial group. The vessel had made no variation in its course in the eight hours Explorer 7 had been following. Explorer 7 had made small gains in closing the gap. The pilgrims had not responded to communications from Explorer 7. The pilgrims had issued no warnings or threats. Andy had allowed messages of hope, regeneration, scenes from human life on Earth, and planet Earth's natural beauty of flora and fauna to be sent. A visual series on the "fruit of the Spirit" had been played, as well as biblical passages with corresponding music and visuals. It was not viewed as propaganda or corny and old-fashioned by anyone in the Kingdom of God. It was simply a true picture of life in the Kingdom, with the invitation to join this place of peace and beauty, kindness and love. All from the heart. As this was taking place, the planets of Thermador and Rau-toon seemed on the verge of exploding—a catastrophe of galactic proportions that would play out not only immediately with the destruction of nearby planets and stars, but over light-years, with the shrapnel of debris reaching far into space.

All on board knew it had been the intention of the belligerent faction of the Pilgrim Alliance to destroy what they could not possess and to cover their flight to another place to begin again their manipulations. A boarding of the alien spaceship had been drawn up for various scenarios. An armed boarding, if the situation turned hostile. An unarmed boarding, if peaceful pursuit of issues was allowed to be maintained. And of course, destruction of the vessel if boarding was deemed impossible and hostility, imminent. All battle stations had been manned for the past eight hours.

Without warning, the face of Sarah, the lady of beauty, came upon the screen.

"Greetings. This is Sarah. We have been enjoying your montage of Earth scenes—especially of our people's original habitation sites and of the people of Earth who share our genetic history. Fascinating. I call to warn you of what may happen when Thermador and Rau-toon explode."

Andy eagerly pushed the respond button, and beautiful Sarah suddenly went silent. Andy spoke. "Do not destroy these planets. They give life to many. The mantis people have a right to exist. Did not God allow them life? Yield to Him and forgo your hand of destruction."

Sarah spoke in the tone of a teacher. "The mantis people began as insects and would be insects now, had we, the pilgrims, not interfered in their history. Our genetic modifications have been slowly lifting them higher in cognizance of self and the world. Without us, they could not have grasped the presence of a soul life or had the power to manipulate the harsh environment they live within."

"Well done." Andy's tone was gracious and circumspect. He would not argue the validity of her claims. "Our Father would have done the same. Yes, He *has* done the same—through His creation—you, transplanted earthlings made by His hand and in His image. You have done the will of God without recognizing His part. I applaud you." Then Andy's face became furrowed, and his voice deepened. "Now, you take upon yourselves the mantle of God, determining life or death. If death, you go against His will. Do not commit such a crime. You will have guilt because you know you are doing wrong.

"Step back from your will to exceed the limits that you should impose upon yourself but can't because the flesh wars against the spirit. Leave the mantis people in peace and take pride in the advancements you have given them, through God."

Sarah spoke. "How you frame life…how clever you are."

"Just honest…honesty is clever, sometimes, in the fallen world…because no one expects it." Andy's voice held sadness. "Think about sparing them. We will not pursue you if those planets live. You would not need to run like criminals. We would not hold the new awakening pilgrims responsible for the acts of the old order of pilgrims. Be 'born again' as a people. The old may die in the past sins, and the new may live in the future's Spirit. Let us come and talk with you and save the lives of your pilgrim soldiers and scientists."

Sarah spoke. "I will call you within three hours with the thoughts of my people." The picture was gone.

***

For an hour, the people of the Explorer 7 prayed. At the beginning of the hour, a call went to all Christendom for prayer. For the second hour, the people of Explorer 7 prayed as well as those of planet Earth and all the space stations and all the inhabited planets and all the Christian military units gathered before Rau-toon for its destruction. At the beginning of the third hour, the lady of beauty, Sarah, was again upon the screen.

She spoke with an optimistic and perplexed tone but with a determined visage. "You have shaken our world, Captain Springs. Many wish to belong to your world, your Jesus. I personally never thought the hunger was there. The leaders see a thoughtfulness in allowing Thermador and Rau-toon to exist and the mantis people to survive. And so the mantis people will live; destruction will not occur. That is the status now. My people are leaving and ask not to be followed. In time, perhaps, we will contact you."

Andy, within seconds, sensed what was occurring: a clever strategy of feint, reconsolidation, and attack. The pilgrim peoples would return and reclaim the mantis people or, by covert acts, never release their hold. The pilgrims would destroy the forces of good within their own society, quash Christianity, and then attack. He knew this from the inner voice of the lady of beauty, for the inner voice clung to the exterior voice—by willful purpose, or an undiscovered duality within the mind, or by subtle tells that Andy could discern by familiarity.

Andy spoke. "We are coming to visit you, unarmed. Prepare for guests." Andy shut off his comms quickly, before Sarah could respond. "Unarmed boarding party, prepare to transport without mechanical transport," he announced to his ship.

The lady of beauty roared in rage in a dead receiver, "Do not come! Flee! Go back! You will surely die!"

The Lord said, "Go."

Andy knew this moment would never exist again. Tip the balance to the scales of righteousness and see a culture, a people, turn to their God. All onboard had watched and heard.

Andy spoke to his crew. "Boarding party, let me hear the ayes."

He listened as all answered, "Aye."

"Let us collect and depart with speed," he ordered.

***

John knew he had landed in a volatile situation before he had fully materialized. The pilgrim people, initially scattered throughout the room, had coalesced, before the arriving Christians, into a battle line of martial arts stances and determined faces of loathing and wrath. Ten to two feet of space separated the lines of the two forces. Miraculously, no weapons were present. John recognized faces from the first meeting—Jared, Enoch, Noah, Sarah, Jemima, Keturah—but most of the gathered were new—men in uniform, security forces. Both sides were tense; the pilgrim security forces were beyond tense and into the realm of fanaticism, where fear and panic roiled into anger and hate.

The pilgrim security detail, though greater in number, was individually outsized, out-muscled by the Christian soldiers; their weakness and puniness goaded their self-worth, even as their numbers were two times greater. John hoped the femininity of Sarah, Jemima, Keturah would be the calm that kept order. His heart sank; even the women appeared tense. Jarod, Enoch, and Noah were believed to be definite friends of the Christian forces, but could they openly betray their own friends, their countrymen? John and his squad of Andy, Mat, and Seth had landed facing the forces around Sarah. Woden and his force of Jack and Paternus had landed facing Kenan, the pilgrim's once-bearded leader, and only feet away. Perhaps Kenan was attempting to hide himself within his altered appearance. The Christians knew they were outnumbered and could expect no help from their shipmates manning the ship's weapon systems.

Woden noticed the unarmed status of the enemy. That was a good sign; someone had ordered disarmament and had been obeyed. He knew it was for him to make the decision. His people were within arm's length of his opponents; this state could not remain long in stasis. Andy would defer, as would John, to Woden's move. He could step back and hope his two crewmen would follow, or he could launch forward into unarmed combat. To withdraw might provoke an enemy attack; and for a moment, his two men would be vulnerable to encirclement, perhaps forced into the enemy ranks and captured. He was subconsciously attempting to speak to them, but some power was interfering. He would not initiate an attack on the pilgrims, though, because then they would gain boldness.

Woden relaxed his body, as did his two men. This show of peace was interpreted as weakness and opportunity, and the pilgrim security forces rushed into the attack. Woden's massive body tensed, and with an inch of movement forward, Paternus and Jack had surged ahead of him by a body length, protecting his flanks, as their fists shot outward, striking heads, necks, shoulders, solar plexuses, and hearts.

Woden stepped ahead to keep pace and acquired the stronger position of being boxed into an area of limited movement, where his superior strength and size would prevail. Using handholds and choke holds, he slammed men to the ground. He trampled on arms, chests, legs. He avoided their heads, as his weight would kill. Behind, and to his left, he saw Andy, Mat, and Seth surging and filling in the flanks. The enemy security forces had immediately engaged and surged. Andy thought it obvious that offense had been their plan from the beginning. Andy gained the only door out and guarded it against all assault; no one could leave and no one could enter. Within four minutes, the room was quiet; the defeated pilgrims stood, exhausted; they sat in chairs, or lay on the floor. The pilgrim men still on their feet included Jared, Enoch, and Noah, who had remained true to their Christian sympathies. They had made a protective ring around their women.

"Now what course will you take?" asked Sarah.

Before Andy could answer, a wailing claxon sounded throughout the ship. He saw dread wash its whiteness over the face of Sarah's beauty. He knew she had heard death and envisioned the horrors of dying in space as her ship blew apart around her. The death of the ship had been preplanned by the pilgrim forces wishing war. What a story to tell the Pilgrim Alliance—trickery and tragedy perpetrated against many of the very pilgrims who wanted peace. Andy bellowed, "All men, even you, form around the women!"

He pointed at the pilgrim men, searched the eyes of the men around Sarah. They could read his heart through his eyes and knew his honesty. Andy grabbed Sarah and hugged her, attempting to cover her body with his massiveness. His hands and arms enveloped her head, pinched tight her upper body, and his legs became one with hers. All his crewman sought out the women, as ordered. Living women assured that the culture, the race would survive. The security men bonded with the women, many joining their former antagonists in embrace around the women or each other. Kenan remained sitting in a chair. He thought it better to die than to cling to the enemy.

Explosions ripped apart the ship.

The dematerializing Explorer 7 boarding party saw the Explorer 7 through the sucking storm of the explosions and black space and struggled for the shelter of their vessel. They fought to keep their conglomeration of bodies together, keep them within the dematerializing sphere surrounding them. If a body floated free, it was quickly killed by flying debris, shredded to vapor. The living began to materialize in the hallways and rooms of Explorer 7 to the sounds of the warning sirens wailing and the sight of the familiar faces of their onboard crew, who, before the returnees could stand, were raising them and speeding them to life-preserver capsules, cramming two, three, four to a capsule. The Explorer 7 had caught shrapnel, or a round, and was quickly losing viability. The capsules as well as the shuttle craft were spewed into space as the Explorer 7 faltered and began a glide.

CHAPTER 19

The capsules had been strewn across the barren surface of the nearest planet with Earthlike conditions for life. The planet's rating was two weeks of viability for humans. This meant that some factor in the environment, either by chance or accumulation, would ultimately, within two weeks, prove hostile to human life, unless the situation could be rectified by means initiated by the human hosts. Explorer 7's crew were popping open their capsule hatches and emerging, many with the rescued pilgrims. The shuttle had landed intact, without a rollover. Scattered across the flat and barren surface of the planet were parts and pieces of the pilgrim's craft and the Explorer 7. Pilgrim bodies, once dressed in dark-blue jumpsuits, were randomly present, scattered in various pieces, many with accompanying flesh, bone, and organs within. Far on the horizon, the living could see a mound of equipment with a flag flying on top. This was the remains of Explorer 7, which had maintained hull integrity and had been landed by functioning members of the crew. The entire onboard crew was already engaged in repairs.

Andy awoke into a cognizance of hazy, disjointed thoughts that readily dissipated. He knew exactly what had occurred; he had memories of the time spent in the capsule and of the clinging form of the lady of beauty, Sarah, uttering words like a prayer. Fear and doubt had pulled feminine cries from her body, which she had attempted to swallow, to hide her weakness. He remembered holding his tribe's infants in his first life, usually when mothers were dying, and the sounds were the same. Such weakness in the flesh, and yet God, in His mercy borne of His loving heart, had brought them peace.

Andy promised the Lord he would sustain her and all his charges male and female, protect them as he had his disabled sons. He studied her face; she was in a sleep compounded by exhaustion. Her long, black hair was now white, and the supple skin now wrinkled. He lifted her out of the capsule and noticed, alarmingly, that she had lost weight. Had an aging occurred? He checked his own skin, studied the face of an approaching crewman, Jack! His capsule had landed nearest to Andy's. No wrinkles.

"Do I look normal?" asked Andy.

Jack smiled. "Yes, but some of our guests do not."

Jack studied Sarah's face and spoke. "She resembles the guest who is sleeping in my capsule."

Andy inquired, "A theory?"

Jack smiled again. "Always, anytime. They are old, and this was hidden by the environment they surrounded themselves within. Whether being outside the protective environment will cause rapid death, a degradation of health, or simply a passive aligning to their proper age, I do not know. Nor do I know if a reversal can take place."

Sarah awoke, saw the two men looking at her with kindly faces. She knew instantly by their eyes that she had changed—had lost her beauty. The desire of others to gaze upon her face was gone. A panic arose; her worth had been compromised. She spoke. "Do not look upon me! I am hideous!"

"No, you just appear differently than how you last appeared," said Jack. "We like you, and nothing can change that."

Sarah looked inward, attempting to find Jack's motives behind his words, and her thoughts simply faded away into peace and acceptance. She raised her arm slowly to Andy, desiring him to grab her arm and pull her to her feet. He obliged. She walked ten steps back and forth. Her balance and strength grew stronger. He surmised her inner-core strength and vitality were still present, and she still had much to offer their survival efforts.

Andy spoke to Jack. "Check on our crew in the capsules and the shuttle, then transport to Explorer 7. Our immediate need is working heat and air-conditioning, as well as an intact hull for sleeping within. Then water, and lastly, food. We will need a shelter to sleep in tonight—the night is probably bitter cold. I'll organize the capsule and shuttle people. Tell them to report to me, please."

Jack aligned his posture and saluted. "Yes, sir." His voice carried respect, as did his stance and snappy salute. He was anxious to get started. Just another barrier to overcome to add glory to his Lord's name. The Explorer 7 would rise and conquer, and the crew would tell of their exploits and of their Lord, who had sustained them. Jack surveyed the debris-strewn planet, saw a cluster of human activity around the Explorer 7, smiled at Sarah, and left.

Sarah spoke. "Are we prisoners?"

Andy humphed. "No, of course not."

She wondered at his largesse. Sarah watched Jack depart; he was one of two dark-skinned crew members. "We knew no Africans in our world, but knew they existed. The same with your white-skinned crew." Andy understood that her people's Mediterranean pigment was uniformly present and matched more closely his and his sons' American Indian coloration, and Paternus and Seth's Mediterranean tones.

Andy answered, "Take the opportunity to know Jack now—all of the crew. You will find what makes us the same. Our relationship with our God is dominant over what once made us different—race, ethnicity, nationality. What makes us different now are individual traits of personality and life experiences. We belong to our Creator; we have our being in His thoughts, His being, His Spirit. He is our Father and supplies our genetics—and, truly, yours, Sarah." He reached over and held her hand.

She thought about Jack's respect for Andy. Was it the respect that came from reputation or the respect that comes from watching and learning? She asked, "How can I be of help?"

He smiled. "Make the rounds with me, gather in your people. I don't believe many of your males survived. I should know if they did and know the leanings of all the survivors—none overtly hostile, I hope. Our mission now is to survive, as a team, and leave this place."

***

Andy's wrist computer rang. It had been completely dead, so that meant power was now on aboard the Explorer 7. "Yes!"

"Jack reporting. Tom says Explorer 7 offers hot food, now, and water. All holes will have patches by sundown, and heat will be available. The outside world knows where we're at—both good and bad people."

"We're coming," said Andy as he calculated the types of responses that might come from their enemies. Andy saw Mat and the woman, Jemima, whom Mat had saved. Her hair was not gray; her skin was supple—proof she was aligned with her age. Andy yelled, "To Explorer 7!"

Mat raised his hand and gave the thumbs-up sign, an ancient gesture from the Roman world of the Colosseum. Woden, Seth, and Paternus had known the gesture in their time. The woman beside him, Jemima, was two hundred years old. She had told him that the woman of beauty, Sarah, was five hundred years old. Most of their kind could reach eight hundred years if they had been raised in stable environments. They had formulated an antiaging vapor, easily reproduced anywhere and suspended in air, which worked magnificently through inhalation, topical exposure, and skin absorption. Jem was anti-God, had never felt the need. She had read all the literature, seen all the holograms made available, and liked to challenge him with what she thought were contradictory facts attributed to God.

Jemima spoke as they walked, and she held his hand, saying she felt slightly unbalanced. "Are you determined to fight again? Another brawl like the one that precipitated this mess?"

Mat laughed. It had been a brawl, but one-sided, as Explorer 7's security detail was trained, experienced, and physically larger and stronger than the foe. He marveled at her word acquisition and her ability to learn a new language so quickly and deeply. "It was the right call. It was your side that was not able to cope with defeat and upped the game to annihilation. We had no intention of taking prisoners or conquering your settlement," Mat said. "It was unfortunate. We are not a civilization of thugs."

Jem spoke. "Well, then, who are you people?"

Mat smiled and answered, "We are Christ's people. We are what we need to be when danger is near. There is a certain excitement and pleasure when life consists of reflex and instinct and training, and we survive and win. But to be here, holding your hand, listening to your thoughts, your people's struggles and defeats…giving you understanding and sympathy…means more to us than hand-to-hand antics do. To share with your people our Lord and Savior, our God, your Maker, who loves you and your people, who is for you and will give you peace, contentment, and victory is why we live. Live forever."

She was caught breathless in her full exhalation of hate for his people and his world, when a clean wind entered her lungs as she inhaled his words. She knew he had no impurity, no deceit, no lie upon his motivations or residing anywhere within. An honest man—who would have thought such a being existed? "Caution!" said her mind. Mat could be a peddler of fables with an honest heart.

He began again, the word flow bearing the cadence of memorization. "'I love to tell the story, of unseen things above, of Jesus and His glory, of Jesus and His love. I love to tell the story because I know 'tis true. It satisfies my longings, as nothing else can do.' Old lyrics," he said, thinking back to the Tribulation and secret praise services with his special group: Dan and his sister, Barb, who had become Mat's wife; and Katie, his sister.

Jemima wondered at this Jesus—or this Jesus concept—that had so consumed, enraptured Mat and all of these current planet Earth dwellers. So odd. They seemed controlled, and yet they weren't; they seemed almost drunk, yet they were deadly conscious and sober. They wished this for her and her people, and yet once hooked, none seemed capable of escape. That is why this was deadly serious: it could not be undone.

He looked at her and spoke. "I learned of this song when the Earth was in the throes of the Tribulation, a period of seven years when God poured his wrath upon the world, a punishment that was meant to awake our dull minds from the stupor of sin and self and turn us toward our true Father, who loved us. As you can see, He saved us. And almost two thousand years from that time of awakening, we are still alive. Proof that His word is true and good." He turned her to him and hugged her. She knew it was not sexual lust or even a needy love. Just love overwhelming—love from another source, a source that could have disintegrated her body, had it wished to hug her tighter. Was this the love of God? Another wave of presence and power overwhelmed her, as if confirming her thought.

"What do your people say…Wow?" She walked on in silence. She had walked with a stoop before, but now her back was straight. She had always felt weak and tired. Now her muscles were strong, and she wondered if this was how athletes felt. She was smiling (she never smiled), and her mind was laughing—she never laughed! "I don't think we have anything in the universe to match this, Matthew, my boy." She looked up at him. "What did you do?"

As she looked up, she caught the flash of objects—missiles—in the sky. Just as quickly, a roiling cloud of whiteness covered the surface space debris, the Explorer 7, and all human life, like a tent. Mat was looking up as yellow flashes of light exploded within the whiteness of the tentlike fabric. The planet shook, and humans crouched to remain on their feet.

Mat spoke. "It seems that someone wants us dead. The angels of my Lord have neutralized the threat." He studied her eyes, happy eyes at that. "Let's get to Explorer 7. And to your question, I did nothing. Heavenly forces are working within you."

***

Andy had called a meeting. All sat, lounged, or stood on the powdery sand on the lee side of the Explorer 7. Security guards with lasers faced outward; the perimeter had been sown with security fields. Many were still eating the excellent meal prepared for them. The gray-haired, wrinkled ladies were at ease and marveled that no one seemed to notice their change in appearance. In their culture, sexual attractiveness was valued more than knowledge, competence, or a sound mind, in worth to others. A spirit of comradery, friendship, a common goal seemed to unite the pilgrims in a spirit they had

not experienced before. Most had not committed to the new philosophy offered, nor joined the course of resistance, for they could not see any danger
in talk, or coexistence, with what they saw as basically just words—words
that people hoped to live for and implement in their lives, with no goals
other than to be pleasant and live a host of virtues that everyone agreed were
beneficial. Had the Christians insisted on a new political party or new laws,
a new police force or judicial code, that would have been a different matter.

Detractors had said those things were coming, hinting that change was
evil, for it would have disrupted the status quo. This was a strong argument,
because the mantis people and their subsequent manipulation had made the
pilgrims rich, had elevated living standards, longevity, creativity, comfort,
and ease. Yet, the Christians had all those things in abundance without sub-
jugating anyone.

Andy, after brief consultations with various members of his crew, addressed the assemblage. "The explosions you heard and felt tremble through
the ground were a flock of thinking bombs, sent by the dissident faction of
the pilgrims. We believe their purpose was to destroy your women, who are
now in our care. They could have blamed the deaths on us or could have
labeled you traitors to your people.

"Within the last twenty-four hours, a referendum has been called for by
our Lord, Jesus, King of Earth and all His subjects. A yea or nay vote for the
allowing of Christian beliefs through all forms of media and human speech,
to include formation of churches and social Christian organizations. On a
separate matter, a referendum was requested for peaceful coexistence with
Rau-toon and Thermador and a renegotiation of all economic ties between
the principal parties.

"We will not be dismayed if your nation votes 'no,'" Andy said. "We will
be dismayed if death and coercion, which have already occurred, tilt the vote
away from acceptance. We expect more threats and deaths. Your lives are in
danger. Tomorrow, you will be transported to a safe zone among your people. We are susceptible to attack tonight and during our voyage tomorrow. I
and my crew pledge our utmost vigor to your safety." He made eye contact
with each woman—and the security personnel as well. "Thank you."

***

John allowed a brief shiver to pass through his body in reaction to the
cold, accentuated by a desolate moonglow on the barren terrain around their
encampment. Temperatures below freezing. Mat, north, at twelve o'clock;
Robin, east, at three o'clock; Jack, south, at six o'clock; Tuck, west, at nine

o'clock. Each armed with a laser rifle, they were the perimeter guard, within sight and sound of the Explorer 7. John sat, hidden, in the center of his men, among the surrounding camp debris of daylight operations, with the Explorer 7 before him. He had a laser pistol strapped to his thigh, as a counter force to an enemy landing into the center of camp. All civilians were in the Explorer, sleeping in individual, explosive-proof capsules. Outside the perimeter were his men Woden, Seth, and Paternus—hidden and ready to operate as a mobile quick-reaction unit.

All had vapor-control masks, airtight and heavy uniforms that hid both heat signatures and electronic pulses from surveilling equipment. Some deep-space and multilayered signals hinted that mercenary Rau-toon assassins led by pilgrim security forces were lurking nearby. The immortal body wasn't dependent on sleep, and everyone was awake, their minds active; internally, they were communicating subsonically in mind talk. The silence and lack of movement upon the planet stimulated conversation.

Even though the mobile unit was half a mile distant, all minds heard the word "sky" come from the unit's direction. Slowly and separately, all eyes moved toward the atmosphere, with its thick backdrop of planets, stars, and moons. A silent, winged object came into view, moving downward in a wide corkscrew flight path, with the encampment the apparent target. The word "no," presented by John, entered their minds. No meant don't shoot. Perhaps this was an unmanned drone to elicit fire and expose positions.

When they had watched the craft circle on its last corkscrew before landing, they heard the words, "I, alone." They knew this came from John, so they would not expose their positions and bodies if and when John opened fire on the enemy. If he was taken from the battlefield by the annihilation of his body because he denied himself supporting fire, so be it. That would be the price a soldier paid to protect the mission.

John's muscular strength was rising and tensing for movement. He knew the model of craft before him, only one door; and standard operating procedure was to position it away from the target to allow the vessel to function as cover for the departing soldiers. He had planned to shoot them with his pistol on "diffused"—enough force to stun or kill but not enough to damage the hull of the Explorer nearby. But it appeared the door would face the Explorer. He began to rise early, needing the time to sidle up to the doorway. He thought the pilot had repositioned the door purposely, knowing an enemy was behind them, and knowing the Explorer was harmlessly in sleep mode. He was the enemy they sought. He needed to rise regardless.

He strode quickly toward the craft, realizing that men, not mantises, were coming around the craft on both sides to kill him, even as another group was before the hull of the Explorer. He saw the enemy movement under the skids of their raised craft. He could not shoot until they burst upon him, limiting his reaction time. He saw bodies falling. Tuck and Robin had disobeyed their orders not to shoot. He smiled at their actions; good call. The door facing the Explorer had changed the previous plans. Too many for him to shoot, and the enemy vessel would stop any round that missed the target. He walked over the bodies of those who had sought him and faced the enemy soldiers who had their backs to him as they placed an explosive charge against the Explorer 7 hull. Two men sensed his presence, turned, and fired at him. Shots pumped from his pistol.

Two shots came at him, and he physically pushed his body forward, into the oncoming rounds, to counteract their backward punches into his body armor. He saw his assailants fall. He fell forward toward the ship. Their rounds hit the edge of the body armor on his back and momentarily tugged him backward.

The bomb squad of pilgrim soldiers congregated by the Explorer were knocked down by Jack's fire. He knew it was Jack, as he heard the shots whiz by over his shoulder from the south. Delicate shooting, individual shots, with the Explorer as backstop. To penetrate the Explorer with an errant shot was unthinkable in consequences. A member of the bomb crew turned, fired at John. John's body armor was hit, his stomach muscles tightened. Then a round hit his back and another, the back of his helmet. Were they shots from Jack? The helmet round was fired low on the helmet, and the trajectory was slightly upward, pushing his helmet up as the front portion of helmet arced onto his face, covering his eyes. Did Jack shoot him? Was someone shooting from inside the troop-carrier doorway? John, as best he could, from his crunched up, prone position, leapt aside, fell and rolled, and in the roll, turning his body, shooting at where he assumed the opened doorway was in relation to him. He thought he heard the massive body of a mantis fall. He grasped his helmet and worked it free.

He saw laser flashes in the barren regions surrounding the Explorer 7 perimeter, flashes on the horizon—grenades, shoulder rockets exploding. Rigid wings were falling from the sky, softening the landings of mantis soldiers, their springy, strong legs taking shocks that would have crippled most machines. The Explorer's air-defense weapons were pounding the sky with exploding starbursts of shrapnel that shredded the mantis wings. He ran toward the satchels of the downed bomb squad. He took the satchels in hand and ran toward the "scamper" parked under the Explorer. John jumped onto this newest weapon system, an invention of Mat and Tim: three laser rifles mounted on caterpillar tracks. A one-person, sit, shoot, drive, low-to-the-ground scamper. Away from the Explorer, he dropped the satchels, thinking their timers may have been activated.

A heavy battle was taking place on the fringes of the seen desert. By the unmoving glow of exploding rounds, John knew Woden, Seth, and Paternus were surrounded, unable to move. John moved toward Tuck on the western point, clearing the west of all enemies. Tuck hopped aboard and held tight with white-knuckled hands. He knew where they were going and what the mission was: to free the "Byzantine three"—the recently created nickname for Woden, Seth, and Paternus. John used the scant cover of the desert skillfully, taking advantage of shallow depressions and slight rises. The enemy died or retreated into the desert to regroup. A sled was made of a discarded fixed-wing, rigid, enemy single glider. The Byzantines sat in a triad formation on the sled, lasers facing out. Then, the mad dash to return to the Explorer, which had moved its position when rounds began to target it.

***

Under Andy's command, the Explorer 7 lifted up and away as soon as the last of the security crew was aboard. An orbiting starship was to carpet-bomb the area before the Explorer's return. The small armada that had come to the Explorer's rescue had already dispersed forces to hunt down the ships that had participated in the assassination mission. The crew members not on duty, the returned security forces, and the guest men and women were gathered in the cargo area that doubled as an auditorium. The planned trip for the pilgrims to register their votes had been canceled while resistance existed.

Tom, as second captain, was casually addressing his security forces, even as his eyes just as casually moved over the forms of the women. Tom addressed John. "Anything stand out during this recent combat?"

John smiled. "Thought it odd the only discharge doorway on the pilgrim's vessel faced the Explorer, and an assault squad was assigned to the bow of their ship, even as a demolition squad went straight for the Explorer's hull. As if they knew I was behind them, and they had nothing to fear from the Explorer."

Andy asked and suggested, "Heat-shield leak give away your position? Had you moved and been discovered prior to your awareness of their approach? Or did they have an anti-ambush tactic planned?"

"I think none of those apply," said John. "The Byzantines, listening to chatter, would have heard the talk."

Woden joined the conversation. "On that subject, the enemy knew where we were, yet we had not broken protocol in any way."

Tom spoke. "Our cardinal-point men weren't known. Why were they missed?"

Diana, eager-faced, who had come to greet John, held up her computer screen. "They were targeted! Look at this overlay of the first wave of gliders. See the clusters around the cardinal-points men? The Rau-toon weren't noticed because they were directed *off* target when rounds began cutting through the air."

Tom tilted his head; he gazed at the pilgrim women. He then turned to the handful of pilgrim men who were guests. The men had aided their Christian cousins in the ensuing combat. One of the women was acting different—wary and frankly, guilty, with the fear of retribution hanging upon her. Tom looked at Diana, "Who had access to this view of our forces before the attack, and when?"

Diana went to the mainframe computer and brought up internal security footage. She studied the screen, then whispered to Tom, "One of the female pilgrims, a full hour before the attack." The security force participants heard Diana, and honed their minds against her words, revealing sharply the culprit Keturah. Jack left the meeting and went directly to the computer in question and found and developed fingerprints.

Tom answered, "No more peeks for her. I will address her in private."

The meeting was over, the crew was streaming out, followed by the pilgrim women. Andy left last, drew close to Keturah, the security threat. Andy spoke quietly. "Keturah." She pretended not to hear. He was about to gently squeeze her arm, when the Spirit warned him that a contrived outburst might be made if he touched her.

"Keturah." He spoke loudly enough that women ahead of her had heard. She was forced to turn.

She spoke sweetly. "Yes, Captain?"

Andy recognized mocking in the tone, but did not react and returned a friendly tone. "May I have a word with you, in private? Or, if alone is awkward, with those of your group present?"

She stared at him forthrightly. "Yes, with those of my group."

Andy noticed Sarah was directly behind, with Jemima, and he knew they were the most open to new thoughts and had balanced, uncommitted minds. Andy stopped as they were approaching and spoke. "These two would be fine, don't you think?"

Keturah nodded her head unpleasantly, knowing the mind-set of the two. To demand others would likely highlight her anti-Christian politics.

Andy addressed Sarah, as he included Jemima in his eye contact. "A small group meeting. It will take only minutes." They were before the door to an empty room with chairs, and Andy extended his hand.

"Be seated, please," he said. "This won't take long, and all is private between us." They sat.

"Some oddities happened during the attack," Andy said. "Prior knowledge of our positions by the attacking forces. A fingerprint, other than a crew fingerprint, was found on the computer screen showing the location of our forces. It belongs to Keturah. Also, Keturah was recorded on camera viewing the location of our forces. I am not angry, as not one of my crew was hurt. I know these are difficult times for your people, your tight-knit nation. I expect you…we all expect you to have feelings and desires, and we understand your views may be different than ours. We are happy that you do care about your people and nation and your course for the future. We only wish for you to make informed decisions, free of bias and hate. Violence clouds judgment and thinking.

"No one on Earth will be disappointed if you do not choose our God, our Savior. On Earth, He was rejected for thousands of years. He sent His son, and His son was hated without cause and crucified and thought to be annihilated. His son rose from death, made a comeback, and eventually was rejected again by many. His Earth enemies are gone forever now. But this spiritual side of our faith can be seen apart from economics, even governance, civility, and morals. Because what is good *is* what is good in a practical sense, concerning human nature and the needs of people. You do not need to belong to Christ to understand that self-determination, democracy, capitalism, and fairness in trade lead to harmony, wealth, and peace.

"Keturah, we care about you and love you. However, the death, even though temporary, of our people would likely bring unpleasant consequences," Andy said. After a pause, he added, "Tell us what bothers you about our assumptions, our philosophy, our understanding of values. Maybe we have just not framed our ideas in a way that resonates with your life experiences. Or in your language."

She answered. "How did I communicate this information to my people? You have no proof, for there is none. So much for your observations. I was simply curious."

Andy knew more was coming.

"You talk of human nature," she said. "The mantids are not human; they are animal. We *use* them. What humanlike traits they have is because we put those traits in them with our genetic superiority. We invest in research to make them more productive. We *should* take the monetary gains as profit."

Andy spoke. "I disagree that you created the humanness in mantids. That's a manipulative lie your people have created. Besides, the mantids are cognizant beings; they have souls; they know there is a God; they have emotion, thoughts that reach beyond their own lifetimes. I am speaking of the Thermadorians. The Rau-toon have a different mind-set—in fact, it's more like yours—that outright conquest and taking by force is a legitimate base for an economic and political system. In the latter years of ancient Earth history, they were called 'communists,' who used force, and 'socialists,' who used mental trickery for superiority. Still, the Rau-toon are cognizant beings with souls. As we wish to coexist with them, they need to embrace a standard that at least encompasses the idea that force does not make right."

"Big challenges," said Keturah, purposely blunting the captain's thrust. "Much debate is needed."

Andy saw her ploy: keep the Christians talking, while the pilgrims took what was theirs. He spoke. "Much debate is needed. But for now, I need to run my ship." He extended his hand, they shook.

Keturah spoke. "It will all work out if we keep talking." She thought, sarcastically, Captain Andy would love those lines.

CHAPTER 20

Ava, accompanied by Dan and Emily, Mat, and Jack, was first to exit the Explorer 7 after the return to the battlefield of the morning. The carpet-bombing mission had been altered to neutralizing specific combat threats: any alien forces whole of body, sound of mind, who wished to fight. This change of mission was in direct response to Ava's request to minimize damage to the enemy dead. She intended to study every corpse. She was one of the few scientists aware that the mantis body had been changing in the last month. Molts had always occurred at regular, foreseeable intervals, but under the leadership of the pilgrims, changes were being introduced. She knew, by rumor only, that her people had tampered with the mantis body for thousands of years. In her training as a pilgrim agent, she had read from official-looking documents that the process was occurring, but as all of pilgrim life consisted of scams, the information had no validity. She had been sworn to secrecy. Dan and Emily would help in compiling the data. Mat and Jack were her security guards and the muscle when bodies needed to be moved.

The Explorer 7 had reduced the engines to pulse, heard only by the crew inside. The entire crew was busy onboard. The silence of the planet was palpable, the strewn corpses, ordnance craters, damaged equipment, body parts—all eerily still, unmoving. Ava strode to the pile of corpses near the first descended alien craft. The pile had been created by John, with assistance from Tuck and Robin on his flanks and Jack to his rear. She had studied the combat footage taken from the Explorer's cameras. She loved forensic work; it felt like Christmas morning, with packages to open—a common Christian phrase her spy-craft classes had relentlessly drilled into her mind to give her authenticity. As a born-again Christian, she now understood the strength and reality of the phrase. Now Christ, once a little baby in a manger, was a grown man conducting business in Jerusalem. His birth and work had truly been a present worth anticipating. That fact was worthy of a "Praise God" to her newfound God, and she audibly said, "Praise God."

Mat laughed. She looked at him, knowing he wanted to know the particular reason for her praise. Though he was a mature adult man, she liked him for his boyish mind that was always searching new avenues of thought. She spoke. "It feels like Christmas-morning expectation, and baby Jesus is fully grown upon Earth in Jerusalem."

Mat and Jack chorused, "Praise God." Ava laughed.

Emily spoke. "Gratefulness never gets stale." Dan was smiling at his party's joy as he studied the pile of dead and said, sadly, "All pilgrims." All present felt a sad longing for potential friendships that would never be made.

Ava's friends' open-hearted love for her people, regardless of the worthless cultural values, confirmed she had chosen rightly. Ava spoke. "Look for ID and insignia. Take note of their armaments. Take their height, weight, and a blood sample. That's all we need from pilgrims. They may be returning to their people for burial."

Emily spoke. "A little DNA wouldn't hurt; their story isn't yet completely known."

Ava stopped in her motion and wondered if this could have processing ramifications. She overrode her caution. She answered, "That is a good idea, Emily. Take samples." She glanced at the alien craft and continued speaking. "The camera showed at least one mantis in the vessel, perhaps more. Need one security man with me—the hull was impenetrable by any surveillance equipment."

"I'll remain outside," said Jack.

"Okay, you're up, Mat." Ava smiled as she spoke.

Mat stepped ahead, and cautiously, quietly moved to the doorway, laser barrel first, and studied the dark interior. One mantis was sprawled on the deck, deep in the shadows. Mat had his life scanner clipped onto his laser barrel. No pulse indicated. In combat, this dead body was what had made the thud John had heard after discharging his laser. Slowly, he proceeded up the ramp, stepped over the body, and then squatted, knowing his profile would be in the light if a living soul was watching from within. The vessel was deep; at least twenty men had exited. His laser light swept the hull. Empty. The pilothouse was above the troop-carrier deck. Seemed too small to hold a man. He placed an explosive charge on the hatch.

Ava quickly spoke. "Could be booby-trapped. Let bomb disposal check later."

Mat nodded in agreement. "Okay. Too small for a mantis, anyway." She began backing out. Mat returned the explosives to his belt pouch, strung caution tape, and attempted to drag the mantis body out of the craft. The mantis's personal combat gear snagged on the craft's floor. He left the body.

As they exited the vessel, the hull shook with an explosion, the vessel lifted off the planet by a foot and settled back down. "Strange," said Mat as Jack came running from behind the vessel. "The explosion was planned by the enemy, a booby-trap."

Jack's voice was flat, matter-of-fact in tone. "All okay, and nothing damaged."

Ava spoke. "Help us drag this mantis into the light."

Dan and Emily came around to join the group. Mat raised his hands; all stared at him. "I repeat, that explosion was a booby-trap. Proceed with caution."

Ava raised her hand. "Take note. 'Caution' is the word."

Mat and Jack partially lifted and dragged the mantis by his arms, down the ramp into the light of dawn. Mat spoke, the emotion of surprise in his voice. "Doesn't he look like Abe?"

Jack opined, "Yes, very much so."

Ava smiled, then stopped abruptly, afraid her emotional face would communicate too much.

Dan sensed something, then blurted, "It's a clone, isn't it?"

Ava spoke. "I cannot comment on that."

Mat surmised and commented, "It's more than a clone; look at the claw finger—it's larger and sharper."

Jack's voice held the excitement of discovery. "Look at the thighs, shorter, more compact, and heavier with muscle. And the lower leg is longer, the calf more humanlike." A boot had been blown off, exposing the foot.

Emily added her revelation. "Look at the knees! They flex like ours—in one direction only. And there is an arch in the feet."

Dan commented, "The skull is larger."

Ava spoke. "Okay, now you know why I am here. But I cannot admit to it and will not confirm or deny any of your observations." All gathered knew the mantis form was becoming human. Ava spoke again. "We wish secrecy for the sake of our Thermidorian friends, as this could revive the argument that they, too, were manipulated many years in the past. I'm sure scientific proof will support the original call of no tampering in the past."

Emily was the only party member listening. Mat seemed absorbed in his thoughts, then returned purposely into the hull. Jack followed. Mat stood at the detonation point of the bomb, within the upper cockpit. He stood on an empty munitions box to look in and realized a man could not have fit into the cockpit. The mantis, standing on the deck? His torso could easily fit into the cockpit, with his head and arms in perfect reach of the controls. Mat exited back to the body of the mantis, saying, "Look at his helmet."

Emily was first to respond. "That's a flight helmet, not a combat helmet."

Ava spoke. "Yes, here is our pilot. He was to blow himself up to be unrecognizable if capture became imminent. He disobeyed, wanting to assess the situation, or wanting to fight."

Mat's voice came quietly. "The secret is that mantises were leading pilgrims." Then he added, "You were aware that a new human-appearing generation was coming."

Ava spoke. "Let's be detailed in our recording of measurements and in our observation notes; lives may depend upon it."

Mat understood that she would not address his thought. Dan remained silent; he had a puzzle that bothered him. That a mantis had piloted a ship meant nothing, even if pilgrims were passengers in the ship. But mantises leading humans? Why would this mantis leave his post to go out and die? Or had he hoped the explosive charges were attached to the Explorer and just needed detonation? Dan decided to check the corpse's body for anything unusual.

***

Sarah and Jem took the seats directly across from Keturah in the cafeteria. Keturah scowled. "No lectures. I know who the enemy is, who will change our way of life."

Jem spoke. "You want us to remain the parasite nation? What a heritage to our children."

Keturah spoke slowly and distinctly. "What is wrong with that? That is the natural world: the clever survive and with much less effort than the slow of mind."

Sarah countered, "'Do unto others as you would have them do onto you.'"

Keturah's chin lifted, and in a lofty tone uttered her words, "The mantids are welcome to try to do to us what we do to them. They don't have the intelligence."

Jem, irritated with Keturah, wished to knock her down to reality. "The Christians very well could return our evil with greater vengeance. They are offering us a chance to live with integrity and fairness, kindness. Those are better options for life."

Keturah spit her words. "The mantis are insects to whom we gave souls."

"That concept has been proven false," said Sarah.

Keturah continued in her rage. "The Christians just want to take what we have as they push their contrived world view, morals, and virtue down our throats."

Jem's voice match Keturah's voice in anger. "They believe and live the words they speak. Besides, they are humans of our very own stock, our genetics, our very own history. You need to look into your dark heart."

Keturah smiled. "My way is natural. All nature follows it, and it is good."

Jem tensed, was about to retort, when Sarah patted her hand, allowed her fingers to rest on the back of Jem's tense hand. Sarah had decided that facts were missing. "We are not to model our behavior on animal behavior, though this view comes easily, for our minds were corrupted by Satan, the fallen angel we called our father. Our true Father meant us to be above and separate. Separate, because our spirit, our souls come from Him, a holy God. Yes, we, our mechanical selves, were made of the stuff of Earth. We even mate in the fashion of apes and other mammals to bring new life into the material world of substance. But we—our minds, hearts, souls—have their birth and home, their *origin* in God. Let us finally live true to that heritage. He is the true vine and that is where we belong: living from His ever-present flow of right thinking and goodness."

"I don't believe the fairy tales." Keturah stood and moved to another, distant seat.

"Nor do I," said Sarah. "Words are of the Spirit realm, of God. When they come from God, they are truth." Sarah looked into Keturah's eyes and knew talk was pointless.

Jem whispered, "We need to track her every movement." Sarah nodded her head in agreement and added, "We need to find out how she communicates with those above her."

***

Dan had meticulously searched the body of the mantis pilot. In a pouch, marked by the first aid symbol and attached to his waist belt, was a creamy liquid Dan had never found in pouches on past battlefields. The plastic container had a squirt top, which he thought odd. Even mantis blood-clotting agents, scab-forming agents, wound-binding agents all had a thickness that needed direct hand application due to the hardness of the skin. The container's directions said nothing but "topical use only." He used a scalpel to transfer a drop of the liquid onto a petri dish. Then a drop went into the analyzer unit. The unit did not produce a quick answer to the composition. Dan left the analyzer on, knowing it would automatically shut down when the analysis was complete. The liquid sticking to the scalpel, he wiped onto the metal frame of the vessel's ramp. Then he just set the scalpel aside on the metal frame, before rejoining his crew, who were expanding outward, wishing to identify more mantis bodies. The mantis soldier's corpses were on the periphery, for they had been brought in to kill the security forces of Explorer 7.

Jack and Mat had disentangled the last and furthest pile of deceased mantis soldiers. Ava had received orders to initiate a more involved evaluation of the deceased soldiers. Jack had already begun pulling off and separating equipment and uniforms so that Dan and Emily could begin recording anatomy changes, wounds. Ava began searching pockets and pouches for documents or personal diaries. Mat held up a large, cylindrical container he had found in one rucksack. "What goodies do we have in here?"

Dan yelled, "Don't open it! Put it down immediately. And take your gloves off and do not touch them with bare skin. Throw the gloves away." Dan believed he saw streaks of clear grease upon the dark-gray container, and his mind had gone to the liquid in the squirt container of the first mantis body.

Mat obeyed, realizing he could have been handling a new plastic explosive or chemical/biological liquids. Dan approached, pulled out of his top pocket a plastic wound probe, and scraped the thinnest coating of the grease from the outside of the cylinder. "Let's take a walk," he said to Mat, as he remembered his chemical analyzer had been left by the first bodies studied. He talked as he walked. "This resembles a liquid I found in a squirt container at the first mantis body. It was in a first-aid pouch."

Mat speculated. "Some kind of mantis ointment or medicine, I suppose. This new to the battle—the mantis was carrying a resupply container."

Dan answered, "No one else carried the squirt container or a resupply container."

"That is odd," Mat said, as they reached the enemy's attack vessel.

Dan stopped and stood perfectly still. He put his arm out before Mat as a barrier to further movement. He spoke. "See that black, squarish blob?"

Mat answered, "Yes. What is it?"

Dan answered, "The chemical analyzer machine."

Mat's mouth went open to form a word. Before he could speak, Dan said, "See that black encrustation on the side of the ramp leading into the enemy vessel?"

"Yes," said Mat.

"That's where I placed the scalpel that held a sample of the liquid from the squirt bottle, which I placed in the analyzer," said Dan.

Mat's voice was thick with surprise. "That was three hours ago."

Dan's eyes were searching, and he found what he sought—an alien weapon that had been kicked under the ramp. He picked it up, pushed the end of the barrel against the analyzer, and grunted in effort. It barely moved. He did the same to the scalpel. No movement: the scalpel had been melded to the metal frame of the ramp by the black encrustation.

Mat spoke. "I wonder what would have happened to Explorer 7 if this liquid had been slapped on the outer hull?"

Dan answered, "It would probably make it too heavy to fly."

"Or make it fly lopsided till stressed bearings cracked and the ship crashed," Mat said. "I wonder if it's done spreading?"

Dan said, "Don't know. But send out pictures of the container, the squirt bottle, and the encrustations, with a danger warning for our people and for Andy to forward to all of our forces."

Mat spoke. "Mr. Mantis left the safety of his ship to spread the liquid on Explorer 7."

"That squad's mission was to destroy the Explorer 7 so that it could not leave this planet," Dan surmised. "Think of the potential for this liquid in covert operations."

Mat spoke in an assumed voice of panic. "Captain, the helm is not responding"

Dan replied in the same voice and tone, "We have lost power, Captain."

"Such is war," Mat concluded.

***

Pete rechecked the sound-monitoring machines in his small cubicle of an office. Grace was standing on a chair in the corner of the room, hands overhead, pressing a replacement sound panel into the vacant area. Their internal-detection duties had increased in importance with the transporting of the pilgrims, and they became critically important when one of the pilgrims was caught retrieving data and sending it to the radical faction of the Pilgrim Alliance. Grace sensed Pete's need for quiet. The panel slipped in flawlessly, a few hard, prolonged, pressure pushes sealed the panel.

She stepped down quietly, pleased with the suppleness of her muscles and the quietness of her joints. She had never experienced any debilitating complaints, as she had been born in the Millennium, but in her readings about premillennial populations and their ailments, she had discovered the vagaries of the body. Ling's comment that pilgrims, for all their knowledge of space and propulsion, suffered heavily from rheumatism, bad teeth, weakening muscular strength, and headaches had bolstered Grace's realization. The medical knowledge of the pilgrims wasn't much above twentieth-century Earth's, and it was nowhere near that of the resurrected body of immortality.

She looked at Pete; he was concentrating so powerfully she could feel the effort vibrating around his head. Headphones on, eyes squinting in concentration. He was on to something. He pressed the headphones more tightly to his ears. He looked into her eyes; his index finger pointed at her and then curled. She lifted her chair and placed it closer to his. She saw him pulling out his ear phones. She quickly tucked her hair behind her ears, and he placed the earphones upon her ears. He picked up her right hand from the table and placed it on a sound dial. He inched his two fingers together till they almost touched. He was giving instruction for minute changes in movement.

She heard clicking, and, as a tablet was on the table and a pen, she began making long and short dashes of profuse sizes. Sometimes she heard a grating rubbing, which a squiggly line would represent. She could only associate the sounds with an underwater sea creature devouring a crustacean, or a boring insect within a tree or chlorophyll plant. Then, the sound stopped. She waited and waited and then turned the room speakers on as she removed her headphones. He stared at her, and she, at him.

He asked, "What were we listening to?"

She had held her breath to better explore the silence for sound, then expelled her breath. She breathed in deeply before speaking. "Let's hope it has nothing to do with the accreting glue just discovered in the enemy's arsenal."

He clamped his teeth and smiled wisely. "I think the minerals blowing in the air would give a sound like blowing snow or sleet on a window or wall. A hissing sound as they stuck to the glue and permeated and rose through the collected detritus."

She thought about his answer. "I think you're correct. We only need to worry under two circumstances: If this is a language being broadcast to our enemies, holding secrets. Or if this is the sound of animal life, or chemical reactions, that are destroying our vessel."

Pete answered. "It could be a benign natural noise that the enemy has discovered and is being used to track us."

"Possible," she said, as she shook her head in disbelief. "But too many traditional ways are easier."

He answered. "Easier but known."

Ling was at the door, and before he could speak, Grace had him by the hand and dragged him into the room. "We need your expertise, Dr Ling. Listen to these sounds." She played the sound over the speakers. She showed him her attempt to draw the sounds.

Ling answered, "A wood-boring insect is my guess, and as we have little wood in this vessel, try the beans in the pantry. Maybe some larvae are feeding." Then his face lit with surprise. "What about mantid corpses? Parasites might be eating their chitin bodies." He sat at a nearby, empty seat and computer terminal, seeking the location of the mantis bodies in the data base. Were any corpses being held in the morgue for future study or stored for transportation? Had body parts and debris cast by ordnance lodged in the outer structure of the ship?

As no mantis bodies were found aboard ship, Ling was standing to leave when Diana walked by the room. "Diana, stop, come back," said Grace.

Diana retraced her steps in reverse without turning around; she was noted for efficient maneuvers of locomotion or with any body movement. Her eyes opened wide—everyone knew that was her sign for willingness and participation. Ling remained.

Grace spoke. "Listen to these sounds." Pete turned on the recordings.

Diana seemed puzzled at first, then, a look of familiarity and disbelief came to her face. She spoke. "I know the sounds, but what do I win?"

Pete answered, "Our eternal gratitude."

Diana smiled. "That will do. Now, the buildup. I lived before the Tribulation. Our physical forms had flaws, as we lived under the curse. Our teeth were a big problem—overbites and underbites, cavities, jaw-hinge problems. Sound recordings were done as a diagnostic tool—I heard many, because I was in training for a short while as a dental technician. That is what you hear; someone sending out code by an array of tooth and jaw noises, clicks and clacks, quick staccato bites, and individual bites. You hear the swallowing of excess saliva, and the handling of nasal secretions. You hear grinding—that grinding is part of the language. Someone is sitting quietly and talking, probably has a metal filling that carries the sound to a nearby transponder. Perhaps the entire hull of our vessel is the antenna." Diana held her hands high. "I knew my four months of dental training would reap vast dividends!"

They all began to clap, and Pete whistled.

After the applause, Ling quietly said, "Now we need a computer program to speed the discovery process. This is probably an ancient Middle Eastern language."

"Or ancient mantis," Diana said.

Grace spoke. "Let's get Ava involved."

***

Andy and Ling were seated alone in the consultation room of the medical facilities area of Explorer 7 as Emily knocked and was granted access. She sat on the remaining empty chair.

"You hit the jackpot," Andy said with a laugh.

Emily smiled broadly and wondered if the laughter negated the jackpot.

Ling chuckled. "You'll get some kind of citation, I'm sure, as your results from the pilgrim soldiers' DNA swabs that I tested show…." Ling smiled as the surprise grew in intensity. "All the soldiers were cloned and produced through ectogenesis!"

Emily's mouth opened wide in surprise, even as her eyes narrowed at the possible implications.

Andy spoke. "Your eyes tell me you understand the questions that might arise."

Ling answered, "Like how many naturally born pilgrims really exist."

Emily added, "Were those pilgrims we have bonded with born naturally? You know, a mantis was the pilot of the craft that landed those soldiers."

Andy answered, "Who is the dominant species, is a relevant question. I will summon an angelic courier to present this knowledge to the Lord in New Jerusalem. Determining true numbers would be an angel assignment."

Emily raised her hand timidly from her lap.

Andy spoke. "Speak, precious Emily."

She grimaced and breathed through her clenched teeth. "Some people in the know say genetic mutations have been shaping the mantids for thousands of years. Mutations were noticed from a specimen on the battlefield."

Andy's eyebrow rose as he stared into Ling's eyes.

Ling said, "Yes, that is true. But also remember the soul cannot be transferred or mutated. We are downplaying the mutations, but justice will come in time. Sooner than you think."

Andy studied Emily's demeanor; he knew she had a final question, and he would answer it. "What our Christian-leaning pilgrims know about themselves or their people, we do not know. They may not know they are clones! It is possible they are all hiding vital information and may not even be our friends, but till that is proven, we will just keep loving them."

A burden fell from Emily. She smiled and, completely relaxed, said, "That is what I will do. Thank you, sir."

Andy spoke. "Ling and I thank *you*…ma'am." He rose and held her delicate hand.

Ling stood and spoke. "If anyone asks about the DNA results, just say the sample was sent to a more advanced site for further testing. That is true." Ling took Emily's hand and wrapped both his hands around it as they moved to the door.

CHAPTER 21

Within twelve minutes, Ava and her team of Ling, Tim, Pete and Grace, Emily and Dan, Robin, Tom, and one AI computer had broken the "tooth" code. Keturah was the spy and messenger. Her sounds had been duplicated, and it was now possible to produce flawless messages with her cadence and in her style. Angelic messengers had notified all starship captains and first officers, all intelligence-gathering operations, and all leaders of departments, of a sound security breach. Past soundtracks were searched, and a select few soon knew the extent of damage, which was minimal. It was determined to simply listen to the communication flow in hope of identifying the time, place, and actors of a future event—the disruption of which could cause significant weakness or collapse of the pilgrim's planned desire for complete domination.

The greatest blessing to date was information pertinent to the accreting glue. Its chemical composition, destructive process, capabilities, production-site locations and capacities had all been discussed, due to the newly uncovered code. Of secondary importance was the revealing of the hostile pilgrim actors, their goals, and timetable. Their sizable underground population on Thermador had been unknown prior to the breaking of the tooth code. The goal of the Kingdom of Christ was to isolate the radical population, pull out the most radical—those who had no qualms about killing others—and banish them to a livable planet, where only peaceful and democratic principles were tolerated. The search for a penitentiary planet was currently underway. This last goal's implementation date was being rushed because of the accelerated effort of the pilgrims to increase their ranks by cloning, and to remodify the mantis people, before taking military action against Christians.

***

Keturah couldn't help but smile as she walked down the ramp from Explorer 7 onto Thermador, with her fellow pilgrim travelers. If any Christian asked about her happiness, she would say she was happy for the approaching referendum. It was to be held tomorrow throughout the Rau-toon Empire, including the former vassal state of Thermador, and on all settlements and outposts of the Pilgrim Alliance. She blithely followed her group to the mass of blue-uniformed pilgrims already gathered on the airport flatness; they were held in place by a fence, with three gates, the official customs registration site for entering Thermador.

She moved into the heart of the gathering till she saw the face of her designated confederate signaling—a blatantly cheery smile. It was code for "stop." She stopped, and individuals began working through the crowd toward her; hundreds surrounded her, tightening their ring. A large umbrella, almost the size of a small, one-person tent, as was common to the inhabitants of Thermador, went up over her head. Then, scores of umbrellas popped open in unison from all who had surrounded her.

Hands quickly removed her outer garments and placed a tight-fitting bodysuit upon her, before draping her in a new blue uniform. She was fitted with a wig. A special facial makeup was applied that appeared normal but deflected light and changed angles on scanning equipment. Shoes with lifts were put on her feet. The circular mass began to spread out, the umbrellas went down, and anyone looking for Keturah would not have spotted her. If someone was tracking Keturah through her heat signature, scent, height, weight, and facial profile, their equipment would receive inaccurate data. The massive crowd had separated into three fast-moving lines of entry. Half the crowd had already dispersed on the other side of the gates. In a minute, the last of the crowd was through the gates. Any agent tracking Keturah would be staring at an empty plot of cement.

Pretty good, thought Ava, watching through a security camera aboard the Explorer 7; except Keturah was clicking away to someone nearby. The clicks could be followed. But even that didn't matter, because days ago the clicks had been tracked into the bowels of Thermador, to a hidden cell of the status quo pilgrims. Most assuredly, that was her destination. The intelligence arm of the Christian forces determined that three million fighting mantids, mostly Rau-toon men and women, were interspersed in the general area of the one hundred thousand pilgrims inside Thermador. The lava-flow canals, the mining tunnels, and the large caverns held the soldiers, machines, and weapons of this advanced civilization of cousin earthlings.

***

The Explorer 7 crew was gathered in the conference room. The pilgrims leaning toward Christianity had departed for a planet chosen for a gathering of their own, where they were to work out their moral and political path concerning the rights of the mantis people and the goal of a newly reorganized Pilgrim Alliance agenda. The Explorer 7 crew were, themselves, attempting to find a path through the delicate feelings and aspirations of three civilizations—Thermadorian, Rau-toon, and Pilgrim—to create a semblance of what Christians knew would be a treaty that worked fairly and satisfied the heart of Christ. Separating the Christian from the non-Christian and giving them their own planets seemed logical, because giving one's life and will to Christ had no formula, and no one could be forced to Him. But external morality, a citizen's code of conduct with other citizens, had to exist. A person of the non-Christian planet could choose to live on the Christian planet when he or she had made the decision to become a Chrisitan. Non-Christians were forced to remain on their planet. A code of conduct conducive to harmony and an agreed-upon economic system that was fair and balanced were essential. The non-Christian planet needed an economic system with agreed-upon rules as to what was acceptable, fair, and good, influenced by the current whim of what those words meant.

"Do onto others as you would want them to do unto you" was the basic premise that could lead to unprecedented harmony. It needed no other attachment to Christianity, if the populace was of balanced mind and goodwill. The greatest part of Judeo-Christian conduct was common sense. Much of what was agreed upon as good—and in use by the unknowing—had been authored by God.

The discovery found in Earth history was that when humankind applauded common sense and they sensed themselves the authors, it was good. But as soon as Christ was attached to common sense, it was then considered loathsome. Cleverly, evil beings would question who the "others" were and whether they deserved the same treatment. Could they even understand the premise? What was their idea of harmony? As all cognizant beings naturally defaulted to the voices of their fleshly appetites, an un-Christian base would always lead to sides being drawn and unfairness practiced. Paradoxically, all present agreed that the non-Christian would not want to be separated from the Christian, as non-Christian machinations needed victims, and their desires needed to be espoused in their fight for domination. Force would be necessary to divide the populations, and a fleet of starships would be needed to keep the troublemaking non-Christians on their own planets.

***

Andy scanned the passenger bay of the Explorer 7, where his entire crew was gathered, all in combat gear. This included Ava, for the time being. Her expertise might cause her to leave for the securing, interpreting of intelligence finds. Behind them were two more platoons, mostly made up of the crews of Explorer 8 and Explorer 6. Andy's ship was being flown and weapons manned by officers and crew new to the conflict. His was the only starship where 100 percent of the crew had opted to participate in the combat phase of separating out the peaceful pilgrims—those who agreed the mantis should be free and an economic system of Christian capitalism should be developed. Some of these pilgrims had already embraced Christ; some were leaning toward this truth. Some had no opinion on the subject and had no interest in Christ but understood that a code of values was necessary for any society, and the Christian ideas of societal codes, including the Ten Commandments, had merit.

Sarah, Jem, and the male pilgrims Jared, Enoch, and Noah, who had been at the first meeting of the two worlds and in the subsequent brawl and rescue, were in combat gear. Their votes had already been tallied; they leaned toward Christianity. They would be crucial in interfaces with their own people and would attempt to arrange peaceful surrender for any who wished it. It was unknown how many of the pilgrims of peace had been bullied into remaining with the belligerents. No one knew what to expect. All knew the hostile pilgrims did not have eternal life and were gambling their existence: they did not believe in an afterlife. Their body armor and newly discovered force-field technology promised survival, as did their highly developed surgical skills. This would ensure a boldness in their attitude.

The Explorer 7 crew had eternal life, and Ava had assured them that even disintegration was not painful, nor was the rebuilding process. Some of the crew had been wounded in past conflicts, and they too added assurances to the group emotion of confidence. The platoon also had what they considered the choice mission. They would be inserted within the subterranean world, which most thought would be easier than forcing entry from the planet's surface into the interior, where booby traps, ambushes, and strategies had been seeded and planned.

Mat had begun to pray aloud, and those around him had joined, till the entire crew of Explorer 7 was deep in prayer, the lead constantly changing as each member continued a theme from the last leader's prayers. The Psalms were read, silently and aloud, and the prophets. Beyond his crew, the other two platoons began their own prayers. The ship began to rock and thump as rounds struck nearby. Lights flickered, darkness came and went.

The green "go" light was on. Andy yelled, "Up!"

They stood, felt a surge of emotion and a resolution to their duty to free the oppressed and serve their King honorably. The green light remained, and then the red light went on, and they wondered what the situation truly was. The lights remained on. The ship began to shudder, and the speed decreased suddenly. There was only a makeshift rope to hold onto, strung at shoulder height down the center of the hold. The rope offered stability, but with so much weight upon it, there was play, and the crew bent down into themselves to push their weight onto the floor through their feet.

There was no fear in the crowded bay. At most, the redeemed could have an emotion of pensiveness and the feeling of time prolonged and dragging, which was remedied with prayer and meditation on the Word. The allied pilgrims aboard knew fear; and looking upon the Christians, knew they did not fear.

The intercom sounded the "pipes." The ship's captain was to speak, his voice came. "Stand down. Intel says there are no enemy forces within Thermador. Acquiring new mission."

All were returning to the floor, and many tumbled as they made the attempt, caught in the arms of the already seated. Andy spoke to those looking at him. "Speculation. Protocol is to send angel forces through on reconnaissance. They found nothing. The battle is on the surface."

Those who heard began to tell those who had not. The intelligence department had never been so decidedly wrong. They shrugged the failure from their minds; God would work something good from this; something anticipated had not happened. It was man who gathered the intelligence, it was man who believed it, and man who was disappointed that he had not been correct. God was God, all knowing, and they were still in Him. The pounding outside became severe; teeth were clamped or jaws would clatter, and muscles tensed. Every individual strained to remain in place, centered above their hips, motionless. All at some time swayed violently into their comrades.

Andy heard the engine rapidly decreasing power, and bodies, though tightly packed, began to move across the floor. Then silence, stillness, nonmovement. The sounds of explosions seemed above the ship. Had they landed on the surface? Would the captain call for them to exit? Were they just sitting, waiting to take a round that would disintegrate them all? Faces began looking at Andy.

Andy spoke. "John, send out two men to find a place of safety. The ship may leave before they can return."

John turned to Jack and Seth beside him, touched their chests with quick jabs. "Find a place of safety, return quickly, as the ship may leave at any time."

Jack and Seth were standing, and then they were gone. Even as Andy had stood, saying, "I will speak to the captain." His intercom channel was dead.

***

Andy had his crew of seventeen hidden and protected by a four-foot ridge, with adjacent single boulders to his flanks and rear. Even standing on dry, barren Thermador was better than being in the ship. His Christian pilgrims, Sarah, Jem, Jared, Enoch, and Noah, were securely in the center of the oval perimeter lines. Ava was beside him. Tom, with his platoon, was to his left; John, with his platoon, was to the right. Tom had Woden, Paternus, Tuck, Tim, Ling, Dan, and Emily. John had Jack, Seth, Robin, Mat, Diana, Pete, and Grace. The other two ships' companies were to his right and left.

The Explorer 7 was a distance behind his lines, its engine now reaching full thrust for a quick getaway to a more hidden and secure location, hopefully within an hour's walk. Communications had been jammed. The enemy knew the location of the ship, as the rounds hitting the ship's force field when airborne had been severe. The captain had dropped suddenly, with the shells bursting above him long after he had descended. The enemy would eventually understand he had dropped below their fire, and they would adjust and begin again. The infantry nearby would then be targeted. The captain would attempt a hover near the ground to reach the new position, in the hopes he could remain hidden by the height of the terrain that was blocking the view of the enemy artillery and rockets.

All eyes were on the Explorer 7, rising just four feet from the ground. The ground was firm, and the dust only two feet off the ground. No one cheered, as the enemy might be monitoring sounds, but all were smiling. As the massive ship moved slowly, it passed over sandy-soil terrain, and dust plumes began to rise into the sky. The hidden audience watched a streak appear on the horizon. It was almost imperceptible, almost imaginary, while it arched, then dropped toward the surface of the planet, striking the Explorer 7. The

Explorer 7 skittered along the dusty ground and stopped. As the Explorer stopped, a barrage of rounds landed upon the spot where it had first been struck, raising clouds of dust.

There were no moans from Andy's crew. They weren't ones to wish and project problems, set-backs. They would let the dust settle and deal in reality. The dust settled. The Explorer 7 sat, touched only by the first round; all others had fallen within a circular area whose boundary was a sizable distance from the Explorer, and boulders had blocked shrapnel. A runner, Mat, was sent to the Explorer. Mat returned with the news that the Explorer would be out of action for three days, if lucky.

Jared, Enoch, Noah, Sarah, and Jem watched everything, every reaction of the Christians. The pilgrims were secretly comparing their humanness to that of their Christian cousins.

Andy moved to John by scampering on his knees, not wishing to break the ridgeline's profile. "Gather in your people. I want to talk." Tom saw Andy with John and heard the request. He understood the reason, though not spoken. Tom called in his people. Andy looked plainly at Tom and knew Tom understood. The two groups coalesced but did not mingle, keeping their unit integrity.

Andy called to the pilgrims, who were sitting alone since the shift had occurred. "Come over here."

Andy spoke to the assembled. "Possibly three days before a fix. Will we be shot down as soon as we move the Explorer, if not before? No promises. Are we familiar with where we are on the map?"

He knew, and some of them should know as well. John, beside Andy, with his crew stretching in a tight line, spoke. "We're only a day or two from the big encampment of Thermadorians by the river, where the angels came to our defense."

Mat spoke. "Where the massacre was to happen."

Paternus's deep voice entered the conversation. "The wide river; the bamboo forests; the four villages of tents; Abe, our prisoner; and Don's corpse wrapped up." He shook his head. "What memories."

Grace 's high, feminine-toned voice added, "And the Lord brought us through!"

Amens came from the survivors—John, Ling, Paternus, Mat, Seth, Woden, Pete, Jack, and lastly, Grace. The entire crew, except the pilgrims, knew the story, as the survivors had wanted to share the glory of the angelic warriors, who watched over them.

Andy spoke as he reached back and put his arm around Ava, who had her head comm over her ears as she listened to the chatter. "Ava has been listening to the Thermadorians dug in and fighting in that area. Don Key and Abe Lincoln are fighting, and the situation is tense. Pilgrims are acting as advisers to Rau-toon warriors, who number six-to-one against the Thermadorians. Should we get involved? That is also a question for you pilgrims."

John was first to speak. "I would get involved. We're soldiers, and theirs is a worthy fight. Don and Abe are our battle buddies; we owe them. But what is our plan for victory? Is it doable by ourselves? Do we need hard resources and/or simply more troops? Let's plan this scenario out."

Tom spoke. "'Exuberance is the handmaiden of carelessness and subsequently defeat,' say the Byzantine crowd. Our emotion should not influence us. But we have a duty to the Thermadorian cause and to Don and Abe. Let's look at the particulars."

Andy projected a topographic map with troop locations and artillery and rocket positions upon a hologram board before the gathered.

Sarah raised her hand tentatively—her knowledge of Andy's openness on all subjects measured against her experientially known values of openness in pilgrim culture, which was to say: none.

Andy spoke. "Speak freely, Sarah. Don't hold back." He saw her face relax and broaden in peace. She now felt free to speak, and this brought happiness to him.

Sarah said, "You have such latitude of command. Is it in your best interests to broaden your fight and suffer material losses and possible long-term down time for your troops? For Thermadorians?"

Andy spoke. "Yes, best interests. That's why everyone has a say, and all your reasons must be discussed except the last—Thermadorians…and I could easily add pilgrims, if following your logic. Can anyone explain this to our friends?"

Mat raised his hand and spoke. "We volunteered to explore the universe and expand God's Kingdom. Freedom to follow Him means freedom to individuals in whatever grouping they belong to or decide to group themselves in. We have worked with Thermadorians, Don and Abe, and though they are not like us in appearance, language, and a host of things, they know right from wrong and are cognizant of a God force. Many have accepted Christ, as did Abe and Don. All are entitled to be treated with respect and dignity."

"Yes," said Sarah, "but they were made by us. *We* gave them 'souls.'"

Tim spoke to his son, Mat's, logic. "And they would resist the taking away of their souls even if your statement were true, would they not?"

Sarah appeared perplexed, though she knew they would resist their souls being taken.

Ling entered the talk. "Suddenly, the awareness of soul life was given them from an outside source. This does not invalidate anything. Every Christian here has experienced the sudden shock of revelation that God is all, and His Son, Christ, is the only reality and clarity needed. All of us were living as animals—yes, us, the perfect allies—lived from and in the ruminations of animal spirits and carnal souls. And then God reached down to us, and like a spark, ignited the realization of our true state. We were Rau-toon. We were Thermadorians. May I say it? We were pilgrims."

Tim spoke. "Treasure this, Sarah. It is not where we come from physically. But spiritually, it is where we are going, the present and the future. And if an insect-appearing life-form comes to me and needs help, wishes to pursue his realization of God who saves, that's enough for me."

The Explorer 7 crew erupted in amens and chuckles. They laughed that they were "fools for Christ." Tim reached over and squeezed Sarah's arm inclusively. Jem, Jared, Enoch, and Noah seemed deeply affected by the words, and all noticed Tim's squeeze of Sarah's arm. To the Christians, pilgrims were their friends, and their words were considered important.

Andy, on his knees, with his telescoping pointer extended to the hologram map, ran the pointer around the perimeter of the Thermadorian forces. "Now, about those other issues. Almost a perfect U shape," he said. "Watch while I do it again." The U shape was the Rau-toon line of encirclement. He looked at his audience. "A rectangle within the U shape. The rectangle represents the Thermadorian defensive lines. The two outlines are sometimes within a sprint of each other, sometimes hundreds of yards away. The enemy is holding slightly higher ground with rocks, boulders, hills, and ridges to hide them. Who sees the strategy?"

Sarah, sitting quietly, realized no one had been upset by her question, and there was no hostility. She admitted, to herself, that the present and future were all, and the Thermadorians seemed to have an embrace of a God force, perhaps greater than her people's. That was the center of these Christians' belief, which she had neglected because she valued their oneness and their virtues and their technology. Her realization was that the Lord Jesus had given them a spark that burned through them, destroyed the old, and brought the light of the God of creation. Her mind rapidly grasped the ramifications of their liberty and freedom, gained not through licentiousness and irresponsibility toward others and life, but by knowledge of their foolishness, blindness, and a steadfast faith in the presence of their God.

John raised his hand, and Andy acquiesced to his request with an open, inviting hand. John spoke. "Let's puncture the enemy trench line in one massive assault, remain in the trench and follow it—just sweep through, follow the contour, dislodging them by a rapid assault that has them running into each other or onto the kill zone of the Thermadorians or toward the desert, where there's no cover. We leave a blocking force where we first assault, so no one can attack our rear and where we can stop any of the fleeing enemy from regrouping behind us and attacking."

Tom spoke. "I second that—if, after the initial attack, we send one squad to the right and one to the left to roll up the lines."

Andy spoke. "I will give that great thought and answer later. Less strength when divided but yes, we won't be bunched up targets for the enemy."

"Fair enough," said Tom.

"I agree with John and Tom," Woden affirmed, then added, "as long as we keep our lasers, heavy machine guns, and self-propelled rockets on the cutting edge of the assault."

Mat and Jack had been having a whispered conference; they looked at each to see who would speak, and Mat raised his hand. Andy nodded his head, Mat spoke. "We need someone with comms ready to call in supporting fire if there is an enemy salient, but more importantly, if there is a reactionary force of enemy troops ready to pounce on us."

Andy spoke. "Yes, that was my concern as well. Level-headed Ava on comms and emotionless Emily plotting coordinates should fill that need."

Emily held up her arms in glee, pumping them upward rapidly. "My home is built on the Rock. I am steady in the Lord!" she declared solidly.

Andy smiled at Ava and Emily, both now chanting the worthiness of their God. "The Lord is good, mighty is He, life is in His hands, He's our victory…" Lyrics without end, pouring from their hearts, as their emotions ignited, from the light seen in the eyes of the other. The words ended suddenly as the peace and assurance of the Spirit descended upon them.

Andy turned to the pilgrims, looking each one directly in the eyes. "What say you, pilgrims? In or out? You may die, so I suggest you give your life to Christ, for He will raise you at an unknown time to eternal life. Or perhaps He will raise you immediately, like He did Ava. No one, I repeat *no one*, will think less of you if you remain. We all clearly see the barriers and empathize with your situation. Pause and think. I will return to you."

He turned to John and Tom. "I worry about transporting. We cannot carry enough ammo or food. The skies will be filled with streaking missiles and shells. It is reported the pilgrims have a radar that can pick us up and so shoot us down." He paused for a moment. "Quickest route to the beleaguered is to send out two scouts, invisible and far apart, after a surveillance-systems check. Scouts ready in fifteen, and the rest, in thirty. Two mechanical mules apiece for ammo, one for a weapons system, and one for advanced first aid.

Spread our people out wherever feasible. The pace will match the terrain, always as fast as orderly. Probably no sleep tonight. And have Ava send a message addressed to Don saying, 'The star-spangled banner yet waves.'"

John smiled. "'Over the land of the free and the home of the brave.'"

Tom added, "I'll have our flag mounted for our arrival or flown by drone over the site."

Andy spoke. "Good touch. Now, about your business." Both men saluted.

Andy turned to the pilgrims.

Jared immediately spoke. "I wish to go."

"Why?" asked Andy.

Jared answered, "To test myself. To be a part of a noble task. And to stop any of my people who would stop you."

Enoch raised his hand. "I, too, will go. Noble it is to free people, and my own people disgust me. Sadly, they are not a part of this."

Andy's eyes went to Noah. Noah said nothing, his eyes downcast in thought. Andy thought upon his own struggles as a young warrior. Noah would fight; he just needed time to think. Andy's eyes went to Sarah.

Sarah spoke. "Jem and I feel this is beyond us in military skills, but we wish to experience the fight and we are physically fit and hardier than we appear. We will take ourselves back to the Explorer 7, if it's more than we can handle."

Andy spoke. "Okay, you four get yourselves ready." Andy had been surprised by their spunk and willingness to risk.

"Hey, I'm coming too!" Noah said loudly.

"Why?" asked Andy.

Noah, tears in his eyes, said, "Christ has bound me to you Christians, and where you go, I will go. The Spirit I've come to cherish as a friend compels me."

Mat cheered with a song in his deep voice, "Hallelujah!"

"And Amen," said Jack.

Paternus merely raised his hand in acknowledgment, moving it like a pendulum, and the Spirit upon him spoke through him, "A loyal band of brothers and sisters we are, through the valley of the shadow of death we go, victorious."

CHAPTER 22

Andy viewed the enemy lines through a wide-lensed periscope. The darkness was dense—few stars and planets, the moon absent. The air was crystalline, absent of particulates. His forces were positioned only one hundred yards from the enemy lines on the plateau lip. Fortunately, the enemy's focus was upon the Thermadorians below, on the opposite side of the ridge. Only one distracted watch of two Rau-toon warriors, faced the earthlings. Not more than twenty yards away, Andy saw one of a line of electronic tripwire devices placed on the open plain and not among the rocks that he and his squads hid behind. Poor soldiering skills were revealed in the placement. His forces were centered at the middle of the enemy's U-shaped lines. The curves of the U would be the keys to success. This is where the plateau met two ridges. The two ridges descended in height. The left ridge was mostly hard-packed sand and soil from centuries of river-borne silt from the river below. The right ridge was caused by the breaking of the plateau against a harder rock as the plateau had subsided in times past.

Within and below the U was the recently built military base of formerly occupying Christian forces, made during the first campaigns of victory, when the Rau-toon occupying forces had fled the Thermadorians. It was not a significant fortress, just soil and rock bulldozed into a rectangular wall, twenty feet high, with gun and artillery placements dug into the walls. Within the walls were landing sites for air platforms and interstellar ships. Beyond the military fortress, where the U-shaped lines did not reach, were the ragged remains of the civilian population centers; they consisted of tents, cave-like holes, furniture, discarded clothes, unburied dead drying in the sands, stores, and watering cisterns. The remains of the Christian force's enterprises:

morgue, hospital, armaments service center, churches, and restorer pods completed the scene of mayhem. It appeared the few remaining civilians were within the fort with their battle-hardened Thermadorian warriors.

Andy signaled John and Tom to come up. John, first up, was invited to the periscope. He viewed and then slowly slid the periscope to his right just a scant fraction from its original resting position on the rock. He lay on the rock, feeling the coldness. He readjusted the focus. The area below looked so small now, but that day when they had landed, surrounded by enemy Thermadorians, the air heavy with the licorice emotions like a haze above them, every Christian had felt the doom wished for them. Then, the angels had come. John chuckled quietly in thanksgiving. That was a sight that would be forever implanted within his mind. Now, the Thermadorians were free of the pilgrims' internal tampering; now Abe and Don were in their right minds and needing help. He studied the position imprisoning his friends, and the planned strategy of freedom unfolded within his mind like a vision. He set the scope down gently and half slid down the embankment. Tom moved up for his look.

Andy spoke in a whisper. "What do you think?"

John answered, "Invisible transport. They won't have time to acquire us as targets. We'll head for the center of the line before us and hit the line hard. Once chaos takes hold, one squad will go to the left, one to the right. We'll roll up the lines, in upon themselves, while moving outward. Knife, bayonet, battle-ax, and long knives, till lasers, rockets, auto weapons must be used."

Andy spoke, "I agree, dividing our attack forces will be to our benefit. Our lasers, rockets, automatic weapons firing into dense masses of bodies will make a massive human attack by us unnecessary." He added an observation and warning. "At the curves of the U, we may be silhouetted against the sky to those lower lines."

John broke in. "We must be aware and stay low."

Andy smiled. "Remember the Harrisburg Airport?"

John humphed contentedly, recalling that battle at the end of the Millennium, when Satan's forces had decided to run and not fight. "Yes, let's pray our Lord takes the fight out of these Rau-toon."

Tom, still at the crest, internally heard his friends' musings. He remembered being told the story, as he had been in Paradise at the time, having naturally died before Satan's last rebellion began.

Andy added, "I'm not counting on it, but I pray it too."

They watched Tom slide down the embankment from the scope. Both noticed the concern on his face, the blank stare of inward thoughts, the furrowed flesh between the eyes and upon the nose. He looked at them. "Saw two pilgrims enter the guard position and converse with the Rau-toon."

Jared was approaching them, and his voice was in a whisper. "Jem, monitoring communications, heard two hostile pilgrims speaking. One among the fortress besiegers and another to a distant fire-support position."

Jem, approached quickly and heard Jared's words. She synced her words into the flow, "Just a routine communications check to a drone-launching and drone-tracking guidance site. Somewhere distant, maybe a fifteen-minute flight away. Ava is triangulating the position."

Andy spoke. "Let's go to Ava. Once she has those coordinates, we will call in a strike, eradicate their drones before they can be called in on us, and then attack immediately."

His forces had taken a day and a half to reach this point, this placement by the enemy's lines. The Christian forces, who needed little sleep, whose energy consumption was regulated by well-tuned bodies that made the most of every calorie, vitamin, and mineral and could lower or raise hormone production, dependent upon demand, were ready for action. Even their seven-mile-an-hour pace, carrying equipment over rugged ground, in high heat, was simply noted within their minds, and automatically the body followed, making all adjustments without thought. In truth, the pace could have been doubled, leaving their pilgrims behind. The friendly pilgrims with them had none of the advantages of immortal health and capabilities.

Andy saw Ava, earbuds in, right hand on her handheld controller and fire-coordinate applicator. Her larger screen was propped up before her on the mound of dirt that gave her cover. She saw Andy approaching, pulled earbuds, and handed them to Sarah, who was crouched down beside her. Enoch, armed, was guarding. Ava approached Andy and placed her hand on his shoulder. She spoke. "Their drone site is to the west, fifteen to seventeen minutes flying time, depending on winds. This was a routine check-in call for status and time on target."

Andy asked, "What assets do we have available to neutralize?"

She answered, "Drones, forty minutes away from target."

Andy spoke. "Call them now, in code, for a strike on the base. While waiting for the strike, take three shoulder-fired rockets and our pilgrims to an interdicting line of fire, in case an enemy drone flies over in the next forty minutes. And be aware, if the missiles are available, they may be needed for a strike against the Rau-toon on the ridges."

"Understood," said Ava.

"Okay. Call me when our drone attack time on target is known," Andy said. "We will attack the plateau and ridges in invisible transporting status thereafter."

***

Andy looked at the timer on his wristband computer. The hunkered-down squads were lined up among the boulders, waiting for the signal to attack. Tom and crew to his left, and John and his crew to the right. They would pierce the enemy lines together, at the center of the plateau, and then begin to kill the enemy, creating a dead zone that would expand as they rolled up the enemy lines in opposite directions. Usually, the enemy fought to the death, but if the ruse of surrender seemed advantageous to the enemy, surrender would likely be initiated. The Christian forces had agreed no prisoners could be taken; there would be no time—speed and confusion were their greatest weapons. His people had been waiting forty minutes; naps had been taken; nonessential gear had been discarded from their bodies, and long knives, axes, and pistols had been strapped within easy reach. Rifles, with long bayonets attached, were in their hands. All had the set grin of clenched jaws upon their faces; the eyes appeared as steel bearings.

Andy stood. The time to strike was now: all was in order and the enemy firebase had been destroyed. He bellowed, "To the enemy with Our God before us!" Andy saluted Tom and John; brief smiles were upon their faces, and peace emanated from their auras. Tom and John returned the salute. They then ran their hands over their gear one last time and followed Andy. Just as Andy was to disappear, he saw Dan, Pete, and Grace moving to their respective platoons as medics or reactionary force, if needed. As he began his transport, rose in height, to his left, he saw Ava, peering at the communications devices before her. Emily and Sarah were huddled together—Emily with her coordinate number pad, and Sarah with her topographic map screen. The pilgrim men had surrounded their feminine teammates with lasers outward, searching for enemy targets. Andy's face was toward the enemy lines, his mind choosing his entry point among the enemy. The soldiers of Christ were airborne and invisible behind the now-embedded Andy as laser flashes, exploding grenades, and the sounds of war engulfed him.

The din increased and separated. He heard the shouts of pilgrim fighters and the strange clicking, guttural language of Rau-toon warriors. He smelled human blood, mantis licorice; he saw red and green blood puddling and heaving, twitching bodies. He heard groans. He silenced them with his laser pistol as he moved to his left, following the course of Tom's forces, down neatly dug-out trenches and firing posts extending off the main trench. He saw the large figure of Woden wrapped upon a thrashing mantis, whose blood was spurting wildly. He saw his son, Tuck, and then Paternus beside him, pistol in hand. He looked behind. Dan had arrived. He saw Pete and Grace moving away, following their squad.

The quiet, interpersonal stage of the assault, hand, knife, axe, pistol, was quickly over. The space gained was necessary for opening up the carnage of laser, automatic weapons, rockets. The enemy had been pushed into a compactness affecting their ability to fight. Andy came upon the large headquarters bunker immediately. Desks and chairs, computer screens and computers were everywhere broken and smashed. Files filled with chitin "paper" lay overturned. A projection from the officelike bunker—an unroofed salient, a firing position—looked down onto the Thermadorian fortress. Someone had planted a long pole into the ground, within the firing position, and on top was the "star-spangled banner," which every Thermadorian below could see. He hoped Don was alive to witness it. He had no time to collect intel, and he had only a rudimentary knowledge of Middle Eastern-based pilgrim and Rau toon.

He moved quickly, following the carnage, and realized he had turned the curve from the U's base to its side. No blockage or slowdown had occurred at this crucial point. The concept of time was left behind. He moved from immediacy to immediacy, constant reflexes and subconscious demands. He stepped over bodies, dispatched the dying with his pistol, dodged laser fire, curled in a ball time after time as grenades were thrown at him. He caught enemy grenades and tossed them back with wicked speed. He shot armed aggressors taking aim at his men. He shot pilgrim and mantis feigning surrender or grievous wounds. He may have been struck, he wasn't certain. He had to keep moving; his men needed him. With a glance, he could see the broad, shallow river hundreds of feet below. He quickly stole a look outside the bunker and saw the position of the Christian pilgrims, who were still watching, guarding the skies. Ava was there; he saw her dark hair braided tightly behind her helmet. Emily was behind her, motionless as a stone. Ava was hurrying toward her women, carrying rockets. Noah was behind, dragging a crate of rockets with each hand. He knew Jared and Enoch both wished to be in the fight when he saw hostile pilgrims running toward them, weapons raised. The weapons of Jared and Enoch fired at the rounds coming toward them; the hostile pilgrims fell. A civil war for them: the cost of honoring Christ more than their own people.

Andy contacted Ava by wrist phone. "It seems the enemy drone site destroyed was the only firebase." He referred to the Christian forces preemptory strike. "Come and join us at the bend in the U. This ridgeline is minutes from being completely ours."

"Aye, aye, sir," came over his wrist phone.

Andy continued to the end of the riverside ridgeline positions. Tom's men had collected Woden, Paternus, Tuck, Tim, and Ling at the last salient. All had superficial wounds that were being treated by Dan and Emily. Tom, looking down at the ruins of the former Thermadorian camps and the morgue and hospital grounds, saw Thermadorian women and children emerging from the below-ground homes and bomb shelters and slowly walking into the former military base, now the fighting position of Thermadorian resistance. Here, men were rising from their foxholes and ramparts and running down the dirt banks, sprinting for the U-shaped, former enemy lines above them. On the ridgeline, on the far side of the U, the flag of the United States had been raised over to the last rampart. Victory was secure, taken by John's command on the plateau side of the ridge.

Andy called, "Tom!"

Tom approached with eagerness in his movements and elation on his face. "Yes?"

Andy answered, "Play the audio stating who we are. No accidental killings needed. Get the help of the Thermadorians for body removal on the ridge and communicate to their leadership that we wish them and their family survivors to man these positions. The old fortress where they had been needs to be emptied. Find out what they need, so we can request it. I'm walking over to John to check on his men and give the same info to his Thermadorians. If you see Abe or Don, tell them we will have a party."

Tom smiled. "Yes, sir."

***

Andy walked to the ridgeline bunker filled with carnage. He walked on bodies sometimes two and three deep. He heard the national anthem of the United States playing. He paused in his walk for a moment of reflection. He faced the flag at John's position, saluted, and thought of the long history of that flag. Countless men had died for what it represented, giving their lives willingly and begrudgingly, and many with no allegiance and understanding of the God who asked for their most precious gift to be spilled upon the ground. Jesus knew what it meant to pour out the last measure—Jesus, on the cross. He looked upon the carnage within the rooved trench line. Debris and pilgrim and Rau-toon bodies and body parts. Such wasted lives, such wasted souls forever living in wandering—or perhaps burning in Hell this very minute. He prayed for his Thermadorian allies, for Don and Abe and their families. He knew Father God loved His children. Andy's men and women would be safe. He was thankful. "Thank you, Lord," he said aloud as his salute returned to his side and the walk continued.

Seeing the faces of John's command at the last bunker confirmed all was well. Pete and Grace were patching up the entire crew of fighters—John, Jack, Seth, Robin, Mat, and Diana. Their wounds were similar to those of Tom's crew: slashing injuries, a few shallow puncture wounds, a concussions from grenades, dust and dirt in the eyes. The emaciated Thermadorians, just arriving, had lined up for medical assistance. Andy ordered John to gather the healthiest appearing Thermadorians and put them to work, cleaning up their new home, the former enemy positions. No one was to remain in their former defensive positions.

Sitting in the medical line, worn and emaciated, were Abe and Don. Andy approached them, with Jack and Mat by his sides. He extended his hand to their shoulders, smelled their scent of licorice mixed with the sticky coating of blood on their skin, pushed to the surface by the intensity of their exertions. He noticed broken bayonets and knife blades stuck in the hard skin. Various slashing wounds had cut deep into their chitin. Their eyes were cloudy, and the red light within them was waning and reviving with the beating of their hearts. Andy spoke. "Good men, lovers of your country, your people. God has brought you through."

"Not all," said Abe, whose wife and two children were with him. The youngest child would have been considered a child in Earth years—a first or second grader. He was shy, tired, and hungry. Mat saw the child's need and pulled a Hershey candy bar from his ruck, peeled the wrapper away, and handed it to the dirty hands of the boy. Jack knew that Mat traveled with Hershey bars simply to give away. The original Hershey's factory had been only miles from his Harrisburg home during the Tribulation. Mat had described, in talks past, the severity of hunger during the Tribulation, and the hunger of his sister, Katie. Jack remembered the stories of starvation told to him by his aunties Tanya, Anya, and Flo, and how a Mr. Johnson, now known as Tim, had given their dad, Tom Sr., a can of beef stew. Jack made the sign to eat, and the boy bit off a piece of chocolate.

Andy responded to Abe's statement. "Did the others live from Christ's power? If they did, then you will see them again. They are not dead."

Abe looked at the ground, his mind in deep concentration, remembering the living Ava, who had once been goo. Don broke the silence. "I believe." Then, Abe nodded his head. "I believe…Don believe, for Ava alive. We prayed for you to come with our friends, our brave friends. Valor men from Christ. You came." Tears flowed from Abe's eyes.

The boy held the candy in his mouth, afraid to chew, then, deeming it safe, moved his jaws, and his face lit up. The boy's first instinct was to give his older brother a piece. Jack couldn't help but laugh in happiness at the boy's delight and his kindness. Mat's emotion was pulled to the young brother's kindness, too, as Mat had been pulled to his sister, Katie's, need. Jack grabbed the boy by his shoulders and shook him playfully, gently. "Gooood, huh?" Jack asked through his tears. Mat smiled, the memory of the love between brothers and sisters in his eyes. God had been good to place His emotions into humankind; to be able to share was of the core of God's being, of His essence. The eyes of Sarah, Jem, Enoch, and Jared, who had just arrived, were upon Jack and Mat.

Sarah addressed the two old Thermadorian warriors. "How long were you fighting here?"

"Weeks trapped," said Abe as his son pulled at his sleeve. Abe bent his ear to his son, who whispered to him. Abe kissed his son's forehead.

Don spoke. "Ate spiders, snakes, ground creatures, death birds. All prayed for you, and you come." Don had just finished speaking when the ground shook and thundered like an earthquake. A glance over the parapet onto the military-camp positions below showed the ground erupting in clouds of dust, soil, rock.

Abe spoke. "Son say, 'Thank you.' He asked why you come."

The old military base had been destroyed in seconds. The bombing of the already-destroyed Thermadorian villages and the new ground shelters began.

Mat answered Abe and his son. "We came because your daddy and Don are good men, and God would want us to help them." Jack translated this into Thermadorian. The child heard and looked with wide, soft eyes at his daddy and Don.

Andy spoke. "Our enemy is making a statement." Andy referred to the destruction of the old base and villages.

Enoch, within his group of pilgrims, said, "Annihilation."

***

The enemy did not bomb the U-shaped positions, erroneously believing these were still held by their forces. Andy studied the dirty faces and sitting, leaning body postures of his gathered crew. All wounds had been bandaged neatly, even if uniforms were dirty, sweaty. Some were drinking, some eating field rations or snack items. Don and Abe were sitting among them, as were Sarah and her crew. Ava had just reported that all communications were down—total deadness; not even distant chatter. No visible damage to their devices. It was as if no one resided on Thermador but their small group. Don and Abe's fighting forces totaled about one hundred, and the civilian population numbered seventy-five.

A pall, a fog of dirt, hung over the entrenchments. Andy sensed a foreboding. A quiet had seemed to settle. There were no distant aircraft, their engines dully roaring or their engine fuselages glinting in the rising sun; there were no lizards scampering in the stony dust, no vultures in the air, no breeze sounding through littered metal fragments or the tattered fabric of tents. No cliff goats were sending debris down the sides of sheer rock faces. No wind turbines were pulling up water in the wells. Even on the broad river, in bamboo brakes, or on grassy shores, nothing was seen. Nothing moved.

Tim, Mat, Emily, and Dan commented to the gathered on a time within the Tribulation, when the volcanic ash came and smothered the sounds of life. Woden, Seth, and Paternus remembered and commented on the snows of their last winter encampment and the abandoned battlefields locked in rigid ice, bodies frozen as they died. Andy, Tuck, and Robin remembered the silent villages of death when smallpox came and stayed. John and Diana remembered their pre-Tribulation desert cave in the winter wilderness.

Andy spoke. "We all feel it. Something is changing, perhaps not for the good. Comms are down. Let us pray for a messenger angel to appear and inform us of the future." Before every head had bowed and a prayer had been offered, a light was within the wide dugout. The angel appeared. Abe and Don's eyes widened—this was only their second sighting. All Christians agreed the presence of angels never became mundane. The light-bearing spirit was equal to Don and Abe in size, yet he made them feel small but protected and loved. The angel spoke.

"Greetings from our Lord in Jerusalem. He wants the Penn's woods people to know that He plans to come to your river and fish this coming summer and hopes Woden, Seth, and Paternus are present, as well as your pilgrim guests, if practicable. He is cognizant of Abe and Don's situation and knows they will be building a nation this summer.

"The Rau-toon, under the leadership of hostile pilgrims, wish to make an example of you—annihilate all, in the hopes of breaking your peoples' will to fight against their cause. You have everything you need to win. His Spirit flows within you. 'The cross conquers.'" The angel studied the faces of the Byzantine men. His eyes locked upon the eyes of Paternus. He was giving something to Paternus through his gaze: knowledge. Knowledge of what, they all wondered. Paternus's eyes widened. The angel smiled.

The angel was gone.

Seth spoke first. "That angel had a Byzantine connection."

Paternus stated, "The cross conquers."

"Aye," said Woden, "a common saying of our armies, started by our first Byzantine king, Constantine, who had seen a cross in the sky before the battle that would define his kingdom."

Mat spoke. "His eyes were on Paternus as if he knew him. Does he know you Paternus? From the past?"

The entire crew was enthralled, quiet and staring at Paternus, waiting for his answer. Paternus seemed agitated emotionally, then empowered physically. He shook his head ,and his body relaxed, his mouth opened. "That angel was with me the day that Justus, the general, requested I come with him and his army to free my family and join my friends in war against the invaders of our home. That angel was the force that lifted me to my feet and moved my legs so that I could walk aboard the ship that would take me home. He was the mover in my legs and my arms until my own power revived, burned through fat and wasted muscle, and I was ready for combat."

Seth and Woden—who were the friends mentioned, who were in the fortress that Paternus helped to rescue, who remembered Paternus embracing his family within the vaulted gate—entered into their own remembrances of that time.

Mat spoke. "Did you know it was an angel at the time?"

"No, I just knew I couldn't move. I begged God to give me the strength. I began to move. My movement was not natural, not my muscle and strength; it was supernatural, and it had to be from God."

The Christian-leaning pilgrims looked at each other, the only souls present yet to be reborn. Each could understand and almost feel the movement Paternus had experienced. Jem asked, "Why did he not fill in any details?"

"It is personal to Paternus, perhaps," said Noah.

"No, I mean about what we should do now. Should we take up the challenge and make a heroic stand against the onslaught coming?" asked a perturbed Jem, who had experienced enough.

"He did fill in the details," Ava answered. "He told us we will be alive when we have finished His will."

Jack smiled. "Because we will be at home in the future, alive and functioning, we *had* to have succeed here."

Enoch added, "God couldn't fail."

"So, now is it about our individual faith?" Noah asked. "He wants us to defend this place?"

Mat answered, "Faith is implementing a plan with and by His Spirit and, I must say, attitude."

Sarah, with incredulity in her tone, spoke. "He wants us to stay, fight, and grind the enemy into the ground, to prove His power?"

Mat smiled. "We have already won, already proven His power. Look at the rows of Rau-toon and pilgrim bodies on the ground. Our Thermadorians are free! It is time for us to walk away, as Jesus did many times when crowds accused Him and were near to attacking him bodily."

"When?" asked Jem.

Mat answered, "When He proclaimed the year of the Lord in the temple of Nazareth, then castigated Israel for their sins."

Tim continued his son's narrative. "They took Him to the hill on which the city was built in order to throw him over the cliff. But passing through their midst, He went His way. This event is found in Luke 4:16 thru 30."

Mat continued, "John 7:30 is another instance, as is John 8:59. If you seek Him you will find Him and there is where His wisdom is found, 'Seek and ye shall find.' Matthew 7:7–23."

Noah and Enoch had their pocket New Testaments out, and pages turned. A conversation began among the pilgrims, with comments and observations from Abe and Don. The Earth Christians slowly joined in the conversation on how to know the will of God.

Tim and son, Mat, quietly thought about the words they heard. Tim had his computer running and was busy with some task. Andy studied his people and could see their attitudes in flux, but no one discounted Tim and Mat's thoughts.

Suddenly, Tim bolted from his seat and approached Andy, and the two of them sat apart, alone, conversing as Tim reopened his computer. Andy lovingly slapped Tim, the geologist, on the back.

Andy stood, raised his hand; all eyes went to him. "Let's get our Thermadorians, civilians and fighting men, washed, clothed in new clothing, and fed; the soldiers are to be rearmed, if need be, and ready to move within an hour, if not sooner."

"I need anyone with mining skills to form under Tim. I also need explosives, portable reactors, boring or mining tools. We have subterranean passages below us from lava flows and water drainage.

We will consolidate our above-ground positions to this bunker complex in the hollow of the U, and some will defend it as a distraction for our escaping Thermadorians.

"Let's get busy, people," Andy said. "God has given us a plan."

CHAPTER 23

John, Diana, Jack, Mat, Dan, Emily, and lone pilgrim Noah rested in the command bunker, from which the most numerous and essential shooting ports projected. A conglomeration of missiles, rifles—both laser and cartridge-powder types—and hand grenades had been gleaned from the trench, quickly cleaned, organized by type and functionality, and protected from possible ricochets and shrapnel. Extra ammo was hidden in holes carved into the bunker's walls. Large carrying bags were nearby. The gathered were volunteers. They would complete the holding action for their positions while the others would make their getaways. Pete and Grace had flipped a coin with Dan and Emily, as both couples had wanted to remain, but both groups needed their first aid and soldiering skills. Tom had wanted to remain, but his language skills were needed by the party leaving. Noah wished to remain to fight, as he believed his combat skills needed to be strengthened. Secretly, he simply wanted to test his nerve.

Now, crawling or walking through subterranean passageways, were Andy, Tuck, Robin, Woden, Paternus, Seth, Tim, Ling, Pete and Grace, Tom, Ava, and the pilgrims Sarah, Jem, Jared, and Enoch. Abe and Don led their tribal people of 175 souls. It had only taken one hour of blasting and boring to reach the large passages moving north to south. They had found the rock walls coated in edible fungi and leaking numerous springs of freshwater, which aided in recovery. They had reached a subterranean level of warmth that was, by chance, comfortable and was well below the penetrating sonar of the enemy forces. Tim was their Moses in the wilderness as he read the rock, tracked the passageways, and kept the pace for their two-hundred-mile trek north, to the next substantial Thermadorian/Christian forces outpost.

***

John spoke. "Are we thinking of any new approach to our defense?" He placed a handful of peanuts in his mouth, sucked the salt; the peanut flavor stimulated his hunger. Everyone was concentrating on lunch. Small boxes, pouches, tins, bags of snacks, crackers, cheeses, nuts, peanut butter, jellies, and dried fruit were opened and resting on makeshift tables.

It was the second lunch since the departure of their friends, early morning of yesterday. Within the twenty-four hours, they had been bombed three times and forced to retreat into their cavern entrance, carrying as many weapons as possible, and reappearing when the bombings had ended. The enemy evidently had no ready forces to follow up the success of the explosives in creating breaches in the defensive line and vacating the trenches of the opposition. Somewhere, an army of pilgrims and Rau-toon were collecting and perhaps even now, rushing to their location, to create a symbolic victory.

Dan spoke. "I'm glad we have the dummy defenders in place, and their little electronic hearts are pumping."

Jack began to laugh. "Yes, nice touch, those water and fuel pumps."

Emily looked to Noah and spoke. "Noah, who's your backup transport buddy if John is unavailable—as in the passageway has caved in?"

Noah smiled at Emily's concern and spoke. "First Mat, then Jack."

"Keep your transport straps free." Said Emily. Noah would be carried in a piggy back rig on the backs of the 'transporter'. His closeness would also offer invisibility when that mode was chosen.

"I will." He said. Emily winked at him as she spoke again, "Good soldier. Planning ahead." She admired him for his presence in this place of danger. Being in the flesh, he could be gravely wounded, creating lifelong, debilitating problems, or he could die....No one knew what his fate would be. Eternal death and Hell because he not yet made his commitment to Christ? Or, if he was one of Christ's chosen, Paradise and a wait...till when?

Mat spoke across the assembled to John. "What about the gap in time?" He referred to the time it took to respond between the bombing's end and the reoccupying of their defensive positions. They were currently using a seismic indicator to warn them of infantry approaching after the bombings. The flaw in this system would be exposed when the infantry numbers were cut and/or soft, spongelike shoe treads were used. In the beginning, they were using the sound of the bombings end till, either by cleverness or accident, the bombings had stopped then began a minute later and caught them just as they gained topside. Disaster was diverted by scurrying back into the tunnel.

John answered. "I was thinking four cameras at the cardinal points, securely anchored, and us in the passage way. The cameras can tell us when enemy troops appear, and we can surface."

"If they get clever and have troops follow a rolling barrage, we might not have enough time to surface," Mat said.

"Are you thinking of a man in the module?" John referred to an empty escape module they had found among the battlefield debris, ejected by a craft weeks ago. Escape modules were extremely projectile-resistant. The module had been repurposed as a storage unit for grenades and rifles.

Mat spoke. "You read my thoughts, and you also knew I volunteered for the job."

"We accept your offer," John said. The gathered laughed; the reading of minds could become confusing but also provided humor.

Emily spoke. "Could we wait out the bombing together, in invisibility mode, outside the bunker's perimeter? We would see the barrage end and could rush back quickly."

Noah, usually silent, spoke up quickly. "No danger of being momentarily trapped in our tunnel."

John answered, "Yes, the idea has merit. The barrages all follow the same track. Plot those previous barrages out, Emily, and we'll pick a spot that is safe."

"Thanks," said Emily to John as she winked at Noah for his support. Her respect for Noah had grown. He had separated himself from his people, his support group, to face one of the greatest earthly challenges, combat. As a child, she had been separated from her family, and her new caretakers had beaten her almost daily. Carl Stasic had saved her, and the Johnsons had taken her in and healed her. She had decided to be Noah's caretaker.

Silence returned to the group; they ate contentedly, happy with the new plan. All were keeping eyes on the security cameras. Diana broke the silence. "Anyone ready for home?"

Mat answered, "Not me. From a physical standpoint, I feel as refreshed and alert as I did the day I signed up. We are inhabiting fleshly machines—no muscle pulls, no aching joints and bones, no decrease in strength or energy, no weariness caused by the stress of combat or unknown situations. No fear of the temporary death caused by total disruption. Less food or more food, I always feel full. Whether I'm sleeping in the dirt or on a mattress, I always get a sound sleep. No emotional ups and downs; the Lord has shown Himself faithful. We have a worthy cause, making Our Lord known and freeing a people from perverse beings."

Dan spoke. "I agree we have no reason to change our course, yet my daydreams are of home, along the river…among faces, locations, and work dear to me. A change of place and people would be satisfying. I'd like to know what they are doing and thinking. I'd like to see the familiar mountains, greenness, gardens producing vegetables. I'd like to taste familiar foods and beverages. I'd like the people and the surroundings to be at that slow, everyday pace. Though our cause is worthy, the cause will always be there—probably almost eternally in such an overwhelmingly large universe."

Emily studied Noah. She sensed he had fears, many fears. She remembered what it was like to fear, living in the flesh. She spoke to him. "Noah, you're coming home with us, whenever you are able. We live in a place of serenity, natural beauty, abundance, and peace. You can be a tourist in New Jerusalem, meet our King, Jesus, and visit your ancestral homeland. Promise us you'll come."

Noah was smiling. He was far from his fears and filled with expectations. "I will visit."

"Make it a long visit," said Jack.

"I second that idea," said Mat.

"All in favor?" asked John.

A raucous "aye" resounded.

Diana, following her own thought pattern, offered words. "We certainly are not suffering hardships in these bodies and minds, for nothing is difficult to our minds and bodies. I guess it's the good feelings that old relationships give us and our desire to help and encourage those in our past that bring us home."

Jack spoke. "And to share our adventures, the sights and sounds of space, new planets, new life-forms. That appeals to adventurers! To be teachers. Maybe the appeal is to self-worth, to hold experiences unknown to others."

John laughed. "What noble and good thoughts, soon to be vacated by the whine of dropping ordnance, flying debris, and the rush to our new waiting area—the coordinates already showing on your transporter hardware."

As if his word were prophesy, all present heard metal cutting through air thousands of feet above them, a tickle in the ears. "Follow me!" said John as he became invisible. They scrambled to don combat packs, and with weapons in hand, they were gone.

***

The bombardment shook the ground for twenty minutes. They watched, their concentration upon the main salient, their soon-to-be position. Then, they witnessed the barrage rolling through the old Thermadorian civilian camps, through the torn-up earthworks of the first Christian fortress, to the ridgetop trenches. They saw the enemy, by the thousands, packed in air platforms, disembark in the dust of the old Thermadorian villages just bombed. Beyond this landing, a mile away or more, they saw a darkened sky descend upon the ground. It could only mean more troops were being landed. These troops were quick, orderly; the platoons formed and moved out, closely following each other at a slow walk, behind the barrage.

The enemy suddenly was moving quickly and had surprised the earthlings with their speed and deployment; one advanced unit had been hidden by a fold in the terrain and was now occupying the position they had wished to land upon. They would need to regain their defensive positions in an air assault with lasers streaking. No gap existed between the bombardment and the enemy's advance. The enemy hugged the bombardment and willingly took casualties from their own forces. Rau-toon troops were still disembarking from an unending flight of air platforms, flooding the flat land of the former villages and military post as the bombing was receding.

The Christians could hear the silence in the sky, even as they saw the Rau-toon warriors congregating behind the last explosions, gathering up, swelling in number. Following John's lead, his squad dropped from the sky till within inches from the ground, then spread out by the back wall of the trenches. The opportunity for a sky attack had passed. To fall upon the enemy from the sky would have been instant death; they would have been exposed to the massed infantry's weapons. The earthlings infiltrated the empty trench, appeared with lasers streaking just as the enemy forces jumped down into the salient. The swelling enemy ranks flowed up the slope and flooded into the trenches, pushing each other by sheer weight of their numbers. As lone rounds dripped from the closed artillery battery faucet, the rounds exploded on the crest, spewing bodies.

Intense laser fire stacked dead mantids in heaps and bought time to regain the trench line and launch a rocket barrage deep into the massed columns of infantry. Many Rau-toon in the back ranks attempted to leap into the trenches. The Christians sent up a small drone over the enemy that pinpointed the leapers by watching for the tells, the tensed legs, the short dip of the body, the arms extended low, elbows straight, as they used their heavy hands as a fulcrum. Many Rau-toon were killed in that crouch, or soon after, before the leap reached its arc. Hundreds of grenades were thrown from the trenches down onto the enemy soldiers, and then shoulder-fired rockets began again, hissing and shooshing. The enemy attempted to crawl underneath the fire. The laser- and machine- and rotary-guns began firing. Tracers streaked the air. Suffering faces appeared in the gunport openings and were blown away, disintegrated by the weapons.

A huge dust cloud had collected from the bombed soil; the moving enemy forces piled up and then swept over the trench line. They saw the lightning streaks of lasers through the dust. They heard the exploding grenades hurtling shrapnel into the debris of furniture, sandbags, bedding, comms equipment. The fighting became hand to hand, rifle parried to rifle, handguns were emptied. The enemy could not destroy the integrity of the fire ports; its mad rush was delayed, stymied by the narrow openings.

A stalemate occurred. The enemy could not enter, and the Christians could not clear the ports for a greater bullet or laser-blast reach. Then, the bombing returned to the dust pall, whether by Christian forces or the enemy firing at its own, no one knew. The Christian forces cleared the gunports of enemy troops, saw them gathering in an artillery-free zone, and fired out into the dust. A rout occurred on the exposed ground, where the enemy milled in confusion and were killed in vast heaps. They broke and ran, some forced to jump off the cliff edges to avoid death. Even in flight, they were killed. On the flat land below, the godless pilgrim soldiers found shelter in the old, rectangular, Christian-forces fortress. The pilgrim forces fired into their Rau-toon allies in spite. Back up the slope went the pilgrim soldiers and loyal Rau-toon to dislodge the Christian enemy in its defensive bunker.

They charged into the bunker and found no one. The Christian soldiers materialized at the rear of the enemy ranks, opened fire. The first targets were the pilgrim advisers, then the ranks of Rau-toon. Each Christian soldier had vivid memories of the mutilated corpses of women and children—Thermadorians—tortured and killed. When all the lasers had burned out, the powder guns were out of ammo, and the grenades gone, with only battle-axes flailing, the Christians disappeared, never to be seen again.

Across the river they went, their bunker portal to the underworld blocked by the debris of battle and substantial cave-ins. They flew low to the ground to avoid new detection devices. They had delayed the enemy and hidden their flight under the false impression they had been annihilated. In a few minutes, they were back at the former location of the Explorer 7. A sizeable cache of water and rations had been buried at this site. Going invisible and flying both used energy at a high rate; the food was appreciated. The cache was untouched, and they ate and drank as they studied Tim's map of the subterranean world. They surmised he was headed north, with the largest Thermadorian settlement as his people's goal. The seven made a calculated guess as to the nearest entry point to the underground highway from their location, and under the cover of darkness, made the hundred-mile flight easily before dawn.

***

Near the perimeter of the Thermadorian settlement, the transporting Christians, plus a carried Noah, saw on the ground a group of Thermadorians and Christians. The group had formed a circular perimeter, with weapons pointed outward. John came down into the center, and as he had expected, Andy's group had camped within the circle. Only Woden, on guard duty, was aware of the transporting Christian, and had his weapon pointed.

Woden spoke. "Thought it would be you."

John was surprised. "How'd you get this far so quickly?" The rest of the party materialized within the circle, and the hugging and shaking of hands proceeded.

Woden answered, "There was an underground river, flowing with a good current, south to north. Boats of mantid chitin, light as a feather, had been sewn together, stationed at various spots. Most fun I've had in a while— obstacles to steer around, little waterfalls to fall from, designed chutes of fast water."

John's spirit was amused. He had been in the heaviest combat of his warring career as Woden was white-water canoeing. John spoke dryly. "Had some fun, huh?"

Woden had not discovered John's humor. Woden's eyes were wide. "That's not the big news. Ava has been tapping into the chatter coming out of the city. They say the war is over."

John was startled. "Over?" The two men could hear laughter; the Thermadorian camp of Abe and Don's people, surrounding the Christians, were on their feet, dancing and hugging. Organized cheers were resounding.

Woden continued, "Yes, the Rau-toon have accepted capitalism as their economy, and trade agreements have been ratified. Religious freedom has been allowed. The pilgrims, both factions, Christian and non-Christian, have agreed on capitalism, fair and free trade, and respect for the existence of Thermador and Rau-toon. They have accepted the creation of a Christian state on a new planet and a non-Christian state on another planet."

John laughed. "I guess it was prideful to think, we, the military, were the only ones working the problem. Well, it suits me. Send me home!"

***

The building of four planet nations proceeded quickly and efficiently, with candor, compromise, and respect for all parties involved. Members of the immortal from planet Earth could choose to remain in space or return home to past lives, including civilian employment. Of course, those who chose to stay could, if they liked, return home for few weeks to prepare for the changes that living on another planet would entail for family finances and businesses and ties of family and friendship.

The crew of the Explorer 7 that remained in space had varied reasons. Dan and Emily, both without a "calling" on Earth, prayed, and were assured their Lord would like them to establish the infrastructure of a democratic government. They hoped to work for the Christian pilgrims or Christian Thermadorians. Pete and Grace decided to remain to establish churches on Thermador and the new Christian-pilgrim planet. John and Diana decided to remain in the field of security and worked to establish a peacekeeping force for each planet and a united force for all four nations. They enlisted Jack and Mat to help.

Mat hoped to bring his former wife, Barb, but she declined after seeing videos and holograms of the planets. Jack interested his friend, Stacie, and she decided the challenge was what she needed. Ling decided to remain, to teach capitalism and business, and he interested his Earth business partner, Carl Stasic, in joining him. Eventually, Tom Jr. joined that group, and the trio's Earth company, TLC Enterprises, was reestablished. Ava remained in space, involved in communications issues among the various factions. She was respected by the non-Christian pilgrims for changing her allegiance without informing on the non-Christians. It was a moot issue, as the Christian earthlings had no plans for vengeance, no need of whispered intelligence. Her former partner, Enrique, had been killed in combat. But her daddy was alive and well. He lived near her, and they discovered who they both were, in personality and life experience, and who they would become with the Holy Spirit within them.

The crew of the Explorer 7 who returned home had their reasons. The Byzantine crowd—Woden, Seth, and Paternus—decided for home and their extended families, though Paternus became interested in quarrying the new, exotically beautiful stone of the four planets and made frequent trips back into space. Tuck and Robin loved their river, the Susquehanna, and their river enterprises. They returned home. Andy, too, liked being near his boys and his former wife, Leaf. Tim also returned home to his former wife, Mary, and their extended family.

The pilgrims Sarah, Jem, Jared, Enoch, and Noah all accepted Christ, grew in their faith, and loved their God with all their hearts, souls, minds, and strength. Keturah remained in her confusion, enjoyed her opposition to Christ and her bitterness. Sarah was the first to physically die of old age, and to the amazement of all, was back the next week in her resurrected body. No "end of the age" waiting. Keturah had a change of heart after seeing the resurrected Sarah, but the time for decisions had passed. The pilgrims had not been given a lifetime to choose a life with Christ. God, who knew all things, saw the evil in the pilgrims' thoughts: to hide from God and live their lives, till they lay upon their deathbeds. It was also revealed that the number of noncloned pilgrims was few—no more than fifty thousand—and of these, most had exceeded their natural expiration dates by their use of enhancers. Although all were capable of sex, the number who were able to produce viable offspring was slowly decreasing.

Don and Abe remained close friends. Their families were joined by the marriages of their children. With Christ, calm entered their lives. They appreciated that they had souls, and it was truly irrelevant whether they had been born with souls through their creator God or their souls were implanted by the pilgrim people. God, who made all, was in control. For the majority of Thermadorians, many aspects of past lives were forgotten, held no importance. They had been redeemed—the past had died when Christ died. New life began within their eternal Jesus when they accepted His victory on the cross. Jesus lived from the present. He was and is the present and the future.

These eternal people had made a pact to gather every five years at the river home of Andy and his sons, to relive that special and curious time when space travel was in its infancy, and eternal life was new.

CHAPTER 24

The river, our rock, and a warm, central-Penn's woods day!" Appreci-ation and thankfulness carried through John's tone. In John's mind, he saw the rock as the unchanging, immovable Christ; the river as the never-ending, flowing power and presence of the Holy Spirit; and the warm day, as the gift of God—unending life. John stepped out of the Susquehan-na's clear waters onto the first ledge of their "relaxing rock." He jumped up, springing from one leg. The tensed muscle propelled him effortlessly; he knew he could have jumped many feet higher. At such times, he remem-bered the "old body" of pre-immortality that would have failed, at maximum strength, to achieve the desired height.

He landed on the smooth, upper level. He reached around behind him, took Diana by her hand and tensed his arm. She sprang effortlessly up to the broad, flat surface of the rock, due partly to his lifting hand. She spoke. "Looks like the vultures have painted our rock." She referred to a white, paint-like excrement on the rock.

"Maybe eagles," he said as his eyes went skyward and were pulled to his left, where the high, looming ridge of the mountain had been abruptly worn away by the river's waters. This elevating had occurred within his brother, Tim's, life on Earth. Even Tim had not seen the earth rise a thousand feet along the existing mountain ridge, as he had been further south, back in Harrisburg, when the big quake struck and tectonic plates shifted. John and Diana had already entered Paradise prior to the beginning of the Tribulation.

The vultures were up high, catching the warmth rising along the moun-tainside, circling so effortlessly. He could not see his home on the mountain ridge; a rock projection hid the view. The sky was blue with a hint of haze and the wispiest of clouds, distanced far apart. "Hey, Mat," called John to a wading Mat, as Barb, his friend and former wife, beside him, pushed her legs through the gentle current.

Mat raised his voice slightly; he knew the water would carry his sound easily. "I was in Harrisburg when the quake came. Our apartment blew apart, Katie broke her leg, and Dad was coming home as fast as possible." Mat had absorbed John's question before it was spoken.

John looked to the far shore, past Mat and Barb, to where his brother, Tim, and Tim's former wife, Mary, were just entering the water for their trek to the rock. John's eye caught a movement up river, among the rocks—Andy coming down, standing in his dugout, the better to see hidden rocks. A broad, straw hat shielded his head from reflected water glare. He held up a bucket in one hand and in the other, a stiff broom. John smiled. Andy had anticipated the need for a cleansing of the rock of excrement and dirt from high waters, and the debris of crayfish carcasses and otter-opened river clams.

Andy floated alongside the rock, tossed the bucket and the broom to John and Mat. John spoke. "Stay, Andy."

Andy answered, "Stop in at my place late afternoon for a cookout. I have a few chores to accomplish now."

"Okay," John said, "and thanks." He noticed that the two solar panels lying across the front of Andy's dugout were attached to two small motors in the rear, where tubes projected into the water.

"Nifty, eh?" said Andy, following John's sight plane as he moved his tiller with his bare foot and steered around the rock. He opened up the motor's quiet power, and his boat moved upriver, slowly but steadily, using the still water behind rock ledges. John and Mat watched him briefly, then surveyed the river islands, as their former mates gave the rock surface a rinse and brooming.

John, uncle to Mat, reflected upon being, over the course of their lives, husbands, fathers, sons, fellow space explorers/soldiers, and men of Christ, who belonged exclusively to their eternal, loving Savior. They were only two weeks back from space, discovery, adventure, and war, and were now surrounded by their former spouses, who had always been and were still true friends. They had occupied the days catching up on landscaping projects and chores, removing downed trees, cutting firewood, planting new trees and bushes. Few home-repair projects filled their time, simply because skilled workers, using modern materials, had built everything to last as near to eternally as possible. They had wiled away their free time on the river, sometimes fishing, sometimes exploring past buried river debris, or American Indian village sites, or pioneer homesteads or mills and barns. This day of sunning, eating snacks, soaking in the water, studying the scenes of wildlife and water around them, sharing thoughts and observations as they pleased usually occurred Sunday afternoons (church services and bible classes filled the mornings).

The sight of Andy had taken Mat and John back to Thermador. Andy had been a great leader, and John wondered if he could someday match Andy's skills, remain in the military, and become a general. Mat knew the need for the profession of police officer was nonexistent on Earth since Satan had been imprisoned. Many opportunities existed on the mantis and pilgrim planets for trainers. Mat's memories focused upon Abe and Don, and then upon himself—a father, son, brother upon a rock.

He laughed softly in recognition and spoke. "I am a brother, a father, a son. Also, an uncle and a grandfather. Then, you get into the greats, times how many? I have lost count. I used that analogy—many personas in one person, all with different responsibilities, relationships, and duties—on Don once to explain the concept of the Trinity. How a lone man will have many roles in his life simultaneously—responsibilities and duties aimed in many directions, all facets of the same being."

John interjected, "Yes, I used that example repeatedly. They really understood that; it resonated within Thermadorian culture. The 'one substance' approach worked less well in explaining the Trinity."

Diana spoke. "Seeing Andy, I went back to our trip, John's and mine, with Andy to New Jerusalem two and half years ago—almost three—when Andy had been called for testing for space exploration. That really was the beginning of our biggest adventure to date in eternal life."

Barb spoke up. "What about Satan's last uprising?"

"That was more of a necessity forced upon us by the existence of evil," Diana said. "Adventure is something you choose to have; free will is there."

Mat added, "At least initially. Once you step into an adventure, you are then in the grasp of its twists and turns."

Tim and Mary had just reached the rock and stood in the water, looking up at their friends. Tim tagged onto the conversation. "Then it is only faith and the light of wisdom from a holy God to guide you."

Diana clarified her purpose. "I was going for a more specific topic. While Andy was testing, John and I toured the Holy City, which was wonderful in one sense. It was John who recognized the not-so-wonderful: that there had been evil men in Old Jerusalem, and Satan, pulling their puppet strings, when their carnal allegiance weakened. Christ and His city council included the stories of the evil men in all the historical site's narratives."

John's voice held a somberness. "I remember my complaint well; I just wanted to forget evil, just wanted the happy parts of the story: that Christ performed miracles and that Christ rose from death and that Christ had devoted supporters."

Diana studied John's face and asked, "Did you get your answer, John? Did this adventure speak to you? I held this in, forgetting it and remembering it, for almost three years, wondering and forgetting where you were on this quest that you probably forgot you were on."

John answered, "We went to space to see exotic sights, moons upon moons, precious stones, sunrises and sunsets of exquisite colors, memorable rock formations, new plant and animal life. And instead, we were involved in a war. I really didn't want that to be part of the adventure—crying and starving young ones and oldsters, a planet that had been raped for hundreds of years. The surety of eternal life lessened our fear, but there was evil, staring us in the face. We rose above it, all our crew; you, Diana, and Tim, Mat, and me, with the presence of our Lord beside us. In short, Jesus and His city council were correct, and even though we occupy Heaven, we must always keep the memory of the bad alive, which Tom Burnell Sr. would have told me, had I asked, before leaving on the adventure. Even more so, our overcoming God who loves us, and all in His creation who honor Him, and any cognizant life-form who welcomes Him knows that the memory of evil must never be forgotten."

Amens were heard. Their thoughts returned to internal reveries, interrupted only by the changing winds and the variance in individual cloud forms and aggregate patterns; the flights of eagles, ospreys, and herons, and above them all, vultures circling, riding the updraft from the mountain. The sound of fish slapping back into the water intrigued them. Some were monster-sized, judging by the sound of the mass belly flopping back into the river. The scents of the water and the vegetation growing from pebbly shallows, flowering and humming with bees and dragonflies, lulled them to semiconsciousness. In awakening, a dip in the water, to then resume their perch upon the rock; where a huge river tree of the bank or island—an oak, or maple, or tulip tree—would captivate them with its mass, its greenness, its limbs as thick as single trees, and convoluting branches of expansive reach. If an explored thought reached the interest of sharing, someone would speak, and the mind would be revived in conversation.

Time was more precious now, when it was forever, than when it had been finite. Luxurious time in a body forever healthy. They realized their beautiful day on the river was setting with the sun, which was now over the islands and within an hour would be over the nearest ridge on the west side of the land beyond the river. The sun went past the islands; the islands cast shadows on the water; and fish began to jump more insistently, taking a bug or small fish along every time they broke the surface. The redeemed of God entered the still-warm waters and waded to shore, smelled the fragrance of grilled food, and followed their noses to Andy's home.

***

Andy and Leaf were grilling beef burgers. Tuck and Charlotte were in the kitchen, preparing a salad of homegrown garden origins. Robin and Deborah, who had been sitting, were up and wiping clean numerous chairs for their guests. Tim and Mary flopped into chairs, thanking Robin and Deborah. Mat and Barb sat, awaiting an opportunity to serve a need. John and Diana stood, looking over the scene.

Andy spoke, and it seemed like a command. "Sit, eat with us."

Leaf added, "We'll build a fire; the river chill is coming, and the wind has a coolness."

John asked, "May I build the fire now?"

Leaf laughed. "Are those wet legs feelin' a chill?"

"Nothing escapes you!" Diana said as she laughed at Leaf's ability to uncover true motives.

Leaf answered, "Just an old river-living lady, born to watch and learn."

Barb responded, "You have many years of life, a life physically more difficult than us moderns, but you're as spry as they come."

Leaf smiled. "Praise to our eternal God, we all are spry, ache-free, and life is eternal."

Barb laughed at herself. "Our health is so surreal…no, supernatural is the word." Her immortal mind easily reassumed the old realities of the past life more readily than most, which made her unique and more readily appreciative than many.

Andy added, "Explorer 7 crew, doesn't it feel good to be upon Earth, to see God's wonders, to have air and space and the living world around us, and not the confines of our ship?"

Tim spoke happily. "I second that."

"We all do," said Mat.

A voice, coming from the river, ascending the bank, said, "Well spoken, one and all." Pete crested the riverbank with a canoe paddle in hand. Behind him, by half a step, was Grace, her purse (where she kept her electronic Bible) strung over her shoulder and today, a large container of homemade ginger-molasses cookies in hand. The other held her paddle, acting as a walking stick.

Grace laughed. "You can't hide a party from us! Our angels keep us informed!" John's fire crackled, the yellow flames cast light, and the wet-legged people gathered near.

Tuck and Charlotte appeared with food trays and uncooked burgers, which Andy immediately tossed on his grill as he unloaded the cooked burgers onto a plate. Deborah ran back to the kitchen for the freshly made buns she had baked and Robin's cherry-flavored fizz water. Barb followed, thinking more hands made less work. Mat was carrying a load of firewood from the woodpile to the fire. Mary called daughter, Katie, and her friend, Paul, as they were home; told them to bring guitars, sweaters, and Katie's homemade potato soup. Tim called the Burnells, as his old buddy Tom Sr. was in the family manse, and Tish, Tom's buddy, was with him. Tom Jr. and his lifelong friend, Lana, were home too. Jack was there with his friend, Stacie. They were nearby, hungry, and organized themselves readily. Tom Sr. had just baked several loaves of bread, still warm, and Tom Jr. had caught that morning small-mouth bass that were filleted, cleaned, and ready for grilling. Jack had just dug up his summer potatoes, and there was a block of local butter in the refrigerator. He brought both items along. A perfect fire to bake potatoes was forming—plenty of coals. Stacie carried her chocolate cake. This would be a long, lazy meal, eaten well past dusk.

Katie and Paul arrived with Emily and Dan, who had just taken the train from Washington, DC. They had brought a friend, George, a tall, ramrod-straight man, who looked a person directly in the face with caring eyes, and whose big, strong hands were full of warmth and love. Emily particularly liked the man and kept her arm entwined with his. Some wondered if this might be her father, whom she had not known as a child, as he was thought dead. Andy, upon seeing George, called his name and noted how he appreciated his presence.

The Spirit of God touched Andy and told him something special was happening. He knew the Spirit had come to him first, as he would be the host of the gathering. The thought made him happy and feel blessed—that he could be the host. Andy looked at his friends. Mat caught his look and saw the Spirit upon him. Mat knew a gathering was occurring, and chills of holiness ran up and down his spine. Barb was the third person to know; she knew her Mat, and what he felt, she felt.

The blast of a shofar echoed from the front yard of Andy's home. The sound stood alone, then reached the mountain behind, and echoed; all talk had ceased. A minute passed before the gathered heard the voices of Woden, Seth, and Paternus calling their greetings. The three men and accompanying partners, Helen, Sara, and Agnella, thought they were merely trying out the ram's horn, which Seth had just bought from a farmer in the valley, and announcing their arrival. But the gathered by the river heard and saw memories of their Savior when He had come as the conquering Christ so many centuries ago. Their hearts had leapt for joy, and tears had come with the memory.

The visitors walked around the corner with happily expectant faces, saw the expressions on the faces of the gathered, and immediately understood what they had done. Helen, Agnella, and Sara rushed to greet the women with embraces and tears of their empathy, as they, too, were carried back to that momentous event. Woden, Seth, and Paternus moved quickly to embrace the gathered men.

Andy was the first to speak. "Welcome. Eat. Stay with us for weeks, if you are able, beloved crewmates of Explorer 7." He had no immediate interest in why they were here; he simply enjoyed their presence. He loved them dearly.

***

The first round of hamburgers and salads had been dispersed, as were the Byzantine guests among the crowd, and the first slices of chocolate cake had been served, along with coffee and Grace's cookies, to the less hungry guests, when it was learned that the Byzantines had had business in Florida and decided to make a quick run to the village of their favorite people. Then, the Burnells arrived, and the third wave of burgers hit the hot grill, accompanied by newly acquired hot dogs and fillets of bass and salmon. At least four conversations were occurring simultaneously among collections of three to five commenting individuals and scores of listeners. The stealthiest additions to the party were Ava and her dad, Ling, and Carl Stasic, the business partner of Tom Jr. and Ling. Andy quietly made certain that George sat near John, to fulfill a request of John's made three years ago.

Briefly, the conversations noted the fact that in this age, no children were present and what peace that created. At the same time, nostalgia brought out tales of each and every adult's party behavior as a child. Much humor was elicited. The conversation was then heavy, with talk of Explorer 7 and her adventures in space and of the dauntless crew among the gathered, who had made the little community proud, and of thankfulness to a gracious God and for the suffering Christ, who had taken the fear of death and destroyed it for eternity. They praised their nation's history, their founders, and everyday people for keeping the memory, if not actual worship, of Father, Son, and Holy Spirit as their guiding light through the pall of sin and Satan's reign. Historically, their nation had run the race, the long-distance marathon of faith. God had proved faithful.

John told the non-Explorer crew, of the Thermadorians nicknamed Abe Lincoln and Francis Scott Key, who fought valiantly for their planet in their revolution, and who had the deepest of souls and were of Christ's family forever. He told the gathered of Abe and Don's love of the American story of a revolution that had changed the course of history.

Mat spoke. "To think that a collection of settlements on the shores and riverways of a vast continent, at a time when technology was simple and rudimentary, when the only thing people had brought with them was the dream to love God with all their hearts, souls, minds, and strength; and to feed their children and create a better world for them—loving your neighbor as yourself—would become the United States of America."

Andy added, "A learning process: 'love your neighbor as you do yourself.' A history of error, introspection, contriteness, change; of shedding the guilt and reaching higher."

Tom Sr. grafted a thought to Andy's. "King Jesus rode onward, moved on in power; we, His people, always moved onward with hearts full of God's love and His dream for what could be."

Mat returned to the narrative. "Think of this river shore, once the boundary between colonization and wilderness. Thirteen struggling colonies at the time, still bullied by their parent, England, would become the greatest nation of the world. Respectful of a person's right to seek God, to love their God. With God's people fully engaged in the life of their country. Only at the end, when the Tribulation was near, had His people felt the wrath of the Jesus haters. The Lord knew it was finished; the root of the tree was long dead and our nation, the final living branch, had finally died. To all the people who loved God, suffered to live His will in a fallen world, who suffered to bring His presence to a new and beckoning universe, we give you praise."

Everyone stood. Jack Burnell took Andy's ever-present American flag upon a pole from its socketed, metal holder and began waving it, and the gathered burst into chants and praises, danced in happiness. Jack ran up and down the lawn before the river. Everyone cheered as the flag stretched in the wind, and the colors were seen complete. Katie and Paul, with banjo and guitar, played and sang "The Battle Hymn of the Republic." Mat sang in his deep, soulful voice. The dancing stopped; the hymn overwhelmed them with the beauty of the lyrics and the tempo of victory. All were singing except one.

Mat noticed one man did not rise, one man stifled his tears as best he could, one tall man became as small as he could in his chair. John noticed too. Emily was bent over him, whispering soothing words into his ear. John came to them both and said, as he ran his hand firmly, repeatedly, over the huddled, sobbing shoulders. "Good man, George. Tell me why you hurt, so that I may comfort you. We must lift you from your distress."

George took a deep breath, took his large hands and his broad fingers to his eyes and pushed away the tears, and spoke with strength in his voice. "I cry in appreciation of a God so loving as to love a worthless man through this gathering."

Emily spoke quietly to John. "This is George Washington...*the* George Washington."

John looked dumbfounded. Mat heard, and from surging emotions, had quickly come to his side; had ruggedly embraced George. To his surprise, George Washington, who didn't like physical contact, Mat now remembered from the history books of his school days, warmly embraced him back. Mat felt the overwhelming power in the bones and ligaments of the man. John woke up, his stupor gone, and embraced George. He, too, felt the overwhelming strength and the presence of the Spirit. John and Mat realized how their heartfelt love for those patriots of the past had touched the very man who had suffered much and accomplished much.

John proclaimed to the gathered, "This is George Washington...who held our army together during the Revolution. Men ragged, without shoes, clothing, without shelter, without provisions or training. Many of his officers wished him to be king at the end of the war. He refused."

"The George Washington who peacefully transferred the power of the presidency to his successor," Mat added. "The George Washington who freed his slaves in the end." John and Mat both made eye contact with their friends as they spoke.

Andy shouted, "The George Washington who just wanted to remain at home on his farm, but dodged bullets, watched his men fight and die, starve, and freeze, as others plotted against him!" Andy was laughing for their joy and the astonishment on their faces. Andy spoke again, "Here is the man most instrumental in forming the United States of America."

Andy thought a thought, and George nodded his head in agreement. Andy spoke in his command voice. "Form a line, introduce yourselves, and whatever praise you have, tell him. Be thankful." Andy knew all would offer thanks; people who could not forgive weren't chosen by God for eternal life. Andy knew George's heart; they had conversed deeply in their sporadic meetings. It was time for George to write his memoirs and tell his story.

Andy knew that people who couldn't hold onto what was good from the issue of a man's life but only his bad weren't chosen by God. Those who believed slanderous and libelous words at face value were not the material for eternal life. In the past, in his first life, Andy had known native people who hated George Washington, for he had brought forces to bear against Native Americans and the French and then English soldiers with whom they aligned themselves. He had owned slaves and was hated for being a part of that reality. The flood of human history in the river of life is always stronger than a man's ability to stand, and the evil debris cast in the waters by Satan will knock the strongest down. Only when the flood has passed into the ocean can a man cross the waters. Through the flood, George had always been a gentleman, had tried to do what was right, and had sought counsel with God.

Solid and resolutely joyous were the Burnells, whose family tree began in slavery—Tom Sr., Tish, Tom Jr., Lana, Jack, and Stacie—when the men shook his hand and the women gave a kind embrace. Tom Sr. told Washington of his ancestors, who had fought in the Revolution—one under George's command (George remembered him), and in every American war since. The embrace returned to Tom Sr. was sincere; the "thank you" was real. All the Burnells knew that if Jesus Christ had vouched for the heart and soul of George Washington, then, that was good enough for them. Tom Sr. remembered all that God had forgiven of his own sinful life. All anyone could do was apologize and live Christ forever after.

When the line was gone, Washington spoke. "Thank you all. I had many highs and lows in my life—for lows, most recall my time at Valley Forge, when I could barely move our nation to feed my men, or clothe them, or give them proper winter shelter. I had a warm house to live in. I had food. I even had Martha visit me. Whatever I suffered, which was mostly the anxiety and worry of keeping my army together and in the field, ready to fight, was small compared to the sufferings of our soldiers, the price they paid for liberty. I am fortunate to know what Christ knows and you know: that our momentary travails can produce the greatest rewards for posterity and, yes, eternity. Thank you for remembering the struggles of my men, the suffering of all our people who cherished freedom, life, liberty. It was worth all the pain, the sadness. Praise our God."

***

The word spread like a wildfire to the valleys to the east—and even crossed the river to western valleys—that Geoge Washington was nearby. Up the river and down, north and south, the early settlers who had entered eternal life and who had, as contemporaries, the name of a living George Washington on their lips and in their thoughts, came all through the night and into the next day to share memories of their common past. Katie and Paul, usually focused on the history of music, realized this was a unique opportunity to gather a history of a time and a man, so they recorded and asked questions. As a bonus, colonial music, unknown till this time, was shared and saved for posterity. The little community along the river, once the boundary between civilization and wilderness, fed the guests; put some up in their homes overnight; allowed tents to be spread on their lawns; allowed their wood to be used for tent poles, cooking, and warmth; offered their water faucets and outdoor showers; shared their gardens' harvests and organized the making of latrines.

On the third day, at noon, when crowds were waning, Jesus and His aides, dressed in outdoor clothing and carrying numerous rods and tackle boxes, came to embrace George Washington. All His friends from the little settlement, all the visitors there for George, received a handshake or a hug, a word of greeting. The prayers of George, all ever thought and ever spoken, turned through the mind of Christ. He had been aware of every word and emotion of the man, and experienced again the culture, the people, the sites and surroundings of George in those days. Jesus had seen it all, the American Revolution, the heartache of death and defeat, the starving times, homes destroyed, refugees, doubts, fears, anxieties. Within, Jesus was wont to cry. But the hard times were gone for the American people, and the present was so glorious.

Jesus stood in a flat-bottomed john boat pulled up on a pebbly sandbar, as the crowd filled the well-kept riverbank and lawn of Andrew Springs, eating Tom Sr.'s homemade bread, drinking Tim's tangy, homemade grape juice. Jesus taught them, reading from the Holy Book, adding to the words, filling in with insightful anecdotes, and miraculously reached into every single soul with insights, healings, and eternal wisdom as yet unknown or experienced. The thousands received communion and had personal meetings with the Lord at altar call, where they discussed the past altar calls in a fallen world and the promises kept. The afternoon went; supper was being served, when the last person said, "Thank you, Lord," and left Christ to himself. Jesus told his aides—and Andy, John, Tom, Mat, and Jack, who had attended to His every need—that He planned to fish till dusk, wading through the warm, low waters. He asked that they keep George from leaving. He told them to wait on shore, as the Holy Spirit would soon well up within and descend from above upon His people.

He was gone, disappeared, only to be seen seconds later, hundreds of yards to the south, standing in the warmth of the Susquehanna. Jesus, with his rod pointed to the south and his back to the distant crowd, waited with anticipation. For he knew the Holy Spirit coming would be a memory they would never forget and would anchor them eternally, refreshing them ten thousand years from this moment. He felt the welling up within them, and He felt the incredible power coming down.

Then, over the water came the soulful, human sounds; the gasps of surprise and joy, the whimpering of unbelief and unworthiness at the incredible love of God poured upon and within them. The raising of arms, the stretching toward Heaven, the faltering postures, the taking of seats and cross-legged sprawls. Thousands of voices ascending into the clean air, heard by God in Jerusalem. Jesus laughed heartily, happily, harmonizing with their overwhelming feelings of love and appreciation. He then said to Himself and His unseen angels, "You don't get that every day." He laughed at His speaking to himself, so childish and so honest. What was being given out, without measure, was God's heart. And the knowledge, the wisdom, the love expressed would change them even more than they had already been changed, which was inconceivable. He had gone to the cross and suffered, and He thanked His Father for the power, determination, grit to have done so. And, yes, it is more blessed to give than to receive.

When Jesus left the river at nightfall, the crowd was still upon the bank, gathered around countless fires. He walked among them, as if on the road to Emmaus, and they did not recognize Him. Their faces were so serene, so calm, so loving, and they were thinking deep thoughts, realizing the truth of the inconsistencies in their past lives, and seeing the great promises ahead. Jesus walked to Mat's home, entered into the home, made his way to a small, first-floor bedroom. The door had a sign: "Jesus lives here." Among fishing gear, a rack of rugged outdoor clothing, a wood table and chair, was a bed. Barb always kept the bedding clean, scented. Jesus knelt by the bed, bowed his head, and thanked the Father for the wonderful day that the people of the village, the surrounding countryside, and the world had enjoyed. Being in the physical body, He thought rest would be good—just a few hours. He awoke before dawn and was gone- to New Jerusalem.

CHAPTER 25

Andy was sitting on his Adirondack, viewing the river from the top bank, when he heard footfalls on the dewy lawn stretching out behind him. The sun had already risen but it would be half an hour before its appearance in the sky as light was effectively blocked by the mountain behind him. Still, the temperature was comfortable, with shorts and a heavy shirt. A gentle mist clung to the river and surrounding, tree-lined shore. He turned to his left, and from the Burnell home, he saw Tom Jr. and Jack, in shorts, with fishing rods, coming toward him. He turned to his right and saw Mat and Pete engaged in talk and moving his way. As he turned to face the river and was thinking of standing and stretching, he realized that John and Diana were standing before him, not more than ten feet away

"Hope we didn't cause alarm," said Diana.

"Just transported down from the mountain," John said. "We brought coffee."

Diana was already gathering the butt ends of burned wood and placing them neatly in the fire pit. Then, she targeted the unused wood from the pile nearby. John emptied his knapsack contents onto the nearest table; four pounds of coffee, two coffee pots, two gallons of water, cream, sugar, eight mugs.

Mat, his grandson, Pete; and Tom Jr. and his great-grandson, Jack, arrived together. Andy smiled. They all appeared so contented and happy.

Andy spoke. "My boys are out on the river, checking fish traps up above our location." His topic changed to the visit of George and Jesus. "The last three days have been lively." Andy realized then that he was holding up Tom Jr. and Jack, who were excited about their fishing prospects. "You two get out there—straight out, along that ledge—and catch some fish. That's where they've been jumping. We will save you some coffee."

The two laughed at their luck in having such a gracious neighbor. "Good idea," said Jack as they walked down the embankment and into the water. "Thank you."

Mat and Pete took the filled coffee pots to Diana's fire, placed the legged grill over the fire, and situated the coffee pots where the heat was most intense.

"What brings you two down here so early?" Andy said to Mat and Pete.

"We just can't stop talking about the past three days," said Pete.

Andy intended to address Pete's topic, when, without warning, the presence of an ancient one was announced, internally, by an angel. Andy had a feeling of gravitas and respect. Pete and Mat seemed oblivious, as did Diana and John, who continued their coffee chores.

Melchizedek stood before him; *was* it Mel? He wore shorts and a T-shirt, sandals on bare feet; his beard had been shaved, his prayer shawl was gone. His hair was close-cropped gray. Andy spoke in astonishment, "Mel, is that you?"

"Certainly. It was time to adapt, especially for summer in central Pennsylvania. 'New wine into new wine skins.' I'm going to take some time off. The Lord recommended your little village."

"What an honor," said Andy.

"I suppose it is when viewed historically. Coming from the beginnings of life. But to me you are a friend as are your neighbors. Now, I present a plan. I would like to visit your Susquehanna Native American Living Museum further up the river, and the Gettysburg battlefield to the south. But that is for later. I want to talk about your crew and space."

Andy looked over at Mat, Pete, and then at Diana and John. They were all standing as if frozen in their movements. Mel spoke. "They are in real time, not suspended. You and I are moving quickly, at break-neck speed between the established realities." He added, "I know your crew is here. I wish to meet all of them, later."

Andy sensed no speeding up of his thought processes or of their speech.

"Tell me your heart," Mel said. "Sovereign God, who knows the deepest passions of men, would love to hear how your opinions differ and meld with His. He enjoys that immensely, and as He is the perfect judge of all things, you can neither hurt nor help your crew by your assessment. You do give depth of understanding, which is always positive in its outcomes."

Andy had wanted a talk like this with someone of authority. He wished to tell the world about the good men and women of the Explorer 7. He smiled broadly. "Thank you," he said, and began. "It was as you suggested at our first meeting; knowing the actions and thoughts of every member made all the difference. Individually, any of my crew could be entrusted to handle any phase of operations. I have mused upon their service many times and have explored the future. They are all the most wonderful people I have ever worked with. I consider them all to be my dearest friends. Logically, while organizing my thoughts, I noticed patterns, groupings.

"My first group, I call the 'up and comings,'" Andy said. "You have four among us this very minute, and the fifth just stepped into the river. Mat and his grandson, Pete. John, uncle of Mat, and John's companion, Diana. The one in the river is Jack, Tom Jr.'s great-grandson. Deep, soulful, and innovative thinkers, Mat, Pete, and Jack. Their minds walk with God and hike and run with the Holy Spirit through all fields of experience. Humble men, all totally unaware of their inestimable worth. John, officer material, knows his worth is based on what he knows. Solid man—steadier or, perhaps, more methodical than the first three mentioned, he weighs more deeply any quick action or sudden plan. His partner, Diana, is much the same. She has the highest math skills, thinks outside the box, and, like John, weighs the consequences.

"All of their futures, their skills, drives, and passions, are most crucial to the success of Thermador and Rau-toon and the destruction of the non-Christian element of the pilgrim peoples. The men are hardened warriors, brawlers when they needed to be. Yet, they have emotions and hearts of love. They are forthright, and they can be subtle. They can read the intentions of alien peoples. They are open to adaptation and fluidity.

"John and Diana meld into the next group, 'the committeds,'" Andy said. "John and Diana, managing peacekeeping forces, are of the same character and have no intention of leaving the mission set before them. Dan and Emily, committed to democratic government, and Pete and Grace, in evangelism, have their minds touching and realizing the crossover into spy craft, intelligence, and the ruses of the flesh and demons. They are the core needed to bring the final victory. Ava is a committed. You know about her, I would imagine."

Mel spoke. "Our sweet Ava. It was touch and go at first, but the Lord's love won her over. Yes, I saw it all unfold. She's solid now. Her father is a good man also."

Andy rejoined his narrative. "The last group are the 'entrepreneur/settler/soldiers.' They wished to conquer the frontier of space and settle into peace and prosperity. My boys, Tuck and Robin; and the Byzantines, Seth, Woden, and Paternus; are excellent soldiers—the best I've ever seen—with settler and frontier backgrounds. They are common-sense combat soldiers. They want raw lands to settle, to exploit the resources, manufacture goods, provide services, and live in peace or conquer those who will not allow peace.

"Tim, Ling, and Tom Jr. are 'all arounds.' They can handle combat, but it is not their greatest strength; they can handle subtlety and intrigue—these things were a duty to Christ they willingly undertook, but not a passion. They share much with the entrepreneurs. They delight in business, in giving people employment and providing for their flock (employees) by way of housing, community goals, education, and advancement. They like being super-sized dads, patriarchs, if you will. I short-changed Tom Jr. He was a superb ship's captain, combat leader as well as corporate boss."

Andy looked over his people, John, Diana, Mat, Pete, and noticed they were moving now. Mat poured a cup of coffee and placed it before Andy. Andy saluted in thanks. He realized he and Mel were in real time. Mat spoke to Mel. "A mug of coffee?" Mel's eyes lit with gratitude, "Yes, with sugar and cream, please." He sat up in his chair, stood. "I will mix my own—much easier, and you have other work." Mat laughed, "You know a guest comes first." Mel responded, "Bless you for your manners," as they went together to the coffee table. On the river, Andy saw Tom Jr. and Jack returning with full stringers clutched in their free hands. The fish had been anxious to be caught. Behind him, Grace and Leaf were coming with containers filled with breakfast foods. The sun had burned off the river mist. Humid heat was upon the earth, and the heavy sweatshirts and long-sleeved shirts came off. Woden and Helen, Seth and Sara, and Paternus and Agnella were approaching from the river trail. They must have been walking. Ling, Carl, Ava and her father, and Tim and Mary were looking at him from Tim's rooftop. Ava waved and yelled, "Good morning!" Andy yelled, "Good morning!" as he waved his hand in the "come down to me" gesture. Another perfect day had begun.

***

Fish would jump and slap back into the water. A bald eagle passed over-head at tree height. A red squirrel chattered angrily from a massive river oak as Baltimore orioles harassed him. A river otter stuck his head above the berm of the bank, bobbed his head, seeking insights into the gathered, then turned for the river. Everyone from the collection of river homes had gathered. Katie and Paul were there with banjo and guitar. Seth's son had a drum; Jack had a harmonica. Food and drink were passed among the gathered, as was conversation.

The conversations were so deep spiritually, due to the recent touch of the Spirit; and the vacation ideas so interesting; and all topics concerning George Washington, the American Revolution, and the frontier were so riveting that no one wanted to disband. Just as anyone felt the need to move on with the day, some new, tempting food would be presented and suddenly, one more cup of coffee or herbal tea seemed a good idea. If motion and change conquered all of the inducements to stay, then the land—the mountains, river, forests, trees, and wildlife—would speak and say, "Remain with us. For we are life, proof of the love of the Father."

Mat spoke. "I wonder how Abe and Don and their families are getting along."

Mel smiled. "Each have added another child, both girls." The gathered smiled too, and "Praise God" was heard. Mel had not been introduced. No need to; his aura spoke his name. He settled into the gathering like a beloved childhood uncle not seen for ages.

"And the pilgrims—Sarah, Jem, Jared, Enoch, and Noah?" John asked.

"All are firmly in Christ," Mel said. "Noah married Jem, and a child is due. Jared and Enoch have found future brides, they are engaged. Sarah is still beautiful, a leader and a Christian. The first to die as a baptized Christian, and the first to be resurrected, as you all know."

"We did good," said Paternus as his mind soothed and eased over so many of the deep accomplishments of their tour.

Robin and Tuck, coming up the incline, just returning from their boats, leaving gear behind, had heard. Robin said, "We did *really* good. We freed a people."

Tuck added, "Plural. Peoples. And we told them about our ever-loving Savior and our God of war, who knows how to kick butt—excuse me—bring victory."

"Who is loving us—and them, still," said Woden.

"All…forever," said Jack, as "amens" sounded.

Andy was moved by the enormity of their past task and the good that was blossoming from their actions, their sacrifices. He understood why George had cried. He wondered if his crew's sacrifices would match the power for future change that George had achieved. God seemed to have a never-ending stream of His people who loved their countries. He had taught them to love their neighbors and to respect governments, especially those that mirrored his values. Men and women always ready to sacrifice seemed to grow out of the ground like newly planted corn. The harvest was always extravagant. He remembered the American flag flying over the battlements of the last engagement and the national anthem playing. He saw the faces of Don and Abe and their families. He shook his head, trying to stop the urge to cry. If he did weep, the tears would be of thankfulness and happiness.

Andy spoke as he gazed at his crew. "I love all of you. You made me look like the captain of a starship." The tears streamed down.

Mat stood, his chin thrust out and lifted. He had scooped up a towel from the back of his chair and held it behind him as a cape. The laughter and guffaws began immediately, as they saw his spirit change into an overripe gravitas, an ego of comedic proportions. He theatrically opened both arms, sweeping the cape before him as he bowed, and in tiny steps, his head down, he inched toward the seated Andy. Mat placed the spread towel before Andy and then offered Andy his hand, even as he remained bowed, as his other hand went behind his back in a flourish.

Andy, a man of mirth, took the hand and stood on the towel. Mat opened his mouth and began to sing operatically in a deep, manly voice, as he faced the audience. The laughter and guffaws rose in intensity. Faces were red, tears were falling. Just looking into Mat's eyes made them laugh, for there was an opera maestro before them, serious and full of self-importance.

Mat sang while sweeping his arms dramatically and pointing toward Andy. "The chief was our captain," he stated in song, undeniably and in the deepest of tones. "Covered in bear grease, he needed the release…" He held the last word forever in timbre and temper, till he began to choke, and then began again. "Of shooting his guns at the unknown ones." Mat bent at the knees, lowered his body, and then began to rise with arms extended as he sang, "That was our captain, so brave and so true. Who knew the end would bring…accreting glue?" The voice, the movements had the crew doubled over.

Paternus and Tuck were on the ground, choking in their laughter. The instantly concocted lyrics, though not special or complete, had poked fun at Andy and his crew's fears that they had overstepped their mandate and had started an intergalactic war, a real fear at the time.

Mat had felt the need to prevent the meeting from sinking into emotionalism, however fleeting it would have been. He remembered his first night back in central Pennsylvania, after the wedding supper of Christ and His church in Jerusalem. He'd been encamped at the Harrisburg Airport with all the new arrivals. Andy had introduced himself as their leader for the start of the Millennium. Andy had danced like an eel that night, explaining why he named his wife "Leaf" and not "Eel." It had all been an act to break the tension of starting a new life.

The laughter and tears of comedic hysteria quieted, as they remembered their captain's bold use of force. Andy laughed at himself—and Mat—and had given him hearty slaps on the back. Everyone sipped drinks and studied the beauty of their surroundings. The warmth was pleasing upon their skin. The slight breeze smelled of river-water scents, and the river mud gave its perfume of sweetly, rotting fish and flowering weeds. Wild cherry trees were in bloom, smelling like perfume.

They had eternal life, and it was very good; so much better than life in the carnality of the flesh. Even as they sat in perfect peace, Hell writhed with the bodies and souls of humanity who had been incapable of giving their allegiance to the Creator God. Not even when His Son was sent to Earth to turn them back to reality would they listen. The gathered men and women knew that individually, they didn't deserve eternal life. Only Christ upon the cross had paid their way.

Mel, the oldest living man among them, who had listened and spoken little, had bowed his head, sensing a river of a song roiling within his soul. He began to hum within his soul through the power of the Spirit—not a song of ancient Israel, for new wine, indeed, needed a new wineskin—but of the Messiah who had come, who had and was ruling Israel and all of His hard-earned servants. Promises kept. Mel looked over the gathered and in a deep, kindly voice, said, "When just a child, I knew God was real. I knew peace among humankind was a treasure of the greatest value. Yet mankind fought among themselves. Terrible murders, raids, wars.

"My reputation was of peace. Yet, I could not avoid war. Neither the laws of God nor men could bring peace. Only God's presence within us can bring peace. Jesus brought that peace through God's presence. 'Sing to the Lord a new song, Sing His praise from the end of the earth!' says Isaiah. So, I sing a song all of you know—perhaps not well, but the Lord will provide remembrance. It appears to be a war song, but it is a war song within the heart, soul, and mind of harvesting souls." He paused and added, "Let it not be lost on us that wars that kill share many attributes with spiritual war, so closely intertwined."

His vision searched and found Katie and Paul, and Seth's son within the crowd. "Play it with a marching tempo. Play it with a Celtic flair, 'Lead on O King Eternal.'"

The band collected within a minute. Mat stood beside his sister, Katie. He would establish the pace of the tune. He looked at Mel, and began the countdown, "One, two, three…"

He and Mel began to sing.

Lead on, O King Eternal,

The day of march has come;

Henceforth in fields of conquest

Thy tents shall be our home.

Through days of preparation,

Thy grace has made us strong,

And now, O King Eternal,

We lift our battle song.

The men had stood, emphasized "battle song" as their fists or open hands were raised to their God. They had faced the terrors of war and won, and to God was the praise. Then the women rose, as the lyrics turned toward the loving Spirit of their God. Their voices as resolute in tone as those of their men.

Lead on O King Eternal,
Till sin's fierce war shall cease,
And holiness shall whisper
The sweet Amen of peace;
For not with swords loud clashing,
Nor roll of stirring drums;
With deeds of love and mercy,
The heavenly kingdom comes.

The gathered sang through their hearts and souls, passionate, appreciative of the presence of their God.

Lead on, O King eternal,
We follow not with fears;
For gladness breaks like morning
Wher-e'er Thy face appears;
Thy cross is lifted o'er us;
We journey in its light:
The crown awaits the conquest;
Lead on, O God of might.

When the song ended, their hearts and souls, aroused in praise, were calling on His name. Hands raised, bodies jumping, arms around the shoulders of their people, hugs, embraces, till the amens came with peace, because God stood among them, within them on the riverbank; satisfaction, because they had served with all they had; and thankfulness, for without Christ on the cross, they would not have existed at this time and place.

EPILOGUE

The people of God, the chosen, blessed with eternal life and health, spent their eternity exploring His endless universe. They became stewards of the universe. They became teachers to less-developed life-forms and cognizant species, some who struggled to touch the blurred form of Jesus and some who easily and readily grasped His reality. They found life-forms who celebrated their physical and mental capabilities, who thought they were gods; and so there was disparity, sometimes slavery, disenfranchisement; there were police, soldiers, kingdoms, wars, heroes, villains, acts of bravery and cowardice, sacrifice, pain, and sadness for them. The cross always conquered. The cross always moved forward.

The people of God found planets three times the size of Earth. They created earths by moving suns to likely planets and learned to keep them in their orbits. Waterless planets were seeded with water, and God's chosen learned to grow rain, multiply what they had into what they needed. God's people made an ocean to cover a planet, the ground first contoured with ocean channels and choke points called gates, corrals. They seeded with water, and the waters grew, and fish were added and farmed and harvested by diverting the huge schools into those underwater corrals. Shrimp, clams, lobsters, every delectable and desirous fish was harvested, and family processing ships took what was sustainable. Plant- and plankton-eating fish thrived in the vast grasslands of sea vegetation. Kelp the size of sequoias stood in vast, watery forests and were harvested as ready-made homes, kiln-dried and trimmed, the natural hollowness expanded, and windows and doors added. They were light and portable, with beautiful natural textures on the walls and ceilings. The homes were horizontal or vertical, trunks laid on their sides or standing upright as they had grown. Vast ocean flats, where people could boat or swim or fish, attracted vacationers from the known universe. There was not a man-eating species present on those planets. Scavenger fish abounded. With the attachment of lightweight fins to hands and feet, and their bodies pumped, infused with oxygen, tourists could swim like stingrays for days without coming up for air.

The people of God made an airy planet from volcanic rock. The hollow core, the vast network of funnels and fissures filled with air that circulated to the surface, where every herbal tree, every tree of spice grew and gave scent, and every plant species did the same. Fungi grew in profusion. The best of the known plant life of the universe was present. Every thousand years, the people of Earth came to refresh and renew their lungs, skin, and digestive systems. A fungi that grew as flat as paper was imbued with an oil like the olive oil of Earth, and a quick toasting made it a pleasant, restorative meal for the digestive tract. It was discovered that certain scents remained upon certain people. Genetics determined the bonding.

Explorers found a planet where the dominant life-forms were dogs, perhaps dropped from some voyaging craft thousands of years in the past. The dogs could speak words, just a few, but enough to know the inhabitants knew a Spirit-ruled life. The canines lived in a city of pumice cones that had been scratched by paws into rooms and steps of all sizes. The males and females mated for life. Only fish and reptiles were native and eaten by the inhabitants, as well as grasses, tubers, nuts, berries, fruits, and wild grains.

They found a planet inhabited by an underground species the size of a man's hand and resembling Earth's moles or voles. With permission, a vast viewing galleria was constructed by removing half of a hillside and erecting a glass retaining wall. The creatures could not stand on their hind legs for long, even when the loft of caverns allowed it, but they could sit; and having dexterous arms and opposable thumbs, they used their bulging stomachs as temporary work benches. They were artistic and entrepreneurial—their actions revealed by the glass wall and available for viewing on the internet. Their small handicrafts, sought after as souvenirs, created a lively commerce.

If you can imagine it, it very well may be true.

***

As eternal means "forever," it is by common sense and necessity that this narrative should end, because life cannot. God is life eternal. He has invited you to the adventure that never ends. Perhaps that adventure will, in some small way, resemble the one presented. I believe it will be better.

In my Father's house are many mansions: if it were not so, I would have told you. I go to prepare a place for you. And if I go to prepare a place for you, I will come again, and receive you unto myself; that where I am, there ye may be also. And wither I go ye know, and the way ye know. (John 14:2–4)